The In-House Politician

The In-House Politician

First Edition

© 2024 by William Robert Reeves

This is a work of fiction. People, places, events and situations are either the product of the author's imagination or are used fictitiously. Any resemblance to events, locales or actual persons, living or dead, is entirely coincidental.

All rights reserved. No part of this publication may be reproduced, stored in a retrieval system, or transmitted, in any form or by any means, without prior written permission from the publisher. Inquiries concerning reproduction outside the scope described should be sent to the publisher.

ISBN: 9798335483100

United States Copyright Office Registration Number: TXu 2-436-253

Printed in the United States of America

Edited by Hugh Cook

Cover design by Katarina Naskovsky

Kindle Direct Publishing

To the residents of Gravesend…..

Long live the armadillo

Thanks to: Laurie, Rick, Barry, Jeanne, Hugh, Leigh, Guy, Charlie, Jim, Ty, and Karen for all your help, encouragement, patience, and proper placement of commas.

William Robert Reeves

The In-House Politician

Table of Contents

Chapter 1 1
Chapter 2 4
Chapter 3 21
Chapter 4 31
Chapter 5 40
Chapter 6 45
Chapter 7 50
Chapter 8 64
Chapter 9 70
Chapter 10 77
Chapter 11 81
Chapter 12 90
Chapter 13 94
Chapter 14 109
Chapter 15 115
Chapter 16 120
Chapter 17 122
Chapter 18 129
Chapter 19 142
Chapter 20 153
Chapter 21 155
Chapter 22 173
Chapter 23 183
Chapter 24 188
Chapter 25 197

Chapter 26	202
Chapter 27	210
Chapter 28	219
Chapter 29	232
Chapter 30	238
Chapter 31	246
Chapter 32	252
Chapter 33	266
Chapter 34	268
Chapter 35	273
Chapter 36	277
Chapter 37	285
Chapter 38	294
Chapter 39	305
Chapter 40	310
Chapter 41	327
Chapter 42	332
Chapter 43	334
Chapter 44	337
Chapter 45	339
Chapter 46	346
Chapter 47	353
Chapter 48	355
Chapter 49	360
Chapter 50	364
Chapter 51	367
Chapter 52	371
Chapter 53	374

Chapter 54 386
Chapter 55 389
Chapter 56 393
Chapter 57 395
Chapter 58 399
Chapter 59 408
Chapter 60 410
Chapter 61 418
Chapter 62 420
Chapter 63 421
Chapter 64 435
Chapter 65 447
Chapter 66 457
Chapter 67 459
Chapter 68 462
Chapter 69 470
Epilogue 472
About the Author 478

Chapter 1

Sally Kessler couldn't get the horrible smell out of her nose, and was wondering if she would have to burn her clothes and fumigate her car. It was giving her a headache. The directions provided for the location of the meeting placed her right next to one of the Scarduzo-owned trash dumps. The whole situation gave her the creeps.

There were no pleasantries. They just stood there and looked at each other in disgust for a few seconds. Sally finally broke the ice. "Well, well. If it isn't Alex Scarduzo. This place becomes you. It looks and smells like shit. So, how many bodies are buried in there?"

"Gee Sally," Alex snarled, "surely you jest. Rule number one is you never let them find the body, and that includes all the body parts. Just ask Jimmy Hoffa's family."

Sally was shaken by his response and was not feeling well from the sights and smells. She said, "That perky little messenger you sent made a compelling case that you had some information I might want. Please tell me I didn't waste my time coming here. Honestly, I don't like standing this close to you."

"Now that's the Sally Kessler I remember," Alex said. "Any more insults before we talk business?"

Sally wanted to shell out more pithy insults, but also wanted to get out of there as quickly as possible. "Let's get this over with. What do you have for me?"

Alex took out some folded papers from his inside coat pocket and gave them to Sally. "Once I get this into the hands of the right people," he said, "you will probably receive a call to confirm those numbers since you're the one who put a gun to Teddy DeMarco's head. You should study up on them, just in case."

"How did you get your hands on this report?"

"C'mon, Sally. We both have our sources and mine will remain confidential."

Sally took a quick look at the report in the dim light. "This report looks like it came directly from the bank. Have you got someone inside? And how do I know if these numbers are accurate?"

"They don't need to be accurate. They just need to be published. Now, do we have a deal?"

"Why do you want to screw Teddy DeMarco? He's my enemy, not yours. I thought you two were buddies. Don't you do business with his bank?"

"Teddy can take care of himself. He's got thick skin just like me. We're both politicians. It's not personal. And there's no reason he'll ever know about me helping you. You can take all the credit for the shit that will rain down from this kind of report. Now, do we have a deal?"

"That depends. What do you want from me?"

"You can consider this a first installment and a freebie. Once it appears in the newspaper, I'll be in touch. I know where to find you."

They both seemed satisfied with this unspecified arrangement.

Sally tried to hand the report back to Alex.

He pushed it back and said, "No, you keep that copy. You'll need it when you're asked for confirmation."

Sally shrugged and turned to go.

Alex stopped her in her tracks and once again yelled to her.

"Excuse me! For the last time, do we have a deal?"

"We do if you get this report published. And next time find a better place to meet."

Alex laughed. "Hey, this is my office. Don't insult it. Remember what I said about the body parts."

On the drive home Sally wondered if any of her comrade forebears had ever conspired with their capitalist enemies. Did the ends really justify the means? She quickly put it out of her mind. If what she had agreed to tonight could help bring down those racist, money-grubbing bankers, and Teddy DeMarco specifically, well, she could live with it. Besides, Alex Scarduzo might be a powerful man, but there was no way he could get a report like that published in any reputable newspaper. The numbers didn't make any sense.

As she drove away, she rolled down the windows and kept them down all the way home.

Chapter 2

The Examiner

Sunday
September 20, 1992

**First Northeastern Delivers
Less Than Promised**

By: Joseph Campbell

One year ago First Northeastern Bank entered into an agreement with bank regulators in Washington D.C., and a New Jersey-based activist group known as People United for Movement and Progress. This agreement was a condition of the bank's acquisition of Peoples Bank & Trust headquartered in Pennsylvania. The combination of these two financial institutions created a super-regional bank with assets of $60 billion. The merger of these two banks was one of the largest interstate combinations ever.

One of the elements of this agreement was that First Northeastern Bank offer $25 million in low- interest rate mortgages to income-eligible applicants in all of the New Jersey cities in which it operates branches. After the initial year of this three-year agreement, First Northeastern Bank has closed only $500,000 in loans. Additionally, the data provided indicates that none of the closed loans were made to minority applicants. In fact, the unnamed source indicated that, to date, all loans to minority applicants have been denied. It should be noted that

The Examiner does not have independent confirmation on the number of minority loan applications.

The Examiner reached out to officials from First Northeastern Bank for comment, but received no response.

When asked to comment, Sally Kessler, Executive Director of People United for Movement and Progress, said, "It was very disappointing to see the lack of progress and performance by the bank. At this rate, 1NEB will never achieve the goal of $25 million in mortgages to these deserving low-and moderate-income homebuyers." Kessler went on to assert that the document she was provided to review appeared to have been prepared by the bank itself. (see bank on A10)................

Tom Donovan was a bit nervous and didn't sleep well last night. It was not out of the realm of possibility he could get fired today. Teddy had singled him out for some kind of rebuke, but it remained to be seen whether it would be a public or private execution.

It was early Monday morning and Tom was driving north on the Turnpike. He was recalling the phone call yesterday from Kelly Giordano, Teddy's assistant. Teddy had called her earlier to make sure she got in touch with Tom and the other staff members to ensure they would all be in attendance for the shit-storm that was about to rain down. The only question was whether it was going to be a normal run-of-the-mill shit-storm, or the type of meeting in which Teddy's head might explode.

Tom's wife Ann took the call from Kelly. Since she didn't know Tom's wife, Kelly formally asked if Mr. Donovan was available. Tom's full name was Thomas T. Donovan. He had just finished reading the article in *The Examiner* when Ann came into the living room and said there was a very nice sounding young lady on the phone. She said, "I know you're not dumb enough to have a girlfriend call you at home." It was good marriage humor.

Tom asked who was calling. Again, he got that same look. Ann said, "It's Kelly from the bank." Now that Tom knew he was no longer in trouble with his wife, he was wondering why Kelly was calling him at home on a Sunday. As he walked into the kitchen, it all came together. It must be about the article.

Tom answered, "Hey Kelly, what's going on?"

"Well, Mr. Donovan, I'm sorry to bother you at home today, but Teddy wanted me to call you. Have you heard about the article in *The Examiner* today? Teddy wanted me to call you and some of the other staff to make sure you would be in attendance at tomorrow's staff meeting."

A chill went down Tom's spine, and after a deep breath he responded in the affirmative. "Just finished reading it. Can I assume that Teddy's not a happy camper? I know I wasn't very pleased with it."

Understandably, Kelly was not in a position to reveal any state secrets, but she did say, "Yeah! He didn't sound like he was in a good mood."

Sometimes Teddy had a tendency to overreact to bad news, but this couldn't be good. The bank had just completed its second acquisition, but this most recent merger had way too many hiccups. This article would not be helpful.

Tom never understood why Teddy thought it necessary to have his weekly staff meetings every Monday morning at the godforsaken hour of 9:00 am. Having a long commute, he could never even think

The In-House Politician

about having a second cocktail on a Sunday night for fear he wouldn't be on top of his game for those early Monday morning love fests. The only acceptable excuse for not being present at these meetings was a death in the family, and even then it felt like you needed a note from the funeral director.

Tom could recall times when Teddy had staffers phone in from their vacations for an update. One time a staffer who was attending a conference in L.A. had to get up before dawn to accommodate Teddy and the East Coast time differential. Tom could hear her yawning on the other end of the speaker phone. Occasionally, Tom thought about asking Teddy if he might consider moving the staff meeting to a more reasonable day of the week. But then he remembered who he worked for.

Since Tom's commute was long he had plenty of time to prepare himself for the meeting. Traffic be damned, he never minded driving the long distance. After all, it was a company car. Tom listened to *Imus in the Morning,* or books on CD. The only real issues for him were the sights and aromas emanating out of Carteret, Linden and Rahway just prior to the Turnpike exit for Newark. Simon and Garfunkel memorialized it well when they sang, "Counting the cars on the New Jersey Turnpike." Anyone not from Jersey wouldn't understand all the Turnpike exit jokes. Tom was Exit 4.

Tom was in the middle of his career in the financial services industry. During his time at the bank, known as 1NEB, it was never his intention to make life miserable for all the formally trained bankers he worked with. It was just the nature of the job. So, he tried to accomplish it with a certain level of panache.

Inside the bank it was Tom's job to encourage his fellow bankers to do the right-thing, but in a manner that would not diminish their annual bonuses or stock options. During this period, banks were hiring professionals like Tom to serve as internal auditors to eliminate any perceived or actual lending discrimination, known as redlining. Part of the job was to bridge the gap between the communities in which banks were doing business and the protest groups who were trying to embarrass the industry into actually making them do the right thing. The job responsibilities naturally morphed into more of an internal cheerleader and activist role.

In 1987, Teddy DeMarco was appointed to head up the bank's department responsible for compliance with the Community Reinvestment Act (CRA). Tom had been with the bank a few years prior to that, but all his assignments were in the southern part of New Jersey, which was also where he lived. Teddy knew of Tom and his work. With his appointment as head of the department, Tom was now reporting to Teddy.

Teddy and Tom did not hit it off at first. Teddy didn't hire him. Tom's original job offer came from one of the bank's top executives who was responsible for steering the prior intra-state merger through the regulatory maze in Washington. In fact, the previous merger included a requirement from the regulators that they hire someone with qualifications that Tom possessed. Indeed, that acquisition was a piece of cake compared to the current inter-state merger.

When Teddy became Tom's new boss, as is the case with most arranged marriages, they did a slow dance trying to figure each other out. They finally agreed that sports was their common bond, and moved on from there. Teddy was a baseball nut and Tom was a recovering gridiron head case with just the normal number of concussions.

As Tom's responsibilities grew, Teddy wanted him closer, so he brought him into the headquarters in Newark, resulting in a ridiculously long commute. As Teddy began introducing Tom to the various executive officers and department heads, they quickly learned there weren't many CRA sympathizers. In fact, most of them viewed it as nothing more than corporate blackmail. It was an uphill battle, but Teddy and Tom saw it as an opportunity to change some hearts and minds, even if it was going to kill them.

As Tom pulled into the underground parking garage, he took a deep breath attempting to relax. He was hoping that after the staff meeting, he would not be led out in handcuffs.

When Tom arrived on the floor, the first thing he noticed was Kelly standing at her desk. She was wearing those black patent leather, stiletto-heeled fuck-me pumps—the ones that say "as good as I look today, you ought to see me on the weekend." She made the art of flirting a full-time profession. No other girl came close in her ability to attract guys to her desk. But everyone knew Kelly could get away with it because she could do no wrong in Teddy's eyes. She was his gatekeeper, and he appreciated the way she kept the Philistines out of his office. Kelly had a hard-as-a-rock talk to the hand personality, which was quick to judge and never forgot a slight—intended or not. If you got on her wrong side—as they say in Brooklyn—"Fuhgeddaboudit!" Kelly had Teddy's ear, primarily because she always got the job done.

The bank was in the vanguard back in the heady days of the '80s and '90s when it seemed like there was a branch on every corner. Banks that wished to survive understood that consolidation was going to happen, like it or not. You were either going to buy, or be bought. And the buyers always survived the process in better shape than those who were bought. Thus, merger activity took off during this period with many larger institutions, like 1NEB, swallowing up other banks in order to gain market share and assets, as well as to eliminate the competition.

Wrapped up in all of this was the fact that over the past few years under the direction of the Chairman, 1NEB had been issuing both preferred and common stock in order to raise funds for further acquisitions. This meant that 1NEB was known to be searching for other banks to acquire. Thus, depending on one's point of view, 1NEB was either a predator, or a bank with vision for the future. Clearly, in the case of Sally Kessler and her comrades, the bank was a predator. She hated 1NEB with a passion. And Sally knew how to convince many of her true believers the bank could never be trusted.

The CRA law had been on the books since it was passed by Congress back in 1977, but until a bank went through a merger it really didn't have much impact. Whenever a merger application was announced it gave all the protest groups an opportunity to point out how badly certain banks were performing in communities of color. Indeed, there were times when the regulatory agencies had the audacity to actually delay the final decision on a merger until all parties: the bank, the protest groups, and in some cases even the regulators, were all satisfied. So, in the "time is money" element of a merger application, any delay could be costly. This meant that the CRA actually had some teeth in it, and some of the protest groups began to growl. 1NEB's merger had been announced two years ago and it took one whole year to negotiate with and satisfy all the parties involved. As a result, Teddy and his staff were now dealing with a new monster in the protest group known as PUMP.

People United for Movement and Progress, or PUMP, had the bank right in its crosshairs. Under the terms of the three-year agreement Teddy had negotiated with Sally Kessler, the bank would make $25 million in mortgages to low-and-moderate income homebuyers located in the cities. As the largest bank in the state, with branches in all the major cities, this meant it needed to make loans to borrowers in some of the toughest neighborhoods imaginable. The bank's Chairman understood the agreement was a cost of doing business and was, in fact, the right thing to do. And $25 million in loans was nothing more than a rounding error on the bank's balance sheet.

Enter Tom Donovan. Teddy brought him in and gave him the responsibility of getting the loans in the door and approved. Additionally, in order to hit the primary goals of the agreement, these loans would need to be made primarily to minority borrowers. And while it was left unspoken, everyone inside the bank, except for Teddy and Tom, believed that the bank's mortgage folks would have to pretty much throw away the standard underwriting rules. A large portion of these loans would end up being "character" loans in the truest sense of the word. And it didn't help that the bank's mortgage department had no experience with inner city lending. These applications were not what they were used to. The learning curve would be long and hard.

The reason Teddy was in such a bad mood this morning was that the largest newspaper in the state, *The Examiner*, had written a front-page article about the bank in the Sunday edition. Of course,

Sally Kessler was quoted in the article, and what she had to say wasn't pretty.

It was now the first anniversary of the three-year agreement with PUMP, and the story was a review of the bank's progress to date. The merger had been proposed back in 1990, and it took a full year to negotiate the deal and receive the regulatory approvals. Now, it was 1992 and the bank had operated under the terms of the agreement with PUMP for the past twelve months. The article described how 1NEB had made only $500,000 in loans during this first year, which meant that it had loaned out just two percent of the commitment, with two years remaining.

Additionally, the article seemed to be told from the perspective of Sally Kessler and PUMP. She made it clear the bank was not living up to its promises. The article also reported that after one full year of operation it had received only a few minority applications and that all had been declined. How *The Examiner* had gotten its hands on these data was a mystery. Of course, the article did not identify any of the sources except for the proverbial unnamed anonymous ones. And the numbers reported were complete bullshit. Someone had made them up. The article made no sense, but Tom felt like he was the only one who knew it.

As the bank's in-house politician, Teddy was responsible for putting the best face on what amounted to an almost impossible task. The article's headline read, "*First Northeastern Delivers Less Than Promised.*" Not good, and Teddy was pissed.

There was an edge to the article. No one likes bankers anymore, if they ever did. Mr. Potter in *It's a Wonderful Life* saw to that. What's more, the reporter who wrote the story was no friend of 1NEB. As

The In-House Politician

the primary business reporter for *The Examiner*, Joe Campbell had written many stories about the bank over the years, including a major piece in 1990, when it was one of the first in the country to test the waters of inter-state banking. At the time of the acquisition, 1NEB had grown into a significant powerhouse with $35 billion in assets. The bank then proposed to acquire another financial institution in Pennsylvania with $25 billion in assets. The two-bank combination would create a financial institution of $60 billion.

As a result of the acquisition the bank was now officially known as a super-regional institution. Outside of the money center banks in New York City, 1NEB was now a force to be reckoned with. This meant the bank had a bulls-eye on its back, with the shareholders, customers of both banks, the regulators, Wall Street, industry competition and, of course, the major protest groups like PUMP, all watching to see how the merger would play out.

The protest groups were the real wild card. The bank's Chairman and General Counsel had the shareholders and regulators under control. And the industry could do nothing but stand by and watch. But Teddy was responsible for keeping PUMP and the other protest groups in line. Thus, the article in *The Examiner* was giving him major heartburn.

Tom referred to PUMP as "the Bolsheviks," which always got him in trouble with Teddy. They knew how to get under the bank's skin. As the leader of PUMP, Sally Kessler was thought to have a magnet implanted in her body. This magnet, or homing device, if you will, always attracted her to the nearest microphone for an impromptu press conference to criticize anyone or any organization who in her mind was robbing the poor.

Sally knew nothing about how mortgages were underwritten, but didn't care. She had people for that. She was PUMP's political voice, so her more knowledgeable staff set forth the terms of the agreement and presented them to the bank—with her final approval, of course.

As Teddy's mortgage guy, Tom was responsible for advising him on whether what was being proposed by PUMP was reasonable. Not that his professional opinion ever moved the needle, since in Teddy's mind there was no option than giving in to their demands. He thought this was the only way the merger would be approved. So the Bolsheviks got pretty much everything they wanted.

Despite Tom's referring to the protest groups as Bolsheviks, he did have some empathy and common cause with them. For one thing, they were responsible for his job. But more importantly, Tom knew that most banks, including 1NEB, were redlining and discriminating in their mortgage underwriting practices. But rather than fighting in the streets, he preferred to take the more respectable route and fight the system from within. Besides, the benefits were better.

Tom had been the beneficiary of a classic liberal arts education. During the late '60s, he had experienced the anti-war movement, the civil rights movement, Woodstock, the environmental movement, and even the women's lib movement. However, since Tom had attended an all-male Ivy League university, the latter movement hadn't found him. It was an interesting time to be in college. Indeed, Tom's college experiences, which included an introduction to logic and ethics, as well as his prior banking positions, had turned him into the old cliché of a fiscal conservative with a social conscience.

Inside the bank, Teddy and Tom were waging a second battlefront. Porter McMahon was the bank's chief residential mortgage officer. He'd never attended charm school. Porter was responsible for underwriting the mortgages under the terms of the agreement. Whenever he heard that Tom wanted to meet with him to review a specific mortgage file that was about to be declined, he was either occupied or out for lunch. Tom's meetings with Porter were as much fun as a root canal. Porter was comparatively young for the job, but had all the credentials required to succeed. He maintained an uncanny ability to always say yes to his boss, no matter the issue. Likewise, he perfected a very snarky way to say no to Teddy and Tom whenever they thought a loan decision needed to be reversed. And while Teddy was more senior in rank, Porter reported directly to the bank's chief credit policy officer Peter Porzio, whose personality mirrored that of Ebenezer Scrooge prior to his Christmas Eve intervention.

Within the confines of his office and sometimes Teddy's, and whenever he thought he could get away with it, Tom began referring to Porter McMahon and his boss, Peter Porzio, as Marley and Scrooge, respectively. Just like in the novel, they were a despicable pair.

Theodore J. DeMarco, Jr. was Executive Vice President at 1NEB. When the merger was announced two years earlier and the Chairman had given Teddy the task of negotiating with the protest groups, he was a bit flummoxed. There was no training manual on how to deal with the Bolsheviks who began every negotiating session with the most outrageous demands they could come up with in order to see how far the bank was willing to bend over.

Teddy came out of the elevator with fire in his eyes and two cups of coffee, one in each hand. Caffeine was his drug of choice. He was a big man in size and stature. Approaching 50 and around six-feet-two, he had at one time been a minor league baseball player, but his career was cut short when he blew out a knee. He then went into teaching and coaching before someone talked him into running for office. Long story short, Teddy DeMarco became a political force in the state. So when 1NEB needed someone to run interference with all the politicians, he was offered the job. It didn't take him long to say yes since his salary, plus bonuses and stock options, was significantly more than he would ever make as a teacher or full-time politician. He also knew that a career in politics could end as quickly as it began.

As he passed by Kelly's desk, Teddy didn't even notice her fine ensemble and grumbled something about whether she had gotten hold of all of the staff for today's meeting. She tried to be funny in her response with a salute and a "Yes, Sir." He responded by slamming his office door.

Althea McBride and Tom had become soulmates ever since Teddy brought him into headquarters, and she had been poached from a competitor bank. She was a smart and sassy gorgeous young Black woman who carried herself with style and grace. As distracting as this was, and Tom being a happily married man, they made sure their relationship remained professional. Althea was at least a decade younger than Tom. They had common goals, though. Tom and Althea both wanted to save the world, to have the bank do the right thing, to keep Teddy from shooting himself in the foot, and in the process, to hopefully move their careers forward.

Tom's friend, colleague, and soon-to-be lifesaver, Althea J. McBride was born and raised in Paterson, New Jersey and had whizzed through the public school system there. It was extremely rare for Althea to bring home a report card with so much as a "B" on it. And her excellent grades were not because her father was the Superintendent of Schools in one of the state's largest cities.

It was because Althea had a combined gene pool that made her one of the brightest students her teachers had ever seen come through the system. With those grades and SAT scores close to perfect, Althea could have attended any Ivy League school of her choice. But she had made the decision a long time ago to follow in her father's footsteps and attend one of the Historically Black Colleges and Universities.

Although her father was a graduate of Jackson State, he never pushed her in that direction. In fact, they both agreed that Howard University in D.C. would probably be more to her liking. For one thing, it wasn't too far from home, and it was in D.C., where careers and connections were there for the taking. And finally, D.C. wasn't Jackson, Mississippi.

Althea double majored in Sociology and Political Science. Upon graduation she received a few job offers to become a staff person for this or that congressperson from some east Podunk district she'd never heard of. Moreover, Althea was more interested in the sociology side of her education since one of her professors had instilled in her the conviction that she could make a difference. Thus, community service seemed to be the path for her—at least for now. So, after graduation from Howard, she was off to NYU's Graduate School of Public Administration to study for a master's degree.

Althea's office was a few doors down from Tom's. At 8:55 she poked her head in and said with a smile that was way too bright and cheery for a Monday morning, "So, are you ready for this?"

Tom felt he was most likely about to be publicly shamed in front of his colleagues, so it was difficult for him to react well to Althea's early morning humor. As they headed down to the conference room, she tried to lighten things up with some gallows humor by saying how nice it had been knowing each other during their short tenure. She went on to speculate on how much they might receive in severance packages. Althea placed her hand on Tom's shoulder and said, "Well, if you do get fired it will definitely shorten your commute. And, can I have your office?"

The department was located on the 7th floor of the bank's headquarters. As they entered the conference room, most of the other staff had already arrived. Since Tom and Althea would most likely take Teddy's incoming fire, the others were kind enough to keep their usual seats open for them.

The conference room was configured in a square with long tables set end to end with open space in the middle. Tom always imagined that the open space in the center might be a place where one of the staffers would conduct a self-immolation after a public dressing down from Teddy. Thus far, no one had committed the ultimate sacrifice.

The corner conference room had three glass walls — two exterior walls that provided a nice view of the city and one glass wall facing the interior of the 7th floor. Tom always tried to position himself in a seat with his back to the outside wall opposite the interior glass wall so he could see directly through to the office floor. He considered it his *Sundance Kid* seat since it meant he didn't have to watch his back and could see anyone roaming the floor looking for a gunfight. Today, Tom specifically wanted to see Teddy's body language as he marched down the hall from his office into the conference room. When Teddy entered the room, everyone fell silent and focused on how well their shoes were shined. Most heads were down in a basic prayer position. They had read the article and no one wanted to make eye contact.

The In-House Politician

As Teddy made his way to his seat the look on his face placed the fear of God in everyone in the room. His first words set the stage for what was coming next. "I received a call from our Chairman at home yesterday. It really made my day. He wanted to know, in very vivid terms with expletives I'll not repeat here, how we'd failed to keep the protest groups in line. And by 'we' he meant me. He went on to remind me that the bank's reputation was on the line and that no one could predict how this article might affect the stock price. The Chairman also asked me what we planned to do about it?" That's when Teddy turned his head ever so slowly in Tom's direction. "Tom, can you please explain to me why I didn't know how poorly we were doing under the agreement?"

"But Teddy," Tom said, followed by a mindless pause.

"Don't, but Teddy me!" he fired back as it appeared his head might explode.

Tom respectfully returned fire. "You receive monthly reports on our mortgage activity, and as you recall we met last week to review the numbers. We agreed it didn't look good, specifically with respect to the zero minority approvals, but we didn't come up with any solutions. But those numbers reported in the article were completely false. And we certainly didn't think Sally was going to sandbag us with a bullshit story like this. She knows how difficult it is to get these borrowers approved, so I'm at a loss as to what she thought this kind of article would accomplish—other than to embarrass us into giving away more of the store."

Tom could tell from his body language and stare-down that Teddy didn't appreciate his last comment. Teddy looked around the room for any heads that were up, making eye contact.

Althea was one of his favorites. She proceeded to save Tom from Teddy's guillotine. "Perhaps," she said, "we should review our outreach plan to determine if we're hitting all the community leaders that might have an interest in getting more loans into their communities." This was a nice save, especially for Tom. He could tell she had something in mind, but wasn't ready to share it with the whole department.

Teddy understood and seemed semi-pleased with this. He looked at Kelly and said, "Set up a meeting this afternoon with Althea, Tom, and myself." And that was it. The meeting was over. Teddy got up and left. Tom guessed that Teddy was in one of his "needing to put out the fires" mode for the remainder of the morning and had no more time to waste listening to any more lame excuses.

With Teddy temporarily satisfied, Tom pledged his undying devotion to Althea. He had made the guest list for Teddy's afternoon meeting. But it was still early, and, anything could happen. And a little gremlin inside Tom's head was telling him that, despite Althea's good intentions, things were about to get dicey.

Chapter 3

THREE WEEKS EARLIER

Tina Washington was Porter McMahon's second in command in the bank's mortgage department. A young African American professional, she had witnessed how Althea had made it to a relatively high officer status inside the bank, having achieved the rank of Vice President. Althea was Tina's new role model. As far as she was concerned, Althea had it all: style, grace, composure, beauty and intellect. But in order to reach Althea's level, Tina knew she would need to complete her degree, dress more professionally, and begin looking around for job openings in other departments. Tina knew she was just window dressing for Porter. He'd made that pretty clear in his many promises to promote her, which as yet had gone nowhere. Whenever she confronted him about it, his excuses were always lame.

Tina's career aspirations were currently taking a back seat, however, to more pressing issues. She was at her wit's end and ready to explode. As the primary underwriter on the affordable mortgage loans under the terms of the CRA agreement, she was not pleased with the credit decisions Porter was making. In fact, many of the loans placed before the mortgage review committee were ones in which Porter had overridden her recommended approvals. In her opinion, he had come up with some of the most insensitive and discriminatory reasons she'd ever witnessed. If Porter kept this up, the high number of minority denials would eventually come back to haunt the bank.

As an example of Porter's heart of stone, he overturned one of Tina's approvals because the borrowers did not have two full years on the job. The borrowers were two African American women who'd met on the job, become friends, and decided to pool their resources. They were both single mothers trying to support young families, and decided to buy a house together. Both women had 18 months of continuous employment with the same company.

Porter rejected the loan because both borrowers were six months shy of two full years on the job, which was standard underwriting practice. But there were always exceptions to the rule—that is, unless you were Porter McMahon. Based on conversations with her boss, Tina determined that his real reason for the denial was that the borrowers were two unwed Black women buying a house together, each with two young children to support. All the children were under the age of four. When he reviewed the file with Tina, Porter said his gut told him they wouldn't be able to afford the monthly child-care expenses on top of the mortgage payments.

When Tina spoke with the borrowers, she was advised that one of the grandmothers had agreed to watch the kids during the workdays. But Porter seized on there being nothing detailing this in the file. Also, he asked how old the grandmother was and was she in good health? Would she have the energy to handle baby-sitting four toddlers? Porter had conferred with his crystal ball, which told him that one of the borrowers would eventually have to quit her job to stay home to care for the children. And without two incomes, they wouldn't be able to afford the mortgage payments.

Porter explained to Tina that he was doing the applicants a favor by saving them from a future default and foreclosure. In his mind, he was the good guy here. But since he couldn't deny the loan on the basis of his crystal ball, he was denying it because they didn't meet the bank's required two-year work history. Those were the rules and he was not about to make a policy exception for "these" people.

Tina looked at him and shocked herself by saying, "Porter, you're just making this up as you go along. You know as well as I do you can't deny this loan on the basis of some unpredictable future event. First, how do you know that one of them is going to quit her job? I told you about the grandmother helping out with child care. We've approved other loans to White borrowers who were just a few months short of the two-year job history. By the time this loan goes to closing, they'll probably be up to 20 months on the job. Come on, really?"

Porter returned her look and revealed his true bible thumping rationale. He said, "Unmarried women should not be purchasing a home together. It's not Christian and it's just not right! I know I can't deny it for that reason, but I have other legitimate criteria on which to base the rejection. I'm on solid ground here denying the loan on the basis of the borrower's failure to meet the two-year job requirement. Don't fight me on this, Tina. We need to go into the review meeting on a united front. Got it?"

Tina said, "And since when have you ever allowed me to speak at these review meetings? Fine, but you need to know that I think you're way over the line on this one."

"I can live with that," Porter replied. "But just so you understand, if this loan gets approved over my recommended denial because of DeMarco and Donovan's whining, then it's not going to have my signature on it. I wish Peter would hand over responsibility for this portfolio to them. All of it. Let them handle all these crappy loans—

from beginning to end." Porter never cursed in front of Tina. In fact, he never cursed at all.

When the second meeting of the mortgage review committee was held, Peter Porzio, Vice Chairman and Chief Credit Policy Officer, made it clear to all present that he considered these meetings a waste of his time. In fact, he was annoyed with everything having to do with the CRA and the bank's efforts to placate all the liberals out there. He announced to Teddy he would no longer be attending these meetings, and was turning over final credit approval authority to Porter for all of these "shitty" loans. He also agreed with Porter's denials of all the loans on the docket that day. It was three more denials to African American borrowers as Porter continued to run up the score.

Tina attended the review committee meetings, but Porter made it clear he did not expect her to contradict any of his credit decisions, or to express any opinions whatsoever unless she was specifically asked by Peter Porzio. About a week after the second meeting in which Porzio announced his disdain for all loans coming in under the agreement, Tina received an interoffice envelope marked "personal and confidential." She gasped when she opened it and read the handwritten note from Peter Porzio himself. In the note, he asked her to call him on his private line, and to not mention it to Porter, or anyone else.

Outside the bank, Tina's best friend from high school was Simone Martin. When Simone called her later that day to announce they were going shopping, and then out for dinner on Saturday, Tina said, "You must have read my mind."

Being best friends, Tina and Simone spoke frequently. They went out together as often as possible, interrupted only on the rare occasion when one of them had a date. Not that they couldn't have all the dates they wanted, because they were both pretty, well-mannered, and well-spoken young professionals. Indeed, these two young women had decided a long time ago they were not going to do anything stupid, like getting themselves pregnant before they were married. But saying no pretty much ended all their male callers after the first or second date, if it ever got that far. Where were all the nice young gentlemen for these fine young women?

On Saturday, after a long and successful day of shopping, they found an Applebee's nearby and settled into a booth in the back of the dining area. As dinner progressed, Tina decided her successful shopping day should be celebrated with a second glass of wine. Why not? She needed it. Simone was driving and she could hold her alcohol a lot better. In any case, they were both having fun and weren't ready to call it a night.

Halfway through their second glass, Simone said she had something she wanted to discuss. Tina sat back. "Sounds serious! You're not…? No, sorry, I would have known."

"Thanks a lot, girlfriend!" Simone said. "No, I just wanted to know if you think this might be a good time for me to buy a house. I get the feeling my parents want to make my basement apartment into a party room. You know, I've been saving a bunch of money living at home, and they may be right about me getting my own place and starting to build some equity. So, what do you think?"

Tina started to laugh loud enough to attract the attention of some folks sitting nearby. Fortunately, the wine did not spill out of her nose.

"Stop it, Tina! You're embarrassing yourself and me."

"We may need another glass of wine" Tina said, "if we're going to really talk business tonight. Because, my friend, have I got a story for you."

Tina began by describing the bank's new affordable mortgage plan that on paper looked and sounded like a great deal. She also indicated that Simone might even qualify for a mortgage based on her current income. But Tina shook her head and looked like she wanted to cry. At that moment it occurred to her it was the wine that was making her spill the beans. She reminded Simone that she could never repeat any of this to anyone under penalty of death, Tina losing her job, and it causing their friendship to end—whatever she thought most important. Tina realized she should have led with that full disclosure, but what the hell, it was time she unloaded her burden on someone. Why not to her best friend, someone she could trust with her life? Besides, she wanted to help Simone avoid the crushing insensitivities and defeat at the hands of her boss, Porter, who would surely find some mindless reason to deny her application. He couldn't care less that Simone was Tina's best friend.

Tina was not shy. "You know, if this guy I'm working for keeps rejecting most of the Black loan applications that are coming in under this new mortgage program, there's going to be hell to pay. Every day I sit there watching him overrule my recommended approvals, and there's nothing I can do about it. The guy is a complete asshole and there are times I'd love to—well, you know what I mean. But in the final analysis, I would hate to put you through the wringer with our bank and my boss. It's just not a very good situation right now. You know I'll help you find a good mortgage lender if you decide to buy a house. I'll even buy you a case of wine as a housewarming gift."

Simone was not laughing. She was livid. She muttered something about how other people outside their direct circle—important people who could do something to right this wrong—should be told the truth about her boss.

Tina said, "Do you understand how much trouble I'd be in if any of this conversation was ever traced back to me? You've got to promise me you'll never repeat any of this to anyone, including your parents. We drank some wine tonight and I said some things I shouldn't have. Things will be clearer in the morning."

But Simone was having none of it. "There's got to be a way to disclose this information to those who could use it for good—in a way that wouldn't hurt you." They agreed to review their options tomorrow, when they were sober and thinking straight.

As they were trying to do their best to sober up with some coffee, Simone decided to give it one more shot. She said, "Tina, you do recall my father is an attorney, right?"

That's when Tina lost it. "Haven't you heard anything I've said? There's nothing I can do that's not going to end up getting me fired. And I haven't even told you the worst part."

"Really? There's more? What haven't you told me? Come on, spill it."

"Okay, but again, you have to promise to keep this just between us."
Simone nodded.

"Well, I received a secret note from my boss's boss the other day. He's the top credit guy inside the bank. He asked me to meet with him, and he's got some crazy plan he wants my help with. And if the plan is successful, I might end up as head of the mortgage department."

"And if it's not successful?" Simone asked.

Tina looked around to make sure no one was nearby. "I'm not exactly sure what the worst case scenario might be, but none of the outcomes are good. And I really can't say anymore. You don't want to know anymore. You'd be a co-conspirator."

Tina tried to laugh, but the co-conspirator remark didn't land with either of them. She said, "Now, we need to get home. Can you still manage to drive?"

Simone said she felt fine to drive, but was still trying to recover from Tina's rant.

On Sunday afternoon, after Tina had taken her second round of aspirin, she called Simone to see how she was feeling. Simone was being a bit sheepish and circumspect, but Tina thought it was just a hangover. That was until she asked, "So, can we just forget about the conversation from last night? I shouldn't have told you all that stuff. I placed you in a bad situation, I know, and I'm sorry. I promise I'll help you get a good mortgage deal if you still want to buy. But can we forget about all that other stuff I talked about last night? Please?"

There was a long pause before Simone answered. "I'm sorry, too. I may already have said something we're both going to regret. Please don't be angry with me? I couldn't help myself. When I told my parents about all the Black applications your boss was rejecting, well, my Dad hit the ceiling. Essentially, he said you weren't doing your job unless you tried to do something about it. So, in my defense of you, I might have said some things you didn't want me to say."

"Oh, no! What did you say? OH MY GOD! WHAT DID YOU SAY?"

"Well, I told them that you had the best view of what was going on with the new mortgage program since you reviewed most of the

The In-House Politician

loans. And then I said that you were really upset with the way things were being handled inside the bank. That you were seeing a lot of applications being turned down, and most of those being turned down were to African American borrowers."

"Is that all you said? Or is there more?" Tina was thinking that if Simone's parents were normal, that comment might possibly be filed under the category of "So, what else is new?"

Simone said, "No. There's more."

"Oh Geez! There goes my job!" Tina said. "Okay. Tell me everything you told them. Don't leave anything out."

"Well, I told them that you were doing everything you could to get as many of the loans approved, but that your boss was being a real asshole. That's what you said, right? He was the biggest problem inside the bank, right?"

"Simone, we drank a lot of wine last night. I don't remember every word I said. But if I said my boss is an asshole, that's a bull's-eye. No doubt about it. What else?" Tina was still thinking the damage was minimal.

"Well, here's where you and I differ on this, because I think someone needs to do something about this. I told them that you knew the whole story—numbers and all. And I might have said something about that crazy plan you said your boss's boss came to you with. I told them I thought you might be getting in over your head and could end up in a lot of trouble."

Tina was now in tears. "Well, thanks for nothing. And I thought you were my friend!" As she was about to hang up, she said, "Have a nice life."

Simone shouted, "Wait a second, please, will you please wait a second? First of all, I'm so sorry about all of this. I can understand if you never want to speak with me again, but just hear me out, please?"

Tina was silent on the other end of the phone now, so Simone took that as her cue to continue. "You remember that my Dad's a lawyer, right? Well, he thinks he can help you. My Dad works for the Department of Justice."

Tina didn't hang up.

Simone said, "Tina, are you listening to me? Here's what he says you can do…"

Chapter 4

After the meeting, Kelly buzzed Tom and said Teddy wanted Althea and him to clear their schedules for the afternoon. She also asked Tom to let Althea know. Kelly asked him to do this in as polite a manner as she was capable of, considering the way things had played out at the staff meeting, including Teddy's door slamming and sour mood. She said he wanted them to be on call for a meeting in his office any time after 2:30. According to Kelly, Teddy had a luncheon meeting outside the bank and had blocked off two hours for it. Tom did not feel secure enough in his relationship with Kelly to ask her who Teddy was meeting with and she didn't offer it up. Not that it mattered, since Teddy never shared his personal schedule with anyone, including Kelly.

This last statement required some clarification. Teddy maintained two calendars. Kelly always knew where he was going, when he expected to return, and how to contact him. He'd begun carrying this new device called a pager on his hip like a six-shooter, and was threatening to get one for all his staff. However, Teddy always kept his own private calendar with the actual names of the persons he was meeting with. What was really laughable were the times he used white-out to delete a cancelled meeting that he had originally entered in ink. Now he could write over it, if need be. Teddy had no appreciation for pencils and their attendant erasures.

Since Teddy was not looking for him until the afternoon, this gave Tom some time to compare notes with Althea. He also needed to play the role of messenger and let her know about their command performance with the boss.

When Tom walked down to Althea's office, he could see she was on the phone. She saw him through the open door and waved him in.

Althea had only recently been assigned to the team tasked with implementing the CRA agreement with PUMP. Tom was the mortgage manager and all-around lending and credit expert in Teddy's department. Althea's role was less defined, but more in line with a sort of outreach and public relations expert helping to smooth the waters with some of the more volatile protest groups.

Althea was the only person in the department Tom trusted. They had confided in each other many times over the past few years and had, as far Tom could tell, kept each other's secrets and feelings about their boss and some of the more unlikable officers at the bank. Tom didn't want to sound like a whiner at the morning staff meeting, so he just kept his mouth shut thinking there would be a better time and place to defend himself to Teddy.

Althea ended the call. "Great! So lunch it is tomorrow."

Tom asked, "Who was that?"

"Oh, just a sorority sister who's in town. We haven't seen each other in quite a while."

Tom nodded and moved on. They just looked at each other briefly and did a simultaneous exhale. They were very familiar with Teddy's rants and had both found themselves on the wrong end of his public humiliations on more occasions than they thought were necessary. Teddy's public executions were legendary.

Althea began by stating the obvious and firing questions rapidly at Tom. "Well, that was pretty crazy this morning. Are you okay now?

You in recovery mode? He didn't give you much time to tell your side of the story, did he? But maybe that's a good thing. Any word on when we're supposed to meet later?"

"Yes, to all of that," Tom said. "Yes, it was a shit show. Yes, I'm starting to calm down a bit. And yes, we're supposed to meet with him this afternoon sometime after 2:30. We've been ordered to clear our schedules and make ourselves available, according to Kelly. We're on call."

Althea was clearly in a better mood than Tom. Perhaps it was because she didn't receive any of the humiliation he had encountered. She also seemed to have calmed Teddy down with her suggestion. She just smiled and said, "I guess that means I'll have to cancel my meeting with the Chairman this afternoon. You think he'll mind?"

Tom was mildly upset with her response because her humor didn't seem to be very empathetic to his situation. He said, "However, the part about maybe it's a good thing that he didn't give me a chance to defend myself, well, I hope you're right about that. 'Cause here's the thing. I'm confident the numbers reported in *The Examiner* article were, at best, a misrepresentation, or, at worst, an outright lie. Somebody just made those numbers up. I think someone's trying to screw us; the bank, or Teddy, or me. It makes no sense. How would *The Examiner* have gotten hold of those numbers? I sure didn't give it to them. And I'm pretty sure Teddy didn't provide them, or he wouldn't have been so upset."

Althea said, "Okay, first things first. Why do you say the numbers weren't right?"

"Because the most recent reports I have from Marley, sorry, I mean Porter, puts us up at around $2 million in closed loans."

Althea laughed whenever Tom referred to Porter as Marley.

He continued. "Now, that's still not any great performance, but it's a whole lot better than the mere $500,000 that was reported in the article. I never talk much about the pipeline since I can never predict the quality of loans that are coming in, or the level of insensitivity we can expect from Marley and his crew. But I know there are some African American loans in the queue. I just don't get it. I thought that reporter from *The Examiner* was a standup guy."

Althea was curious. "Did you keep copies of those reports from Marley?"

"Sure I did. And I gave copies to Teddy. Only question is, did he read them?"

"So who would want to screw us, and why?"

"Oh, okay, so you want me to come up with a list of all the suspects, both inside and outside of the bank, that would like to see us fail? That list is as long as your arm. Well, on second thought, the prime suspects would be a pretty short list. I guess top of the list would be Sally Kessler. She hates us with a passion and would love to see us fail. But I don't know what her definition of failing looks like. If we don't make the numbers under the terms of the agreement, our reputation may get tarnished, and I would probably get fired, but the bank isn't about to go under. But maybe she gets some kind of redemption in the Bolshevik world if she makes us look bad, right?"

"Yeah, well, Sally can be a real bitch when it comes to banks in general, and us specifically, but I don't see her as desperate enough to make up some false data report, do you? And how about the reporter from *The Examiner*, Joe Campbell? Don't you think that if someone provided him with our mortgage data, then he would have tried to confirm it with us? When I said us, I mean Teddy, of course."

Tom knew she wasn't trying to make him feel bad, but that's the way it came out. He was Teddy's mortgage professional in the department and was the go-to guy in charge of getting the affordable mortgages in and closed under the agreement. So, naturally Tom would have been the guy to double check the numbers. But everyone knew the rules. Staff didn't speak to the press about anything. That was Teddy's job. But if *The Examiner* had contacted Teddy, he hadn't asked Tom to confirm the numbers.

Althea saw the look on his face. "Sorry, Tom, you know what I mean."

"Yeah, yeah. I know. Then there's always my good buddy, Marley. He would love to see Teddy and me fall flat on our faces. I can't imagine what kind of stories he tells Scrooge about me. First of all, there's the fact that I've had no formal credit training in mortgage underwriting. Then there's the fact that all the mortgages we're making under the terms of the agreement are riskier and less profitable than the conventional loans he closes every day. And God forbid that Scrooge is telling him that our portfolio numbers and performance will be combined with his. If that's part of the equation, then Marley would be my top suspect. Remind me to ask Teddy about that, will you please?"

Althea's eyes were glazing over. But she was still engaged enough to ask, "About what? Ask Teddy about what?"

"We need to get some clarification on whether our portfolio is being combined with Marley's. If it is, Marley is never going to be patient with us, and me in particular. And when I say patient,

I mean his willingness to process, underwrite, and give the benefit of the doubt to the type of applications we take in. On the other hand, and I expect he knows this, if too many of our loans are declined, that makes us all look bad, including him. Especially if most of those denials are to minority borrowers. It puts the bank's reputation at risk. The regulators and the press would make a field day out of a high minority denial rate as compared to the number of White denials."

"Really!? Althea said. "Tell me something I don't know."

Tom got up and started pacing. He braced his arms on the chair and asked the big question. "You think Teddy's gonna give me a chance to explain those bogus numbers in *The Examiner* article when we meet this afternoon? I drafted a quick and dirty memo providing him with an overview of the actual numbers, which were considerably under reported."

"How did you have time to do that since this morning's meeting?"

"Actually, I started it at home last night. Like I said, it was quick and dirty. Hey, it's my job to know the numbers."

She smiled. "Let it go, my friend. You didn't get fired over the article, right? So he must still have confidence in you. I repeat, let it go. If he's okay with it, then you should be as well. But in answer to your question, yes, you should document the numbers and send him the memo. Always good to cover your ass. But if I know Teddy, he's already moved on. Teddy doesn't do damage control like most guys. He plays offense all the time, no defense. How'd you like that sports analogy? Yeah, I grew up in a house with all brothers. I learned from them."

"That wasn't bad."

Tom thought about her response and concluded she was right. Teddy's ego would never let him make a general apology to all the staff for his benefit. This left him hanging out there a bit, but what could he do? "Okay," Tom said, "let's say I agree with you that he's fine with not talking publicly about the numbers in the article. But what about the fact that there seems to be someone out there, or possibly inside this bank, who is feeding Joe Campbell bad numbers on us with Sally Kessler's consent. And what's more, *The Examiner* is printing them without our confirmation. I'd like to know what Teddy plans to do about that. Wouldn't you?"

Althea looked at Tom as if he had two heads. "Listen to me," she said firmly. "Teddy gets paid very handsomely to be the political eyes and ears for this bank. It's his job to look out for all the landmines out there. Let the man do his job. If he needs our help, I'm sure he'll ask for it."

"So, it doesn't concern you that he's not…?" Tom didn't finish that thought, because he didn't know where it might land.

Althea said again, "Let it go."

"Okay, okay, got it. So what's this idea of yours about reviewing the marketing plan and that thing about community leaders and all that?"

She laughed. "Hey, I really pulled that one out of a hat, didn't I? And you're welcome, my friend. My comment seemed to shut Teddy down for the moment. The look on his face when he asked you why he didn't know how bad the performance was—well, it was a bit frightening. I was just trying to change the subject and save your lily white ass. You owe me."

"Yeah! Thanks. Put it on my tab. No really, I appreciate it. Hopefully, it results in a full pardon rather than just a of stay of execution."

Althea was still trying to formulate a plan to present to Teddy. She stated it would only work if all the credit gods were on their side. She said, "Have you ever heard of Rev. Lloyd Ogletree? He's the pastor of a megachurch down at the Shore. But more importantly, he's also the current chairman of the New Jersey Chapter of the African American Ministry for Justice and Economic Development, or MJED, as they call it. If we could somehow convince him and all of the Black churches who are members of MJED to help us promote our affordable mortgage program, well, then we might just get our numbers up, especially our Black application numbers."

"Not bad," Tom said. "So how do we do it?"

"You need to understand something, Tom. Pastor Lloyd, as he likes to be called, is not a friend of ours, or any bank's for that matter. He sits on the board of PUMP, and Sally Kessler is one of his chief advisors. Whatever bilge Sally makes up about us, and the banking industry, she feeds it to him directly."

"So, what makes you think we can turn him in our favor?"

"Oh, I leave that kind of political B.S. to Teddy. That's why they pay him the big bucks. If there's a deal to be made, Teddy will figure out a way to get it done."

"Right, but what I mean is, how does Teddy get in the door to meet with Pastor Lloyd?"

She was smiling ear to ear. "Well, Pastor Lloyd and I are both graduates of Howard. And, despite your so called Ivy League alumni connections, we graduates of Historically Black Colleges and Universities play well in that sandbox, too. As a well-known alumnus,

The In-House Politician

Rev. Lloyd Ogletree is often invited to come back and speak on campus. My senior year he spoke and I introduced myself to him afterwards. I'm sure he won't remember our brief interaction, but who knows. It can't hurt, right? Hopefully, once he hears that Teddy's got a Howard alumna on his staff who would like to reconnect with him it might lead to a meeting. You never know. We'll see. So, what do you think?"

"I think I should get back to my office and finish that CYA memo. We'll need the correct numbers for any future meeting with your Pastor Lloyd. And who knows? Maybe the actual numbers will save me."

Chapter 5

Teddy returned about 2:15. He quietly called Kelly into his office and, completely out of character, apologized to her for his earlier door slamming. Apparently, whoever he'd met with for lunch had put him in a much better mood. He told Kelly to alert Althea and Tom to swing by his office at 3 pm. Teddy had a few follow-up calls to make and an urgent need to powder his nose. It was a big lunch.

After Kelly left his office, Teddy opened his briefcase on his lap since there was no room on his desk due to the large stacks of papers and files. He had no wish to disturb the organized chaos that was located there. As he looked through his briefcase, he noticed a file Kelly had given him prior to leaving on Friday. The file was labeled "Weekend Reading" and was one of the required staples he always took home. However, depending on his plans for any given weekend, there were times when the file never saw the light of day. This past weekend was one of those time-eaters, which had included a daughter's soccer game, a birthday dinner for his wife, and a political fundraiser for the New Jersey State Democratic Party.

When he opened the file he saw the report Tom had received from the Mortgage Department. This was also the report Tom had referenced at this morning's staff meeting. "Oh shit," he said. He didn't have time to review the file right now, since nature was calling, and he hadn't yet triaged today's edition of *The Examiner*. He wanted to make sure there weren't any follow-up articles on the bank's alleged poor performance. Better yet, in the wishful thinking

The In-House Politician

department, maybe there would be a retraction for upsetting his and the Chairman's Sunday at home.

Speaking of which, Teddy remembered one of the high profile obituaries he'd seen in the paper. As he was recalling it now, it wasn't so much an obituary, but a story about a young lady who had gone missing on a vacation in Italy. She hadn't been heard from for two weeks, and the Italian police were still searching for her. The young lady's name was Michelle Mitchell and she was the political aide to Alex Scarduzo Jr., the Ocean County Executive.

The head shot of Michelle Mitchell looked very familiar. He thought he'd met her before. And this was quite possible since Alex Scarduzo Jr. was an up and comer in the New Jersey Republican Party. Teddy had attended a few fund-raisers in which Alex was connected in some way, since Ocean County was Teddy's biggest customer. Indeed, the banking relationship between 1NEB and Ocean County, which included payroll accounts, deposits, and bond issuances totaled close to $50 million in balances in any given month.

The mystery of Michelle Mitchell's disappearance had Teddy's attention. Alex always seemed to have a nice-looking young lady attending to him, who was not his wife, but who always looked like she was taking notes. Likewise, Teddy had been inside Alex's office on many occasions and met many of his staff. And while he didn't recall Michelle Mitchell specifically, the amount of income produced from the banking relationship with Alex and Ocean County was such that Teddy felt the need to call him to say he was thinking about him and Michelle. He buzzed Kelly to see if she could locate a copy of yesterday's *Examiner*. He wanted to re-read the story and have it in front of him when he called Alex.

At the appointed time, Althea picked Tom up and they walked down to Teddy's office. They hovered around Kelly's desk since the door to Teddy's office was closed and she indicated he was on a call. The cardinal rule was you never entered Teddy's office without Kelly's permission. Tom learned that one the hard way one time when Kelly was not at her desk. He knocked politely on the door before entering and was given the glare by Teddy and the arm motion to exit immediately. Tom apologized afterwards and they never spoke about it again. Message received, loud and clear.

Teddy's office was always dark, like some sort of inner sanctum. Not being Catholic, Tom had never been inside a confessional booth, but entering Teddy's office brought that vision to mind. While Teddy had a nice view of Main Street with a big picture window behind his desk, it still always seemed dark in there. Maybe it was because the sun never seemed to shine through his window since it was always arcing through the sky on the opposite side of the building. Or perhaps it was because Teddy installed a set of heavy retractable curtains on the glass wall facing the office floor and they were always closed. So, the only visibility into his office was through the glass entry door. Whenever you were summoned to his office for some unknown reason, your first thought was that you were about to be taken to the woodshed, another rather dark venue.

Teddy operated at two temperatures, hot and four alarm. However, his temper alternated with a great sense of humor. He loved to play practical jokes on some of his favorites in the department. Also, there was that rare occasion when he brought you into the confessional booth only to say he had tickets for the ballgame that night, and asked if you wanted to go. Of course, the offer was always at the last

The In-House Politician

minute and he insisted on you taking a customer. Okay, so how were you supposed to get hold of your customer on the afternoon of the game in the off chance that customer was just sitting by the phone thinking you might call for an invitation to tonight's game? And, of course the customer had no other plans for the evening, right? But it was still nice that he offered.

Teddy's office was filled with all kinds of sports and political memorabilia. He was born and raised in Chicago, but came East for college and had stayed after his ball-playing days were over. A lovely young co-ed was also involved, who may have had something to do with his remaining in the Garden State.

As a Chicago native, he was a life-long Bears and Cubs fan. His office was essentially a shrine to all things football and baseball, with great photos of Dick Butkus, Gale Sayers and "Sweetness" himself —Walter Payton. Likewise, Ernie Banks and Ron Santo were held in high esteem on his office walls. You might be asking, why no mention of Michael Jordan and the Bulls? Well, Teddy was already out of college and working in Jersey by the time "His Airness" reached the NBA. But he was still a big fan.

Then there were all his political photographs. It seemed as if Teddy had had his picture taken with every U.S. President since 1980. Photos with Governors, Senators, and Congressmen adorned his walls and took up all the remaining space that was not occupied by Da Bears or the Cubbies. However, a special place was reserved in the middle of the wall opposite the entry door. If it was your first time visiting, you couldn't miss it. It was a picture of Teddy and his wife with the Pope. In advance of Teddy's visit to Rome, the Archbishop had performed a small miracle. He had asked for and received a special audience with the Pope for Teddy and his wife, photo included. Every time Teddy entered his office in the morning, he genuflected and blessed himself.

When Teddy ended his call, Kelly let him know that Tom and Althea were waiting. Kelly followed them in with what appeared to be an article from yesterday's *Examiner* and handed it to him. From the brief discussion between Kelly and Teddy, Tom believed it was the story about an aide to Alex Scarduzo who had gone missing. Tom recalled seeing it in the paper yesterday, but hadn't read the full article and didn't make the connection until now.

Chapter 6

Teddy was in a much better mood, but one couldn't call it jovial. The bar was set pretty low, so anything was an improvement after the morning staff meeting.

He started off with what one might consider a semi-apology. He waved the mortgage report in his hand and said, "Tom, I didn't know this report was in my briefcase until a few minutes ago. Seems to me that if I knew about the report, I could have better defended our department's performance to the Chairman when he called me yesterday."

This statement didn't allow Tom much wiggle room. He didn't want to throw Kelly under the bus by asking if she'd alerted him to it before he'd left on Friday. On the other hand, he couldn't say what he really wanted to say, which was something like the line from *Cool Hand Luke* about "a failure to communicate." It wasn't his fault Teddy hadn't read the report, but he kept that rejoinder to himself. In his own defense he said, "I told Kelly about the report when I handed it to her, and she confirmed that it would be in your weekend reading package. The mortgage data on that report will show you that the numbers quoted in *The Examiner* article were total bullshit."

Teddy put his hand up and stopped him right there. He apparently had more to say. He continued to inform them sheepishly that he'd had a busy weekend and never opened his briefcase. And this is where the semi-apology seemed to take on actual form. He waved another document in front of them. Neither one of them had any idea what it was.

Their boss had a hang-dog look that was always accompanied by a shrug of the shoulders and a slow sideways negative shake of the head, which typically indicated some modicum of guilt. He said, "This is my call sheet, which Kelly pulls together for me from the call tickets I give back to her when I haven't been able to return them. This is my fault. There's a call on here from late last Thursday from Joe Campbell at *The Examiner*. Now, I've asked Kelly if he said anything about wanting to get my reaction to an article he was writing. Kelly didn't recall him saying it was important for me to get back to him immediately, just that he wanted to speak with me and to please have me return the call. Not thinking it was critical, I gave the call ticket back to Kelly to put it on the call sheet. So I guess it's my bad that I never called Joe Campbell back. And well, you guys know the rest."

Tom and Althea looked at each other in disbelief. They also wanted to get some further clarification about supposedly knowing the rest.

While he rarely used profanity in Althea's presence, Teddy bellowed, "Goddammit, I should have opened that briefcase! Worst case, I would have been able to defend us to the Chairman, and best case, if I'd returned the call to Joe Campbell I might have been able to dispute the numbers he was reporting. Who knows, maybe he would have delayed the article until he checked back with his sources on the data—not just Sally. Sorry."

Tom was trying his best not to look like he wanted to take a victory lap, or at least high five Althea. He couldn't help smiling.

When he saw Tom's grin, Teddy pointed his finger at him and said, "Tom, you find this funny?"

Tom said, "No. I sure don't. But you did place much of the blame on my shoulders at this morning's staff meeting, and, well…" Once again, Tom provided Teddy with a sheepish delay.

"You're right, Tom, I did, and I'm sorry about this mix-up. Now tell me about the numbers in the mortgage report, and who you think might be the source of those false numbers. It makes no sense to me that Joe Campbell would report those numbers without getting confirmation from me. If that's why he was calling me last week, well, he wasn't very forthcoming in trying to get a response before he published it. But that doesn't do me any good right now."

Tom was about to advise him on the numbers but Teddy stopped him. "On second thought, let's you and I talk about those numbers later. For now, I want to hear Althea's plan to get our mortgage numbers up."

As usual, Althea was right. No defense. All offense—at least for now. She said, "Well, I'm sure you've heard of Rev. Lloyd Ogletree, right?"

Teddy was trying to recall him.

Althea continued. "Let me tell you a little bit about him. Rev. Lloyd Ogletree is the shepherd of some 3,000 members of The Evangelical Church of the Living God located down at the Shore in Monmouth County. It's a megachurch and has the largest African American congregation in the State. Pastor Lloyd, as he is known to his congregants, friends, and enemies alike, is a big man at six-foot-five and well over 300 lbs. He has an intimidating presence in the pulpit, and even more so when you're face-to-face with him. On Sundays when he's in the pulpit preaching in his black robe and purple stole, he can really bring the fire and brimstone. And when he looks down at you either preaching or in conversation, it's as if you're speaking directly with God. He's got the voice of James Earl Jones, the size of Roosevelt Grier, and the confidence of Adam Clayton Powell,

Jr. Pastor Lloyd doesn't need to charm you, because the minute he engages with you, you're putty in his hands. And if you're wondering how I know all this, I've been down there to his church a few times to hear him preach."

Teddy's eyes grew wide in astonishment. "Yes, I've heard of him, but we've never met. I've also heard some rumors that he's been making the rounds at many of the Democratic fund-raisers. Some say he might be considering a run for Congress down there in Central Jersey. And if that's true, he's crazy. That's Ed Blake's district. But now that Blake's running for Governor the seat's up for grabs. Anyway, you were saying? What about Ogletree?"

Althea was fine with Teddy's interruption. She said, "Well, there are two things you should know about Pastor Lloyd."

Teddy seemed amused. "So you two are on a first name basis?"

"No, but that's what he likes to be called. So here's the thing. We're both alums of Howard University and we met briefly years ago. Obviously, we're a few years apart, but I'm not being too modest when I say that we alums of Historic Black Colleges and Universities tend to form very close bonds. We look out for each other and like to promote each other's careers. It's kind of an unspoken bond between all of us."

"That's nice to hear," Teddy said, " but what's it got to do with improving our minority loan volume?"

Althea knew how to play Teddy, and she wasn't sidetracked a bit. She came in with her closer. "You may not be aware of this but about six months ago Pastor Lloyd was elected Chairman of the New Jersey Chapter of the African American Ministry for Justice and Economic Development. Membership in MJED, as they like to call it, includes many of the largest Black churches in the State, most of which are located in the same cities where we have branches." Althea sat back in her chair and let that sink in.

Teddy's eyes lit up. A moment passed before he spoke again. "Alrighty then! So, how do we get in to see your good friend Pastor Lloyd?"

"I did not say we were friends. But once he learns that you have a Howard alum on your staff, it may help to open some doors. You should also know that he's no friend of ours. He sits on the board of PUMP. You'll need all your powers of persuasion to get him to help us."

Teddy didn't appear to be shocked by this. He smiled. "Well, I guess I'll just have to charm him."

He thanked them and said he had some phone calls to make. He also said he was going to try to get in to see the Chairman and let him know about the false mortgage numbers that were reported in *The Examiner* article. The discussion of the mortgage report would have to wait.

Althea was two-for-two now and seemed to be basking in the glow of her recent successes. On the way back to their offices Tom complimented her on her Roosevelt Grier analogy. He said, "How did you come up with that one? You weren't even born when Rosy Grier played for the Giants."

She said, "My Dad."

It appeared as if Tom's head was no longer in the guillotine—at least for now. He was still employed. Althea had come through again.

Chapter 7

After the meeting with Tom and Althea, Teddy buzzed Kelly and asked her to get Fitz on the phone. He needed someone of stature to reel in Rev. Lloyd Ogletree. It was time to bring in the big guy.

Patrick M. Fitzgerald, or "Fitz" as he was known, was Teddy's mentor. In his younger days, Fitz had been a star lineman for the State University. Today, however, his height could not support the weight he had amassed wining and dining all those important bank and political customers. Fitz was still trying to fit into some suits that were clearly designed for a lower weight class and an earlier period in his life. The chain on his pocket watch stretched the entire width of his vest and much wider girth. Fitz was in his mid '70s, and he still had a full head of salt and pepper hair and prominent bushy eyebrows that seemed to move in tandem with every facial expression he made. He was larger than life.

Fitz was semi-retired from all the roles he previously served at the bank, and was the best public relations man in the world this side of P.T. Barnum. He had an uncanny ability to remember your name and the name of your wife after only one brief greeting and handshake in a reception line. He knew everyone who was important, and they knew him. He had been a congressman, had served as a cabinet official for two governors, and eventually became the best-known banker in the state. He had spent the last decade of his formal career at 1NEB, and was the person most responsible for bringing

The In-House Politician

Teddy to the attention of the Chairman. Once Teddy arrived, the two worked side-by-side for a few years until Fitz decided it was time to semi-retire and hand things over to his protégé. Fitz went on to do more volunteer work, which was his real passion, while continuing to serve as a consultant to the bank and to Teddy.

Fitz was the person of stature Teddy called to see if he could help in setting up a meeting with Pastor Lloyd. As it turned out, Fitz did know Pastor Lloyd personally. He also knew his reputation.

"Yes. I've known that S.O.B. for a number of years. I met him in D.C. on two occasions when we both sat on the dais at the National Prayer Breakfast. It was back when I was Chairman of the National Fellowship of Christian and Jews. I asked Ogletree to provide the opening prayer and benediction at the first event and then to give opening remarks at the second."

"He's a grandstander," Fitz continued. "He'll do anything to get his name in the paper and burnish his reputation. In fact, at the second prayer breakfast he had the balls to put out his own press release and placed copies of his opening remarks on a back table for the reporters to pick up. And if that wasn't enough, he then held his own press conference orchestrated by his staff assistant who attended with him. Can you believe that? He brought his own entourage to a prayer breakfast. I haven't spoken with him since that last event."

Teddy said, "Whoa, my friend! Are you done with your rant? I don't want you to kiss his ring, and I sure don't want you to ask him out on a date. I just wanted to know if you knew him, and it sounds like you do."

"Unfortunately, yes! Once again, how can I help you?" Fitz apparently knew where this was headed.

"Well, my good friend, I was hoping you could reach out to Ogletree and ask him if he would agree to meet with me."

"So, I've got to actually call and speak to that S.O.B., is that right?"

Teddy took the humorous route. "Well, there are other forms of communication, like writing him a letter or hoping that you'll run into him on the street somewhere, but we're kind of in a hurry. We're hoping to set up this meeting ASAP."

"You're gonna owe me big time for this one. Even if he doesn't take my call or call me back, I'm gonna hold this over your head until I'm satisfied you truly recognize what you're asking me to do. But I'll do it because it's for you."

Fitz was successful in reaching Pastor Lloyd by phone. In the course of their short conversation, Pastor Lloyd indicated he'd heard something about 1NEB's troubles with some of the protest groups. He was playing it close to the vest with Fitz since his friend, Sally Kessler, was always complaining about that bank. He agreed to contact Teddy as soon as time would permit.

Once Fitz reported back on his success, Teddy ordered Kelly to do whatever it took to accommodate Pastor Lloyd's schedule. This included rescheduling any of his meetings other than his weekly update with the Chairman. Everything else on Teddy's calendar was fungible. Kelly was to keep Teddy apprised of the negotiations for when and where the meeting might occur.

Kelly's level of exasperation with Pastor Lloyd's assistant was only matched by Teddy's anxiety and hovering over her desk whenever he knew she was on the phone with the other side. It was like negotiating a Papal visit. It became clear to Kelly that Pastor Lloyd was not inclined to meet with Teddy at the bank. In a moment of pure honesty, Pastor

Lloyd's assistant confided in Kelly that if word got out about this meeting, and he was somehow spotted by the press, his reputation might be tarnished. Bankers were the devil—you know—the current day equivalent of the temple money changers. But Pastor Lloyd was pragmatic enough to understand that following the money could sometimes lead to good things, even if it meant sitting down with those same money changing sinners from time to time.

After a few back and forths, the other side's assistant indicated that Pastor Lloyd was invited to speak at an all-day seminar at the Abyssinian Baptist Church in Harlem the following week. Perhaps it could be arranged for the Pastor and Mr. DeMarco to meet for dinner after the day's events. But the meeting would have to be a very private affair. Teddy's eyes lit up when he heard this was a possibility. He told Kelly to suggest the two men meet for dinner at a great little restaurant in the Down Neck neighborhood of Newark where the food was great and no one would recognize him. The other side agreed and the meeting was set.

Teddy knew all the restaurants in the Portuguese section of Newark, as well as the owners, head chefs, and maître d's. After all, the bank was headquartered in Newark and Teddy spent much of his time entertaining some of its biggest customers. He selected the restaurant he thought would do the trick. It served an amazing rodizio, a Brazilian type of dinner experience that was beyond a feast. In fact, Teddy had taken the entire department there for a holiday luncheon. It was the only time in Tom's life he had to cry uncle because he couldn't eat another bite.

In this case, though, Teddy needed some privacy, so he asked the maître d to set him up with a table in a quiet little room upstairs. It was a room that few customers knew existed unless you were Teddy DeMarco. The bank had recently financed the restaurant's kitchen renovations to the tune of $250,000. In return, Teddy got whatever table he wanted, whenever he wanted it.

Tom was not included on the guest list for this meeting, which was something he never let Teddy forget. However, Althea was kind enough to fill him in the next day. In her recap, she made it clear that once her introductory role was completed, she was politely asked to leave. This debriefing was designed to alleviate Tom's jealousy. It did not.

When Pastor Lloyd arrived at the restaurant, Teddy and Althea were waiting for him outside. Not too many things surprised Teddy. But when the Pastor's entourage pulled up in front of the restaurant, two security guards dressed like *Men-in-Black* with matching wrap-around shades, hopped out of the two black SUVs. One of the security guards opened the door for the Pastor, while his staff remained inside the vehicles. Teddy found it laughable that the Pastor wanted complete privacy at the meeting and then showed up in a parade. Likewise, he was not aware Pastor Lloyd was bringing anyone else to the dinner meeting. But always being the perfect host, Teddy quickly invited whoever was in his party to join them. That's when Pastor Lloyd whispered something to one of the security guards, resulting in three more staff persons climbing out of the SUVs. Teddy made a mental note to have a conversation with Kelly the next day.

As part of the negotiations for the dinner meeting, Teddy made sure Kelly had determined that Pastor Lloyd was not a vegetarian, and that he enjoyed some good red meat, because there would be plenty of it. The assistant advised Kelly that the Pastor's appetite was legendary. In fact, the women in his congregation always found new recipes to keep themselves in his good graces. These women considered it a part of their religious duty to keep the Pastor well fed.

The dinner party for the evening had now expanded from three to six. Teddy had assumed it was only going to be Pastor Lloyd, Althea, and himself. It was a good thing he'd secured the upstairs room since it was easy to increase the size of the table. The main dining area was filled to capacity, and Pastor Lloyd had received assurances from Teddy they would dine inconspicuously.

That Pastor Lloyd had brought along three staff persons and two security guards to the Harlem seminar was beyond Teddy's comprehension. But bringing these same folks to dinner as uninvited guests was exceptionally rude. Teddy recalled what Fitz had told him about Pastor Lloyd. It wasn't as if Teddy was worried about the dinner bill, since the Chairman had given him a blank check to get the job done. And Teddy was no slouch when it came to entertaining. But in this case, Pastor Lloyd was not a customer, at least not yet, and his not-so-subtle inclusion of his three additional staffers for dinner led Teddy to believe he might be in for a tough evening of negotiations. He was just glad he didn't have to feed the two security guards as well. Teddy assumed they took their SUVs to the nearest fast-food joint and waited for a call to pick up the Pastor and his entourage. Teddy was impressed that Pastor Lloyd also made use of a pager.

As they all climbed into the elevator, Althea reintroduced herself to Pastor Lloyd. She reminded him of when they had last crossed paths when she was still an undergrad at Howard. She also noted the specific topic he had lectured on that night. Pastor Lloyd was gracious and nodded in agreement trying to remember the topic of his lecture.

He did so many appearances it was hard to keep track of them. He apologized to Althea because he didn't recall their conversation. She completely understood and they continued to talk about the good times at their alma mater. Teddy watched and listened in a state of euphoria. It seemed like Althea had successfully wrestled the bear and had him eating right out of her hand.

The arrangement with the restaurant for the upstairs room included their own private waiter who doubled as bartender. A small bar stood in the corner of the room; a big picture window behind it overlooked the street on which the restaurant was located. They all had a drink at the bar, and when Teddy saw the conversation between Pastor Lloyd and Althea slowing, he suggested they all sit down and order. It might take a while for the guests to understand the culinary delights they were about to enjoy, so Teddy recommended they let him order. This was a wise move since the Pastor and his staff were not familiar with how it all worked and how much food they were about to consume.

Teddy placed himself at the head of the table closest to the bar so he could speak with the waiter whenever needed. He invited Pastor Lloyd to sit opposite him. Althea sat to the right of Pastor Lloyd, which suited Teddy just fine. This left Pastor Lloyd's three assistants to sit on the sides, two of them were on either side of Teddy. That left the third member of the entourage seated next to Pastor Lloyd, opposite Althea. And while Teddy was introduced to these three individuals when they first met, he had no recollection of their names, and no interest in getting to know them any further other than to appear as a polite and gracious host. They made small talk until the food came. Meanwhile, Teddy watched and listened to what the Pastor had to say, trying to gauge his temperament for the business discussions to come.

It wasn't as if the Pastor needed to say anything—it was just the reverence of his body language that both Teddy and Althea witnessed that made them adhere to the same code of waiting until everyone was served. It was only then that Pastor Lloyd offered up his traditional prayer prior to anyone picking up a utensil.

The feast proceeded with sparse conversation. To Teddy's delight everyone seemed to be enjoying the food. He had, in fact, selected the best restaurant for this meeting. The food kept coming and Teddy's guests were dumbfounded by the quantity and quality. He kept reminding them to go slow and sample everything because the meal was nothing more than a feast that could easily have fed a third-world country. Oooh's and ahhh's were abundant from Pastor Lloyd and his staff as they continued to see more food arrive. And just when they thought the meal was over, the waiter brought more. He would slice the meat off the rodizio stakes, and would come back whenever someone's plate was empty. At some point, perhaps an hour into the meal, Pastor Lloyd finally cried uncle just as Tom had done at the holiday party.

Teddy asked to see a dessert menu, but Pastor Lloyd said he couldn't eat another bite. He nodded to the man sitting immediately to his right and opposite Althea. Teddy thought he recalled his name was Isaac and that he had been introduced earlier as Head Deacon of the church.

Deacon Isaac, which is how Pastor Lloyd had referred to him during the earlier conversation, had an Old Testament look about him that said the God he worshipped was a vengeful God. It appeared that

Deacon Isaac had made peace with a faith that required him to repent and to urge others to do the same. With a nod from Pastor Lloyd, Deacon Isaac invited the other two staffers to join him downstairs while their boss and Teddy conducted business. This left Althea in the awkward position of wondering if she should also excuse herself so that the men could make their deals.

Since Teddy didn't know if Pastor Lloyd wanted her to be part of their conversations, he nodded and whispered his thanks to Althea and said it was fine if she wanted to take a taxi back to the bank where she had left her car. Upon Althea excusing herself, Pastor Lloyd got up from the table and in a manner perhaps a bit too forward for a Man of God, indicated to Althea how much he enjoyed their conversation. He also wanted to express his desire that if she ever wanted to contact him directly on any matter, spiritual or otherwise, to please do so. As they were about to say their goodbyes, Pastor Lloyd extended both arms in the gesture of an embrace, which was accepted by Althea without thinking. With that exchange completed, Pastor Lloyd reached into his vest pocket and handed her his personal business card.

Teddy had also excused the waiter. He and the Pastor were now alone.

Pastor Lloyd initiated the discussions. "So Mr. DeMarco, I understand you've been having some problems with my friend Sally Kessler. Do I have that right?"

Teddy played the astonished card and replied with a little white lie. "I didn't know you two knew each other. How do you know Sally, and may I ask if you let her know we were going to meet?"

"No," Pastor Lloyd replied with a smile and a shake of his head. "I don't typically run my plans by her. However, you should also know that I sit on the board of PUMP. And Sally has made it perfectly clear that she considers you and your bank to be, well, how shall I put this as delicately as I can?"

"I know, I know," Teddy said. "No need to explain any further. She thinks all bankers are evil, and as for me, well, since I work for the largest bank in the State, she considers me to be the devil incarnate. I've tried my best to educate her on how banks operate and get her to at least understand that while we may be a necessary evil, the key word there is necessary."

"Yes sir," Pastor Lloyd said. "Sally Kessler can be a major pain in the ass, if you'll forgive the expression. I've often thanked the Lord that I've never found myself on her wrong side. And now that I see what she can do to you and your bank, I'm going to redouble my efforts and my prayers to make sure that I never do."

"So how do you know her, I mean before you joined her board?"

"Well, as you know, I serve on a lot of committees and advisory boards. A few years back, Sally and I were appointed to one of the Feds' community advisory committees. The committee met in D.C. a few times a year and we typically went out to dinner afterwards. One night I ended up sitting next to her. We somehow got on the topic of the type of banking industry protest activity she was conducting using the CRA as her cattle prod. When I look back on that now, I guess she's successfully castrated a few of you guys!"

They both laughed. "So then you know what I'm dealing with?" Teddy said.

Pastor Lloyd laughed. "Yes sir, I do! And I hereby grant you absolution from the sinful thoughts you are having right now about

Sally and her friends. I read the recent article in *The Examiner* and feel your pain. So, how can I help you?"

"Well, as you know from the article, we've been having some trouble in generating demand for loans under the terms of the agreement we have with her, which is unbelievable when you understand what we've agreed to do. For example, all the loans are at below-market interest rates. We're also not requiring any mortgage insurance, which reduces the amount of cash a borrower needs for closing. We're taking all the risk into the bank's portfolio. Additionally, we're providing loans to borrowers with as little as five percent down payments. But please forgive me, I'm boring you with too many details. In the final analysis, we really don't understand why folks aren't lined up at our branches. We've marketed this agreement to all the real estate agents. We've put advertisements in the newspapers, and we've held marketing events with nonprofits whenever and wherever we could find folks interested in listening to our pitch. We've done events in front of only five people when we had 50 registered. But, as you read, our volume has been less than expected and, now, as a result of the article, we have Sally, the regulators, and the press, if you'll pardon the expression, up our butt poking around to see what other crap they can find! Oh, and for what it's worth, the numbers cited in *The Examiner* article were all wrong. We think someone is trying to, well—"

"I'm sorry for your troubles," Pastor Lloyd said. "So here's what I suggest you do, and I assume that this is the reason you invited me to dinner. Our group of pastors call themselves the MJED, which stands for the African American Ministry for Justice and Economic Development. We have many missions and I won't bore you with all of the details, but suffice it to say that we strive to improve the economic conditions in the African American community in as many ways as we can afford, and that are part of God's grace and blessings here on earth. I think I can testify that our member churches represent and speak for a large portion of the African American population in New Jersey. And I think I can rightly say that the leaders of MJED would probably want to hear about this new mortgage plan of yours."

Pastor Lloyd paused a moment, then said, "Let's have our people talk about a meeting date, as long as you agree to come down to my neck of the woods, and you give me enough time to pull in as many of the members of MJED that are available. How does that sound? One other thing, though. Let's keep this meeting with MJED just between us for now. I don't want any of my members to hear about this from anyone other than me. Okay?"

Teddy couldn't believe it. He wanted to plant a kiss on the Pastor for making everything go so smoothly. But he contained himself. "Wonderful, terrific, I can't thank you enough. I've got to believe that we can do some great things if we team the bank up with MJED. I really do."

Pastor Lloyd sat back in his chair and wiped his chin one more time. "One more thing, Mr. DeMarco. And I hope you will not take offense. You have to understand that I don't really know much about you or your bank. I also don't know that much about your agreement with Sally. All of which is to say while it sounds to me like you're doing the right thing with this agreement, my professional reputation relies on trust. If I were to find myself crosswise between you and Sally, or if I were to find out that your mortgage program was just for show and did not suit our African American brothers and sisters, well, that would not be a good thing for me, or my followers."

Teddy found it revealing that Pastor Lloyd's concerns put his reputation first. It confirmed what Fitz had warned him about. He turned on his best political skills and said, "Pastor, I can assure you that the affordable mortgage product we've developed with Sally Kessler and PUMP was designed specifically to help your folks become homeowners. They won't find a better deal anywhere. Now, as for our mutual friend Sally Kessler, you know her as well as I do, and you'd have to agree she can be unpredictable at times. I cannot say how she will react when she learns that you and I met. But I will leave that up to you. She won't hear about it from me. I'm fairly certain her initial rection will be to hold you in contempt for sitting down with the enemy. But I'm also certain that you'll be able to calm her down and explain that it's a win-win-win. The bank gets access to more Black homeownership prospects, Sally gets to take a victory lap, and if all goes well, the members of MJED have happy church members who now own homes."

Pastor Lloyd smiled. "Well said, Mr. DeMarco. Well said."

Teddy was on a roll and as the consummate deal maker, he couldn't help himself. It was embedded in his DNA. He just came out with it because it was just part of his process. "So, Pastor Lloyd, please let me know if there's anything we can ever do for you. Okay?"

There it was right on the tip of his tongue, and Teddy went for it. "Pastor, there are some rumors out there that you may be considering a political career. I've been there and done that, and can testify that it ain't easy. I just wanted you to know that if you were to decide to make a run, you could have a real friend with 1NEB. In case you didn't know, one of the many hats I wear is that of chairman of the bank's Political Action Committee. I control

The In-House Politician

the purse strings and would be happy to assist you should the time come and you needed our help."

Pastor Lloyd was surprised by this. He had not given any thought to asking for money as part of his agenda for the meeting. But he also wasn't shy about his plans. He said, "Well, Mr. DeMarco, it seems you have some pretty good sources. I am considering a run for office, but I haven't made any final decision yet. However, knowing there might be some financial support from your bank would certainly be helpful in making such a decision, and I thank you for that. I'll get back to you if the need arises. Sincerely, thanks for the offer."

They got up from their seats and walked towards each other, shook hands, and agreed to be in touch. Teddy wanted to hug him, but thought better of it. Pastor Lloyd thanked Teddy immensely for what was a feast of a dinner and apologized for bringing all his extra guests. Teddy said it was fine.

Pastor Lloyd's cars had been summoned by Deacon Isaac and were waiting for him in front of the restaurant. As the caravan sped off Teddy began to wonder if his offer of the bank's financial assistance would come back to bite him in the ass. Never one to question his own instincts, he reminded himself to check in with the powers that be at the New Jersey Democratic Committee. He was sure they would advise him that Rev. Lloyd Ogletree had no chance of winning the nomination, and presumably would not attempt such a crazy stunt. Teddy thought, what could possibly go wrong if Ogletree decided to run for Congress? Then it occurred to him. "Oh shit. What have I done?"

Chapter 8

The first time Peter Porzio, Vice Chairman and Chief Credit Policy Officer of 1NEB, had a serious conversation with Alex Scarduzo Sr. was at the rehearsal dinner for the wedding. Porzio's son Francis was engaged to Leigh Ann Prezutti, niece of Alex Sr. The event was held one week prior to the wedding to accommodate everyone's schedule, and was held at the private club both families had been members of for years.

Leigh Ann was the daughter of Morgana and Anthony Prezutti, with Morgana being the second and younger sister of Alex Scarduzo Sr. When Leigh Ann and Francis were younger, they met at the private club and grew up despising each other. They both went away to college, but upon returning home ran into each other again at the club. That's when the old sparks turned into a romantic flame.

Anthony Prezutti was a well-known general contractor who grew up in South Philly with Alex Sr. They went to school together and were friends for life. In fact, Alex Sr. provided Prezutti with an early cash infusion that he grew into a multi-million dollar enterprise with road construction contracts in many of the Mid-Atlantic states. There were plenty of rumors about how Prezutti had secured these contracts, but nothing was ever proven. He was also godfather to Alex Jr.

While the Scarduzos and Porzios knew each other as members of the same club, they did not socialize prior to the engagement. Peter Porzio wanted to maintain his distance from Alex Sr., knowing his

The In-House Politician

reputation and that of his company. Porzio was a well-known and highly respected banker who was not inclined to sully his reputation by being seen with, or in any way associated with, his son's new family by marriage. Likewise, Alex Sr. heard through the club grapevine that Porzio and his bank were not inclined to do business with him. Other than the slight insult, Sr. thought the whole idea of bank financing was amusing. He had no need of it. His waste hauling business was a cash cow. And if, on the odd chance he ever needed financing, he knew how and where to get it. But now that Porzio's son would soon be married to his niece, family interactions would become unavoidable.

All these family relations were well documented on a whiteboard in the FBI's Newark Area Office. A Venn diagram illustrated all the family histories and their overlapping connections.

The conversation at the rehearsal dinner was pleasant enough between the two families. At the mid-point of the evening after all the speeches were done, Old Man Scarduzo requested that Peter take a walk with him so they could chat and enjoy some fine Cuban cigars. Porzio didn't see how he could refuse. On the patio overlooking the 1st hole, Sr. was very generous in his compliments about the rehearsal dinner. He had never been impressed with the food at the club, but maintained his membership in order to entertain customers and other guests in a manner expected and appreciated by all. Indeed, he was of the opinion that no other club would have him.

Scarduzo looked directly at Porzio and said, "Well, now that we'll soon be related, you can't keep avoiding me, you know. I know you don't like me because of my reputation, and I understand that. You an impressive banker and your position doesn't permit you to do business with the likes of me."

Porzio was surprised by Scarduzo's candor and was about to respond, but Sr. did not let him interrupt.

Scarduzo continued. "No, no. That's okay. I understand, and there's no hard feelings on my part. I just want us to be friends, or if we can't be friends, then at least we don't want to be enemies. So let me get to the point since the folks inside maybe wondering where we've gone off to. Peter, I truly believe that we can help each other. I really do. The fact is that I've been pretty lucky in my business. I've never really had any need for bank financing. But some of my friends and associates haven't been so fortunate. From time to time they can use some bank financing to get them over the hump. In fact, they tell me there are times when they're bidding on contracts that one of the criteria for selection is that they have an established relationship with a bank—you know, as a kind of reference. In some cases they might also need a letter of credit."

Porzio was in full stop mode. He held up his hand and said, "Alex, I don't think I can help you."

"C'mon, Peter. Just hear me out. Seriously, this can be good for both of us. Now, I promise you I will never ask you for any financing for me or my company. But some of my friends and associates can bring your bank some pretty hefty loan balances, resulting in some big fees and interest income. And I assure you there will be no overlap with me in any projects they bid on and you agree to finance. That's my pledge to you. In return, you should know that my son Alex Jr. plans to run for the congressional seat in our district—on the Republican side, of course. And I can assure you he'll be running unopposed. If he's successful and wins the general election, he can be a very good friend to 1NEB. And it won't cost you a dime. How's that, you ask?

Well, it's very simple. All these friends of mine who I refer to your bank for financing will also be donating to Jr.'s campaign. It's all legal and above board. My friends and associates know how to return a favor. So, you help them with their financing needs, they help Alex Jr. get elected, and you have a friend in Washington, who will be taking Blake's seat on the House Banking Committee. It's a sweet deal all around. Oh, and one last item for your consideration. For all these guys who you provide financing to, I will personally guarantee the repayment of their loans. Now, I'm sure you wouldn't want anything like that in writing. But you have my word and my handshake on it. And you can ask anyone that my word is my bond. So what do you say? Can we do some business together?"

Porzio was reeling. The fact that he'd had this impromptu conversation with Alex Scarduzo Sr. was rather intimidating. The deal sounded pretty good. Except for two things. First, there was the part about Scarduzo personally guaranteeing repayment. It could work only as long as the money owed went from Scarduzo directly to the borrower and then to the bank. That was a deal with the devil, but it surely sweetened the pot. The second item was more of a question than a problem. What if Alex Jr. lost the election? Sr. couldn't promise his son would automatically become the next congressman from their district. And the bank would still be saddled with all the loans to Scarduzo's friends.

Porzio asked, "What happens if your son loses?"

"We don't like to lose. We fully expect him to win. But, who knows? Worst case scenario, you've got a terrific portfolio of interim loans, which will continuously roll over and bring 1NEB lots of good income—at virtually no risk to the bank. But we fully expect him to win. And I can assure you he'll be a friend of 1NEB in D.C. So, what do you say?"

"Let me think about it," Porzio said. "I'll give you my answer next week at the wedding. But I have one absolute condition, and it's a deal breaker for me. You and I will never talk about this again. This meeting never happened. Never. Agreed?"

Scarduzo looked at Porzio with a frown that could not be interpreted either way. "You wound me, Peter. You really wound me. But I understand why you need to do it this way. So I agree to your condition."

As they returned to the party, Scarduzo wanted to put his arm around Porzio as a sign to all his associates present that the deal was done. But he thought better of it. Sometimes even families needed to keep their distance from each other. This was one of those times. But he did wink at Anthony Prezutti. The Old Man knew how to read body language. In his mind, the Vice Chairman of 1NEB had already said yes. He just didn't know it yet.

At the wedding the following Saturday, both men positioned themselves in seats at their respective tables that allowed them to see each other clearly across the room. There came a point after the toasts as everyone except the bride and groom were eating their meals when Porzio looked over towards Scarduzo. In keeping with their agreed upon covenant that there would be no further conversation about the proposal, Porzio just nodded in agreement. With a half-hearted smile, Sr. returned the nod, and the deal was done.

With the wedding winding down, Peter Porzio found he was not alone in the men's room. He had been followed by a young man. As they both dried their hands, the young man produced an envelope from his inside suit jacket pocket. It was a plain white envelope with nothing written on it. The young man did not look at Porzio directly, but in a deferential tone stated, "Please pardon the interruption, sir, but Mr. Scarduzo Sr. sends his regards, and said you would know what to do with this. Thank you."

The young man exited quickly, leaving Porzio alone to open the envelope. It was the list of friends and associates of Scarduzo Sr. who might be requesting financing from 1NEB in the future. At the bottom of the list was a handwritten note from Scarduzo introducing the young man as his designated intermediary. His name was Mark Trasotti and it listed his phone number. Scarduzo's note recommended that Porzio memorize the young man's name and number, as well as the names of the companies cited on the list. He also suggested Porzio might want to burn the list. Of course, Porzio would never consider such a thing. That would make it appear as if he was doing something illegal or underhanded. In his mind, all he was doing was bringing in new business to the bank. He put the list in his pocket.

It also occurred to Porzio that having a Republican Congressman in Washington, D.C. would certainly be helpful to the bank. If elected, perhaps he could do something about that CRA law that was causing his bank to make bullshit loans to "those" people.

Chapter 9

Alex Scarduzo Jr. was heir to the fortune spewing out of the family business known as New Jersey Waste Hauling, Inc. At 75 years of age, Alex Scarduzo Sr., Founder, Chairman and CEO, still ran the company, and appeared to have no intention of slowing down, or, god forbid, retiring. As such, Alex Jr.'s title and office at the family business was mostly for show. As Vice President and Director of Accounting, he had few responsibilities. He had people on the payroll, as well as outside firms, that performed the bulk of the company's accounting and financial tasks. Alex Jr. had plenty of time on his hands.

As a heavy contributor to the New Jersey Republican Party, Alex Sr. made overtures to the leadership about finding something important for Jr. to do to keep him busy and out of his hair. And since the Party enjoyed a constant replenishment of its finances from Alex Sr., his son was offered various opportunities to serve.

Alex Jr. had come up through the ranks with the usual apprenticeships, starting at the local Board of Education, then Town Council, followed by County Freeholder, and ultimately graduating to his current position as the elected full-time Ocean County Executive.

Jr. enjoyed politics and was quite good at it. However, since the County Executive was a full-time job, he had to resign from his position at New Jersey Waste Hauling, Inc. In return, his father appointed him to the board of directors and granted him a limited partnership in the company.

As County Executive and now Republican candidate for Congress, Alex Scarduzo Jr. caught the attention of Teddy and Fitz. And while Fitz was not a fan, he watched Alex's rise within the Republican Party with interest. Teddy, on the other hand, was more interested in his role as County Executive. In this position, Alex Jr. held the county purse strings, and had agreed to a business arrangement in which 1NEB became its primary bank. And while Teddy had always run as a Democrat in his past political life, there was no Democratic Blue or Republican Red when it came to securing government banking and payroll accounts for 1NEB. Indeed, the Ocean County coffers were no exception. That color was always green.

The congressional district that covered most of Monmouth and Ocean Counties was geographically situated for Alex's political ambitions, except for one thing. No Republican had won in this district in a very long time. The district had some wealthy communities located along the Shore which could always be counted on to vote for the more conservative candidate. The remainder of these two counties tended to vote Democratic. The Party saw this as an opportunity for Alex, Jr. to get his feet wet in a national campaign, albeit one in which he would most likely serve as a sacrificial lamb. Someone had to take one for the team.

Despite the odds against him, Alex was fearless and had every intention of winning. First, though, he needed to determine who his Democratic opponent was going to be. The rumors were rampant that Rev. Lloyd Ogletree was going to announce his candidacy soon. The primary was a year away, but Alex spent every spare minute strategizing how to run his campaign. Indeed, item number one was determining ways to limit his opponent's financial resources, and secondly to make them spend what resources they did have in the Democratic primary.

The Republican leaders promised they would reward Alex Jr. handsomely in the event he lost, but no one indicated what that prize might be. He was already County Executive. More importantly, no one was indicating that he had any chance of winning. So, Alex figured that his best chance of getting the Party's attention was to, in fact, win.

Alex had a few things going for him. First, he had all the money in the world and could therefore self-finance his campaign. This meant he didn't necessarily need to toe the party line in order to solicit campaign funds. His father's business was a cash cow, and Jr. was the primary beneficiary.

Second, Alex Jr. was a street fighter, both literally and figuratively. He'd been suspended in grammar and middle school for fighting, and had almost been kicked out of the exclusive boarding school his father sent him to. Alex's problem was that he was small in stature. He never grew past five-feet-four inches, and was always the smallest boy in his class. As a result, he got bullied and picked on to the extent that his father insisted that he learn how to defend himself. Alex was then trained in karate and the other martial arts. The bullying stopped in the 7th grade when Alex took down the biggest knucklehead in the middle school with a few swift kicks that laid him out before he could surrender. Alex Jr. enjoyed his time at home under suspension. Upon his return, all the former bullies gave him a much wider berth.

However, the incident at boarding school was a bit more serious since the parents of the injured boy, a student named Joe, called in the police and pressed charges. The school had no choice in the matter

The In-House Politician

since Alex hit Joe so hard that he almost lost an eye. No one seemed to give any credence to Alex's story of self-defense, even though the other boy was known for making ethnically charged insults to all those of the Italian persuasion. It was supposed to have been some kind of hazing ritual by the upperclassman that went sideways when Alex thought this Joe person was making fun of his size and ethnicity. When it came time to gather witnesses to hear Alex's side of the story, all the boys in the dormitory, led by Joe and his parents, clammed up. It was common knowledge that Alex didn't fit in, and they all wanted him gone. Then Alex Sr. stepped in and made a deal with the school and Joe's parents. All of Joe's medical bills were paid and magically, all the charges against Alex Jr. were dropped. Likewise, a substantial donation to the school's endowment was made by the Scarduzo family. But most importantly, Alex's juvenile record remained clean. Unfortunately for Joe, though, he would have minor problems with his damaged eye for the rest of his life, requiring that he sometimes wear an eye patch.

Alex's enemies never bothered him again. The result, however, was that his final prep school years were a lonely time for him. He had no friends. But he remembered all the names of those who never came to his defense in case they ever crossed paths again. Just like his father, Alex Jr. had a long memory.

And finally, Alex had spent his entire childhood, teenage, and college years watching how his father dealt with members of the Sanitation Workers Union. A number of situations had arisen over those years that seemed to be resolved only after his father had met with some guys who "tawked" funny, and dressed like funeral attendants. They were very good at resolving issues and restoring peace in the workplace.

After Alex Jr. had somehow graduated from a college no one had ever heard of with a degree in accounting, his father brought him into the company. When he asked his father about the labor unrest he had witnessed in his youth, his father just shrugged his shoulders and said that sometimes the ends justified the means. Alex didn't quite understand what this meant, so his father took him aside. "Sometimes you just gotta get tough with these troublemakers. They understand it when management plays hardball. You can't give in to these punk-like socialists. Never! You'll understand better as you get to know how this business works."

While never a fan of his father's waste hauling business, Alex also didn't look a gift horse in the mouth. He was fine with earning an excellent no-show salary while honing his political skills before turning thirty. He was a quick study and found the art and practice of politics to be child's play. He loved getting down and dirty, slinging mud at his opponents and always finding ways to deflect the consequences and place the blame on others. He understood quite clearly that the road to political success required a thick skin and always knowing where the bodies were buried. Oh, and that nutty saying from some old Chinese dude about keeping your friends close, but your enemies even closer—or something like that.

Assuming that Ogletree might run, Alex knew he needed to spend some time looking into his past in order to uncover some of those proverbial skeletons in the closet. Everyone had some. You just had to be better than your opponent in uncovering them. Fortunately, Alex Sr. called his son in to have little chat about campaign strategy. When they began discussing the topic of opposition research, Sr. advised his son that the resources of those men who helped to secure the labor peace, the ones who dressed like funeral attendants, would be made available to him for the campaign. Their Americanized names were Nick and Joe. Only Alex Sr. knew how to pronounce their actual Sicilian names. These guys had special skills that were typically not included on any business card or resume.

Initially, Alex Jr. was hesitant about using the services of these unknown gentlemen until Alex Sr. made it clear that they worked in the shadows. They would be paid in cash by Sr., so there would be no trail of funds ever traced back to his campaign, or, more importantly the Federal Election Commission.

As it turned out, these guys were good. Apparently they weren't as dumb as they looked. Within a few weeks of being deployed by Sr., they came back with some items of interest that both Sr. and Jr. thought might be useful in the campaign.

The first item was that, while still not an officially declared candidate, Ogletree was lining up possible campaign funds. They had discovered that Rev. Lloyd Ogletree had recently met for dinner with Teddy DeMarco at 1NEB. This could mean only one thing. Ogletree was looking for PAC financial support from the bank. And secondly, rumors were circulating about the bank not performing well under the terms of its agreement with Sally Kessler and PUMP.

Alex Jr. confided in his father with a few rhetorical questions, like, "Why would an African American politician running for office take money from the same bank despised by Sally Kessler and her PUMP friends? Wasn't the bank supposed to be making lots of loans to minorities in the cities of New Jersey? What kind of a deal did those two make?"

Alex Sr. not being a man who understood the difference between a rhetorical question and a real one, said, "Beats the hell out of me.

But if you say that those Commies at PUMP hate the bank, but support the minister, then you've got a wedge issue you can use to your advantage if that minister looked like he might win the primary."

Alex Jr. smiled at this. He thought, Maybe Dad isn't as... He let that thought drop off. This was his father and he owed him respect.

Finally, and on a more personal level, Nick and Joe were in possession of information about Pastor Ogletree's sister, Karen, who was an unwed mother and had spent time in a drug rehabilitation program, paid for by her brother, the would-be candidate himself. Could there be more to Karen Ogletree's story that her brother would prefer not be made public? All these juicy items could be useful. But he needed more.

Alex Jr. thought it might be wise to reach out to Teddy DeMarco at 1NEB and have a little chat. After all, Teddy was Ocean County's primary banker. Moreover, based on the business relationship and a desire to maintain it, he assumed Teddy would tell him what he knew about Ogletree's political plans. Likewise, he would ask him if the bank planned on supporting Ogletree with a PAC contribution. Alex was hoping the answer to the latter question was no. And if it wasn't an unequivocal no, then he would have to subtly remind Teddy that he would take it as a personal insult if Ocean County's bank of record was financially supporting his political opponent.

And then there was the Michelle Mitchell matter. Alex had held a press conference announcing a reward of $25,000 to anyone with information leading to her whereabouts and recovery. He quickly amended his recovery remark by saying of course he hoped Michelle would be found alive and well.

Chapter 10

Alex really missed Michelle. They had been together for the past two years, ever since he offered her a job as his assistant and stolen her away from a life worse than death working for one of his father's managers at New Jersey Waste Hauling, Inc. She was a perky and petite redhead with an associate degree in business from her hometown community college. She thought about going for a full four-year business degree, but decided to take a year off before making the leap. Besides, she didn't have the money for two more years of college and didn't want to take on any more student loan debt. Alex paid her well and there was a certain excitement attached to the job since she was always attending political dinners and fundraisers, which played right into her curious and fun-loving personality.

It was at one of those State Republican Fundraising Workshops held in Atlantic City when she and Alex had one too many cocktails and they ended up in his suite. The rest, as they say, is history. Michelle was always at Alex's side whenever he was required to attend a political strategy meeting or fundraising dinner. He always introduced her as his assistant, and she consistently brought a notebook with her in order to appear to be doing her job. The couple knew they had to be careful and always registered and paid for two separate hotel rooms.

Water cooler chatter started to take on a life of its own when Alex and Michelle were often out of the office on the same day and at the same time when no official meeting was on his calendar. No one on Alex's staff ever questioned him on his whereabouts.

However, an unsigned note from an unknown source sent to Michelle put them on notice they'd been found out. After receiving the note, they decided it was time to end their afternoon trysts. They were too easily traceable. They would have to do a better job of concealing their affair.

The end came when Alex's wife found out. Her name was Catherine, with a C. Not Cathy, or Caty, or even Cat. It was always Catherine. She came from money as well. But Catherine came from old, established money. It was the kind of money that included a coat of arms over the fireplace and a few Mercedes parked in the circular driveway. Catherine's parents were not happy she would be changing her name from Whitman to Scarduzo.

It was a National Republican conference to be held in San Francisco with some side trips to Napa Valley that did Alex in. Catherine really wanted to accompany him since she had never experienced the wine-tasting delights of Northern California. In response, Alex said he would have a very busy schedule cozying up to wealthy donors who would be keeping an eye out for young up and comers in the Party. This meant she would be alone most of the time and would have to visit Napa Valley by herself. When Catherine seemed okay with this, he laid a guilt trip on her about the kids still being in school. He reminded her that his parents were getting older and couldn't really be counted on to watch them. Catherine finally relented and agreed to stay home.

Alex's mistake was giving Catherine his pager number. He'd made it clear he always wanted to keep the pager limited to business contacts, and asked her to use it only in case of an emergency. When one of their girls received a concussion at her soccer game, Catherine thought he would want to know about it right away. It was nothing serious, but she didn't want him to call home and be surprised. Alex wasn't thinking clearly when he called her back since he was clearly slurring his words. He had to come clean about having found the time to go on a quick tour of one of the vineyards. Catherine was upset, but not nearly as upset as when she called his office the next day to leave a message updating him on his daughter's condition. It was then she learned that Alex's assistant, Michelle Mitchell, had traveled with him to San Francisco.

Catherine had seen too many photos and TV appearances of Alex with Michelle standing in the background. The San Francisco business trip was the last straw. She confronted him when he returned home, and he denied it. But Catherine was a determined and jealous wife. She advised Alex that if he was not having an affair with Michelle, then he should prove it by either letting her go, or transferring her to another county office where they wouldn't be working together. When he said no to her demand, Catherine hired a private detective.

Now she had the proof. When she confronted Alex with the photos, he was done. He couldn't deny it. Catherine gave him an ultimatum. Either end the affair and fire Michelle, or find himself in the midst of a very ugly divorce. And she would take the children and the house. She reminded him that he was currently running a national political campaign. What would the affair and a divorce mean to his voters and campaign contributors? His national political career would be over before it got started.

Alex didn't really care that much about the house, but taking the kids? No way! He didn't even care that much about his own personal wealth, but he had to protect the family business. He knew that any good divorce lawyer would hire a forensic accountant to review the books of New Jersey Waste Hauling, Inc. Inasmuch as his father had granted him a partnership in the company, a significant portion of Alex's other income came from these distributions. He had received a waiver from the county on this additional income based on his full disclosure and pledge to never consider his family's business for any county contracts. And since Alex had no idea what a forensic accountant might find, he decided he would have to end it with Michelle. He would then spend the rest of his life making amends to Catherine. Hopefully, his girls would never find out about his indiscretion, or at least until they were of an age to fully understand the source of their trust funds and lifestyle.

When he broke it off with Michelle, she didn't take it well. As the "other woman," she had plenty of stories to tell. Alex pleaded with her to keep silent about the affair, but could only be certain of containment once he enticed her into signing a non-disclosure agreement. The NDA came with a very handsome payoff.

Hoping his father knew nothing about the affair, Alex hired an attorney who had no connections to the family business. In fact, Alex wanted the lawyer to sign a blood oath that his father would never learn anything about it. He was certain Catherine would never reveal anything to her father-in-law since this would only lead to more questions. And they both knew Alex Sr. didn't like loose ends.

Chapter 11

Teddy reached Alex first. When Alex picked up the phone, Teddy immediately indicated it wasn't a business call. He said, "Alex, I read the story about the disappearance of Michelle over in Italy. That's awful! I just wanted to call to find out if there was any news about her and if there's anything I can do to help?"

He didn't wait for a response. "I'm pretty sure I've met her before, right? At one of those endless fundraising dinners? Little redhead, if I recall her correctly. She was your political aide, right?" Teddy finally took a breath.

It took Alex a moment to recover. He was still working out his story to tell all the callers to determine how things were going with the search. He kept telling himself they knew nothing about the affair, but he still felt like he needed to get the story straight anyway. Michelle had always been at his side and regularly sat at his table at all the rubber chicken dinners he was required to attend as Ocean County Executive and now doubling as a candidate for Congress. The callers all seemed to be genuinely concerned.

"Thanks for the call, Teddy. I really appreciate it. We're all pretty upset here since she was such a vital part of the campaign. You may have heard that I've put out a reward to see if that will motivate anyone in the search for her whereabouts."

"So sorry you had to do that," Teddy said, "but since you're here and the investigation is over there, well, maybe it'll help."

"Yeah!" Alex said. "And if we don't get any leads on her whereabouts soon, I may send a guy over there to serve as a go-between to make sure we're getting up to the minute information. My dad has some guys who speak Italian, so hopefully, there won't be any difficulties in translation. They work at the company and are distant relatives who came over on the Italian *Mayflower*. But we'll see how it goes over the next few days.

"There is one thing you should know, though, in terms of full disclosure. And I would really appreciate it if you'd keep this just between us. Michelle had just decided to leave her job here before she disappeared. It was kind of sudden and it took me by surprise. She never let on that she was unhappy. And her performance was, well, let's just say she will be difficult to replace. Everything seemed to be going fine until she told me she was leaving. Then she decides to take a quick trip to Italy. Now this. She disappears. It's just crazy. I'm still processing it. I guess I'm still in a state of shock. I don't know what else to say, but again, thanks for the call."

Alex was pleased with himself and the explanation he had recited spontaneously. But there were still some holes in the story. Michelle had never handed in a formal written resignation. There wasn't enough time—what with the breakup and NDA. Everything happened so fast. It was just a verbal agreement between the two of them that she would turn in the paperwork once she returned from her trip. The NDA required that she leave her job with Alex's campaign immediately. She met the attorney at an undisclosed location, signed the document, then booked her flight to Rome. However, she didn't board the plane until she'd checked the balance in her recently established Swiss bank account.

The trip was all Michelle's idea. Just prior to the breakup, she had been looking into various travel packages to Europe, and was hoping she could convince Alex to go with her. He could make up some excuse for the trip—like new business recruitment for the County. He'd never made her any promises, and never said anything about ever leaving his wife. The idea that he might take a trip overseas with her was a romantic pipe dream and he told her so. She was devastated by the breakup and wanted to get as far away from Alex as she could.

Another hole in the story was whether Michelle had discussed with anyone why she was leaving her job and going on the trip alone. This was covered in the NDA, but he probably should have reminded her of it before she got on that plane. Michelle was an emotional mess. The what if's could go on forever. He reminded himself that was why he was paying the attorney big bucks.

Alex was questioned about Michelle's abrupt departure and disappearance by local detectives working in tandem with the Italian authorities. He thought it best to come clean and tell them that she'd quit her job suddenly before she left, and that they'd agreed to put in the paperwork when she returned. She would provide him with a back-dated notice once she returned. Alex had no idea why Michelle had gone missing, but was hoping the NDA had nothing to do with it. God forbid if the police somehow got wind of it. Worst case scenario? He didn't want to think about it.

Teddy seemed satisfied, but then had one more question. And this was a harder one. He said, "If you don't mind me asking, what happened over there on her trip? What are they saying about the events leading up to her disappearance?"

Alex wasn't prepared for this semi-intrusive question. He felt as if he was being interrogated by the police again. His response was a rather abrupt. "Well, the answer to that question is that I have no idea what happened over there. And you've got to understand that, god forbid, she's never found, or—well—you know the worse thing happens, then I'm most likely going to be asked a lot of hard questions since I'm one of the last persons she spoke with before she got on the plane. She was a great person and a terrific employee. I just don't get it. I really don't get it. But, again, thanks for your concern. I gotta go, Teddy. Lots of phone calls to return. Talk to you soon."

As Alex was hanging up, he remembered he needed something from Teddy. He quickly yelled into the receiver, "Hey Teddy, you still there?"

Teddy heard him, "Yes sir. Still here. What do you need?"

Alex was a bit embarrassed about what he was about to ask given the current circumstances surrounding Michelle's disappearance. This was going to be an awkward conversation, but he decided to dive right in. "Sorry to keep you any longer, but I did have one business-related question for you. I should rephrase that—it's more of a campaign question."

"Uh oh!" Teddy replied jokingly. "This call's not being recorded is it? Just kidding, my friend. How can I help?"

"Well, I'm kind of embarrassed to ask this, what with all this Michelle stuff going on, but, business is business, right?" He didn't wait for a response. "I wanted to know if you've heard anything about Rev. Lloyd Ogletree having decided to run for the Democratic nomination down here in my neck of the woods? You know I've been waiting to hear about an opponent for some time now. And

The In-House Politician

if he is going to run, whether your bank is going to support him—financially, I mean? Will 1NEB be giving him a PAC contribution?"

Teddy couldn't believe what he was hearing from Alex. He said, "Now why would you think I would have any more information about his candidacy than you? I'm sure you've got better sources than me. You're the Republican candidate in that district, so what have you heard?"

Alex's tone seemed to be bit harsher now. "Well, the fact is that I haven't heard anything definitive. That's why I'm asking you."

"Why me?" Teddy said.

"Because my sources tell me that you recently had dinner with Ogletree, that's why."

Teddy smiled at this revelation. "Oh, you're good. You must have spies everywhere. We did our best to accommodate Ogletree's request to meet privately and under the radar. No fanfare. He's got his reputation to uphold, you know. He couldn't be seen breaking bread with the evil bankers. Such a meeting with the largest bank in the State could be misconstrued by a lot of different people. But to be honest, the meeting was all my idea. I met with him in his capacity as the leader of the New Jersey Chapter of the African American Ministry of Justice and Economic Development. I know you've seen *The Examiner* article about how we haven't been closing enough mortgages under our agreement with Sally Kessler's group, PUMP. It's all a bunch of bullshit. But the members of Ogletree's organization represent the largest Black churches in the state, so I met with him to see if he and his organization would help us market our mortgage program through their churches. He agreed to round up his members for a big meeting so we can present the mortgage plan to them and solicit their support. I'm still waiting to hear back from him with a date for the meeting. That's why we had dinner."

Alex was pleased to hear that his plan was working keeping Sally Kessler happy and Teddy groveling to do her bidding. "Oh, I see," he said sheepishly.

"So, you two didn't talk about his potential political campaign at all?"

Teddy now found himself in an awkward situation. He couldn't really lie to one of the bank's best customers, as well as someone he considered a friend. What if Ogletree actually did decide to run? Teddy had promised him some financial support from the bank. But he only said that to encourage the Pastor to agree to a meeting with his MJED members. He couldn't believe Ogletree would actually run. Teddy said, "Well, we did have a very superficial discussion about a possible run. In fact, I brought it up and asked him about the rumors. But his response was a definite undecided. He was quite clear he'd not made any decision one way or the other. Now, for my full disclosure, I did indicate that we might be interested in helping him if he decided to run—financially that is. Are we okay now?"

Alex's response was decidedly not what Teddy was expecting. "Actually, no, we're not. As far as I'm concerned, if Ogletree runs, I want his campaign finances to be on life support. And as for what funds he can actually muster, I want him to spend every dime of it during the primary. So, I hope I'm not being too subtle when I say this, but if the primary bank of Ocean County supports my political opponent financially, well, then I wouldn't be a happy man. And if you do end up supporting him, I hope it will be the smallest amount you feel you can get away with."

The In-House Politician

Teddy recovered quickly. "Alex, I think we may be getting ahead of ourselves. First, Ogletree hasn't decided to run yet, and second, if he does run he's definitely not a shoe-in to get the nomination, what with the primaries and all. Ogletree doesn't have the luxury of running unopposed like you. Besides, you know that if we were to support Ogletree, we would also support your campaign. We don't like to take sides."

"Teddy, you know I don't need the bank's money. I've got enough funds to cover two or three campaigns. Now, I don't want to talk about this anymore. I've got more important matters to attend to. Like finding Michelle."

"Okay, Alex. Message received. Please let me know if there's any news on her whereabouts."

There was no response from Alex. He just hung up.

Teddy was concerned. He knew Alex well enough to think that he was holding something back. He didn't hear any emotion in Alex's voice about Michelle. And for him to switch from her disappearance and then go directly to the political recon and campaign finance, well, maybe there was another side to Alex he'd not seen before.

In fact, after Teddy ended the call, he was recalling how they had first met and what he had subsequently learned about Alex and his father.

Teddy remembered back in the day when he was first introduced to Alex Jr. They'd hit it off immediately. During his courtship of Alex, as Ocean County Executive, Teddy had invited him to a few Yankee baseball and Giants football games. In one of his other jobs at 1NEB, Teddy was also the head of Corporate Entertainment. It was all rolled up into the job of romancing new and existing customers. As such, he was responsible for doling out tickets to all the home games, which were in high demand since the bank's boxes at Yankee Stadium and Giants Stadium were at a premium. Every officer in the bank was constantly badgering him for tickets for their best customers. But in the case of his recruitment of the Ocean County Executive, it was Teddy's wife's meatball recipe that finally sealed the deal. At least that's what Alex, Jr.. claimed. He reminded Teddy that his wife's maiden name was Whitman, and that she grew up having her meals prepared by a chef and served by a butler. His wife's culinary skills were limited to boiling water. Thus, the meatball recipe was precious to Alex. Teddy never believed it for a minute.

And while Alex Jr. never requested it, Teddy took it upon himself to inform Peter Porzio when he had secured all the Ocean County business accounts for the bank. In a subsequent meeting on another matter, Teddy took the occasion to ask Porzio if the bank might be interested in any financing opportunities for the Scarduzo family's waste hauling business.

Without a word, Porzio got up and shut the door to his office. He pointed his finger at Teddy with a menacing look and said, "Listen to me, DeMarco. You can do whatever you want with Alex Scarduzo Jr.'s business accounts for Ocean County, but don't ever think this bank will have anything to do with Scarduzo Sr.'s company. I'm really surprised at you. I know you've heard the same rumors about his father's connections. Don't ever mention his name in my presence again. Did the son put you up to this? You know what? Never mind. I don't want to know. You just play nice with the son, and forget about the Scarduzo family business. If the company needs any financing, which I doubt, Old Man Scarduzo has plenty of other sources. The unregulated kind, if you get my drift."

Teddy said, "Gee, Pete, I'm sorry. I'm always looking out for new business opportunities for the bank, and I just thought that—"

Porzio held up his hand indicating he wanted silence from Teddy. He said, "DeMarco, I've got no more time for this. Are we clear?"

"Loud and clear. And thanks again for your time, Pete."

Chapter 12

Michelle knew her disappearance would create serious troubles for Alex, but she didn't care anymore. She thought she loved him, but then came to the realization that it was just a one-time fling. It never occurred to her that such a large payoff might come as part of the break-up package. Alex, and perhaps his father, must have really wanted to buy her silence. And the money rapidly overcame her initial hurt feelings.

Michelle believed that the number of zeroes included in the NDA payment meant she would be able to live very comfortably in Europe or wherever else she wanted to go outside of the U.S. She conservatively estimated that if she wanted to go wild, the money could last ten years. Alternatively, if she wanted to live the quiet life and invest it, she might be able to stretch it out much longer. Living off the income from such an investment might require that she find another job, but she would deal with that another day.

She knew there were staff members back in the campaign office who had come to the conclusion that something was going on between her and Alex. Eventually they would begin asking questions about her whereabouts, and would all speculate as to what might have happened. The only question was whether their assumptions would ever be shared with the police. Moreover, Michelle would always smile whenever her thoughts turned to those late night pillow talks between Alex and Catherine about what might have happened to her—that is, if they were still sharing the same bedroom.

The In-House Politician

Michelle knew about Alex's father and his connections. One night when Alex had one too many drinks he had confided in her that Alex Sr. was not someone to cross. He was the kind of boss who didn't like loose ends. And Michelle was definitely a loose end.

Michelle thought that Alex was pretty naïve about his father. She was pretty sure he knew about their affair. Indeed, Alex Sr. kept his eyes on all things related to his son's political future. So, she couldn't take any chances. Her gut told her she needed to go off the grid. Her best option would be to disappear completely.

In her mind, Michelle calculated that she had perhaps two weeks before folks back in the campaign office would start asking questions. Specifically, she had told Alex she would return in a week or so to complete the paperwork on her sudden resignation. When she didn't appear, he would then have to come clean and say that she had verbally resigned to him. That's when her actual disappearance would begin to take form. Her failure to return would precipitate calls to the U.S. Embassy in Rome, as well as to the Italian authorities who would have to retrace her steps after her arrival. It occurred to her that she should pay cash for everything. No credit cards that might be traced. She'd learned that from Alex.

Michelle was looking at a map of Europe trying to decide how best to travel north to Zurich. She wanted to get her hands on the money as quickly as possible. Then she would have enough money to pay for a new identity. But she had no idea who might perform such a task, or, for that matter, finding someone she could trust. She had seen too many spy movies and, well, that was another problem she would deal with tomorrow. She had to get somewhere to think through her next steps.

She found a little coffee shop and pulled out her map. Staring down at it, she became terrified at how little Italian she knew. She had picked up a book on Italian common words and phrases at the airport gift shop, but none of it helped her with the map. There appeared to be a universal symbol for a train that ran from Rome up to Milan with a connection to Zurich.

Perhaps it was time to speak with someone who might help her better understand the map. She saw a uniformed poliziotto, but it occurred to her that speaking directly to someone who might eventually be looking for her was probably not a good idea. She looked around for other travelers with a touristy look. Hopefully, they spoke English and would take pity on a young American travelling alone.

Michelle spotted two young men chatting at a nearby table. She couldn't tell what language they were speaking, possibly German or Swedish, but their backpacks definitely indicated they were fellow travelers. She went over to their table and asked if they spoke English, and of course they did. They were very accommodating and showed her where to get a taxi to the train station, and wrote down the specific train she needed to head north.

During the train ride, she had time to think. It occurred to her that she would be a wealthy young woman by the time Alex's father figured out that his son had left her out there as a big risk. But then her worst fears began to take over. Alex Sr. wanted to protect his son's political future and fortune at all costs. More importantly, he didn't know what Alex Jr.. might have told her about the family business. The most likely scenario was that once Alex Sr. found out about the NDA and her travels to Italy, he would probably send someone to kill her and dispose of the body. Michelle began to weep when she thought about what she had gotten herself into.

Time was of the essence. She needed to get her money and then obtain a new identity. But how? She knew no one in Italy, Switzerland, or the rest of Europe. She was on her own.

As the train hurtled through the countryside north of Rome, Michelle looked up and saw a tall man in a grey business suit walking toward her. He did not look like a local traveler. He returned her gaze and then sat down in the seat next to her. As he reached into his suit pocket for something, her brain told her it was too late. The man then pulled out his credentials and showed her his identification. The FBI had found her. So much for going off the grid.

Chapter 13

It took two weeks of phone tag between Deacon Isaac and Kelly to finally get a date on the calendars of Pastor Lloyd and Teddy. As expected, the toughest part was to agree on a date that would maximize the number of MJED members in attendance.

Over the phone, and then with a follow-up fax in advance of the meeting, a protocol was proposed by Pastor Lloyd and agreed to by Teddy. Again, he didn't see where he had much choice in the matter. If he wanted the support of Pastor Lloyd and MJED, he needed to play by their rules. Teddy agreed there would be no individual follow-up to the member churches of the MJED until Pastor Lloyd gave the green light. This was because Pastor Lloyd was going to conduct a post-meeting debriefing with the attending members to obtain a consensus as to how they wanted to respond to the bank's request for assistance. This ruled out any of the normal business card poker always played at introductory meetings. Likewise, there would be no attendee sign-in sheet for Teddy to take for his records. It was clear from the pre-meeting conversations that Pastor Lloyd wanted to control his members' response to the bank, and for them to agree on a united front. There might have been some genuine mistrust of bankers mixed in there as well.

As part of his pre-meeting planning process, Teddy asked Tom to develop a PowerPoint presentation to cover all the important elements of the new affordable mortgage product. Then he gave Althea the job of presenting it. He wanted Tom to coach her on the finer points. Althea confided in Tom that she was a bit embarrassed by the way Teddy had handed off the presentation responsibilities to her since he was the department's residential mortgage expert. But they both knew why he had selected her. They let it drop and moved on in order to put their best foot forward.

Pastor Lloyd's megachurch was located on the outskirts of Asbury Park and Neptune along the Rt. 35 corridor in Monmouth County. His congregation was drawn from all parts of Monmouth and Ocean Counties, with many coming in from the two aforementioned cities and others travelling down from Long Branch in the North and from Freehold and Lakewood to the West. His church membership was estimated at 3,000. He proudly announced that on any given Sunday there were typically between 600 to 800 at each of his two worship services; one at 9:00 am and the second at 11:00 am.

Tom's first impression of Pastor Lloyd was that his nose had been broken on more than one occasion since it was flat and directionally challenged. When he spoke, it was apparent he needed long breaths through suboptimal nasal passages in order to get the proper amount of oxygen into his lungs. Tom suspected that if he had not been a gangster in his previous life, then Pastor Lloyd had spent more than a few rounds in the boxing ring. The latter was confirmed by some photos of his younger self on the wall of his office. A former man of violence had been converted into a man of peace.

As Althea had described it, Pastor Lloyd's voice sounded like James Earl Jones, which was quite appropriate to convey the Word of God. Once again, Althea was right on the mark.

Pastor Lloyd's mission outpost was the size of a small college campus. On Sundays twenty or so deacons directed traffic in order to properly fill the parking lots and to maintain vehicle flow and crowd control. It was like attending an NFL game in the Meadowlands, but without the tailgaters. The church also owned a number of large golf carts, which accommodated twelve comfortably and twenty snugly. These carts were stationed at the outer edges of the parking lots for those latecomers and disabled who could not find a handicapped space close to the sanctuary. Those spots were at a premium.

Inside the stadium-like sanctuary, another ten deacons served as ushers and security guards. Not that any crimes were being committed inside the church on Sundays, but from time-to-time certain members of the congregation had been known to get upset when they found people, other than their own family, occupying the pews they thought were their personal property. The deacons had to mediate these disputes.

Likewise, Sunday services could get rather boisterous and spirited at times. The deacons tried their best to manage the faithful reciting all their Hallelujahs and Amens to keep them from passing out, especially during hot summer months when the air conditioning was not operating at optimal levels. This process involved handing out water and fans. Indeed, all the deacons were trained in CPR. And the decibel levels coming out of the huge pipe organ and the congregation's responses often made Pastor Lloyd's message difficult to hear. Fortunately, attendees could always follow the sermon with the closed captioning on the two massive TV screens suspended from the ceiling on both sides of the altar. Tent revival meetings were tame compared to Sunday services at The Evangelical Church of the Living God.

The sanctuary itself was built to seat 1,500. The only time this became a problem was the overflow on Christmas and Easter.

The In-House Politician

The church had invested in sound and video equipment for use in the adjacent parlors to accommodate these "Creaster" attendees. Otherwise, the two services on Sundays seemed to accommodate all worshipers wanting to glorify God. In addition to the sanctuary and the expansive parking lots was a Sunday School building connected by a covered walkway, which also doubled as classroom space during the week for all the other programs administered by the church. There was a day care center and, of course, the administration building that housed Pastor Lloyd's office and those of his staff.

A church of this size employed an assistant pastor, a music director, and a Sunday School director. With the exception of the assistant pastor, all the other staff were volunteers. But since these folks spent so much of their personal time at the church, Pastor Lloyd and the Board of Trustees thought that their commitment to the Lord was important enough that they deserved an office of their own. There was also an office for Head Deacon Isaac, but he had to share this with his deacon captains on Sundays.

Pastor Lloyd's office was bigger than Teddy's. In fact, Teddy whispered to Tom that the office was bigger than the Chairman's. Tom could not independently confirm this statement since he'd never been invited inside the Chairman's office.

Teddy was determined to be all business today and would not let his guard down. That was right up until Pastor Lloyd called on the Lord to bless them all and the business they were about to conduct. Teddy then melted into all sweetness and smiles as he was confronted with another true believer. Politicians were easy to deal with—but a Man of God? Not so much.

After everyone had exchanged pleasantries, Pastor Lloyd escorted Teddy, Tom, and Althea to the ultimate destination, which was the church's boardroom. This boardroom rivalled that of any Tom had previously witnessed in his banking career. The plush leather chairs and fine mahogany conference table easily accommodated 25, with additional chairs lining the perimeter of the room for another twenty souls.

Like any great boardroom, the walls were adorned with portraits of previous pastors and former chairmen of the board of trustees. One portrait was particularly haunting. It was that of Pastor Lloyd's predecessor, the legendary Rev. Holt Higgins. He was the person most responsible for building the church out of a storefront in Asbury Park into its current status as a megachurch. Rev. Higgins was retired and living in Florida, but returned from time to time to serve as a guest preacher. These events were publicized well in advance, and needless to say, filled the sanctuary to capacity.

Pastor Lloyd was never a fan of his visits, since Rev. Higgins was such a large presence in the church. Jealousy always got the better of him, and he always prayed for forgiveness. Rumor had it that Rev. Higgins had not been in favor of hiring Pastor Lloyd to fill his shoes. Only those board members who served at that time knew for sure, but it was a private ballot, and no one was talking.

Pastor Lloyd managed to get representatives from eight of the fifteen member churches of MJED to the meeting. In fact, Pastor Lloyd was pleased he was able to get this level of attendance since trying to round up all the churches was like herding cats. And not all of the churches were represented by their pastors. Some sent their head deacon since their pastors had other legitimate commitments, while the remaining few just didn't trust sitting in a room with bankers who wanted their help. Bankers had all the money, so why did they need our help, they were asking themselves. Something was wrong with this picture. So, they sent their deacons to hear what the sinful money changers wanted from them.

Tom entered the conference room first, followed by Althea, then Teddy. Tom was taken by surprise when all the men in the room, wearing their black, grey, or dark blue pinstripe suits, crisp white shirts, cufflinks, and power ties, stood up in unison. It didn't take Too long to figure out that this courtesy was not intended for him. Althea was right behind him, and looked very fetching in her dark blue business suit, white blouse, and gold jewelry. She'd pulled her hair back in a severe bun, and the board members couldn't take their eyes off her. Althea was the reason for this uniform display of chivalry. In fact, Tom could see a few of the attendees conferring and nodding with each other in whispers about how impressed they were with this fine-looking young Black woman who had found herself in what they could only imagine was a very well-paying, high-powered job at the largest bank in the state. Althea was the object of their attention and they all smiled and looked in her direction. It was quite a show. And Althea couldn't help but appreciate it. She was in her glory.

As the gentlemen were taking their seats, Teddy tried to do his politician thing by going around introducing himself and shaking hands with everyone. He couldn't help himself. But Pastor Lloyd was having none of it. This was his meeting. Before Teddy got halfway around the conference room Pastor Lloyd invited him to sit down in the chair next to him at the head of the table. Althea and Tom took seats behind Teddy against the wall. There were no chairs for them at the adults' table.

The meeting was scheduled for 10:00 am. It began at 10:02.

Once everyone had settled into their seats, Pastor Lloyd folded his hands and bowed his head. He offered up a prayer, which could have served as a short sermon at Tom's church. Pastor Lloyd then asked each of the attending representatives to introduce themselves, to indicate where their church was located, its size, and to say a little something about their church's mission.

The nine churches in attendance were located in Newark, Trenton, Jersey City, Paterson, Atlantic City, Camden, Bridgeton and New Brunswick, as well as Pastor Lloyd's. From the introductory comments, their congregations ranged in size from as small as 500, to as large as Pastor Lloyd's 3,000. And they all voiced their support for Pastor Lloyd's leadership of MJED in their own personal way. It was as if it had all been rehearsed. Teddy's takeaway from this was that perhaps Pastor Lloyd had made his decision to run for Congress, with the full backing of MJED.

Teddy's short bench really came through for him. When the deacon from the Paterson church introduced himself, Althea let it be known she was a Paterson native as well, and that her father was Superintendent of Schools there. She stated that while her family was not a member of his specific church, she knew it well, and the name of its pastor. Althea had them all eating out of the palm of her hand. Tom was surprised Teddy didn't promote her right on the spot.

Once the attendees had completed their introductions, Pastor Lloyd asked Teddy to introduce himself and his staff. When he stated that Althea was a Howard graduate, the attendees couldn't

The In-House Politician

stop smiling. As a graduate of one of the Historic Black Colleges and Universities, their admiration for Althea now shot up into the stratosphere—not that she needed any more help in that regard.

Teddy and Tom were the only two White men in the room. He was quite comfortable in this role. As a former politician, Teddy had spent many late evenings campaigning in African American communities, and was well versed in the issues facing them and their neighborhoods. In fact, he campaigned so many times at social clubs and bars in Newark's South Side and Central Wards that this meeting was like a reunion of old friends.

Tom, on the other hand, was a fish out of water. That's why Teddy had asked Althea to lead the presentation. He was there for back-up coming off the bench if there were any specific questions about the affordable mortgage program.

Althea handled the presentation beautifully. No curveballs were thrown her way—just a few softballs, which she was able to hit out of the park. Teddy was all smiles. Things were going well.

After Althea's presentation and basic Q&A session, Teddy looked at his watch and sensed it was time for him to start wrapping things up. He closed with his campaign pitch by saying that the bank needed their support with their congregations, extended families, and any other residents they ministered to in their respective communities. Trying to be funny, he indicated that the bank would take anybody off the street with a pulse, as long as they were qualified borrowers. He said that the team would be happy to follow up with them personally if they had any more specific questions. Teddy added that bank staff would love to be invited to come out to make presentations at their individual churches on whatever dates worked for them. He pointed to Althea and Tom as the staff he was referring to. When Teddy suggested that Althea might make a personal visit to their churches, all the gentlemen seemed to perk up.

If Pastor Lloyd was not pleased with this egregious violation of the agreed upon protocol, he let it pass. He most certainly knew what was coming. Teddy expressed how grateful he was to all who attended, and his sincere appreciation to Pastor Lloyd for hosting the meeting.

And that's when it happened. One very stately looking gentleman with a full head of silver-grey hair sitting at the far end of the conference table stood up, cleared his throat, and let it be known that, as far as he was concerned, the meeting was not over. Teddy did not recall his name from the brief introductions. The distinguished looking gentleman looked like Zeus about to throw down a bolt of lightning. He was a big man, well over six feet, and was dressed in a three-piece blue pinstriped business suit with a gold-plated pocket watch tethered to his vest.

The gentleman proceeded to fire a 100-mile an hour fastball at Teddy. It was the kind of question Teddy could typically handle with ease. In front of a group like this, however, men of God who were well versed in the long unfulfilled promises perpetrated on the African American community by White politicians and bankers, well, Teddy knew that the pleasant part of the meeting was over. These were some angry Black men who wanted to know what these White bankers were going to do for them. It was going to be the tap dance of Teddy's life to come away from this meeting with the full support of MJED.

The unidentified Mr. Zeus said, "Mr. DeMarco, if you are requesting that we return to our congregations to help you promote

The In-House Politician

the bank's affordable mortgage program, then can you assure us all of our members' loans will be approved? That's what the program is for, right? It's to help our brothers and sisters finance the homes they want to buy, correct?"

Tension now filled the room and Pastor Lloyd did nothing to bring down the temperature. All the men in the room nodded in agreement and said Amen to this question. They all had war stories from members of their congregations about how their loans had been denied by some lily-White bankers whose institutions had redlined their neighborhoods. And inasmuch as Tom respected Teddy, he found himself wanting to know the answer to this question as well, since it was his job to get these loans approved. That's when Teddy turned, pointed, and said, "Tom, here, is our mortgage expert, so I'm going to ask him to address that question."

Now it was Tom's turn to tap dance, and while his mother had sent him to social dancing class in grade school, tap was not part of the curriculum. And he was never light on his feet, as his former football coaches could attest.

As Tom tried to show no evidence of soiling himself, he had this vision of his mother looking over his shoulder to critique what he was about to say. She forever drilled into him to never open his remarks with the ubiquitous "well" or the proverbial "umm." Likewise, she always reprimanded him for not looking into the eyes of the person he was addressing. So, with all this baggage rattling around inside his head, Tom dove right into the deep end of the pool, looking straight into the eyes of Mr. Zeus at the other end of the table.

Tom said, "Gentlemen, as you know, not every mortgage application gets approved." He could see Teddy squirming in his seat, but he soldiered on. "There's no mortgage lender in the world who has a 100 percent approval rate on all applications. We would love to tell you that we have a 95 percent approval rate, but even that wouldn't be truthful. However, I can assure you that we're doing everything we can inside the bank to get as many of these loans approved—I mean the ones that come in under the terms of our agreement.

"As part of the agreement, we established an internal mortgage review committee, which Teddy and I both sit on. And this committee is empowered to review all denials before they're final. So, in the case of any proposed rejections, we have every opportunity to turn those decisions around—if they're savable."

This last statement sparked some whispering among the attendees, as well as some eye rolling. Tom's statement about the internal review committee was a one Pinocchio since the committee had only met twice in the first year of the agreement, and no loans were overturned. In fact, at the second committee meeting, Peter Porzio announced that he thought all the loans were shit and that he would no longer attend these meetings since they were a waste of his time. He gave full authorization to Tom's favorite mortgage officer, Porter McMahon. Essentially, this was a violation of the agreement, and if Sally Kessler and PUMP ever got wind of it, she would make Teddy's life miserable. So they decided to keep this their little secret.

Tom looked Mr. Zeus right in the eyes when he answered his question. It didn't work. Tom felt like his face was just six inches from his. Zeus sat back in his chair, turned his head from side to side, and folded his arms as he said, "I've heard all this B.S. before." Then he pounded both fists on the table in the manner of an exclamation point and went on to say, in a very loud and condescending tone,

The In-House Politician

"So you can't promise us that all the loan applications from our members will be approved?"

Tom said, "Sir, I can assure you we are trying our very best to approve every viable loan application that comes to us under the agreement. But I—that is—we, cannot make any guarantees." Tom was taking on water and sinking fast. He looked for any help he could find, saying to himself, "Where are you, Teddy? C'mon, man, I need you now!" Nothing. Not even a look that said you're doing fine! Go get'em! Or, attaboy! Nothing.

It was at this point that Althea threw Tom a life-line. She stood up and said, "Gentlemen, what Tom is trying to say is that we are being a lot more flexible in the underwriting of these loans, but we are still a bank and we still have credit standards we must adhere to. If you were a depositor or stockholder in our bank, I'm sure you wouldn't want us to be making any loans to applicants that weren't credit worthy, right?" She was the only one of the three of them who could get away with this response. She looked around the table to see if any of the assembled disciples were objecting to what she had just said. Seeing none, she sat back down.

Still standing there, Tom looked over to Althea for further support. She pointed to his chair, and silently mouthed the words, "Take a seat and shut up!" But she said it with an air of confidence. Tom couldn't tell if he was off the hook yet.

Tom was then saved by the second bombshell. Seeing his opportunity, Pastor Lloyd jumped in. "Mr. DeMarco, am I correct that this agreement is with Sally Kessler and her organization, People United for Movement and Progress?" The Pastor already knew the answer to this question. He was just playing to his audience. Not only did he now have Teddy's full attention, but his continuing use of the formal "Mr. DeMarco" in his question was just what his members wanted to hear. It was, in fact, a Come to Jesus moment for Teddy. After a big laugh and a smile, both of which were defensive in nature, Teddy said, "Yes, but why do you ask?"

"Well, I hope you don't mind," Pastor Lloyd said, "but I let Sally know we were going to meet. I wanted to get more information in order to prepare for this meeting. As you know, we are ministers of the Word, not bankers. I thought it would be good to get a better understanding of what was in your agreement. By the way, Sally said to say "Hi!" She seemed pleased to know you were reaching out to us as representatives of the African American community." When he was done and recalled their previous conversation about Sally Kessler, Pastor Lloyd looked at Teddy and winked.

Teddy showed no outward signs of being upset. This was good because his internal temperature was bordering on melt-down. In as calm a manner as he could muster, he said, "Well, I'm glad you two were able to connect. Despite what you may have heard, Sally and I actually do get along. We have the same goals. We just come at those goals with different constraints."

"Wow!" Tom said to himself. "That was a big three Pinocchios. Teddy will definitely have to go to confession for that one."

Pastor Lloyd clearly had the upper hand now, but Teddy remained focused. The Pastor then lobbed in the next grenade. "Sally offered to send me bullet points summarizing the primary elements of the agreement. Would you mind if we talked about them?"

Teddy had been warned about Pastor Lloyd. He was getting sandbagged by a professional. He wondered if this was the same

The In-House Politician

man he had broken bread with recently. This Man of God was now in full politician mode.

And once again, the head Bolshevik had reared her ugly head. But then Teddy had a revelation and the peace of understanding that comes with seeing an opportunity. He said, "We would be glad to have discussions about the other points of the agreement. It's just that it could take a while and you might want to consider reconvening at another time for those discussions." He was playing for time and praying that some of the attendees had other commitments. Pastor Lloyd quickly surveyed his members to determine if they could stay longer. All agreed to stay. Teddy was stuck.

Then Althea saved the day, again. Sensing that Teddy and Tom were getting anxious, she knew they needed a time out. She got up and announced to Teddy that she needed to go freshen up. With this, it was as if a four-star general was exiting the room. All the attendees stood up. Their mothers had raised them well. As she left, Althea was, once again, given a standing ovation, sans applause.

Teddy turned to Tom and told him to go find a phone and call Kelly to cancel his afternoon appointments. With a nod from Pastor Lloyd, Deacon Isaac led him to a phone.

After successfully accomplishing his mission and returning to the boardroom, Tom witnessed Althea holding court with the deacon from the Paterson-based church and four of the other gentlemen, including Mr. Zeus. Althea was clearly having a much better time than Teddy and Tom. Apparently, Althea was also exempt from Pastor Lloyd's rules of engagement.

As Tom was about to sit down, Teddy whispered in his ear that he was going to have Althea assist him on the currently non-existent mortgage review committee. Additionally, he was going to announce this to the attendees right now. Teddy was also playing to the room.

When Althea returned to her seat, she leaned into Teddy and Tom and whispered, "Don't worry. I got this. They're impressed with the affordable mortgage program, and will all vote to help us market it through their churches. They all gave me their business cards and I returned the favor." So much for protocol.

Hearing this, Teddy was all smiles. Tom was also a happy camper. Althea had won the day, again. She had made it possible for the team to live and fight another day. It also occurred to Tom that Althea was a pretty good street fighter, and he could use all the help he could get with Marley. The currently non-existent mortgage review committee would never know what hit them.

Chapter 14

The meeting lasted another hour before Pastor Lloyd decided it was time to begin the second half of his day. He still had to meet with his MJED members to decide whether they wanted to assist the bank in marketing its affordable mortgage program through their churches.

It was way past lunch and Teddy apologized for this. But they were all travelling in the same car and he had to get back to the office. Food would have to wait.

As they drove north on the Parkway, Teddy seemed to bow his head as if he was about to take a nap. But this was just a prelude to what was coming next. After a long silence, he raised his head and began to laugh out loud. In fact, he laughed so hard he had to wipe away the tears that came with his memories. He was about to reminisce about how he and Sally met years ago. They had a long history together.

Teddy said, "You know, Sally Kessler could easily have been a CIA operative—say, somewhere in some banana republic in Central America riling up the Sandinistas to overthrow one dictatorship only to replace it with a more repressive regime. Or better yet, she could have been one of Nixon's dirty tricksters, like Charles Colson or Howard Hunt of Watergate fame. Sally knows how to stir the pot. She's a pro at it."

He went on to describe how Sally spent her early childhood in the small Jewish enclave known as the Weequahic section of Newark.

Leon Kessler, Sally's dad, and his brother Sol, her Uncle, owned and operated a liquor store and small grocery store. The two brothers were business partners, and the stores were located next to each other, which made them easier to manage. Sol operated the liquor store, while Leon ran the grocery store. As small business owners, the Kessler brothers made a good living, but were never going to be rich. The liquor store brought in the bulk of the revenue, but it was also a prime target for thefts and burglaries. After the fourth robbery, Uncle Sol said he'd had it with Newark and wanted out of the partnership. The neighborhood was changing with the African American population growing and the White and Jewish populations departing. But since Leon couldn't afford to buy out his brother, they both decided to sell and head West to the suburbs of Essex County.

Thus the two Kessler families, their relatives, and friends all followed the out-migration of Newark to the Oranges, Maplewood and Irvington. Farther out, West Orange and Livingston were the promised land, but even back in the late '50s, real estate prices there were relatively expensive. So Sally's parents rented an apartment in Irvington, hoping it would just be a temporary stop along their way to a better life.

Tom interrupted. "How do you know all this about Sally?'

Teddy's response was surprising. "Sally Kessler was a student of mine. Yup! That's right. After college and baseball, I began my career as a teacher and taught civics at Irvington High School. But the main reason I went into teaching was because I wanted to coach. So when a teaching position opened up in Irvington, I jumped at it because I knew the baseball coach there was talking about retiring. I had a handshake agreement with the Superintendent that I would have the coaching job once my predecessor finally pulled the pin. The job was mine two years later.

"Sally was in one of my civics classes. Man, was she smart. Then during her senior year they asked me to fill in for one of the guidance counselors who'd become ill and was out on leave. I said okay and that's when I really got to know her. She was assigned to me so she told me all about her family history."

Althea asked, "So, what was she like in high school?"

"In high school, Sally was an outsider, an odd duck, always ready to pick a fight with someone she thought was a bully. It was kind of funny to watch, since she never grew past five-foot-two. She kept her hair short because it had frizzed out at an early age. And she always seemed to be carrying around a few more pounds than her weight class permitted. It wasn't like she was heavy, just a bit rounder than the typical teenage girl wanted in order to look good in a mini-skirt. So she always wore pants. Oh, and those coke bottle glasses she wore painted the picture of a young girl who was probably not getting invited to the prom. That is, not unless she asked her friend Howard. I forget Howard's last name. They were good buddies. But she really didn't care about the prom, anyway.

"Sally had a small circle of friends, and she picked a lot of fights with the bullies who made fun of her and her friends. They were picked on a lot because they were the smart ones and didn't always fit in. Today, you might call them dweebs or nerds, but back then, they were just the odd ducks in high school who flew under the radar, but who really blossomed once they were unchained in college."

He continued. "When I was counseling Sally, she would open up to me from time to time. She said that when she got together with her friends they would put on the phonograph and listen to Peter, Paul & Mary, Bob Dylan, Simon and Garfunkel, Joni and Judy. They would read Russian poetry and discuss Dostoevsky, Tolstoy, and Chekhov. The music and literature got them all fired up and pointed them in the direction of joining a movement, any movement, as long as it appeared to be a good cause, whatever it may have been at that time. Sally said that one day one of her friends came home with a recording by Lenny Bruce. His social commentary really struck a chord with her. It was around that time she decided she needed to leave her small universe behind, and that high school was just something she needed to get through."

Teddy stopped for a moment and took a deep breath. He gazed quickly out the window to get his bearings.

Tom asked, "Did you follow her time in college?"

"No. But I got reports on her from mutual friends who knew her during her college years. That was a crazy time. Kennedy was dead, and the country was spinning in lots of different directions."

Tom smiled when Teddy said this because it meant Sally wasn't much older than him. And Tom knew what the late 1960s were like. For a brief second he thought that perhaps their experiences were not so different. Then he remembered that he was an evil banker. At some point their paths diverged.

Teddy said, "One of the legendary stories about her was that she claimed to have attended the March on Washington in August 1963. Who knows? She never provided any proof. However, it seemed unlikely since, as her guidance counselor, I knew she didn't graduate from high school until June of '64. I'm guessing she thought that, true or not, it was important to have this item on her official protestors resume since it gave her some credibility in her future role as spokesperson for the poor and disenfranchised. It was during college that Sally decided her mission in life would be to correct all the economic ills caused by capitalism."

Teddy's disclaimer was that all the stories he'd heard about Sally in college were anecdotal, and he had no knowledge if they were actually true or not. But they all seemed fit the profile of the person they knew as the leader of PUMP, and the one Tom lovingly referred to as the head Bolshevik.

Teddy said, "There were rumors that during her four years of college she lobbied for the establishment of a Women's Studies program at her alma mater. She also attended every protest held in D.C., with the anti-war movement being her largest time commitment. Another story was that she tried to gain membership in the Association of Black Collegians on her campus, but they would have none of it due to her—how shall I say—lighter pigmentation. She thought that just because she was sympathetic to their cause, they would let her in."

They all laughed at this, including Althea.

"If there was a cause, a perceived slight, or an injustice, Sally was there to protest against it. With the amount of time she spent organizing against everything she thought was wrong, and the amount of time she spent traveling to various demonstrations, it's amazing she ever got to class and completed her course work. I have no idea if this is true, but when she first heard about the Columbia University protests in April of 1968, she was on the first train to New York City to join in. It made no difference to her that she was just a few weeks away from her senior year finals. She was already well known on campus. No professor dared give her a less than satisfactory grade for fear of being brought before the Dean for some alleged infraction. She'd done it before to one unsuspecting professor and the word spread like wildfire. Sally was a student you didn't want to mess with.

"You know, Sally actually worked for my campaign at one time. In fact, we campaigned together for political candidates we both supported. I would say there was a time in the past when we were actually friends and political colleagues."

Without coming right out and saying it, he was thinking that perhaps there were still some qualities in Sally that made her a respectable opponent. Teddy didn't want to hate Sally. They had too much history together. But now, she was a major thorn in his side, and was trying to bring down the entire financial services industry one bank at a time, with 1NEB being her current target.

The fact that Sally Kessler was connected with Pastor Lloyd Ogletree and MJED was no surprise to Teddy. But it still got under his skin. Once again, she seemed to be one step ahead of him.

They exited through the toll booth and were on the direct glide path into the bank's underground parking garage. Tom looked over at Teddy and saw that the smile that had come with his memories was gone. He was all business now. It was time to get back in the game and focus.

Chapter 15

The second meeting occurred at the same location and Sally recalled its wonderful aroma. It was hard to forget. As they performed their precautionary premeeting protocols by exiting their cars and patting each other down, Alex was careful not to get too frisky. She didn't like any man's hands on her, and the fact that they were Alex Scarduzo's paws only made it worse.

Alex said, "You owe me. You owe me big time, lady!" He was trying to intimidate her again. It had worked the first time, but now she felt like she had some cards to play.

"Oh really, what makes you say that?"

Alex smiled. "That made-up mortgage report really hit the jackpot for you. I'm still wondering how *The Examiner* fell for it hook, line and sinker. But it worked, and it worked especially well for you, didn't it? That front page story put DeMarco and his bank on the defensive. Made the bank look bad, and you guys—well, the article turned you into Robin Hood, right?"

Sally knew he had a point. She just didn't want to admit it. She was having the same thoughts about how the story was published without any independent confirmation. Joe Campbell from *The Examiner* did call her about it, but they weren't friends exactly and she couldn't be considered an impartial third party. It was a brief conversation. She just said the numbers sounded right to her. "Yes, I guess it did help our cause somewhat. But we'll need a lot more like that to bring 1NEB to its knees."

"Don't worry," Alex said. "There's plenty more where that came from."

Sally paused a moment while he gloated, but then bore in with the harshest tone she could muster. "I thought we'd agreed not to meet here anymore. I can't stand this this place or being this close to you."

Alex was getting tired of her banter. "Sally, your insults may give you some satisfaction, but they don't win you any points with me. It's understood we don't like each other, but let's try to be civil, okay? I agree we need to find a better way to communicate and a better place to meet. Problem is that phones are no good since they can be traced, and someone might be listening. You never know. And I recently lost my go-between, but I needed to speak with you on an important matter."

Sally smirked. "And was that go-between your little cheerleader and political aide, Michelle Mitchell? The one who's gone missing in Italy? I saw the newspaper report. She looked awfully familiar."

Alex was getting angry, but knew he had to control it. They were in this too deep to get out without major damage to both of them. "Sally, you should be careful what you say to me. I might get the wrong idea. And you do recall our last conversation about who may or may not be buried in that trash heap?" He used a sweeping and expansive arm gesture to place an exclamation point on where they were meeting.

"I'm going to let that last comment go, but believe me when I say that it's in my file on you. Now, can we get back to business?"

"So, I'll ask you again, what do you want from me?"

Alex smiled. "I'm proposing that we swap opposition research. I give you information on DeMarco's bank. In return, you give me information on whoever gets the Democratic nomination in my congressional district. And I suspect that's going to be your friend, Rev. Lloyd Ogletree. Have you heard whether he's made a decision to run yet?"

Sally laughed. "So that's what this is all about?"

Alex wasn't in the mood for games. "You didn't answer my question. Have you heard anything about Ogletree's plans?"

"Nope." Sally said. "Nothing. If he's running he hasn't told me."

"You two are buddies," Alex said. "Doesn't Ogletree sit on your PUMP board? I'm told he considers you to be one of his closest political advisors. You two subscribe to the same communist social welfare bullshit."

Sally was doing her best impression of being bored by folding her arms over her chest. But she couldn't quarrel with his assertions. He had good information. "Yeah! He's on my board, but he hasn't confided in me on whether he plans on running. Sorry, I can't help you. So are we done now? Can I go? And find a better location to meet. This place smells like shit. I feel like I need to burn these clothes. Evidence of our meeting, you know."

Alex laughed, but it wasn't funny. She was right. What if he had another meeting tonight? Someone might ask him about that stink on his clothes, and that would not be helpful if he needed a good alibi. He looked at Sally and said, "You know, you and DeMarco are a real pair. He said the same thing—that Ogletree hadn't decided yet. But if he does decide to run, DeMarco said he might help finance him with a PAC contribution."

Sally was caught off guard. "Wait! What? What's DeMarco got to do with Ogletree?" She was playing only half dumb. She had already spoken with Pastor Lloyd about his meeting with DeMarco, but nothing about his political ambitions or accepting money from 1NEB.

"Well," Alex said, "that article in *The Examiner* lit a fire under DeMarco to reach out to Ogletree to see if he could get his Black churches to help market some cockamamie mortgage plan you forced down his throat. He met with Ogletree and asked him to arrange a meeting with his Black churches. At that meeting DeMarco asked him if he was planning to run, but your guy said he hadn't decided yet. And that's too bad, since I would really love to see your guy Ogletree and the other Democratic candidates spend all of their cash in the primary, if you get my drift. So here's what I'd like for you to do. I'd like you to do whatever you can to convince Ogletree to run in the primary. I want to see all the Democrats fighting each other. Got it?"

Sally was incredulous. "So you think I've got enough pull with Ogletree to convince him to run for Congress? And if he does run, what makes you think I would ever betray him to the likes of you?"

Alex ignored this and said, "Well, all I'm asking is that you give it your best shot, okay? Besides, wouldn't you like to see Ogletree win and represent that district in Congress? He's your guy, right?"

"Yes, but I don't think he's got much of a chance to win the nomination."

"You never know. Ogletree could catch fire and give the field a real run for their money—emphasis on money. Give him a chance and see what he can do. Even if he loses, at least he'll have made a name for himself, and will have the experience of a national campaign under his belt. All good for him either way, right?"

There was a certain logic to Alex's supposition, but Sally didn't want to seem so agreeable. "What if I say no? Or what if I can't convince him to run? What then?"

"Sally, we've been all through this before. I help you and you help me. That's our deal, right? I held up my part of the bargain with that article I got published in *The Examiner*. Now it's your turn. Try to get Ogletree to run. That's all I'm asking for now. And I can assure you that there's more information coming your way on your favorite bank and your favorite banker, Teddy DeMarco."

"Oh really? And what kind of information are we talking about, and who's your source?"

"C'mon, Sally. We've both got our sources and mine will remain confidential. As will yours. Now go home and wash those clothes. They probably stink."

On the drive home Sally was beginning to think her relationship with Pastor Lloyd needed some retooling. She could not imagine any scenario in which a member of her PUMP Board of Directors would ever take money from 1NEB and Teddy DeMarco. If that happened, Ogletree would be giving in to the dark side.

Chapter 16

Michelle was still in a daze trying to understand how and why the FBI had found her in Italy. The FBI agent's name was Steve Inbusch and he seemed like a reasonable guy. And as to how and why they had found her, it was pretty simple. Inbusch advised her they were investigating the Scarduzo family and that she'd been under surveillance for the past six months. He made it clear she was not a target of their investigation, but they believed she had important information relevant to their investigation. The agent also said they had certain information that might entice her to want to cooperate.

Agent Inbusch said, "Here's a photo of a guy who works for Old Man Scarduzo. This guy just boarded a plane in Newark headed for Rome. Do you recognize him?"

Michelle braced herself on the armrest and placed one hand over her mouth. "That's either Nick or Joe. Even Alex couldn't tell them apart. He's one of the two guys Alex said his father had assigned to help him with the campaign. But I really don't know him or what he does for Alex."

"Old Man Scarduzo made inquiries with the authorities in Rome regarding your whereabouts, but the locals have no idea of where you are. This guy in the photo—his name is Giuseppe LiVecchi. Giuseppe is Italian for Joe. He and his brother are bad dudes. Sicilians with nasty reputations. Now we have no idea what this Joe's intentions are, but we can assume he's not come over here to welcome you back into the family and return you to the States. Trust me. We've got it all under control."

The In-House Politician

The agent confirmed Michelle's worst fears. Alex's father did know about their affair. Then Inbusch said if she wanted their protection, there was a deal to be made. Her life was in their hands, and the Feds very much wanted to keep her alive in order for her to testify. Inbusch was very good at flipping witnesses.

There was one subject Michelle did want to talk about. She wanted to know about the money. Inbusch smiled at this comment. He was waiting for her to bring it up first. The agent revealed they were aware she had signed a Non-Disclosure Agreement with Alex, Jr., but the Bureau's legal team said it would not prevent her from testifying in a federal criminal case.

Michelle turned to Inbusch. "So, what about my money? Can I still get my hands on it? And how do I know you're not just making this story up about Old Man Scarduzo wanting me dead?"

"We're going to be here for a while," Inbusch said. "This investigation is ongoing, and these cases take time. We believe that you're an important piece of the puzzle. And just so you feel better, we have eyes on Scarduzo's man. Our agent is on the same flight with him. We won't let him near you, I promise."

Michelle asked the question he'd been expecting. "So what did Alex and his father do to have the FBI after them?"

"Like I said, we're going to be here for a while. We'll have plenty of time to discuss it, provided you cooperate with us. I'm hopeful we can come to some understanding that benefits both of us. And by both, I mean you and the United States Government."

"Do I really have a choice?" she said.

Michelle put her head in her hands and looked out of the window of the speeding train. She was wishing she could be anywhere else.

Chapter 17

Forty-eight hours had passed since the meeting with Pastor Lloyd and the members of MJED. Teddy was not a patient man. There had been no follow-up call regarding their decision to help market the affordable mortgage program. Teddy was getting crankier by the hour. In fact, Kelly was now finding any excuse to personally deliver memos, and to visit friends located on other floors in the building. But Kelly's absence from her desk just made Teddy angrier. If she was away from her phone, then she would miss the expected call from Pastor Lloyd.

Teddy never answered his own phone. Who knows who it might be? Could be anyone and Teddy didn't talk to just anyone. That's what Kelly was for—to screen his calls and play point guard on his team to distribute the messages to the right staff person. If Kelly wasn't sure who the call should go to, then she would just take a message and ask him who to pass it on to. Likewise, Kelly knew who Teddy would take calls from. One time she took a message only to catch hell for it, and had to get the caller back immediately. Only Kelly could work for Teddy. And they both knew it. Kelly was the only person on Teddy's staff who could talk back to him and get away with it. In the case of Pastor Lloyd, though, she knew enough to steer clear of her boss until he figured out how to get things under control. He was ready to erupt and the smallest misstep could get the lava flowing.

Teddy had to do something. He picked up the phone and called Fitz for some advice. Fitz, as it turned out, was on his way to Trenton

The In-House Politician

for some innocuous board meeting. He was employing a driver now since his eyesight was causing him some depth perception problems, and he could get more work done as a passenger in the back seat. He indicated to Teddy that he could be available for a late day meeting at the bank, unless Teddy wanted to take him out to dinner. But Teddy had already promised his wife they would have a rare evening out, though he was not in the best of moods. She'd seen it all before—many times before.

Kelly was relieved when Fitz showed up at the bank later that afternoon. She knew he had a calming effect on Teddy, and damn if he didn't need something or someone to help him settle down. When Fitz entered Teddy's office, Teddy poked his head out and told Kelly, "No interruptions and no calls, unless it's Pastor Lloyd, of course!"

Kelly rolled her eyes. "Got it!"

Fitz was very good at getting to the heart of the problem. After Teddy summarized the situation, Fitz zeroed in on the fundamental question. He said, "So at the end of your meeting with Pastor Lloyd you left with the understanding that he would be getting in touch with you to let you know if they would work with the bank? But you also said you had some discussions about a possible grant from the funds in the agreement, right? Did you make him any kind of offer—you know, an actual dollar amount?"

Teddy said, "Yes, we talked about grants, but I didn't offer him a specific number. We ended up covering that element of the agreement after Ogletree extended the meeting's agenda. He actually had a copy of the agreement in hand, or at least a summary of it. And guess who provided it to him? I know where you're going with this. But it occurred to me that having that kind of conversation in front of the other MJED members might have every one of them wanting their own individual grant. And I'm pretty sure we have branches in all the cities represented by the churches at that meeting. I guess I should double check that. No, that doesn't matter. Even if we only have branches in half of those cities, we can't afford to give them all separate grants. Can't do it. There's not enough money in the agreement to satisfy all those churches, and there are other member churches that didn't even attend the meeting. What if they want grants, too?"

Fitz smiled. "Would you please calm down, my friend? You need to make them an offer they can take with them as part of their assisting you with your problem. C'mon, Teddy! You know it's all about the money. They need an incentive to help you out. And since you're saying you don't have enough money in the agreement, then you need to give Pastor Lloyd a big grant for the whole MJED organization and leave it to him to decide how they divide it up." Fitz paused to think for a moment. "And who's to say you can't find more money in the bank's general philanthropy budget, or, why can't you go back and get more money from the Chairman to give out under the agreement? Didn't you tell me he said, 'Whatever it takes to get the job done?'"

"No. I can't," Teddy said. "I'm already in trouble with the Chairman for that *Examiner* article. The timing is not good asking for more blood money."

On second thought, it occurred to Teddy that the amount of grant funding in the agreement was a minimum. If he was successful in prying loose more funds from the bank, well, that would make him a hero with Sally Kessler and Pastor Lloyd. But it would also set a bad precedent for any future negotiations with the Bolsheviks. Teddy knew the Chairman was looking at other acquisitions to grow the bank, so negotiations with the Bolsheviks were just in Round One. He knew that every new merger would cost more.

The cost to Teddy would be more sleepless nights. But while the cost of the next agreement would be even larger, these funds were nothing more than a rounding error on the bank's balance sheet. He would have to think this one through. In the end, he knew Fitz was right. He would have to bite the bullet and find a way to sell it to the Chairman.

"You might want to run this idea past the Legal Department," Fitz said. "There are people out there who might consider your donation to MJED as, well, as a payoff. You'll need to put some language in the grant agreement that makes it clear it's merely a grant for the terrific things MJED does in their communities, only one of which is to help you market the affordable mortgages through their churches."

"I'm sure Legal will work with me on this," Teddy said, "especially if it means keeping PUMP from demonstrating in front of the bank. What if I went back to Pastor Lloyd and said the bank is prepared to provide MJED with one large grant to train all the churches who want to participate in referring loans? We would only do this under his careful eye, of course. What do you think?"

Fitz laughed. "I think that's what I just said. It's something real you can take back to Ogletree. Let's hope he likes it. Just make sure you run it all by Legal first."

"Yeah! Yeah! Details! We'll find a way to get it done. But whatever the final method, I just need to make sure I've got all my bases covered with Sally Kessler and her friends. Fitz, I love you, man! You certainly earned your consulting fee today, my good friend."

"Glad I could help," Fitz said, "but we could have accomplished this over dinner, you know."

They laughed at this and Teddy was feeling better. His temperature was dropping and both Kelly and Teddy's wife would be the beneficiaries.

The next day, Teddy called Tom in and brought him up to speed on his plan to gain the assistance of the MJED. His anxiety about not having heard back from Pastor Lloyd was again front and center. The calming effect of Fitz from the day before had only lasted one night. Additionally, Teddy's dinner out with his wife may have helped a little, but its shelf life had expired with his first cup of coffee.

Teddy gave Tom the assignment of meeting with the Legal Department to talk about the grant to MJED. He didn't mind it, though. Mary C. Connolly was a statuesque young attorney just a few years out of law school who was assigned to Teddy's department. "MC," as everyone called her, was easy on the eyes with her long legs and beautiful long dark hair. She was the type of young lady you couldn't help staring at whenever she entered or exited a room. There were times, however, Tom wished she would confer with Kelly on some fashion tips. Then he reminded himself that she was not only an attorney, but an attorney working for a bank, and one of the few females in the General Counsel's office. There was a dress code, like it or not.

MC was smart and never as condescending as most of her male colleagues in the Legal Department. She knew her banking law and was undaunted whenever Teddy needed Tom to ask her the most ridiculous legal questions.

When Tom explained Teddy's problem with providing MJED a grant in return for their help in marketing the affordable mortgage

The In-House Politician

program she was unconvinced. She said, "It might look worse than a quid pro quo. In fact, someone might see it as a fee for the service of originating loans, and these churches are not licensed to act as mortgage bankers in the State."

When Tom returned and debriefed Teddy on the results of his meeting with MC, he once again shot the messenger, but this time in his humorous way. He asked Tom how many concussions he'd suffered during his gridiron playing days. Among his many talents, Teddy had perfected the fine art of ripping you a new one, while at the same time making you believe it was a good and proper medical procedure.

Either way, Teddy was out of options. He needed the Black churches to help 1NEB get the word out about the affordable mortgage program. But Pastor Lloyd had gone radio silent. It was now time for Teddy to swallow his pride and call him to beg. Pastor Lloyd had certainly seemed interested in the grant portion of the agreement, as well as the mortgage product for all his and MJEDs brothers and sisters. And there was also Althea's understanding that her little band of followers liked the plan and would support it.

Kelly was the bearer of the good news to Teddy. She waltzed into the confessional booth with a small pad in hand. She didn't want Teddy to quiz her without her notes. She said, "Pastor Lloyd's guy, Deacon Isaac, just called. He said that Pastor Lloyd wanted to get a message through to you, Mr. DeMarco."

Kelly had Teddy's full attention.

She said, "The message was that Pastor Lloyd received a favorable response from all the attendees after your recent meeting. However, he's now in the process of reaching out to the other members who did not attend the meeting in order to get their agreement on the plan as well. He said this could take a few days. He also wanted to apologize for the delay in responding. And that's all he said." She looked up from reading the message and shrugged her shoulders. This last remark was stated with emphasis to let Teddy knew she had no further information, so there was no need for any more questions.

To say that Teddy was pleased was an understatement. And while he wasn't ready to move to a full-on touchdown signal, he did jump up out of his chair and ran around in front of his desk and performed the safe sign, in all its fundamental baseball animation.

As Kelly left Teddy's office, she turned and said to him, "You really are weird."

Chapter 18

Three months into the arrangement with the MJED, on a day when Teddy was out of the office, Kelly took a message from Pastor Lloyd indicating he wanted to set up a private meeting with him. Teddy understood the code. Pastor Lloyd would host the meeting on his home turf, and no one else would be in the room. No witnesses. This made Teddy a bit nervous since each time he spoke with Alex Scarduzo he was quizzed about whether Ogletree was running. Pastor Lloyd gave Kelly his private number so that Teddy could call him directly. Teddy then called the Pastor and they set up a date to meet the following week. The Pastor reconfirmed with Teddy that he would be coming alone.

Teddy now needed to speak with Fitz. Due to the clandestine nature of this upcoming meeting, Teddy believed that Pastor Lloyd had finally decided to jump into the race. If Fitz didn't know anything more about Ogletree's political aspirations, he could easily find out. Both Teddy and Fitz were no rookies when it came to Jersey Democratic politics—who was in, who was out, and who were the rising stars. But so far, there was no intelligence out there on Pastor Lloyd's plans.

Over the next few days, the reports Fitz received indicated that Pastor Lloyd Ogletree had been appearing at many Democratic fundraisers throughout the state, apparently trying to curry favor with party officials. Pastor Lloyd's membership on the Governor's Civil Rights Commission was an excellent resume starter, but neither

Teddy or Fitz thought it sufficient to provide him with the kind of experience he would need for a successful run for Congress. But crazier things had happened, and they were open to all possibilities.

When Teddy arrived for his appointment the following week, he was surprised the Pastor wanted to meet in the chapel. Teddy felt a bit confused about the apparent change in venue, and asked why they weren't meeting in his office. Pastor Lloyd winked and whispered, "Because I have an automatic recording device in my office. Just like Nixon's, but for doing God's work, not dirty tricks. It starts immediately whenever someone speaks in my office. Problem is that I don't know how to turn it off. If I asked one of our deacons to come in and disable it, well, then he's going to want to know why. And that's not a question I'm prepared to answer right now."

Teddy laughed. "So this is the type of meeting you don't want to have any record of, is that right? I take it you only put your trust in the Lord?"

Pastor Lloyd nodded. "Amen to that."

As they entered a small, ornate chapel, Pastor Lloyd followed Teddy in and locked the doors behind them. Teddy found this curious since no church he attended ever locked its doors. Two large Queen Anne chairs were positioned on either side of the podium. Pastor Lloyd motioned for Teddy to sit in one. He rolled the podium forward a few feet so their line of sight was not blocked. They were situated at an oblique angle to each other so it was easy for them to make eye contact. After the Pastor took his seat opposite Teddy, he invoked the Lord with a quick prayer.

When he was done, Teddy spoke up. As all good politicians do, he wanted to set the tone of the meeting. He said, "Pastor Lloyd, I

The In-House Politician

just wanted to say a big thank you to you and your fellow members of MJED. Althea and Tom tell me the volume of loan applications coming in from the churches has been more than we ever expected. We're very pleased with this level of activity and hope you are, too."

Pastor Lloyd said, "Yes, well that's great, Mr. DeMarco, and we hope it all continues in this manner, but that's just one of the reasons I asked you to meet with me. I've got one to add to your total."

"Please Pastor, call me Teddy."

"Well, we'll see about that after today's meeting. You see, I'm personally delivering this mortgage application to you so that you can make sure it gets into the right hands at the bank. Unfortunately, I have some history with your branch manager in Plainfield and, well, I figured since we were meeting anyway, I might as well deliver it to you in person."

Teddy was a bit surprised, but was sure there was a good explanation. He asked, "Plainfield? History?"

"My family goes way back in Plainfield, back to the riots in the '60s. I guess I shouldn't say riots, should I? Civil disobedience and protests, which included some rioting by a few, how shall we say, overly zealous participants. My father was one of the local protest leaders to speak out at the rallies about the injustices we were facing. Some folks still say my father was one of the leaders who incited the crowds. I was just a boy then and don't remember much of it, but folks tend to have long memories. And your branch manager in Plainfield, well, she remembers quite well what happened during those days of rage, as some like to call them. We went to the same high school, although she was about ten years ahead of me. Just like the Hatfields and the McCoys, only the Black version. Her family and the business leaders in town don't particularly care for the Ogletrees, if you catch my drift. So, I thought I would bypass all the old animosities and give you the application directly. Is that okay with you?"

"Sure thing," Teddy said. "I can take it for you, but I'm still a little confused. This is Monmouth County. Why would you be taking an application to our Plainfield branch?"

"The application is for my Mother," Pastor Lloyd said. "She still lives in Plainfield. Mildred Ogletree, or Millie as she likes to be called by her friends. She and my sister Karen and my niece live together in a house they rent there. I've been trying for years to get my Mother to move out of Plainfield, but that's where she was raised and that's where the rest of the family still lives."

Teddy raised an eyebrow. "So where's Momma Ogletree intending to buy? You understand there will be no favorable treatment by handing it off to the boss, right?"

Pastor Lloyd didn't get the joke and forged ahead. "My mother and sister want to buy the house they've been renting for the last ten years or so. I was not aware of this, but the owner of the property, who by the way is a friend of mine, was putting aside a few dollars of their rent every month in the hope they would eventually save enough for a down payment in order to buy the place from him. Apparently he's wanted to sell the property for the past few years. You'll be able to count their rental funds the landlord put aside for their down payment, right? No rule against that, is there?"

Teddy performed his traditional soft shoe. "Pastor Lloyd, we'll work with you and your mother to try and get this done. I'll get my staff on it as soon as I get back to the office."

The In-House Politician

"That's great, Mr. DeMarco, that's great. But there are a couple of things you should know about this application."

"Okay, hit me with your best shot. And believe me when I say that we've seen lots of tough applications. I'm sorry. I shouldn't have said that. Sounds like I'm prejudging it before you tell me more about it."

Pastor Lloyd finally got Teddy's humor. He said, "Well, here goes then. First, my sister and I don't get along much. Whenever the family gets together, we normally go to our respective corners, if you know what I mean. You see, she got pregnant by this guy who she thought was going to marry her. Turned out, he was a—well, forgive me—but not a good man. A real scoundrel, if you will. Once he heard about the baby coming, he stole all her cash and credit cards right out of her purse and left for parts unknown. Now she's got the baby, no husband, no credit cards, no health insurance, and no child support. I call my niece a baby, but she's growing up fast. Great kid! Smart, polite, cute, she's got it all—except no father. My mother, Millie, is helping to raise her. I do what I can to help them out, but my Mother and Sister don't like taking any money from me. In all honesty, I've probably not been as understanding and—in her mind—forgiving as a Man of God should be. But it's a very difficult situation to navigate. I assure you that I'm trying. Oh! And my sister's not working right now. She got laid off from one of those big box stores a few months ago. Sorry, I can't remember which one. She's been slow to get back on her feet to find another job."

Teddy said, "Yeah! You don't get to pick your families, do you? Okay then—so I guess that leaves your mother's income to pay the mortgage? What does she do to pay the bills?"

"My mother is retired and on Social Security. She also receives a small monthly pension. I'm not sure how much, but it was transferred over to her when my dad passed. She also cleans houses for extra income. Problem is that all the housecleaning work is paid under the table. It's a cash business—that is unless you work for one of those big cleaning services. But she's on her own and likes it that way. She takes jobs whenever and wherever she pleases. No bosses, except the homeowner and her own schedule."

Teddy had a quizzical look on his face and asked the fundamental question. "Well, unless your mother's Social Security and pension checks are rather large, how does she plan to cover the monthly mortgage payment? It seems to me that might be a problem—you know—insufficient income to cover the monthly bill. But there I go again. Please excuse me. I should not prejudge. What's she is paying for the house?"

"It's a two-family house. And as far as the price is concerned, I'll let you guys figure out if she can afford it. My sister and her daughter are living in the upstairs apartment, but they'll move in with my mother downstairs, so they can rent out the upstairs unit for additional income."

Teddy was still a bit uneasy. "Okay, what kind of rent do you think they can get from the unit?"

"Not sure," Pastor Lloyd said. "I'd like to say that the Lord will provide, but I know you bankers get nervous whenever we invoke the Holy Spirit, so I'll refrain from doing that—or guessing about the rent."

Teddy was still not sure about this one and wished he'd not been as confident as he'd sounded earlier. He tried to put a good spin on it. "Well, Pastor, you really know how to challenge us, don't you? We may need some divine intervention with this one. But I assure you, we'll do whatever we can to try and make it work. Just remember that we have bosses we report to inside that bank as well. Your mother's application doesn't sound like a slam dunk. But we'll do our best."

Pastor Lloyd looked very seriously at Teddy and said, "Mr. DeMarco—this is important to me. After all, it's for my mother. Please do whatever you can, and keep me posted."

Once again, Teddy assured him that he would do everything he could.

As a politician with a social conscience, Teddy sympathized with working folks who had a tough time making ends meet. He counted his blessings. He was fortunate enough to have found not one, but two callings. His political career focused on assisting his constituents with every resource at his disposal. He even had his staff pay into a small jar for minor infractions, including poor grammar—spoken, or in writing. He used the money to pay some hardship rent cases for deserving constituents, or to help with heating bills during the winter months.

Then he found a second career as a banker with that same social conscience. Here he had all the resources to do even more than he could as a politician. But there were times when his hands were tied. And when he thought about Millie's mortgage application, his gut feeling was that if his hands were not already tied, they soon would be. This was not a good thing, since he needed Pastor Lloyd to trust him. It would be extremely difficult to maintain the support of MJED if he lost Pastor Lloyd's confidence.

Teddy was about to wrap things up and head back to his car when Pastor Lloyd surprised him by saying, "Now let's talk about the real reason I asked you to come in."

With the conversation about his mother's mortgage application over, Teddy had forgotten that Pastor Lloyd's primary agenda included something that required complete secrecy. And his mother's mortgage application did not require a top-secret clearance.

Teddy adjusted himself in the chair and did his best impression of a good and interested listener. He recalled there were no recording devices in the chapel. He put on his political hat for what he expected was coming next. He said, "And what, pray tell, might that be? I guess when I asked you before to hit me with your best shot, you hadn't even gotten up to bat yet, huh?" There was nobody better than Teddy in the use of sports analogies. But his sense of humor did not find its target in the Pastor, who was all business.

Pastor Lloyd sat up firmly in his chair, looked Teddy in the eye, and said in a very serious manner, "Mr. DeMarco, I think by now you have figured out what this conversation is about. Prior to this, I was not ready to commit myself to the kind of personal journey this next phase of my life will require. I spent the last few weeks in quiet prayerful reflection. I asked my Lord and Savior for guidance, and I truly believe he answered me. On a more worldly basis, I have spoken with a number of trusted colleagues and friends to assess their level of support for me moving forward. At this point, Mr. DeMarco, I think it's time for a Man of God, and a Man of Color, to offer the people of Central Jersey some real political leadership. We've had nothing but unfulfilled promises and higher taxes with nothing to show for it, and only moral indignities and gridlock. The politicians we've elected are lifers. They do nothing but raise money for their next election. Mr. DeMarco, nothing gets done by these people in Washington. I intend to run for the Democratic nomination for this Congressional District. I will be making my official announcement next week."

Teddy raised both hands in the universal sign of surrender. It appeared he was about to hear another political speech. In fact, it sounded like the Pastor was trying out a stump speech on him just to see how he liked it. But he'd heard it all before. In his opinion, what they really needed to talk about was a strategy for fundraising, and then more fundraising. So Teddy interrupted the Pastor and said, "My apologies, Pastor Lloyd, but you had me at Man of God. No need to practice your speech on me. What we really need to talk about is a plan to get you better name recognition, how to get your name on the ballot for the primary, and how to raise money for the campaign. Would it be too bold of me to ask how much you've raised thus far?"

"The campaign has about $10,000 in the account. Additionally, MJED is currently setting up its own fundraising apparatus and I will be their primary beneficiary. We haven't determined how it will operate yet, from a legal standpoint that is. We could really use a good campaign finance attorney to help us with that—pro bono, of course."

"Of course," Teddy said, "but I'm afraid I can't help you there. None of our bank lawyers have any experience in campaign finance regulations. Sorry."

"Yes, yes! I understand."

Teddy forged ahead. "Pastor, you're in a difficult situation in this Congressional District. There are any number of challengers who would love to get this nomination. I expect that you'll have a pretty wide open primary, which means you will need a solid campaign war chest. And I'm sorry to say that a mere $10,000 is not going to do it for you. But you can depend on a contribution to your campaign from 1NEB."

"How much?" Pastor Lloyd asked.

"I'm sorry?"

"How much will your PAC be giving me?" It appeared he expected a specific number.

The conversation had now turned very formal and Teddy was not sure he liked where it was going. He said, "Those decisions are made by the PAC Executive Committee inside the bank."

Pastor Lloyd pressed him hard. "But Mr. DeMarco, I thought you were in charge of the bank's PAC?"

Teddy was tap dancing again. "That's true. I am the chairman of the PAC, but I only make recommendations to the Executive Committee. They review my recommendations and then vote on them."

Both men were getting a bit testy with each other now. Pastor Lloyd said without thinking, "So then you're not really in charge of the PAC, Mr. DeMarco, are you?"

Teddy decided it was time to bring the temperature down a bit. He responded in as calm a voice as he could muster. "Pastor Lloyd, the Executive Committee relies on my judgment to bring them the best candidates for the bank's financial support. I have never had one of my recommendations turned down. Ever!"

Pastor Lloyd wasn't backing down. He asked again, "Okay then, so how much will you recommend that your PAC contributes to my campaign?"

The In-House Politician

Teddy paused a moment to determine how best to answer this question. He didn't think the Pastor would necessarily like what he was about to say. So he started out very deliberately. "You must understand that our PAC funds are limited, so we typically contribute to those candidates who we think, first, have an excellent chance of winning, and, second, who are supporters of the banking industry's agenda. We have a long way to go before I can place your name before committee. I hope you understand that, right? You're just beginning your campaign." Teddy decided to avoid the second part of his previous answer because that conversation could get ugly. As a member of PUMP's board, Pastor Lloyd Ogletree's positions could not be classified as friendly to the financial services industry.

Pastor Lloyd had a look of betrayal on his face. He turned away from Teddy.

Teddy said, "I know that sounds like a Catch 22 situation, but like I said, our PAC funds are limited."

"So, you're not inclined to support a dark horse candidate?"

Teddy didn't know what to make of this comment—whether the Pastor was making a joke, and he should laugh, or he was being serious and was looking for confirmation from Teddy that no funding would come unless and until he had shown himself to be a viable candidate who deserved the bank's support. Teddy said nothing and let the conversation settle down.

Pastor Lloyd's annoyance was building. He said, "You know why I continue to refer to you as Mr. DeMarco, and not by your first name? It's because of times like this. You're the one with the money and I can't have any of it until I prove myself to you, isn't that right, Mr. DeMarco? But how can I prove myself to you without any campaign funds to accomplish this task? Sally Kessler told me not to trust you. I told her, no, I think he's a man of principles. He's a man with integrity, and he's a man of outstanding moral judgment. And above all, I said he's a man I feel I can trust." Pastor Lloyd was pouring it on thick, but Teddy had heard it all before, especially when people wanted money from him.

Pastor Lloyd continued. "Please tell me, Mr. DeMarco, that I haven't misjudged you. Are you, in fact, the person that Sally Kessler tells me will not honor his commitments unless you put his feet to the fire?"

Teddy was pissed and wanted to get up and leave. No one had ever called him untrustworthy—at least, not to his face. No candidate seeking funds from the bank's PAC had ever insulted him like that. And if that wasn't enough, this Man of God had just invoked the name of Sally Kessler, Teddy's arch enemy, as an authority on Teddy's conscience. Really? This was one of those moments when whatever was said next could either blow it all up, or give peace a chance. Teddy called on all his restraint, and very quietly but firmly said, "Pastor Lloyd, I think perhaps we've let our emotions get the better of us. I believe the two of us have developed a good working relationship in which we're trying to help each other reach our ultimate goals. We should probably both take a step back and take a deep breath before we both head over the cliff."

This got a slight smile out of Pastor Lloyd and seemed to lighten the moment. They both exhaled.

Teddy continued. "I want you to know that I came here in good faith. I truly believe in the work that you and the MJED are doing. And I believe that from what I have heard and seen, you will make

The In-House Politician

an excellent candidate for Congress. But regardless of what you've heard about me from Sally, I am not the devil. I promise you I will do whatever I can to get you funding from the bank's PAC. I may have to bend some rules to get the funds to you earlier than we typically do, but I'll see what I can do. And I will do my best to get your mother's mortgage application processed as quickly I can. She will be hearing from my staff ASAP. Now I would like to leave here thinking that you understand my position. Do you, in fact, understand where I'm coming from?"

Pastor Lloyd's body language told Teddy he was not satisfied, but he had concluded this was all he was going to get out of today's meeting. "Sure, Mr. DeMarco, I understand."

They got up from their chairs and shook hands.

As Teddy was moving towards the door, Pastor Lloyd said, "Okay, then. So, what's next? When will I be hearing from you?"

Teddy turned and faced Pastor Lloyd. "We'll be watching you to see how your campaign progresses. We'll be in touch after that. And my staff will be in touch with your mother for any additional information needed."

"Goodbye, and the Lord be with you. Safe travels, Mr. DeMarco. I have a lot riding on your safe arrival back at the bank."

They laughed. Then Teddy said, "Even with all that we discussed today, you still can't call me Teddy?"

"If you want us to be friends, Mr. DeMarco, you will need to prove it to me first."

Teddy dropped his head and put up his hands up again in full surrender mode. He turned and left.

Chapter 19

Teddy summoned Tom to his office by way of Kelly. Her message was that he should be available to meet with Teddy as soon as he returned to the office. She added that he was on his way.

It's a good thing Tom was in his office when he arrived. Teddy was never a happy camper when he couldn't locate one of his staff at the exact moment he wanted them. Patience was not his strong suit. Tom was on the phone when Teddy pounded on the door. The door was open and Tom could see him clearly, but he still thought it important to announce himself anyway. Teddy hadn't been to his office yet, and was still holding his briefcase and overcoat in one hand. Was he giving Tom a message, in his erstwhile manner, to be prepared for another shit-storm meeting? As Tom was ending the call, Teddy raised his hand fully extending the five fingers, again for emphasis, and then pointed to his office and mouthed the words "five minutes."

Despite Teddy's attempt at miming, Tom clearly got the message. It wasn't like Teddy to come directly to someone's office. He always sent Kelly with the summons, so Tom was getting a bit nervous. He didn't recall doing anything to anger him recently, but you could never tell with Teddy.

After waiting 4 minutes and 30 seconds since his hand gesture, Tom picked up his note pad and walked the twenty paces or so down the hall to Teddy's confessional booth. The door was open, but he wasn't there. He looked at Kelly, but she was on the phone. When she saw him, she gave him the okay to head into his office.

She knew he was expected back, and hadn't been called away to another meeting.

Whenever Tom was in Teddy's office he liked to sit on his couch. It was really comfortable and was located against the back wall with two Queen Anne chairs flanking it on either side. There was also a long rectangular coffee table in front of the couch, making the work space looked formal, but still casual. Teddy often ordered Tom to take a seat at the front of his desk where two more formal leather chairs were situated. This always meant he was about to take up a defensive position directly opposite him so as to minimize the casualties. But today, Tom was alone to make his choice of seating arrangements for what he hoped would be just a small skirmish without leaving too much blood on the carpet.

When Teddy returned to his office he did not say a word or even acknowledge Tom's presence. Ah, yes! The silent treatment was all part of the dance. He was in one of his moods. Just to break the ice, Tom thought about asking him how his meeting had gone with Pastor Lloyd, but then thought better of it. Teddy barked at Kelly to hold his calls.

After he shut the door, Teddy pulled a file out of his briefcase and came over and sat down opposite Tom. He slapped a file down onto the coffee table and said in a rather harsh tone, "Don't open that file yet!"

"Okay?" Tom said, sitting back in the plush couch.

"Look at me, Tom. I need your word that you will do everything you can to get this mortgage application approved. This file is extremely important to our work here, and I don't want it getting fucked up by Porter and his minions. So, what I want you to do is to review this file with a fine-tooth comb. Then I want you to draw up a list of additional information you think the Mortgage Department is going to need to get this deal done. But before you talk with anyone down there, you come back here and meet with me so the two of us can figure out the best way to proceed. I don't want those knuckleheads who work for Porter talking directly to the applicant unless it's absolutely necessary. This is your #1 priority, so please get on it as soon as we're done here, okay?"

"Sure, Boss, but can I at least know who this application is for and why it's so important?"

Teddy's mood changed now from the serious to the boy's club. He said, "Fine, but it's a good thing you're sitting down. Pastor Lloyd personally handed this to me today. It's a mortgage application for his mother. Her name is Mildred "Millie" Ogletree. And this application is a real winner. You may need to think about taking Porter out to dinner in order to get this one across the finish line. In fact, if I thought I could get away with it, I'd pay his way down to Disneyworld. We need to get it done. I can't imagine any scenario in which I have to pick up the phone and tell Pastor Lloyd that we can't approve his mother's application. That would most certainly put an end to our relationship with him and MJED. So let's not place ourselves in that position. Got it? I'm counting on you."

"Yes Sir! Got it!" Tom saluted for emphasis. "No pressure there," he mumbled to himself.

"Okay. Thanks," which was always code for "we're done and you're dismissed."

Tom returned to his office, thinking about how many mortgage applications he had reviewed during his career. Most were hard cases

The In-House Politician

that could only be salvaged with lots of tender love and care. Then there were others that fell into the category of "why are we wasting our time?" The way Teddy explained this one to him, he wasn't sure which category it was going to fall into.

Tom always took solace from remarks he once heard from the bank's Chairman speaking at an officer's meeting. He was asked a question about discrimination in the lending business. His response was that in our jobs as bankers we needed to be right 99.9 percent of the time in order to protect the funds entrusted to us by our depositors and shareholders. Furthermore, he said we discriminate every day. This was the real shocker to Tom. He had never heard a banker admit to discrimination in any setting, public or private. But then the Chairman went on to clarify that we discriminate on one basis, and one basis only. We discriminate on the basis of the borrower's ability to repay the debt. He went on to say that if there was any one working at his bank who was discriminating on any other basis than that, and he found out about it, they would be gone. Immediately! No questions asked.

The Chairman looked around the room to see if he had everyone's attention. He related the story of how his grandparents had immigrated to America. He said when they tried to get a loan to start a small business, they were turned down by every bank in town due to their status as immigrants, or in other words, on the basis of their ethnicity. They ended up getting the money to start the business from friends and family who had also come over from the old country. The Chairman said, "So my family knows what it means to be discriminated against. Now I'm the one calling the shots. There will be no discrimination by anyone in this bank, other than on the basis of the borrower's ability to pay. Understood?"

Tom wanted to jump up and scream, "Amen," but figured Teddy would fire him on the spot.

Tom believed those were words to live by. In fact, he was sure that in his efforts to help some applicants get to a final approved status, he had violated some regulations that were established to prevent bankers from unnecessarily spending an applicant's fee when it was pretty clear from the outset it had no chance of being approved. But Tom always thought he was doing the right thing. Besides, the bank's affordable mortgage portfolio was so small that he just figured they were flying under the radar. So after he first glanced at Millie Ogletree's application, Tom smiled, shook his head, and closed the file.

Tom felt like he might need some nourishment before diving into it further. At the risk of Teddy seeing him sneak off to lunch AWOL, he decided to hit the cafeteria and bring something back to his desk as part of the ritual of being a good soldier. He opened the file a second time and began what could only be described as a spiral downward into Dante's Nine Circles of Hell.

By the time Tom finished listing all the additional information needed for Millie Ogletree's application to be ready for review by the Mortgage Department it was five o'clock. But he knew Teddy was waiting to hear from him so he tiptoed down to his office hoping he was either gone for the day or at another meeting. This way Kelly could serve as his witness, testifying that he'd stopped by to brief him before leaving for the day. Tom could then put off the bad news until tomorrow. Perhaps—just maybe—Teddy would arrive at the office in the morning in a better mood.

But Teddy was still in his office, and Kelly advised Tom he would be off his phone call momentarily. She said he could either wait or she would come get him when he was done. Tom opted to wait so he wouldn't risk Teddy getting on another call. He waved Tom in, finished his call, and then they got the party started.

Tom entered the confessional booth thinking Teddy was probably still in an ugly mood. Teddy started off the conversation with a joke about Tom's college football career saying, "You know those Ivy League teams haven't yet figured out the appropriate balance in the student/athlete equation. Too much student and not enough athlete." No matter what, Teddy could always be engaging and funny. He was always ready to talk sports, anytime, anywhere. Off balance, again. He was in a good mood now, so they got down to it.

Once he saw the laundry list of items Tom had pulled out of Millie's file, he said, "So, did you wave your magic wand over the file and turn it into a doable deal?"

"Teddy, I think we're going to need more than a magic wand for this one. We may actually need that trip to Disneyworld for Marley, I mean Porter, in order to get this approved. I've seen some tough cases before, and this one ranks right up there."

"Okay! Okay! I hear ya! But we're not paying you the big bucks to say no."

They both laughed at that statement.

"First, you need to understand that anything I say here is without the benefit of seeing

Millie's credit report. At this point, we don't know if she's been a good payer or not, and that will be crucial in her case."

Teddy nodded. "Understood."

"Fundamentally, she can't afford to buy the property. Millie agreed to pay $125,000 for the place, but her income won't support that kind of payment. Additionally, we're being asked to take the seller's word for it that he's been putting some of her rent money aside on a regular basis into an escrow account for Millie's down payment. We're going to need to see some verifiable records from the seller to prove that the money in the escrow account came from Millie's rent, and wasn't just deposited recently by the seller to make up the five percent down payment. And I don't see any additional funds to cover the closing costs. There's only $300 in Millie's checking account. And it's with another bank by the way."

Teddy shrugged. "Is that it?"

"No, I'm just getting started. Millie's daughter Karen, Pastor Lloyd's sister, is on the application and sales agreement as a co-borrower. But she has no income right now, and she hasn't listed any assets on the application—not even a car or a savings account. According to the application, she's been out of work for about six months. She's not bringing any strength to the transaction."

"Yup! Pastor Lloyd mentioned that when he gave me the file."

"According to the file," Tom continued, "Millie's monthly Social Security check amounts to $1,000. She's also receiving her deceased husband's pension, which is another $400 per month. So Millie has a monthly income of $1,400. But the monthly payment is $750, including taxes. So, with just her stable sources of income, her housing debt ratio is over 53 percent. That won't cut it. Now, Millie put down on the application that she has additional income from various housecleaning jobs. Unfortunately, it's sporadic, a cash business, and I don't know any way to verify it, not unless she can somehow substantiate regular deposits into her account as coming from these jobs. Certainly, the employers aren't going to verify the payments since they didn't report them to the IRS, and there'd be too many of them for us to track down. So, it will be up to Millie to prove this additional income if she wants us to use it. If we can somehow substantiate this additional housecleaning income, we may be able give her an additional—say, average of $300 per month. This would get her monthly debt ratio down to about 44 percent—which helps, but still doesn't bring it down into an acceptable range."

Tom paused a second. "Then there's the rental income. We have no idea if, let's say, $500 a month is the market for a unit in Plainfield. We won't know this until we get the appraisal in. So if we assume the appraisal confirms a $500/month rent, this would bring her monthly debt ratio down to 34 percent, which is still high. Again, this assumes a lot we don't know yet. These assumptions are that she can prove $300 in housecleaning income, and the appraisal will support that rental income. And hopefully Millie doesn't have a huge car loan on her credit report that she forgot to include on the application. Oh, and I almost forgot the part about proving the monthly set aside of her funds by the landlord for her down payment. So, as you can see, there's a lot of major holes in this application. I'd say it's currently on life support."

"Okay," Teddy said, "then let's resurrect it. Tell me what you need to spruce this baby up, then we'll decide our next steps."

"Well, first we need to see what the seller has in terms of documentation on the set-aside of rent monies for the down payment. Typically, you only count the rent paid towards the down payment account as long as they have a formal agreement stipulating how much of the monthly rent is being set aside. Call me crazy, but I don't think there's any written any agreement. Let's hope I'm wrong. Additionally, we need to have Millie provide us with bank statements going back two years to show any monthly deposits coming from her housecleaning jobs. And if we're successful in getting this income verified, Marley is going to have to look the other way about Millie not reporting it to the IRS. What are the chances of that happening?"

"Who is Marley?" Teddy asked.

"Porter McMahon," Tom said. "That's what I call him."

"Be careful with that," he barked. "Anything else?"

"Well, we can't really know about the potential rental income until we complete the appraisal. But by then it's the same old story. It means that we've spent her application fee on the appraisal and credit reports, and we may still have to deny the loan if we can't make the numbers work. You know sometimes when we see, right up front, that we can't make an application work, we refund the application fee with the denial. But in this case, we can't get to that point unless we spend the money. By the way, where is Millie's application fee? I didn't see it in the file."

Teddy laughed. "How the hell should I know? I didn't look at the file when he handed it to me. If it's not in there, I guess we'll have to take it out of your pay this week."

"Right! Because I get paid the big bucks."

"Put that on your list of items we need to resolve. We may have to ask Porter to eat this application fee, if Millie can't come up with it. It doesn't sound like there's a whole lot of extra cash lying around."

"Speaking of Porter," Tom said, "you do understand that assuming all the things I listed come together, he's still the wild card here. I'm sure that he's never done a loan where the down payment came from a monthly set aside of rental funds—kind of like a lease-purchase agreement. And I can't imagine he's going to like the idea of averaging her monthly housekeeping income. Finally, I can't see him being thrilled with crediting her $500 a month rental income when she's never been a landlord before. What happens the first time she needs to fix the toilet upstairs? Where's that money coming from? Not to mention when one tenant leaves and there's a few months without any rental income? There's no cash reserves. And where's the daughter in all of this?"

"It sounds to me like we've got our work cut out for us on this one," Teddy said.. "Hopefully, we can get Porter to work with us to order the reports we need with the understanding that we'll find a way to reimburse him—one way or the other."

"Are we talking about the same guy? Marley?"

"Stop it!" Teddy said. " Okay then, here's what we're going to do. I'm going to meet with our senior credit folks to plow the road for this application. I'm going to ask them to put a bug in Porter's ear, so he knows it's important to work with us to get this one to the finish line. Once that's done, I'm going to want you to meet with Porter to explain to him the same information you just briefed me on. That way he knows what the situation is on this deal. Then, once I have this approved from credit policy, you will take the lead on getting the additional information we need to approve the loan. I only want you talking with Millie Ogletree. If any of those knuckleheads in the Mortgage Department start tearing this application apart and talking directly with her, well, you know what will happen. And we don't want that. *Capisce?*"

"Got it."

"Good job today. You see. That was easy."

As Tom got up to leave, Teddy said, "So, why do you keep referring to Porter as Marley?"

Tom laughed. "Sorry, that's my nickname for him. I call Porzio Scrooge, and I call Porter Marley. You know, from Dickens' novel? Just to myself. I never use them with anyone else—well, maybe Althea. Scrooge and Marley were in business with each other until—well—you know how the story begins—with the ghost of Marley."

Teddy laughed in a somewhat sinister way, but he still laughed. "Yeah! Yeah! I know how the story goes." Then he got serious and said, "Tom, be careful with that and keep those nicknames to yourself."

"Understood."

It was way past five o'clock. Tom called his wife and told her not to wait with dinner for him.

Chapter 20

Joe Campbell considered himself a good business writer. He'd been with *The Examiner* for ten years and had published some hard hitting pieces about politicians on the take, bad cops, priests who'd gone over to the dark side, and, more recently articles on mortgage discrimination in the banking industry, also known as redlining. There had been some overtures in the past from the *Wall Street Journal*, but he thought he'd stay right where he was, as head business writer for *The Examiner*. He didn't want to become a small fish in a big pond. He could do more to accomplish change by shining some light on power right where he was.

Indeed, part of his decision to stay was his ambition. He knew his beat, and was well respected in the profession. From time to time, he was asked to serve on panels at conferences with other business experts and writers. And he'd received some favorable reviews related to these appearances. But Joe assumed he had a better shot at the big story—the one that makes your career—by staying right where he was.

The story he had published a few years back on the acquisition by 1NEB of an out-of-state bank had all the makings of a real in-depth analysis on how banks had been heartless when it came to lending in distressed low-income communities, as well as the closing of branches in minority neighborhoods. Banks shied away from making loans in these communities because of the perception of higher risk. In Joe's mind, as a result of the industry's disinvestment, or redlining, in these communities, it became a self-fulfilling prophecy as they continued to decline. But whenever he thought he might have a real opportunity to make good on his promise to expose the effects of these banking practices, he got pulled off on a different assignment his editors thought would be more interesting to *The Examiner's* readers.

Joe didn't think of himself as a liberal, despite the slant his stories always seemed to take. Exposing the bad guys just seemed to fall into that same old category of progressive muckraking. He saw it as reporting the facts and letting readers judge for themselves. There were times, though, when he found himself in situations where he was essentially in bed with the lefties, the liberals, and the social welfare types who always wanted the press to help them with their agenda. It was the nature of the business. In fact, it was these types of stories that just might lead him down the path to a Pulitzer with its attendant fame and glory. So what if he had to spend time with the likes of Sally Kessler and her PUMP acolytes. She was always good for a rumor about some new evil con the banking industry was perpetrating on the unsuspecting public.

And then there was his eye thing.

When Joe was first hired by *The Examiner*, the editor who interviewed him asked about the eye patch. He wanted to know if it would inhibit him from the amount of reading, typing and driving to interviews and stories required for the job. Joe's response was that it hadn't prevented him thus far from serving as the editor of his college newspaper, or in his last job as a reporter for a newspaper in the Midwest. In fact, he didn't wear the eye patch all the time—just on certain days when that one eye went a bit lazy on him. Otherwise, his vision was fine.

Joe found it interesting that his editor never asked him about what happened to his eye. He was glad he didn't, but if he had, Joe would have been truthful. There'd been an accident when he younger, when he was in prep school. And he would have left it at that.

Based on the sample stories he'd sent in prior to the interview and the recommendations from his previous employer, Joe got the job.

Chapter 21

The Mortgage Department had been notified Tom would be handling the application and that no one was to speak with Mildred Ogletree or her daughter Karen. Teddy had successfully plowed the road, and presumably the issue of the application fee as well. No one asked Tom where it was. Porter's staff would input the file into the system, and once Tom gave them the go-ahead they would order the required credit reports and appraisal.

The application fee statement requires some clarification. While it was true that no one asked where the fee was, or if the proverbial check was in the mail, in a moment of downright honesty, Tina Washington admitted to Tom that Porter had a real hissy fit when he found out the Mortgage Department would have to eat the fee on the Ogletree application. Tom sensed that she was smiling on the other end of the phone when she reported this, but he couldn't be sure.

If Porter wasn't pleased when he heard about this decision, it must have eventually occurred to him that if Tom screwed it up, he couldn't be blamed. So, what the hell. Either way, in the end it was a win-win for himself—except for the application fee.

There was still some question in Tom's mind as to whether Millie's daughter Karen should be a co-borrower. She was unemployed, and brought no strength to the application. Nowhere on the application was there any indication she owned a car or had any savings of her own beyond the combined checking account with Millie, the one with a balance of $300. Likewise, she didn't list any jewelry or furniture under her own name. However, it seemed that Millie wanted to keep her daughter on the application.

Given there were some important income verification issues yet to be resolved, Tom thought it would be a good idea to set up a face-to-face meeting with Millie. Since this was going to be a "character" loan if there ever was one, he felt it made sense to meet with her in person in order to gauge her commitment to the transaction. Tom asked Teddy if he thought Pastor Lloyd should be invited to the meeting. His only advice was to be sensitive to any family issues that might surface when discussing it with Mrs. Ogletree. If she didn't want her son at the meeting, that was her right. For the moment, though, Tom still thought Millie would make a better applicant on her own. There was no telling what might come up on Karen's credit report since Pastor Lloyd hinted about some past problems she had encountered.

Tom called Mrs. Mildred Ogletree to let her know the application was in process, but he would need additional information to get it in good enough shape to render a decision. He made no promises. When they set up a time to meet she was very gracious, although reserved and businesslike. At some point in the conversation, she told him he could call her Millie. She made it known that she had never purchased a house on her own, and sounded quite anxious about the process. Based on the conversation, it appeared she wanted to meet Tom without Pastor Lloyd. He said this was fine. However, when she asked him about whether her daughter needed to be present, Tom said that wasn't necessary. He wanted an opportunity to speak with Millie alone. He needed to get a clearer picture of why she wanted Karen on the application. And he had no intention of getting involved in any family disputes without the knowledge or consent of Pastor Lloyd. At least that was his plan.

They set an appointment for the next day.

When Tom arrived Millie was sitting on the front porch in her rocker surveying all she could see from her elevated perch. They greeted each other formally. She was Mrs. Ogletree to Tom, and he was Mr. Donovan to her. She then reminded Tom he could call her Millie.

She was a striking looking woman for 70 years of age. While she was not tall, she appeared so by her slender, statuesque figure. With her silver-gray hair pulled back into a severe bun, she needed no make-up for her lovely face, which had a smooth, silky texture. She reminded Tom of Lena Horne or Diana Ross. She wore her finest Sunday go-to-meetin' long dress, but without the accessories and required hat. Clearly, she wanted to make an impression and she was quite successful in doing so. He asked permission to quickly walk the exterior of the property. She responded with a laugh and a shrug, saying it was fine with her since she didn't own the place yet—so he should do whatever he needed to do. Tom was glad to see she had a sense of humor.

The neighborhood was a typical older urban setting with properties in close proximity to each other. The subject property was located on Third Street in Plainfield, one house in from the corner of Park. It was a two-family property that had seen better days. The roof appeared to be in relatively good shape from what he could see from his street-level view. The clapboard siding had a few cracked or missing shingles, but nothing serious from his perspective. All the adjacent properties had small side yards separated only by long dirt driveways leading to old detached wooden garages, which, most likely, were only used for storage. Cars were mostly parked on the street, and the front yards were small.

Once Tom completed his walk-around, Millie invited him inside and offered him a cup of coffee. He accepted only to be polite. He'd already had his daily dose of caffeine and was dreading the long ride later. As they sat down in the kitchen, Tom looked around to see the quality of the cabinets, the flooring, the sink, fixtures, and appliances. Nothing seemed out of place other than the need for some new flooring. It occurred to him that what he was doing at that very moment, sitting in the kitchen having coffee with an elderly Black woman who was trying to purchase a home, was a very small piece of his plan to save the world. Heck, he was full of himself! Tom quickly came back down to earth when she asked him if he thought her mortgage application was going to be approved soon.

From his initial observations, it was clear that Millie Ogletree suffered no fools and could easily read all his signs, both verbally and from his squirming body language. After all, she had raised a son to be a Man of God. And no matter what happened, Tom was convinced Millie Ogletree would still pray for him.

Tom smiled at her question, and while he was considering a proper response, Millie threw him another curve ball.

"Mr. Donovan, I have to say that I'm thrilled with the opportunity to buy this house with a loan from your bank, and through this special mortgage program y'all have put together. But frankly, I'm also a bit confused, since most of my friends and neighbors have told me that your bank has redlined this neighborhood. I'm not quite sure I fully understand what that term redlined means, but my friends have said it means your bank and others have rejected all the loans that have come from folks trying to buy homes here. Is that true?"

Tom was looking for some divine intervention. "Well, Millie, it's a bit complicated, and, I'll admit the banking industry doesn't have a good history when it comes to making loans in neighborhoods like this one."

"You mean neighborhoods where there are lots of folks who look like me, don't you?"

"I can't defend our past lending practices to you. But if I had to, I would start by saying there are many older neighborhoods like this one where the homes, which were built many years ago, have seen better days. And sometimes the folks who own them haven't had the money to keep them up, or to fix them up. Over time, these homes start to, well, deteriorate further. So when lenders send appraisers out to establish market values on these older homes, many times the lender doesn't obtain a high enough collateral value sufficient to cover the loan. Do you follow me?"

"Mr. Donovan, seems to me that's a fancy way of saying your bank doesn't like to make loans to Black folks, right?"

"Like I said before, I can't defend past practices of the industry, and, well, my bank specifically doesn't have a long history of making mortgage loans to anyone. In the past, 1NEB only made these loans to wealthy borrowers with large down payments as an accommodation since they were important customers."

"So, why are you here then? We don't have a large down payment, and we don't want to be your charity. But we do want to buy this house."

"Mrs. Ogletree, I mean Millie," Tom said, "it's a long story, and it has a lot to do with all those past practices, and my bank wanting to grow larger. As a result of all those factors, the bank put together this special loan program to help borrowers like yourself buy a home in neighborhoods like this one."

As those words came out of his mouth, Tom was hoping Millie would not be offended by them. She was not.

"Okay. Let's leave it at that. My son says that your boss—I wrote it down so I'd remember—Mr. Teddy DeMarco, has made a good case for us to take advantage of your special loan program. So let's get back to my original question. When will my loan be approved?"

Tom did his best to explain the situation to her by walking her through the numbers. First and foremost, he added up all her regular and verifiable sources of income—her monthly Social Security and pension amounts. Then he added in the rent she expected to receive for the upstairs apartment. She could see now how this monthly income compared to what her monthly mortgage payment, including real estate taxes, would look like. As diplomatically as he could, Tom explained to her that even with those two sources of income and the rental income, she would not have sufficient income to pay all her bills—at least not from the bank's perspective. This was why they needed to dive deeper into her housecleaning business to determine if they could find some additional income that could help her to qualify.

At this point, she began to have that look—the one that tilts your head off into the distance looking for solace somewhere because you don't want to make eye contact for fear of saying something you'll regret while still maintaining your dignity. Millie was proud she was able to make a living cleaning houses while still raising a family. She explained that when her husband was alive and they had two incomes, they were able to make ends meet with a few dollars left over every month. But when he died at age 60, she was on her own. While she continued to receive his pension from the Railroad, the reduced amount wasn't nearly enough to cover all the bills. So she made the heartbreaking decision to sell their home and become a renter. Her son, Pastor Lloyd, was doing well by this time and helped her out whenever she was in need. But Millie's pride would not allow her to take any charity and she always endeavored to pay him back.

When she finished explaining how things had arrived at this point, they returned to the task at hand: how to verify her housecleaning income. Tom asked her if there were any records of the amounts she was paid, like cancelled checks or some bookkeeping entries she might have kept. She confirmed his worst fears that all her payments were in cash and there were no separate records. In fact, Millie said, many times she would just take the money down to the utility company to pay the gas and electric bills. She wanted to make sure that her daughter and granddaughter were always warm in their upstairs apartment.

Great! No records, Tom thought. He asked her how many times she cleaned houses per month. Again, she had that look of being grilled by the vocational police. She said she had some regulars whose homes she would clean twice a month, and others who called her as needed. When all was said and done, it sounded like she was working an average of eight days a month. She got up from the table, went into another room, and came back with a monthly planner which she used to verify that number. Tom said, "Whoa, Mrs. Ogletree, I asked you earlier if you had any financial records of your housecleaning work."

She lowered her reading glasses and looked down at him over her perfect nose and said quite correctly, "No, Mr. Donovan, you asked me if I kept any records of the amounts I was paid for these jobs. I did not. I can tell you how much each customer pays me, but I don't have any formal records. However, I do need to keep a record of my work schedule so I don't double book any customers. It's also helpful to know where I'm traveling to work so I know what bus to take. I rarely drive my car. It sits out there in front of the house most of the time."

Tom said, "You're right, Mrs. Ogletree. I apologize." Lesson learned.

She responded in a very gentle tone. "Oh, that's quite alright. Just a little misunderstanding."

He asked, "Say, would it be alright if I took a look at that planner with your work schedule in it?"

She paused a few seconds and quickly leafed through the pages. She laughed and said, "Well, I guess it's alright. I just wanted to make sure there's nothing bad in here. I keep my gentlemen caller's numbers in another little black book. But please don't say anything to my son. He thinks I'm a saint." She paused and winked at him. Tom couldn't tell if she was pulling his leg. It was none of his business, but they both laughed out loud.

She handed it over to him and politely asked if he wanted more coffee. Tom said, "No thank you," and started looking through the planner. It did, in fact, seem to verify that she worked about eight days a month—sometimes nine or ten, but never less than eight. The problem was that this was her personal planner and Porter McMahon could always say she just constructed it to support her unverifiable income. Porter was like that. Unfortunately, he was right. But sometimes you just gotta trust people. And Tom found Millie Ogletree to be as trustworthy as they come.

The second problem was that the planner covered only the current year. When Tom asked if she had kept planners from previous years with this same kind of information, she said she might have them somewhere, but it would take her some time to find them. He would have to wait for that additional information.

"So Millie, how much do you make cleaning these houses. Do you charge all your customers the same amount?"

"Oh my goodness, no! You should see the size of some of these mansions. Oh, I could tell you stories about how some of these White folks keep their—" She stopped, as quickly as she started, remembering who she was talking to.

Tom said, "Please go on. I'd love to hear those stories."

She demurred. "No Sir! I shouldn't be telling tales about my customers. Just not right. I charge those folks $150 a day to clean those big places because of the size, number of rooms to vacuum and dust, number of windows to clean. I charge extra if they want me to do their laundry and some ironing. But ironing is rare these days. Everything goes out to the dry cleaners, you know. I charge $100 a day for the smaller, regular size houses."

Based on his quick calculation, and giving her credit for four mansions and four regular houses, Tom came up with a monthly average of $1,000 in additional cash income. He asked Millie if this sounded right and she nodded. It wasn't a nod of "Yes, absolutely," but more of a nod with a shrug of the shoulders, which implied, "Sure, whatever you say."

"Millie, were there any occasions in which you deposited the full amount you were paid in cash directly into your bank account? Like on the same day or the next day?"

She said, "Oh sure, I do that sometimes. But there are other times when I need to pay some bills. Like I said before about paying the utility bills."

"Okay, now we're getting somewhere. Can you please let me see copies of your monthly bank statements? If we can track some regular monthly deposits in the amounts you were paid by your customers, we may have a chance at including some of your housecleaning income on the application."

Millie gave him that look again. "We have one of those low balance checking accounts that only charges you a small monthly fee as long as you don't use the account much—you know, like write a lot of checks. You're the banker. You know how those accounts work, right?"

"Right," Tom said without much enthusiasm. "But I'm confused. You said, "we." Who is we?"

"My daughter Karen is the other person on the checking account. She looks after the monthly statements and balances the checkbook. I'm way too old for all that. Karen pays the rent check and lets me know how we're doing. From time to time, she tells me if we're a little short for the month. Then we either cut back on groceries a bit, or sometimes I take another housecleaning job or two that month. But this has only been a problem for the last few months since Karen lost her job. Things have been a little tight since then. Before that, when she was working, we were doing just fine."

"Okay. I understand all that, but does your daughter have copies of your monthly checking account statements going back in time—let's say for the last two years?"

The In-House Politician

"Like I said, I really don't know about all that stuff. You'll have to talk to her."

"Please understand that those bank statements are your only way of supporting the monthly income you get from your housecleaning jobs. If we can get those statements and the work dates in your planner to match up, then we might have a chance, and I must emphasize it's a slim chance, to be able to give you credit for some of the housecleaning income. When will you be seeing your daughter again?"

"Karen will be home for dinner tonight. I'm not sure where she's off to right now. Hopefully looking for a job. But my granddaughter gets home from school by four, and we like to have supper together. I will see her then."

"Can you please ask her about those bank statements, and have her call me with any questions? She's going to have to make copies of those statements for the last two years, and get them to me."

Millie wrote that down and nodded, but she still had a puzzled look on her face, which seemed to be saying, "Is all this really necessary, don't you trust me to pay my bills?"

With the housecleaning income hopefully on the right track, Tom said to himself with fingers crossed, they could now move on to the next big item: the source of the down payment. The bank's affordable mortgage program was permitting loans with only five percent down, but borrowers still needed some additional cash to cover the closing costs. In Millie's case, her down payment of five percent on the purchase price of $125,000 was $6,250. However, this was going to be another one of those cockamamie transactions where the source of the down payment was supposedly coming from funds her landlord was setting aside from her monthly rent payments.

"Millie," Tom asked, "do you have any monthly statements from your landlord showing the amounts he placed in an escrow account for your down payment?"

She frowned. "What's that? An escrow account you call it? You're going to have to tell me what that means, Mr. Donovan." She was still not inclined to call him Tom.

After he explained what he was looking for from the landlord, she appeared to be on the verge of tears. Through glistening eyes, she said she was not aware of any such account. He asked her where the money came from for the deposit on the house when she and her daughter signed the sales contract to purchase the house. The glistening eyes were now in need of a tissue.

"I really don't know where the money came from. That's another item you're going to have to ask my daughter about. She handles all that."

Tom was getting a bit frustrated. Had he known the level of involvement Karen Ogletree had in the transaction, he would have asked her to be present at this meeting. But he was still operating under the assumption that if Millie was the sole breadwinner, then Karen was not needed on the mortgage application, and might be a problem. It was becoming clear to him that Millie depended on her daughter for lots of things, and in this case, she was the keeper of the family finances. However, the one big question Tom really wanted to ask was whether she and her daughter had any separate savings to be used for the closing costs—assuming they got that far.

He said, "Well, it seems like I'm going to have to set up a time to speak with your daughter in order to get more information about your financial statements. However, before we have that

The In-House Politician

conversation, I did want to ask you why you want to keep Karen on the application, since she is currently unemployed, and can't help you pay the monthly mortgage."

And there it was. Knucklehead Tom, who did not want to get involved in family matters, just came out with it. As the words were coming out of his mouth, he couldn't stop himself. Even before he finished saying them, he was already wondering how they would be received.

Millie took a moment to compose herself, then looked at him directly and spoke plainly. "Mr. Donovan, do you have a family?" Up until now, the meeting had been serious and businesslike with a few laughs mixed in from time to time. It was clear Millie Ogletree was now about to give him a stern emotional lecture. He felt like he was back in the principal's office in grade school. He saw it coming and there was nothing he could do about it. After he nodded his assent, she continued. "And do you have children who are still at home and dependent on you?" Again, Tom nodded and tried to say "yes," but she was on a roll and it was time for him to just to sit back, shut up, and listen. If he didn't, it seemed like she was going to send him to detention.

"Mr. Donovan, I am currently the sole supporter of my daughter and my granddaughter. I believe my son told your boss the story about how Karen got herself in trouble with a no-good man, who left her high and dry after he got her pregnant. I love my daughter and I adore my granddaughter. I will do anything for them that's in my power. Becoming an unwed mother without a husband to support her was not the end of my daughter's troubles. I'm not sure how much you want me to go into our family history, but it's safe to say that I'm pretty much responsible for helping to raise my granddaughter. Do you understand what I'm trying to tell you?"

She sighed. "There were times when Karen was gone for months. I didn't know where on earth she was. She always came back and my granddaughter was always happy to have her back in her life. But there were times when Karen came home dead broke, and she was clearly strung out. Fortunately, my son, a Man of God, stood by the family. Against her wishes, he got her into a rehab program, and she's been clean ever since she got hired for this last job. I don't know what this last job loss is doing to her self-esteem. I pray as hard as I can, Mr. Donovan, that the Lord will guide my daughter through this tough time in her life. But Mr. Donovan, I want to include my daughter on the mortgage application for a few reasons. First, I want her to know that when I'm gone, this place is hers, no questions asked. Second, I want her to know that her daughter, my granddaughter, always has a place to call home. And finally, as God is my witness, I want Karen to see her way clear to getting another job, in order to help me and her daughter keep this place. I'm hoping that all of these reasons will help her keep clean. I know that my daughter has some pride. And she's not happy when her daughter sees her sulking around the house with nothing to do. My granddaughter is getting to an age where she's noticing these things and starting to ask questions. If Karen is on the mortgage with me, then she's also responsible for her portion of it. Do you understand what I'm telling you, Mr. Donovan?"

This time Tom actually got to respond sheepishly with a nod and a quiet, "Yes, I do."

"Good, I'm glad that we understand each other, Mr. Donovan. Now, what else do we have to talk about?"

Tom was still recovering from just having been taken to the woodshed and needed a moment. After a deep breath, he moved on.

"Well, I'm going to have to speak with your landlord about the down payment issue. And I'm going to need to speak with your daughter as well. How do you want to work this? Should I call your landlord, or do you want to have him call me?"

"I'll call him and give him your number."

"What's his name so I know who to expect the call from?"

"His name is Mr. Isaac Robinson. I believe you two have already met."

"Oh really? When was that?"

"Mr. Isaac Robinson is the head deacon at my son's church. As I understand it, Deacon Isaac was the one who helped you find a phone the day y'all met there."

"Yes, I remember him from our brief encounter at the church. He seemed like a nice man." Tom thought that was the politically correct thing to say since he and Deacon Isaac did not have any long discussion over world events, or the meaning of life. He just said "Follow me" and pointed him to the phone on his desk.

"Okay then, I'll expect a call from him. Thanks." He did not want to press any further on how this whole transaction came together. It was none of his business and he had a feeling he really didn't want to know.

Since they had been at it for at least an hour, Tom felt the need to ask Millie about her schedule and if she was okay with a few more questions.

"I'm all yours today, Mr. Donovan. No other appointments until my granddaughter gets home from school."

He asked about her assets. Together they came up with a value of $3,000 for her car.

Next, Tom asked about her jewelry. She had listed it as being worth $5,000. In response to his question, Millie got up from her chair and was about to go into the bedroom to bring a few pieces out to show him, but Tom said she didn't need to bother. He would take her word for it. When would he ever learn? She wanted to show him her prized possessions and he didn't seem interested. She was trying to make a connection and he blew her off. He tried to recover. "Perhaps you can show me some of your pieces when we're done here, if time permits."

This seemed to console her a bit, but he still felt like an idiot.

Tom moved on. "Okay. Let's talk about your credit history." He turned over the application and chuckled. "Millie, it appears that you don't have any credit history. You didn't list anything on the credit side of the application. Does this mean that you haven't borrowed any money over the last few years? No credit cards?"

"That's right, Mr. Donovan. I don't believe in debt. If I need something, I save up the money to buy it. No loans!"

"That's very admirable, but without any credit history, we can't evaluate how well you pay back the people you do owe money to. We need to assess that part of your life in order to judge whether we think you're going to pay us back. You know what I mean?" He did his best to smile.

"Oh, yes! I understand, Mr. Donovan, but like I said, I don't believe in owing people money. It's not good for the soul. The Bible is pretty clear on this, you know?"

Tom couldn't let that pass. After all, he was a banker. He said, "No, I didn't learn that in my Sunday School. But I am curious. If you don't believe in owing money, why do you want to borrow so much money from us to buy this house?" It seemed like a logical question.

"I have no other choice, Mr. Donovan. If we hadn't agreed to buy the house from Deacon Isaac, then he would be selling it to someone else. He decided he didn't want it any more—you know—all the headaches of being a landlord. But out of deference to my son, Deacon Isaac said he would wait to sell it to us when we had enough money for the down payment. And then your bank's new mortgage program came to our attention. It seemed like a sign from the Lord above. What's more, I'm too old to move and I didn't want my granddaughter to have to change schools. She's suffered enough with her mother's issues."

"Understood," Tom said. "So, you have no credit? You've never borrowed any money, ever? No credit cards, car loans, appliances purchased on a layaway plan? Anything?"

"Well, my husband and I were both on the mortgage for the house I sold after he died, if that means anything. But that was ten years ago. And I'm thinking I may have purchased that refrigerator on a layaway plan a few years back. But if I did, I have no idea where the paperwork might be. Might have thrown it out."

"Okay, here's what we're going to have to do to build up your credit record," Tom said. "Please speak with your daughter tonight about getting copies of your gas and electric bills. When I speak with Deacon Isaac, I will ask him to give me a letter identifying how much your monthly rent has been and if you paid it on time. This will be part of the conversation I have with him about the funds he's been placing in escrow for your down payment. And if you can locate any information about that refrigerator layaway plan, that would be most helpful."

Tom could see she was tearing up again. He was letting his frustration with her lack of credit experience get the better of him, and he was letting it show. He was a banker, after all, and dealt in credit. It was one thing for him to be bending over backwards to make this mortgage application work, but it was another if the borrower was telling him she didn't like being indebted to anyone. In fact, she was entering into this transaction only because she had no other choice. If push came to shove and he was asked about this application strictly as a character loan, Millie did not exactly plead her case very well. And Porter could read him like a book. But then he recalled Porter didn't make any character loans. Ever! Tom was the shepherd on this loan. This one was on him.

It was time to finally tackle the tough question. He asked her if she still wanted the bank to run a credit report on Karen. And assuming the response was the same, he couldn't really leave without asking if there was anything he should know that might pop up on Karen's credit report. He said it would be better if he knew about any problems in advance since bankers never liked surprises. Millie said that since he would be speaking with Karen about their joint checking account, he should ask her directly about any issues that might come up on her credit report.

Tom looked over the file and couldn't think of any more questions. They had been at it for a good two hours and his bladder was about to explode. While driving in he noticed a gas station on the corner of Third and Park, and he needed gas for the trip back to the bank.

He said goodbye to Millie and assured her they would be talking again very soon. He also indicated that he looked forward to hearing from Karen and Deacon Isaac.

On his way out of town, he stopped at the gas station on the corner to fill'er up and powder his nose. Then he drove back to the office.

Chapter 22

Later that week Tom received the expected call from Karen Ogletree. In their conversation he got the sense that Karen thought she was being deposed, believing that every answer was going to come back to haunt her—possibly even sending her to jail for perjury. Tom was happy when he got more than a one-word answer to his questions. He began the conversation by saying how much he was impressed with her mother, Millie, and that the property they were buying seemed like a good fit for them. This seemed to calm her down and they began to have much better give and take. Karen said she was very grateful for all the things her mother was doing to help raise her daughter, to keep a roof over their heads, and to put food on the table.

Millie had prepped her on why Tom needed to talk with her and why the bank account information was so important.

Tom said, "So, Karen, it sounds like your mother knows what I need to move the application forward. We need to determine how much income we can give her credit for in her housecleaning business. Were you able to get hold of copies of your combined checking account statements?"

"Yes, Mr. Donovan, I have them, but not all the deposit dates match up with the amounts my Mother earned based on the dates in her scheduling book."

"Well, that's not good," Tom replied. He knew this wasn't going to be easy.

"My mother compared the bank statements with her scheduling book. It's pretty much a hodge-podge of entries, some of which she has explanations for and others—well, she can't really remember why on a certain date the reason she may have kept the money in her pocketbook. Her explanation for the dates when there was no deposit, or only a partial deposit a few days later, was that she probably needed cash for groceries. If there was money left over, she deposited the rest on a later date."

It all sounded reasonable to Tom, but he knew if Porter was going to give Millie any credit for this income, it was only going to be when the deposits corresponded exactly to her scheduled work dates. Then it occurred to Tom, once again, that Teddy said he was calling the shots on this loan. But in order to not fall flat on his face, he needed to review the application as if he was Porter. He had to anticipate all the underwriting questions and concerns. Someone would eventually audit this loan, especially if it ever went south.

Millie's housecleaning income would be a leap of faith since there was no back-up documentation stating the actual amount she was paid on those dates. Tom would end up averaging the actual deposit amounts in order to come up with a reasonable monthly estimate. Since he didn't have the information in front of him, he could only speculate that this income, even if it were included, would still not be enough to qualify. But again, he was recalling Teddy's encouragement that he'd seen a Hail Mary work before.

Tom asked Karen if she could send him copies of the bank statements, as well as copies of her mother's work schedule book. He also asked Karen to have her mother write up a separate report identifying which deposits corresponded with scheduled work

The In-House Politician

dates. She should also include explanations of other deposits made that were partial amounts left over from previous housecleaning payments. Tom still wasn't sure it would pass the Porter laugh test. He and his underwriters would never give Millie credit for any of those extraneous deposits, since the exact amounts did not match up. But he needed to give it a try. Karen agreed to do all this and get it into the mail to him by the end of the week.

While Tom was hoping they were done with all of the bad news, he still needed to ask Karen about her credit history. Millie had predicted it wasn't going to be pretty. Tom had seen his share of ugly credit reports before. He asked himself, "How bad could this one be?" Things were about to get radioactive.

As Karen began the explanation of her credit history, Tom could hear sniffling in the background. She didn't like to talk about it, and, she really didn't want to talk about it with someone who was not a family member or friend, or in this case, someone who might be judging her. Tom's best approach was just to listen, and ask clarifying questions when needed.

Karen said, "What would you like to know?"

"Well, according to your mother, most of your credit problems started when you met the guy who ran out on you. I apologize for describing it that way, but I don't know how else to phrase it."

"Oh, that's okay. Your description is right on target. He turned out to be a real scumbag. When I met him, he was running with a tough crowd. I should have known better. After a while, the guys in his gang started to accept me and things seemed to be going well. I was beginning to fit in. But these guys played hard, drank hard, and once you gained their trust, dabbled in hard drugs. I was young and found it all exciting. You have to understand, this guy was my first real boyfriend. I overlooked a lot of bad stuff that was going on in the gang. I won't bore you with the details, but it ended badly when I got pregnant."

She paused a moment, and Tom could tell this was all very emotional for her.

"That must have been a very rough time for you," he said.

"Well, yes, but I haven't told you the worst part. I was living with this guy, on and off, for about six months. When I told him I was pregnant, he left one night after I'd gone to bed. He stole my credit cards and all my cash. I never heard from him again. He was gone and none of his buddies knew where he was—or so they said. And to make matters worse, it wasn't until a few days later that someone reminded me to report that my credit cards had been stolen. I was so upset that it never crossed my mind. In that short amount of time, he'd purchased $2,000 worth of clothing and some audio equipment."

She paused a moment and took a deep breath. "I did report it to the police and it turned out he was working with a female accomplice. The merchants interviewed agreed there was a woman with him. She was the one who forged my signature. I now owed $2,000 in credit card debt, and had lost $500 in cash to that scumbag."

Tom tried to be sympathetic. "I understand that's a tough story to tell. But I'm guessing the bad credit part of it was just the beginning, right?"

"You got that right. I was about to have a baby and had no health insurance. I went home to live with my mother because I had no other place to go. She provided a roof over my head and food on the table. But my mother didn't have any extra cash to help me pay off the debt. After a few months of missing payments, I agreed to an extended repayment plan with the credit card companies.

"After my daughter was born, I was able to find a job working nights. My mother was able to babysit during the day by cutting back on her housecleaning work. And she could only do this because I was bringing in some extra money. I felt like I was in a good place, or at least a better place. But—and here's where I know it sounds a bit selfish—when I was working nights and had a child at home to care for, it didn't leave me much time to get out of the house, if you know what I mean. The night shift got to be a real drag. So, about the time that my daughter entered pre-school, I began looking for a day job. But as you can imagine, there weren't too many openings for a young Black woman, with a child at home, no college degree, and bad credit."

She kept talking and Tom did not interrupt her. Karen was getting into the real personal stuff. "I really hated working the night shift. It was awful. After a while I needed a little daytime pick me up from time-to-time in order to attend my daughter's school events and parent-teacher conferences, as well as a night out every once in a while with my girlfriends."

Tom was thinking that Karen was a proud young woman, and was not about to delegate school activities to Millie—even though Millie was the emergency contact, and the one who made her daughter breakfast every day. Millie also made sure the girl got to school on time and finished her homework. Karen freely admitted that her mother was the real parent here.

Karen asked, "Why does all of this matter? My credit is what it is. It's not going to get any better by me rehashing these horror stories."

Tom's response was perhaps a bit pricklier than it should have been, but he was reacting to her selfish behavior. "Well, Karen, based on what you've told me so far, it sounds like your credit report is not going to look very good. As bankers, we don't like surprises. So, it's best to tell us in advance the reasons for the bad credit report before we review it. Sometimes it helps us better understand the circumstances for the credit issues."

"Okay, you asked for it. As I was saying, those little pick me ups eventually morphed into a much more expensive habit. The money I needed to pay the loan I took out to buy a used car was now going to buy drugs. Once I stopped paying the loan, the car was repossessed, and I had no way to get to my job, other than public transportation. My mother could see what was going on, so she called my brother to get me some help.

"My brother may have told you that we don't really get along. His righteous indignation over my drug habit tended to go in one ear and out the other. I wasn't ready for his intervention. By the time he got involved, I was getting ready to file for bankruptcy, but he talked me out of it. At first, my brother tried the gentle Jesus Loves You approach to get me to agree to a drug rehab program. He even offered to pay for it. I told him I could kick the habit on my own. But when I almost set the house on fire one night, strung out, smoking a cigarette and falling asleep, my brother advised me that if I didn't enter the program voluntarily he would call the Department of Youth and Family Services to have my daughter removed from the home. That was his version of tough love. And it's the reason why we're not—how shall I say, loving siblings."

Karen ended by stating that after she completed the rehab program, she found a new job. "My brother came down pretty hard on me, and I suppose I should be grateful. Tough love and all that stuff, you know. But threatening to have my daughter taken away from me, well, that was pretty harsh. I made it through the rehab program and thought I was getting my life back again. I know this sounds like a pity party, but I really felt like I was getting my feet back on the ground when I got laid off. And it wasn't anything I did wrong. I was just last in, first out. Now I'm no longer able to help my mother with the rent and monthly expenses."

Karen was in tears.

Tom gave her a moment to recover. He said the bank would order a credit report on her, and, based on what she said, he was pretty sure her credit score was not going to make the grade. He was trying to be kind. Tom asked her if she had any other credit accounts that she could show a good repayment history on. She said no and confirmed what Millie had told him, which was that they paid cash for everything other than the rent, which was the only check they wrote.

Once again, Tom was at the point where he needed to say something that he knew was none of his business. He justified it by telling himself he was really trying to help Millie qualify to buy the house on her own. "Karen, did you ever think about withdrawing your name from the application? Seriously, with your poor credit history, you're not helping your Mother's case. On her own, your Mother doesn't have a very strong application, but your lack of employment, job history, and poor credit could very well sink the ship. I'm sorry to be so brutally honest with you, but those are the facts as I see them. So, you might want to have another conversation with her about whether you should take your name off the mortgage application. I can't say with any certainty that Millie is going to be approved on her own, but I can almost guarantee that the application will be denied if you stay on as a co-borrower."

He had made this statement in an effort to help. Now, with Karen sobbing on the other end of the phone, he was regretting it. He had just crossed over two lines that were very high on the Not-to-Do list. Under consumer banking regulations, he had, in effect, discouraged a mortgage application. That was a big no-no. It typically required an adverse action notice to be mailed out to the applicant. But in this case, and since he was practicing law without a license, Tom believed that the bank did not technically have a completed mortgage application since no application fee had been paid. He was positive that if this conversation ever came back to haunt him, his favorite long-legged attorney, MC, would back him up.

Secondly, he had gone over the line and inserted himself into the family counseling business without authorization from Millie or Pastor Lloyd. Millie was quite clear with him that she wanted to have Karen be part of the application despite her credit issues. Most likely, Tom was now about to encounter the wrath of Millie Ogletree. Again! And he had no one to blame but himself—oh, and Teddy—since he got him into this fine mess.

There was silence on the other end of the phone, which seemed like an eternity. He heard Karen let out a big sigh. "Mr. Donovan, I will have that conversation with my mother tonight at dinner. But she warned me that you might try to talk me out of being a co-borrower on the application. And while I don't disagree with your assessment, my mother has been pretty clear that she wants me to go in with her to buy the house. I don't think she's going to change her mind."

The phone call ended with Tom advising Karen that he would be in touch once her credit report was in hand and he'd had an opportunity to review the documents related to her mother's housecleaning income. He informed her he would need a written explanation from her related to all the poor credit information expected on her report.

Tom was exhausted after that conversation and saw this loan sinking fast. It had nothing going for it, except that it was located in a city where the bank had a branch and needed loans. Also, it was a loan to a nice elderly Black woman, and the bank needed more loan approvals to African American borrowers. It certainly didn't need any more denials. But most importantly, she just happened to be the mother of Pastor Lloyd, who was providing the bank with all the affordable mortgage business it needed to fulfill the goals of the CRA agreement with Sally Kessler and PUMP. 1NEB needed this loan.

And in order to tie up one of the other major loose ends, Tom had spent the last few months explaining and directing Deacon Isaac on how he could make the best of what started out essentially as a lease purchase transaction with absolutely no documentation. Tom counselled him to take the money he said he'd put aside from Millie's rent for the down payment and give it to Pastor Lloyd. As a direct relative, the bank would then permit a gift of the down payment from Pastor Lloyd to his mother to assist her with the purchase. There were plenty of problems with this loan, but Tom would have bet his firstborn that Porter was never going to approve a lease purchase deal with no backup documentation.

Technically, with the advice Tom had given Deacon Isaac, he had probably violated any number of banking rules and regulations. But it was all done in the interest of getting Millie's loan approved. He was now drawn into a conspiracy of his own making. But, what the hell! He was already in over his head, and was wondering how long he could tread water. Indeed, there were times when he had to stop Deacon Isaac from saying anything more so he could maintain some level of plausible deniability. As Teddy had asked him to do, Tom had put a plan in motion that could only be described as a Hail Mary. But in this case, even if the Hail Mary was successful, it might still be called back for twelve men on the field. Take your pick on who the twelfth man might be.

Tom looked at his watch to see it was five o'clock yet.

Chapter 23

It had now been six months since the bank had begun working with the MJED member churches. Everything was a complete blur. It took a while to get them up to speed. Althea and Tom spent a lot of time together training the deacons and other church staff on how to market the program, and what to look for in an initial screening of an application. Under a grant Teddy had provided to Pastor Lloyd, the funds were then distributed to the member churches for prepurchase counselling activities, including travel expenses, postage, copying, and reimbursement for refreshments served at the marketing sessions.

Althea and Tom made a good team. When it worked out logistically they liked to travel together. No sense taking and risking two cars when one would suffice. Of primary concern was that many of the churches were not located in the best of neighborhoods, and they liked their cars. They liked driving them. And typically they were parked in dark, unlit lots adjacent to any given church's administrative offices. By traveling together Tom was the secondary beneficiary of the same chivalrous deacon escorting Althea back to their car since they were a package deal.

At first, he and Althea were excited to get out and meet with prospective homebuyers, but during the first few months, attendance at these evening events did not attract the numbers they had hoped for. Sometimes there would be a local real estate agent or two in the audience who'd heard about the program, and may have had a potential FHA buyer in mind. In fact, the bank's affordable mortgage program was a much better product than any FHA loan, but it took the realtors a while to figure this out.

While everyone in attendance had a great desire to become a homeowner, it was rare to find many of them with the required five percent down payment and closing costs. As a result, it appeared the bank would be waiting some time before these potential homebuyers could put aside the money to buy their first home.

Once the word began to spread, however, the applications started to come in at a steady pace. The MJED churches were doing a good job of finding potential applicants. Unfortunately, few were of the AAA credit quality Porter McMahon was looking for.

The bank was now flush with applications. But the tremendous increase in volume was both good and bad. It was good to have volume that exceeded all expectations. At the current rate Teddy and Tom felt they would easily meet the agreement's goals. Likewise, the majority of these applications were to minority buyers, which was exactly what they were hoping to see to keep Sally Kessler happy.

On the other hand, Porter wasn't pleased. He didn't have the staff to keep up with the demand. And if he didn't have enough people to process the loans in a timely manner, Tom's fear was that they would be declined at first glance before they received a full underwriting review.

Moreover, when Tom had a conversation with Teddy about whether the performance of the affordable mortgage portfolio was being combined with Porter's, he said he wasn't inclined to discuss this with Peter Porzio. "Let's let sleeping dogs lie," he said. This meant he didn't want Tom talking to Porter about it either. Tom's second greatest fear was that if Porter was having to eat these high

The In-House Politician

risk and less profitable loans in his own portfolio, he would be even more ruthless in his denials.

Millie Ogletree's application had come in during the middle of this six-month period, and Tom was still working on it three months later. Millie and Karen were very patient and trusting with him, understanding that their application was not in the best of shape. They believed he was doing his best to get it approved despite its rather difficult characteristics.

Tom had made no promises, but it became clear to him that Millie was putting all her faith in him to get her loan across the finish line. But he still had his doubts about it, especially since they still had to deal with Porter McMahon and Peter Porzio. Issues like the down payment had been resolved by having Deacon Isaac transfer the funds to Pastor Lloyd who then gifted it to his mother. Tom also did his best to help Millie document her monthly housecleaning income by coordinating some of her bank deposits with her scheduled work dates, but there was still Karen's nightmare of a credit report.

With a full eighteen months of operations under the agreement completed, Tom's worst fears about Porter and his staff were coming true. They were denying minority applications by the bushel—specifically African American loans, and to a lesser extent, Latino applications.

Teddy knew how badly this minority loan denial information could hurt the bank if it was ever made public. Tom provided him with copies of the same weekly reports he received from Porter. Sometimes he just passed them along. Other times when there appeared to be some proposed declinations he wanted to save, Tom would make an appointment to see Teddy. When he began to alert him of his concern about the number of rejections, however, Teddy didn't seem overly concerned. As it related to possible bad press he seemed to think *The Examiner* had already done its hatchet job on the bank. 1NEB was old news, Teddy thought, assuming no new leaks.

They still hadn't determined who provided the initial false report to Joe Campbell at *The Examiner*, or why he would have printed it without some serious efforts to confirm its validity. And while there was some truth to Teddy's pragmatic approach to the public relations risks, Tom still pressed him on how they could get the minority mortgage approvals up and the denials down. Teddy indicated an off-site meeting for senior officers was scheduled for the following month. He promised he would pull Peter Porzio aside to test his willingness to move the internal credit culture to a more accommodating stance—at least as far as the affordable mortgage product and Porter were concerned. Tom was impressed with Teddy's strategy. But it was still at least a month away, and there were no guarantees of success.

One thing was crystal clear. This whole issue of the minority denial rate needed to be kept a closely held secret. Information like this was incendiary, and they needed to address it internally. People could lose their jobs based on bad press like this, and Tom was definitely a target.

The last few months had also been good for Pastor Lloyd. Since his announcement to run for the congressional seat, he seemed to have hit the ground running. Indeed, his campaign finances were in good shape after he'd found himself a sugar daddy developer from New York who was trying to muscle his way into the New Jersey real estate gold mine. This developer, who specialized in affordable rental units, was savvy enough to understand he needed support from the African American community in order to be successful. However, the

Pastor's initial campaign funds were now running low, resulting in an urgent call to Teddy.

Teddy now had to decide if, when, and how much he wanted the bank to contribute to Pastor Lloyd's campaign. Pastor Lloyd reminded Teddy of his promise to see how his campaign was faring before donating any PAC funds to help him. He made sure Teddy acknowledged that he was currently leading the Democratic pack in the polls at 45 percent. Pastor Lloyd indicated that no one else in the race could catch him as long as his campaign finances held out. Additionally, there were all those affordable mortgage loans that both he and his MJED members had directed to the bank. Surely, he had proven himself to be a friend of the bank. If he did know about the high number of minority loan rejections he didn't mention it on the call.

Indeed, Teddy was convinced that Pastor Lloyd had proven himself. He had checked all the boxes needed to convince the PAC committee to make a contribution.

The two major issues facing Teddy were that he didn't want the State Democratic Party angry with him if they were supporting other candidates. And secondly, he didn't want the political contribution to appear to be, at best, a quid pro quo to Ogletree to help the bank meet its affordable mortgage goals, or worse, a bribe to keep the candidate silent on the high number of minority denials. Either way, he wasn't sure how best to convince the PAC to support Rev. Ogletree. Teddy wasn't looking forward to the next meeting of the PAC.

Chapter 24

It was never Tom's intention to piss off Porter McMahon. It just came naturally. Porter's personality could never be described as charming. In fact, Tom guessed that in high school Porter was voted most likely to strangle a cat, or, most likely to be changing the oil in his muscle car rather than attending the prom. He was not a pleasant person to be around. And due to Tom's responsibilities as Teddy's mortgage guy, he had no choice but to spend more time with him. Indeed, with the volume of loans picking up based on the bank's partnership with the MJED, the loan denials were also increasing at an alarming pace.

Tom's prime directive from Teddy was to get as many loans approved under the agreement as possible—within the constraints of prudent underwriting, of course. Right. And Porter's directive, it seemed, was to take pleasure in denying as many loans as possible. Tom's mentor, Jim O'Brien, kept telling him that Porter was only doing his job. He understood that to a point. But it took every ounce of restraint for Tom not to put a contract out on the guy. And he did know someone from high school who'd gone into that line of work.

What Porter didn't seem to understand, or perhaps chose to ignore, was the issue of the minority denial rates. All the affordable mortgage program loans that crossed his desk for a decision ended up on the Home Mortgage Disclosure Act. HMDA, as the acronym goes, was a bank's primary report card on how many loans were approved, denied, or withdrawn during a given period of time. It identified the

The In-House Politician

loans by census tract and by the race of the applicant. These reports contained all kinds of data, which were then used by regulators and the public to determine if banks might be discriminating in their mortgage lending activities. To be politically correct, one should say "allegedly" discriminating. The regulators then compared a bank's minority denial rates with its peer banks to see how they were doing in similar situations. Certainly Porter knew all this. He just didn't seem to care.

Tom believed that Porter had taken immense pleasure in reading the article in *The Examiner*. Likewise, he thought Porter was hoping to see a follow-up article declaring the bank just couldn't manage to get the job done. Hell, it wasn't his fault. He hadn't been part of the negotiations that put in place the affordable mortgage program. And, to the extent he was trying to protect the bank's conventional mortgage portfolio performance, Porter seemed very confident in denying every borderline case that was put in front of him.

Tom kept Teddy apprised of the volume, locational activity, and denials by race. The comments section of the spreadsheet provided him with the reasons for all proposed denials. Tom had an understanding with Porter that no formal declination would be mailed out until he'd had an opportunity to review the report. Whenever a denial was proposed with questionable factors, Tom was able to retrieve a hard copy of the file for his review. This put that specific decision on hold. If Tom believed that a file could be saved, he requested a meeting with Porter to review it with him. It was their own little impromptu Mortgage Review Committee. Of course, loan files that Tom considered borderline were slam dunk denials from Porter's viewpoint. And since Porzio had disbanded the official review committee, this left Tom at the mercy of his favorite mortgage officer.

Tom always tried to have more than one file to review whenever he met with Porter. In fact, he tried to have a minimum of two, and on a few occasions, he actually brought three. His thinking was there might be strength in numbers. Tom was thinking Porter might feel guilty about being such a hard ass, and was hoping he might want to show some mercy every once in a while. Hey. Batting .500 or even .333 would put Tom on Teddy's All-Star team.

Case in point: title wise, Porter and Tom were at the same officer level. They were both senior vice presidents. But whenever they met, it was always in Porter's conference room. He explained that he needed to have access to his staff resources and data systems to answer Tom's questions. Additionally, he claimed he couldn't be away from his office for long periods of time. Teddy had ordered Tom to play nice, but it wasn't easy.

Similar to Teddy's conference room, Porter's had a glass wall which opened onto the floor of his Mortgage Department. This meant all of his staff could see them whenever they met. It also allowed them to witness Tom's various hand motions used to argue his points. By now, Tom's reputation as the guy who was always trying to overturn their denials preceded him.

Whenever they met, Porter always let Tom sit in the conference room for 5-10 minutes to wait and stew, just to show his staff who was boss. But what Tom really loved was whenever Porter finally did enter the room, he never said a word—not a "hello," not a "how's it going?"—not even a "nice weather we're having today." There were times Tom thought he expected a red carpet, rose petals and trumpets.

Tom was fearful that word might have leaked back to him about his nickname for him. When Porter came in, he just sat down, opened the first file on the agenda, and said, "So tell me how you think this file can be saved." Tom wanted to smack him upside his head.

They were now at the point where their meetings were getting contentious. Porter snickered whenever Tom either forgot or tried to work around some key underwriting standard. And Tom smirked whenever Porter seemed to backtrack when offered a legitimate work around that might save a file. Tom recalled a meeting in which Porter would not waver on his denial of an otherwise good credit report, but showed one 60-day delinquency, and a failure to pay a government-guaranteed student loan for a few months. There were reasonable explanations in the file covering both credit issues, but in Porter's mind student loans were sacrosanct. It really didn't matter what the explanations were. It was only when Tom reminded him they were trying to make homeowners out of folks who hadn't been born with silver spoons in their mouths that he would sometimes reconsider. But then his patriotic fervor kicked in. He reminded Tom that he was the bank's chief mortgage officer and was responsible for the overall performance of the portfolio. And although Porter had supposedly agreed to use the more flexible underwriting guidelines under the terms of the agreement, it was clear that traditional credit standards were still being used by his staff.

No one had ordered Porter to have a social conscience, and in fact it was Tom's understanding that his hard-nosed boss, Peter Porzio, would never hear of it. But even if he thought he had any leeway in his underwriting of the affordable loans, he couldn't have played that role. It just wasn't in him. Porter was a hard-ass. Tom could almost hear the *Stars and Stripes* playing in the background as another one bit the dust.

The minority loan denial rates were now mounting up faster than the approvals. And it wasn't as if Tom hadn't kept Teddy in the loop. But the coach in Teddy always wanted to put the losses in the rearview mirror, because tomorrow would be a better day. Teddy kept saying, "We can't lose them all, right?"

There was one day when Teddy actually seemed to be listening. Tom advised him the bank's Black to White denial ratio was now approaching 3:1. And the Latino denial ratio compared to Whites was over 2:1. Tom brought in the cavalry for this meeting with the attendance of Althea. She knew how to drill home the point. She looked at Teddy and stated in as serious a tone as she could muster, "You need to do something about this guy Porter McMahon. He's a bigot and a racist and he's going to take us down with him. We have no control over the credit decisions he's making even on our marginally good loans. And once our minority denial ratio goes public, we're screwed big time!"

They now had Teddy's attention. He asked, "How bad is it?"

Tom gave Teddy the rundown. "Based on the most recent report, 75 percent of all the African American loan applications have been rejected in each of the last three months. And all of these denials were to applicants referred by the MJED." Tom was waiting for Teddy to say something, but he kept silent for now.

He continued. "On a stand-alone basis, these denial ratios are a nightmare. If our approval ratio doesn't turn around soon and the regulators see our HMDA reports, the bank could easily find itself sanctioned with a cease and desist order. And if that leaked out—

The In-House Politician

well, that wouldn't be pretty from a public relations standpoint. It would be even uglier than the initial article."

"Teddy," Althea said, "if this news leaks out, the press will eat us for lunch, and no doubt PUMP will be demonstrating out front. Is that what you want? Seeing Sally Kessler and her PUMP disciples on the 6 o'clock news calling us out for too many African American loan denials? And there's Pastor Lloyd and his MJED members. I've got to believe that he's hearing about the number of rejections from their church leaders. You can't depend on him keeping silent much longer, can you?"

Teddy was trying to think it through before responding. Until now it was Tom's understanding that if Teddy thought Porter was being unreasonable with the files, he would take it up the line to Porzio. But Teddy's idea of Porter being tough, and Tom's opinion, diverged when it came to some of the more difficult character loans. And while Teddy agreed in principle, he also knew that his fight with the chief credit policy officer was the equivalent of trying to hit a Nolan Ryan fastball. At best, he might hit a few foul balls, but eventually he would strike out.

Porzio had made it clear he thought all the affordable mortgage loans were shit. Moreover, Teddy was playing the internal political long game. He did not want to appear to be the bank's liberal bitch to the PUMP Bolsheviks. If he was going to be successful, he needed to be thought of as reasonable and pragmatic. He assigned the liberal bitch role to Tom.

Teddy finally said, "First off, we can never let this minority denial rate ever see the light of day. I mean to the public, of course. The regulators will eventually see it, and do whatever they do. We really can't do anything about that. But secondly, are our loans really that bad that so many get rejected?"

Tom wanted to ask Teddy if that was a rhetorical question, but he knew it wouldn't sit well. "Teddy, you and I have talked about the primary underwriting issues most of our applicants face. I could go over many of the loans that are denied and give you good reasons why they could have been approved, but do you—?"

Teddy cut Tom off. "Okay. This is what I want you to do. I want you to bring up the minority denial ratios with Porter at your next meeting and see what kind of response you get. And you should tell him you've raised this issue with me and that I'm inclined to speak with his boss, if that's what it takes to get him some religion."

Teddy was still operating under the assumption they had to be careful about not using their nicknames in front of Althea. But when she asked him "So you're actually going to bring up this issue with Scrooge about Marley?" Teddy couldn't help himself and laughed out loud.

In a rare moment of heartfelt honesty Teddy came clean. "I know you guys are fighting the good fight, and I'm really proud of your efforts. But I'm just not ready to have this conversation with Scrooge. At least not yet. My greatest fear is that his response will be to go to the Chairman to ask him to shut us down— you know— the whole program on the basis of low profitability and poor asset quality. Now, the Chairman would never allow this to happen, but this kind of whining will only serve to ruin our reputation with the big boss. It's a no-win situation. We've got to try to work this out. I've got to think long and hard before I take the complaint against Marley upstairs."

The In-House Politician

Tom and Althea weren't shocked at Teddy's response. Althea, who could get away with more direct confrontation with Teddy, said what they were both thinking. "Okay, but just so we're clear, you do understand the full public relations risks involved here?"

Teddy said, "I do and thanks for the update. Let me chew on it for a bit," which was his way of saying this meeting was over.

At their next meeting with Porter, as expected, he was not moved by the minority denial rates. His response was simple. "If you continue to accept applications from folks who do not meet the bank's underwriting standards, then you will continue to have large numbers of denials. And, if it turns out these denials are primarily to Black and Latino applicants—well, it's not my fault."

As far as Porter was concerned, he wasn't discriminating by race. And while he never actually used the "N" word in the review meetings, there were many times when he did refer to "those people" or "these people" to describe what in his mind were across the board unqualified applicants. It was all Althea could do not to throw him out the window.

Althea was now attending these review meetings with Tom to give him moral support. As a counterbalance, Porter began including his senior mortgage underwriter, Tina Washington. She really knew her stuff. It also didn't hurt that she was Black. Porter was sending a message that he didn't consider himself a racist or a bigot. Indeed, he could play the race card, too.

Occasionally, there were times when Porter was unprepared to discuss some of the nuances of questionable files. He would ask Tina to brief them all on the particulars. She knew the files inside and out. Additionally, the staff who reported to Tina were responsible for producing the weekly spreadsheet on their portfolio. And while there was no overt evidence of it in these meetings, Tom always thought that Tina had a special place in her heart for these borrowers.

Whenever Tom had background questions on a specific file he called Tina to get the answers. She was always very accommodating, while at the same time letting him know that her boss would not necessarily agree with her thinking. Tom was shocked Porter allowed Tina to speak with him separately on these files. Apparently, Porter had no fear she would ever move over to the enemy. Tina never spoke in the review meetings unless Porter needed something specific on a file. She always deferred to her boss, even if she didn't like him very much.

Chapter 25

Michelle didn't know where to turn. She was grateful for the protection from the FBI, but the fact that she needed it was a chilling thought. Conversely, she still had a healthy level of skepticism. For all she knew, the Feds could have taken that photo of the alleged hitman back in the States. There was nothing in the photograph that proved he was in Italy searching for her. It could have been taken at any airport. She was thinking the Feds might be trying to intimidate her into testifying against Alex and his family. But why would they do that? She'd seen this tough-looking guy hanging around Alex's campaign headquarters, but she never knew his name or what his job was. He was always there with another guy who looked just like him. Agent Inbusch had provided her with his actual name, Giuseppe, or Joe in the Americanized version. More importantly, Michelle couldn't figure out what information she had that would help the Feds with their investigation of the Scarduzos.

She recalled the times serving as Alex's courier delivering messages to and from that Sally person. Michelle couldn't remember her last name. She never did know what was in those messages. And wasn't that the point? If she had no knowledge of what was going on between Alex and that Sally woman, then why would the Feds think she could help?

Michelle had been at Alex's side for the past two years. What had he done that she did or didn't know about? Apparently, the FBI thought she knew about all his misdeeds. She asked Agent Inbusch again what they had on Alex and his family, but he just smiled and said, "All in good time." He was playing it very close to the vest and kept her completely in the dark. Except for the part about the hitman.

One thing bothered her though. As far as she could tell she was still not under the full 24-7 protection. If she was, there would have been an agent posted outside her apartment. Perhaps they were very good at concealing their surveillance. Or were they using her for bait? Did the Feds actually use witnesses as bait? Michelle convinced herself that she'd been watching too many TV shows where the witness never made it into the courtroom to testify. But really, did they actually want Scarduzo's hitman to find her to use as proof against the family? This was something she wanted to ask Agent Inbusch about as soon as the time was right—and preferably before the hitman showed up.

Michelle never met Alex's father. During the affair Alex had often said his father was fully vested in his political career. Indeed, he indicated his father was a ruthless man who would do almost anything to protect his son's reputation, as well as that of the Scarduzo family name. They never talked about whether Scarduzo Sr. knew about the affair. But based on how Alex described him, she was certain that if his father knew about it he wouldn't have kept quiet. Or would he? Michelle could not believe that her former lover could be so heartless as to put a contract out on her. They were in love—once. But his father—that was another matter altogether.

There was also the issue of the money, and the NDA itself. Agent Inbusch advised her that the document was not a barrier to her testimony. The NDA was a civil matter unrelated to their criminal case against the Scarduzos. Michelle's testimony would be compelled by a subpoena issued under seal, which would provide her with some

The In-House Politician

level of anonymity. The judge would compel her to answer questions in court that would also counter the secrecy of the NDA—none of which was her fault.

Michelle asked Inbusch if she should obtain an attorney to advise her on the terms of the NDA just to determine the risks. He told her it was entirely up to her. The FBI would have no involvement on the issue of the NDA or the money associated with it. Their only concern was that she not divulge anything about the investigation. The implication was that if she were to say anything to imperil their case, her protection would quickly vanish.

She was too smart to believe this kind of implied threat. If the Feds thought she was important enough to follow all the way to Italy and then to Switzerland, she was confident they wouldn't abandon her. And she knew enough about how the attorney-client privilege worked that any discussion with a lawyer would not stand in the way.

Inbusch also hinted that she owed them since, first, they were protecting her from the Scarduzos, and secondly, there was always a chance she could be charged as an accessory. If it was determined she knew about any of Alex's wrongdoings and did not report them to the authorities, then she could be in trouble. However, Agent Inbusch indicated that if she cooperated, the Feds could grant her immunity and keep her out of jail.

This was not the life Michelle had briefly thought was possible when she first saw the size of the insurance policy Alex had provided for her silence. In the short time between when she had signed the NDA, seen the amount of money deposited in her account, and then flown to Rome, she'd had visions of living in high-end hotels, going out dancing every night, and living the good life of a wealthy

American ex-pat in Europe. How bad could it be—becoming a Parisienne? Expensive, yes, but she could afford it. But within a few hours of her arrival in Rome that dream had vanished. The FBI was now in charge of her life.

Michelle was skeptical about going out at all. But Agent Inbusch assured her they had eyes on the hitman. He was still looking for her in Rome, and had been in touch with the local police there. They were keeping a careful watch on him. What's more, Inbusch suspected that the hitman would eventually give up and return to the U.S.

Then it finally dawned on her. Scarduzo Sr. wasn't dumb enough to make her disappear just because of her affair with his son. This could only mean that Alex's father knew about the investigation and decided she was a loose end. Now she was pissed. Inbusch had not been straight with her. If Scarduzo Sr. knew about the Feds investigation, then the hitman wouldn't stop in Rome. He would eventually find her. She needed answers from Inbusch, and was beginning to feel like the walls were closing in.

That was when Michelle finally called "bullshit" on Inbusch and confronted him. "So when are you going to level with me? Old Man Scarduzo knows about your investigation, right? That's the only reason there's a contract out on me. He doesn't care about the affair with Alex. That's meaningless compared to your investigation. You need to come clean with me. And you need to do it now!"

Inbusch said, "All in good time. All in good time. At this point all you need to know is the hitman is still in Rome. Our biggest concern is whether the Old Man knows about the NDA. If he does, then he probably also knows the name of the bank in Zurich. We think there's a chance the NDA is still a secret known only to Alex Jr.. and his attorney. But if the hitman buys a ticket to Zurich, then all bets are off. Then we will have to place you under full-time protection and move you to a safer location."

"So I'll ask you one more time," Michelle said. "What is it you think I know about Alex's alleged criminal activities? And I will tell you, once again, that I know nothing about his father's business. Please listen to me. I know nothing!"

Inbusch decided it was time to come clean. "Well then, let's talk about what you may or may not know. Tell me one thing. While we had you under surveillance, when you were with Alex Jr.. you always carried a notebook around with you. Did you actually write down notes from Alex's meetings? And where is that notebook now?"

Michelle finally understood. She just laughed, and winked at the agent. She had something the Feds needed and wasn't about to give it up without a good deal. She was beginning to think she really needed an attorney. But first things first. She needed some money to live on. It was time to make a withdrawal. She also needed to find a pharmacy since she was feeling nauseous.

Chapter 26

Joe Campbell couldn't do Alex's bidding anymore. He just didn't know how to tell him. The article he'd written on the bank had nearly gotten him fired. Indeed, the story on how poorly 1NEB had performed during the first year of its agreement with PUMP was published by pure luck. When his editor asked him about his source for the article and his confirmation process, Joe told one little white lie and two big Pinocchios.

The little white lie was that Sally Kessler, the leader of PUMP, had semi-confirmed the numbers in the report. It was true that Joe had spoken with Sally, but she deferred, saying that if the mortgage data had originated from inside the bank, then it must be accurate. She never did ask Joe how he'd gotten his hands on it. She just assumed it had been provided by Alex Scarduzo, just as he had promised. Sally's non-confirmation confirmation was good enough for Joe because he wanted the story to vindicate his previous articles on the bank, which were not complimentary. He also knew he had to try to get some level of confirmation from the bank. But how much effort he put into it was minimal and he felt bad about that.

The first big Pinocchio was that when he attempted to get confirmation from Teddy DeMarco, he had not returned the call. What Joe failed to tell his editor was that he never let Teddy's assistant, Kelly, know the specific reason for his call, or the deadline for the article. Joe's editor was very curious as to why there were no comments from the bank.

The second big Pinocchio was that the data report on the bank's performance had been anonymously dropped off at the front desk in an envelope addressed to him. And while this was partially true since the delivery person was unknown and the envelope didn't say who it came from, Joe's response to his editor's question was that he assumed it had come from some disgruntled worker inside 1NEB. It must be an anonymous whistleblower. Joe was not about to reveal his relationship with Alex Scarduzo Jr..

"All the more reason you should have worked harder to get a reaction from the bank," his editor said.

When the editor pushed harder on why the bank never returned his call, Joe shrugged his shoulders. "I can't explain it. You know I've got some history with that bank from my previous pieces. Teddy DeMarco doesn't like me very much and probably assumed he wouldn't get a fair hearing from me. So why bother?"

His editor still wasn't satisfied, but it was too late to pull the story. Joe's editor said he would be watching him more closely to make sure *The Examiner* could always defend itself. Thus, the article went to press without any comment from the bank.

Joe had written the story because Alex said it came directly from 1NEB, and Alex wasn't the kind of guy you said no to. Besides, the data supported Joe's past stories confirming his previous articles on the mergers. And what better way to take down the largest bank in the State, or at least give it a black eye, than by revealing it declined all of the African American loans it had received during the initial year of the agreement. Indeed, the articles Joe had previously written about the interstate acquisition by 1NEB had raised specific questions about how it was going to affect minority communities in both states. The bank's poor performance at the end of the first year was definitely news.

Joe wore the eye patch when he walked into the dive Alex had selected for their clandestine meeting. No one would recognize either one of them in the dark and dingy place. Joe didn't really need the patch, but was using it as reminder to Alex of their history. They both had information on each other that would not be good for either of their careers if it was ever revealed.

Joe knew the information related to Alex's attack on him in boarding school would not be helpful to his political career. Alternatively, Alex knew how ambitious Joe was and how eager he would be to publish the article. He assumed that Joe would bend the rules, and he was right. Moreover, Joe had no idea Alex had made a separate deal with Sally Kessler to confirm the report. Alex was pleased with how well he had manipulated Joe.

Alex carried the reason he had almost blinded Joe Campbell in his back pocket. In prep school, Joe had said some nasty things about the Scarduzo family name as well as Alex's size. If this was ever made public it would not reflect well on Joe's character as a supposedly impartial reporter. Additionally, Alex was sure that Joe Campbell knew it was not a good idea to incur the wrath of the Scarduzo family, especially Alex's father.

But something inside Joe was telling him that he couldn't continue down this path. He was a changed man ever since prep school. In fact, he had chosen a career that would allow him to identify the bad guys, and to perhaps help to right some wrongs. He believed that the story on 1NEB was true because he wanted it to be. It made sense to him based on everything he knew about how bankers operated.

Indeed, he had made himself believe that no serious confirmation was necessary. But in his heart of hearts, he knew he had violated all kinds of professional ethics by short-cutting the process. He convinced himself it would be the last time.

Alex smiled when Joe sat down opposite him wearing the eye patch. "Joe, you look like a friggin' pirate with that thing on. I hope you didn't wear it for me. I've seen you out in public before, and most times you're not wearing it. Sorry if I'm not intimidated. I really do feel bad about what I did to your eye back then, but you deserved it. You said some really shitty things to me back then. But, that's all in the past. You can't hurt me, unless you hurt yourself as well."

Joe said, "Well, hello to you, too. I guess that means I can remove the patch now. It's dark in here. I'm thinking I'll need two eyes to read the menu. By the way, where did you find this place? It's not on any map I have."

Alex laughed. "Hey, you wanted this meeting, so I selected a place where no one knows us. Now, let's get to it. What's on your mind?"

Joe turned serious. "I can't be doing these stories for you anymore. I'm not your stooge inside *The Examiner*. That last story almost got me fired. My editor wanted to know where it came from and I didn't have a good answer for him. I told him it just dropped into my lap from some anonymous source, presumably from some whistleblower inside the bank. So, just let me say thank you for all the information you've provided me in the past, but I'm risking too much. If anyone ever learned about our relationship, I'd never get another job in the industry. So, that's why I wanted to meet—to tell you this in person."

Alex's smile turned sour. "Well, thanks for the in-person courtesy Joe, but that's not going to work for me."

"Oh, really?"

"Yup. You see, that last article you wrote on 1NEB, the one you say almost got you fired, well, if truth be told, you actually should have been fired. That article was fake and yet you still printed it. Oh, the bank may not have performed very well during the first year, but not that bad. I can't tell you how happy I was when I read it. You found a way to get it done. Impressive. And I was amazed at the way you made a readable story out of a bunch of dry bullshit loan data. As I expected, you wanted to print that story just as much as we wanted you to. You know how much Sally Kessler hates that bank and Teddy DeMarco. Nice job, by the way."

Alex saw that the waitress was about to come over to their table. He put up his hand and said, "Please give us a second to look over the menu." She nodded and turned back.

Joe said, "So let me understand this. Are you saying that Sally Kessler made up that report? And then she gave it to you? And then you used me to get it published knowing that it would support my original articles? You and Sally Kessler are sworn political enemies. How's that possible?"

"Yes and no! The no part is that Sally didn't make up those mortgage numbers. She doesn't know squat about the mortgage business. And she didn't know I was going to ask you to write the article. But you got her to confirm it, right? And as far I can tell, everything is working out just fine. You got a great storyline continuing the thread about those evil bankers at 1NEB, Sally got to polish her resume as a bank killer, and I made a useful new political ally in Sally Kessler. You can just file that one away for future reference if you need it. All's well that ends well, right?"

The In-House Politician

Joe had to take a moment to let it all sink in. Across the table from him was the very same person who had almost blinded him in prep school. Now this same guy had him and his career over a barrel. Joe had that deer in the headlights look and began to shake his head in disbelief. "So who pulled those numbers together and prepared that report on the bank's performance?"

Alex smiled. "Let's save that discussion for another day, okay? I know that was a lot to take in, but as long as we both understand our mutually beneficial situation, then we can move on and make the best of it. Right? No reason to dwell on the past. We can help each other."

In as compliant a voice as he could muster, Joe said, "What do you have in mind for this evil partnership you're proposing?"

Alex looked around to make sure no one was within earshot. "It's simple. I provide you with stories and you write them. Now that we've gotten past the fact that you'll need to do a better job of checking your sources, I can promise to feed you plenty of newsworthy stories. I can't say they'll all be completely accurate, but that's your job to check before you publish them, right? Hey, there's always some level of truth in any rumor. I'll become one of your confidential sources. These stories I provide you will either make or break your career. It all depends on how you handle them."

"Yeah! They'll break me alright."

"No, no. C'mon, Joe. You're a good writer. Who knows? Maybe one of the stories I feed you finally gets you that Pulitzer you've been angling for."

"So these stories you're going to provide me, will they be real, or will you be sending me on a wild goose chase, wasting my time?"

"Listen. Anything I give you will either be real, or at least more than just a rumor. I've got plenty of operatives on the ground who provide me with good intel. Just part of the political process, which I'm sure you understand. And you should understand this. This is very important. I do have someone inside 1NEB and this source is very reliable."

"Oh yeah? Who?"

Alex looked amused. "Didn't we just talk about confidential sources? You'll be able to tell whether my source is real whenever you do your own independent confirmations. Next time you should really do your best to get the bank on the record. I can understand why your editor wasn't pleased with you. But I get a sense you've learned your lesson. Oh, and not all my stories will be on the bank. I might also have some insider intel on the life and times of Rev. Lloyd Ogletree, Democratic candidate for Congress. I'm betting he's got some skeletons in his closet, just like you and me."

"And what if I can't satisfy myself or my editor on one of your stories?"

"Then you don't print it. No more fake stories, Joe. I promise. That was a one-time deal just to get us on equal footing. I've got something on you, which I swear I will never reveal unless I'm forced to. Your racial epithet was not very nice, if you recall. Likewise, you've got something on me, which I would hope will never see the light of day either. But the eye patch as a reminder was rather silly, don't you think? We need each other, Joe. I help you obtain your Pulitzer and you help me get elected to Congress. It's pretty simple. And if you can't confirm a story I give you, then you don't publish it. But just remember one thing, okay? While you're my go-to guy, there are other newspapers and other reporters out there who may not operate in the same ethical universe you think you do. So do we understand each other?"

"I've changed, Alex," Joe said. "I'm not the same guy who bullied you in prep school. And as long as you understand that I'm not going to write any more stories that I can't confirm, I guess I'll leave myself open to using you as a confidential source. I really don't have much of a choice, now, do I?"

Alex wanted to pound his fist on the table for emphasis, but thought better of it. He didn't want to draw any unnecessary attention. Through a gritty smile he said, "Now that's the right attitude. I'll have a new story for you in a couple of weeks. Good talk. And don't worry. I'm picking up the check for lunch today. How's that for a reliable confidential source? Now, let's order some lunch."

Joe stood up from the table. "I've lost my appetite."

Chapter 27

After three months of back and forth with Millie, Karen, and Deacon Isaac, Tom was pretty sure there wasn't anything more he could do to make their loan look any better. It was time to brief Teddy on its status. In turn, Teddy said he would schedule a meeting for the two of them with the bank's chief credit policy officer to get his approval. He thought it best to leave Porter out of the process as an intermediary and go directly to Porzio. Teddy said he would leave it up to Porzio as to whether or not he wanted Porter at the meeting. Upon completing the briefing, Teddy's last words were, "Tom, just remember one thing. Scrooge doesn't give a rat's ass about this loan. We're just going through the motions and kissing the credit king's ring. Relax!"

From time-to-time Teddy would fall into Tom's trap of referring to Peter Porzio, Vice Chairman and Chief Credit Policy Officer, as Scrooge. But whenever he did it and then caught himself, he would make Tom put a dollar into the jar he kept on his desk because, of course, it was all Tom's fault. The jar was already pretty full from all of Tom's previous indiscretions. But there were times when Tom felt it was well worth the price.

Teddy certainly gave him the impression that things were under control. Tom, on the other hand, was a nervous wreck. This loan for Millie Ogletree, was most likely going to make or break the bank's relationship with Pastor Lloyd and MJED. If the loan was declined, Teddy would lose all credibility with the Pastor, and it would most

The In-House Politician

likely result in a significant decline in the number of loans coming in. It would also be time for Tom to update his resume.

As for his career at the bank, it also occurred to Tom that it was either Porter or him. Tom's job responsibilities were to fulfill the goals of the agreement, which primarily meant closing loans that were high-risk and less profitable. Porter, on the other hand, ran the mortgage department, which was one of the most profitable units in the bank. If Millie's loan went down in flames, it would most likely be Tom's head on the chopping block.

Tom knew he needed to bring his A-game. Millie Ogletree's loan application was not exactly triple-A quality. Indeed, no one was going to make this loan unless Teddy convinced Porzio of the political necessity. According to Teddy, Tom's presentation on the loan was pure window dressing. He promised him on numerous occasions it was already a done deal.

So, as Tom was walking back to his office he thought, if this is a done deal, then why are we still having this meeting with Scrooge and possibly Marley? He was getting more anxious by the minute.

Teddy wanted him to script out his presentation for the big meeting. Tom already had his cheat sheet typed up and ready to go, but Teddy wanted it in narrative form. He understood the words better than the numbers.

Tom knew Teddy would begin the meeting by connecting the dots, summarizing it all for Porzio—just as a reminder why they were wasting his time. Then Teddy would hand the ball off to him.

Tom had to assume Porzio would invite Porter to the meeting. So, as tough as it would be, he thought he should start out by saying thank you to Marley. Oh, right! It would be good to call him by his given name—so he would say thank you to Porter. Hopefully, Tom wouldn't gag on his insincere gratitude. He had no knowledge of whether Porter had complained about him to Porzio. But once again, it really didn't matter since, according to Teddy, this was a done deal.

Tom would then go into the positive aspects of Millie's application, or the pros on his cheat sheet. First and foremost was the fact that the borrowers met the agreement's overall debt ratios and could, at least on paper, afford the house—that is, if they gave Millie some credit for her housecleaning income on the side. Secondly, Millie had two solid sources of income from Social Security and her husband's pension. Additionally, they would have the rental income. But most important, was the fact that Millie was a hard worker and would do whatever it took keep a roof over their heads. The property appraised out at $10,000 above sales price, and Millie's credit was spotless—mainly because there wasn't any. Tom wanted to insert some humor into the presentation just to take Porzio's temperature. Then he would go on to explain that both Millie and her co-borrower daughter, Karen, advised him that whenever they needed to purchase something, they would save up their money and pay cash for it. He wanted to emphasize that they seemed to be very frugal borrowers. But Tom would then have to admit that the primary reason Millie's credit was spotless was that she didn't have any—no credit cards, no car loans, and no other outstanding debt. She had a ten-year old mortgage that was paid satisfactorily, and a three-year old lay-away plan for the refrigerator, which had also been paid as agreed. But nothing current.

Next, Tom would turn to the negative aspects of the loan. The cons included two major items. First was the fact that the borrowers had no equity in the transaction. Until now, Millie and Karen had not

The In-House Politician

invested a penny of their own money into the purchase. It occurred to Tom that he could go into a rather long explanation about the original lease-purchase agreement between the borrowers and the landlord, but he didn't necessarily want to subject himself to what would, no doubt, make him look like a fool if Porzio asked him if he really believed that story. That's when Tom had become a co-conspirator in the plan to have the down payment money pass from Deacon Isaac to Pastor Lloyd and then be gifted to his mother.

Secondly, on the negative side was Karen's credit report and life story, which played out like a never-ending soap opera.

Finally, Tom would end the presentation with his so-called compensating factors. Karen had recently found a new job, which would provide them with additional income. And he had exacted a promise from Millie and Karen to save up half of the closing costs over the next two months in return for a conditional approval.

Teddy got back to him the next day. He started out with "great job." After that, he said Tom should tone down the part about the borrower's lack of equity. He thought it might be a hot button for Porzio. And by toning it down, he meant leave it out completely.

Later that day, Teddy and Tom had an impromptu meeting in the men's room. Tom button-holed him on the issue of Millie's lack of equity in the deal. He reminded Teddy that Scrooge would ask to review the file ahead of time, in which case it would reveal there was no real borrower equity in the transaction, and that he—Tom—would appear to be a total incompetent if he left it out of the presentation. Alternatively, Tom said that if Scrooge didn't ask about the equity, then his not-so-charming mortgage officer, Marley, certainly would. Once again, Tom would look like a knucklehead.

As Teddy was drying his hands and about to exit, he said, "Tom, remember what I told you yesterday. And this is very important. Scrooge doesn't spend one second of his day thinking about our affordable mortgage portfolio. I'm so confident in this that I'll bet my Yankee ticket that he hasn't looked at the file, and won't ask to see it in the meeting. In fact, he couldn't care less about the quality of this specific loan. He knows why we need to make it, and as long as the co-borrowers have a pulse, he's not going to care one bit, other than to give us some shit about the quality of our portfolio, which I'm sure he's heard about from your good buddy Marley. Don't worry about it. Relax. And if Marley brings up the issue of the lack of hard money in the purchase, you have my permission to talk about the original 'so called' lease-purchase agreement, which you restructured. You can even connect the dots for him about who the seller of the property is and how he's related to Pastor Lloyd. If Scrooge doesn't get up and say this meeting is over, I'll really be surprised. I fully expect he's forgotten all about the purpose of the meeting, and when he understands that it's about one small mortgage loan in our portfolio, he'll say, thanks for coming, but I don't have time for this. So, we go up there, kiss the ring, and get out of there with a win. Hopefully." Teddy now had his hand on the door knob indicating the meeting was over. But before he left, he winked and gave Tom one more, "Relax!"

According to Tom's calculations that fine would be six dollars into the jar. The references to Scrooge and Marley were two by Tom and four by Teddy. He was hoping Teddy would forget about it since they all occurred outside his office. But it would be worth it if Millie's loan was approved.

The In-House Politician

When they arrived for the meeting the next day, the door to Porzio's office read, "Peter M. Porzio, Vice Chairman and Chief Credit Policy Officer." Tom had forgotten about the first half of his title, or maybe he'd just blocked it out.

As they entered the inner sanctum, Porzio's assistant led them into a small conference room off to the side. It had a separate entrance for the king to arrive in all his glory. As small as this conference room was, it still had its own view of the Manhattan skyline.

Tom was nervous. He noticed that when Porzio entered the room, his body language and failure to look at them directly was indicative of a powerful man who did not respect anyone below his level. There was a big red pasta stain on his white shirt that no wide tie could cover up. Porzio made no mention of it and didn't seem to care. Indeed, Tom thought Porzio had the appearance of a man who never missed a meal, and who didn't think the gym was worthy of his time. He looked like a heart attack ready to happen at any moment. Tom wanted to ask Teddy if he knew CPR.

They were both relieved to see that Porter McMahon had not been invited to their little love fest. Tom didn't ask where he was and Teddy just smiled when Porzio said, "Let's get started."

After Teddy reminded him of the reason for the meeting, Porzio sat back in his chair looking bored and said, "So you're here for my approval on this loan, is that why we're having this meeting?"

Teddy said, "That's right, Pete, and we appreciate you taking the time to hear us out."

"So you're going to tell me about one residential mortgage loan? And this loan is for how much? $500,000? I don't typically get out of bed for anything less than $5 million, but I'll make an exception for this one since you thought it was important to get my approval."

Now despite Teddy's assertions of a done deal, Tom had spent the last few days preparing for this meeting. He knew every detail of Millie's loan. He had put on his best dark blue banker's suit with a red and blue-striped power tie. He was going to impress Porzio with his appearance, if not his expertise. Tom assumed Porzio had no idea who he was, what he did for the bank, and, what's more, didn't care. There had been the two prior mortgage review committee meetings, but Porzio and Teddy did most of the talking. Tom had also shared a few elevator rides with him in the past, but Porzio never appeared to be in the mood for elevator chit chat, so he just kept his mouth shut. It was now time for him to impress the Vice Chairman and Chief Credit Policy Officer of First Northeastern Bank with his talents. Tom said, "Sir, this loan is for $118,750."

Porzio did not laugh. And he did not give Tom permission to call him Pete. He just looked out the window, then back at Teddy, and said, "Tell me again why you're wasting my time with this loan?"

Teddy was sitting close enough to hand signal Tom under the table to stay calm. He knew Tom was feeling like Rodney Dangerfield—getting no respect—but he didn't want him to blow it by letting Porzio know he thought he was an asshole.

He reminded Porzio why they needed this loan to be approved. Teddy again connected the dots for him on how the borrower was the mother of Pastor Lloyd, and how Pastor Lloyd and his group of churches had been supplying the bank with good loan volume under the terms of the CRA agreement. He also reminded Porzio that he had promised to come back for his final approval on the loan.

The In-House Politician

Porzio said, "DeMarco, you know what I think about CRA and the bullshit position it places us in. The asset quality of your mortgage portfolio leaves something to be desired. But I guess we don't have any choice in the matter, right?"

Tom wanted to speak up and defend the benefits of reinvesting the bank's money in revitalization efforts in the cities it operated in. Teddy could tell he was about to respond, so he kicked him under the table, which was his elegant way of telling him to shut the fuck up. And he did, and Tom's opportunity to impress Porzio flew right out the window.

Teddy said, "So how do you want us to proceed, Pete?"

Porzio looked in Tom's direction, pointed, and said, "Is that the file?"

Tom responded in the affirmative—even though Porzio didn't have the courtesy to say his name or look him in the eye. And that's when it dawned on Tom that Teddy hadn't even introduced him at the beginning of the meeting. They just delved right into the business at hand without any pleasantries.

Porzio waved his hand, indicating Tom should give him the file. He looked at Teddy and said, "I'll send this down to Porter and tell him to put it through the system and spit out the approval." Then he got up and left the room. No "Good bye, or thanks for coming." The meeting was over.

Teddy was all smiles. And while Tom was happy about the loan approval from Porzio, at the same time he wanted to reach across the table, slap him and say, "Get some manners, you M-F son of a bitch!"

As they got into the elevator, Teddy had a big smile on his face. "I guess my Yankee ticket is safe."

Tom waited for the elevator doors to close. "You know, it would have been nice for you to introduce me to that man."

Teddy apologized. "I thought you two knew each other. Didn't you meet him at the mortgage review committee meetings? Gee, I'm sorry, Tom."

Tom wanted to say something snarky like, "Oh sure. Scrooge called me for lunch last week, but I couldn't make it. I told him I had too much work to do on Millie's loan presentation." But he thought better of it. What he did say was, "We never really made a connection at those review committee meetings, if you recall. And for the record, that man is the reason why the banking industry is despised."

"See," Teddy said, "I told you he doesn't give a rat's ass!"

He was right. And once again, he told Tom to, "relax." It was really getting annoying.

Chapter 28

After he received a plaintiff call from Pastor Lloyd about the promised campaign contribution Teddy knew he needed to act fast. It was the classic case of a good candidate with a good message and little money. Without a big war chest, Pastor Lloyd was limited in getting his word out over the airwaves. He needed more funding and he needed it fast. Alternatively, his two opponents seemed to be flush with cash. Neither one, however, seemed to be connecting with the voters.

The current Congressman, who was not running for re-election, had not yet endorsed anyone, and the leadership of the State Democratic Party had not tipped their hand as to which candidate they preferred. It was a jump ball, but somehow Pastor Lloyd's message seemed to be resonating. He was currently leading in the polls at 45 percent. With that level of support, he had qualified for the League of Women Voters-sponsored debate.

Teddy had asked Fitz to monitor the Pastor's campaign, and let him know when the time was right for the 1NEB PAC to come in and save the day with its contribution. He had already cleared it with the State Democratic Committee, indicating that any amount the bank might contribute was as a thank you for past considerations, which he declined to specify. He didn't need to. As the head of the bank's PAC, Teddy DeMarco was well known to everyone in the political game as a man of conscience and a man who always picked winners. If Teddy DeMarco was going to contribute to Ogletree's campaign, then he must think the candidate had a good chance to come out on top in the primary. The general election, which might pit Ogletree against the Republican Alex Scarduzo, well, that was another story.

The major concern for Teddy was to make sure the bank's contribution to Pastor Lloyd did not appear as a payoff. Pastor Lloyd's efforts in directing mortgage business to 1NEB was not widely known, but there were always investigative reporters out there trying to become the next Woodward and Bernstein. Such reporters might be able to piece together a story that some readers might misinterpret. There were a few who might have already put it together, like Sally Kessler. But why would she make a fuss since she wanted to see Pastor Lloyd elected and to take credit for more minority homeowners. Of course, Sally could always put this coincidental business arrangement in her back pocket and use it against Teddy and the bank if she ever needed it. Teddy was confident he was doing the right thing and was fairly certain the contribution would not come back to bite him in the ass.

Teddy received a call from Fitz. He said the time was right for the bank's contribution. Fitz claimed Ogletree was burning through cash like a drunken sailor, and if he didn't get an infusion of funds soon, he might have to drop out of the race. If that were to happen, Pastor Lloyd would not be a happy camper if he had to close his doors before receiving any funding from Teddy DeMarco and 1NEB.

Fitz had a spy inside the campaign who'd heard the candidate railing against Teddy and the bank for their failure to come through thus far. Pastor Lloyd was under the impression that Teddy had promised him a contribution, if the campaign looked viable. And Teddy couldn't deny it. Pastor Lloyd had delivered big time with the

The In-House Politician

volume of affordable mortgages. And he was also leading in the polls. He couldn't afford to make an enemy of Rev. Lloyd Ogletree. Teddy also assumed this would keep Sally Kessler off his back and in turn, the press.

Teddy was going to need about a week to round up members of the PAC Board of Directors to rubber stamp his recommendation. He couldn't cut a check until they met and approved the amount. He had decided that a $5,000 donation from the 1NEB PAC wouldn't raise any eyebrows. Additionally, this amount should keep the Pastor going for a few more weeks, at least until the debate. Teddy was also considering a second contribution of $10,000 if it could be matched 2 for 1 from other supporters and Ogletree continued to lead in the polls after the debate.

MC was also legal counsel to the PAC. Teddy wondered if she would have any problem with the contribution since she knew about the business relationship between the bank and Pastor Lloyd. He was certain she would understand and provide him with cover, if it ever came to that. "Maybe it won't even come up," Teddy thought. Right. Murphy's Law. So Teddy charged Tom with the responsibility of selling MC on the matter, and Tom was okay with that.

Teddy had Kelly contact all the assistants to the members of the PAC's Board to schedule the meeting. Separately, he phoned Pastor Lloyd to let him know the bank would be providing his campaign with a contribution as soon as his committee met.

He was surprised by the Pastor's lack of enthusiasm to this news. Maybe the campaign was already out of cash and Pastor Lloyd knew that even with the additional funds he was about to crash and burn. When Teddy asked Pastor Lloyd how his campaign fund was faring, the response was a curt, "That will depend on how much you're giving us, Mr. DeMarco."

Teddy was now caught between the proverbial rock and a hard place. He had just committed to providing funds, but it sounded as if no amount was going to be good enough. That is, unless the amount he provided was well beyond his self-imposed limit of $5,000. However, any amount higher than the $5,000 would raise questions from the PAC members and possibly place MC in a no-win situation where she could not necessarily go along with Teddy's request.

Teddy said, "The bank is willing to contribute $5,000 now, and then, after the debate—" He paused here for moment wondering whether what he was about to say next was worth the risk. He continued anyway. "If after the debate things continue to go well, and by that I mean you're still polling well, then we might be willing to ante up another $10,000 in matching funds. We would want you to find other contributors to match this amount $2 for every $1 from us. So, on the upside, in the best-case scenario, you could be receiving a total of $35,000 from 1NEB and other matching contributors. How does that sound?"

This seemed to put the Pastor in a better mood. His voice and attitude perked up. "Any chance you could reverse the order of those two offers?" he asked. "Could you see your way clear to giving me the $10,000 in matching funds now, and then if polling goes up after the debate, you could give me the other $5,000?" He seemed to be grasping at straws.

"Sorry, Pastor, but I can't do that. You have to understand that even the initial $5,000 is more than we normally give to any one candidate. Typically, we only give $2,500 or maybe $3,000. We don't

The In-House Politician

ever want to be viewed as a bank that buys favors from elected officials. You know what I mean, right? And we would expect you wouldn't want to be seen as beholden to us either." Teddy wasn't about to negotiate the additional $10,000 match, since he didn't know if his PAC Board would even go for it. This whole campaign finance thing was costing him a bundle of money he hadn't planned for. It was money he couldn't spend on other candidates who were proven friends of the bank.

Before Teddy hung up with Pastor Lloyd, he needed to say one more thing. "I just want to remind you of something I told you when we first met on the issue of our bank contributing to your campaign. And I want to be very clear on this, okay? We only give funds to candidates who are, or will be, friends of the banking industry. We know Sally Kessler has your ear. Now, we hope that we've convinced you we have all of our customers' best interests at heart. We wouldn't want anything to jeopardize our working relationship with you and the MJED. I know from experience how ugly politics can get. We are your friend and we hope you will continue to be our friend as well."

Teddy ended the call. "Goodbye, Pastor Lloyd. You'll be hearing from me soon."

"Amen to that and God bless you, Mr. DeMarco."

While Teddy assumed that if Pastor Lloyd was aware of the high number of minority loan denials, he wouldn't bring it up on this call since it was to discuss a campaign contribution. And he was right. No discussion of any loans. He didn't even ask about his mother's loan.

Teddy always held meetings of the PAC directors in the boardroom on the top floor. It was situated between the Chairman's and Vice Chairman Porzio's offices making their commute to the meetings short. And, the General Counsel's office was just down the hall. Teddy assumed they would not condescend to meet anywhere else in the building, but in fact he was merely continuing the tradition established by his predecessor, Fitz.

The boardroom faced east with a full view of the Manhattan skyline. On the interior wall hung portraits of all the previous Chairmen. The seats were plush and the table top so shiny you could see your reflection in it.

The 1NEB PAC Board of Directors met a few days after Teddy's conversation with Pastor Lloyd. Since the Chairman was out of town, Porzio was the ranking officer and assumed the role of chair for the meeting. When he entered the boardroom, Porzio took the seat at the head of the table where Teddy usually sat. Teddy had to defer to the Vice Chairman who had not checked his ego at the door.

The first order of business was to vote on the $5,000 contribution to Rev. Lloyd Ogletree's campaign. Teddy made his case and it was approved unanimously.

Now, it's rare when Teddy makes an error in judgement, but in this case he should have been happy with the win and ended the meeting. Unfortunately, he did not.

Teddy said, "I want to thank you all for your vote to assist Rev. Lloyd Ogletree's bid for the Congressional seat in Central Jersey. I also want to alert you to the possibility that if, and this is a very big if, Pastor Lloyd's polling continues as we expect, after the televised debate, I think we should consider giving him another $10,000 as a contribution to be matched on a 2 to 1 basis by other supporters. If he comes out a winner in the debate, we want to be considered part of his team. This would illustrate great leadership on our part, and it would show good faith to him and the New Jersey African American voters."

He should have ended his pitch right there. But he did not.

"However, and I can't emphasize this enough, there's a lot riding on his performance in this upcoming debate. It's quite possible that he could fall flat on his face since he has no previous experience in a debate like this. TV cameras can be intimidating to the uninitiated. So this second $10,000 matching contribution may never be needed."

This last argument didn't make much sense even as the words were coming out of his mouth. But Teddy wanted to give the PAC members an out if the Pastor didn't do well. Ogletree preached every Sunday into a TV camera and his flock of 3,000.

Teddy's last remarks left Porzio with the impression that Ogletree might not do well in the debate. Additionally, he seemed to know the connection between Ogletree and PUMP. He raised his voice and stated his position firmly. "DeMarco, listen to me. We need to conserve our limited funds in order to donate to candidates who are actually friends of the banking industry. Isn't your candidate, Ogletree, in the pocket of those crazy radicals called PUMP? They hate our bank. Didn't they have something to do with that last article in *The Examiner*, which made us look like heartless bigots? And wasn't PUMP the group you negotiated that ridiculous CRA agreement with, which we're still paying for in blood money in all kinds of shitty loans?"

Teddy was not prepared for this tirade from Porzio. But Teddy being Teddy, he was quick to recover. He made it clear that he agreed wholeheartedly with what the Vice Chairman was saying about the conservation of limited funds. But he defended his recommendation with confidence. "Gentlemen, the bank needs to maintain good relations with the African American community and thus far, Pastor Lloyd Ogletree has been a great friend to this bank. It is true that Ogletree works in tandem with some of the folks at PUMP. It's also true that the article in *The Examiner* on our performance made us look bad and made PUMP look good. But that's all in the past. We need to keep Ogletree as a friend, or at least not make him our enemy. He's leading in the polls. We don't want his train to leave the station without us onboard."

That's all the confirmation Porzio needed to hear. It was like telling him to make a loan to Bonnie and Clyde in order to finance their careers in robbing banks. In Porzio's mind, if Ogletree was with PUMP, then he would never become a friend of the bank. It made no sense to him.

Porzio began shouting. "If this guy is not our friend, then why are we giving him any money in the first place? I would like to reconsider my original vote for the initial $5,000 based on this new information."

Teddy was now in panic mode and looked over to MC for help. The other board members were starting to grumble as well. They were all taking their lead from Porzio. Finally, MC spoke up. "While it's true we might be spending money on a candidate who doesn't have the best regard for the banking industry, there were other considerations for doing so."

"What other considerations?" Porzio demanded.

Teddy's ship was taking on water fast. MC had opened that door and there was no going back. Coming into the meeting Teddy was hoping he wouldn't have to disclose his business arrangement with Pastor Lloyd and MJED. All the PAC members understood the need to maintain good relations with the minority community, but it would be difficult to convince them that the contribution was not a political payback for the Pastor's partnership with the bank in the affordable mortgage program. Teddy and MC needed to explain this arrangement without making it sound like a bribe. But Porzio saw right through it.

He hated the idea of the bank paying what in his mind was blackmail money to get the merger approved. He was of the opinion that the regulators would have approved the merger without any CRA agreement with the protest groups. However, he only mentioned his objections to the Chairman and General Counsel. Teddy did not operate in Porzio's orbit. When it came to keeping the Bolsheviks at bay, Teddy reported directly to the Chairman. On this matter, the Chairman had given Teddy a wide berth to do whatever it took to get the deal done. And so far, it had worked. In fact, in a certain way *The Examiner* article had helped Teddy accomplish his mission internally. Except for Scrooge and Marley, it had the effect of alerting everyone inside the bank that business as usual was over. It was time to rethink past practices, and it gave Teddy the opportunity he needed to get the message across—whether they liked it or not.

Porzio looked like he was about to explode. "What's this all about, DeMarco? What other considerations is she referring to?" If Porzio knew MC's name, the chauvinist in him merely saw her as "she" and that was all he thought he needed.

He said, "If this has anything to do with that CRA agreement you negotiated with those extremists, you won't get my vote. I've seen the results of that mortgage product you put in place. Porter told me some horror stories about those loans. I really think it's time to put an end to all this liberal bullshit, giving away the store to some radicals who know nothing about how banks operate and want to redistribute the bank's profits to the poor. This Robin Hood philosophy doesn't sit well with me." MC's presence in the room was the only thing holding Porzio back from using the "F" word.

Then MC spoke up again. She was insulted by Porzio not recognizing her as the legal expert in the room. MC was not looking at Porzio when she said in as firm and lawyerly a tone as she could muster, "Sir, are you quite finished with your rant?" MC could give it back as good as she got. By just referring to Porzio as "Sir," she was being respectful of his position, but not giving him the satisfaction of reciting his name or title back to him.

Teddy had never seen or heard anyone speak to Porzio in this manner.

MC turned in her chair, smiled, tilted her head, and looked directly at Porzio. "Do you really think that an expense of $5,000 to a minority political candidate, who may or may not be a friend, as well as a commitment to make $25 million in mortgages, will be problematic for what is now a $60 billion financial institution? I would say that in the overall scheme of things, these commitments are not even a rounding error for a bank of our size. And we should all congratulate Teddy on the great work he has done to keep the protest groups at bay."

While her tone did not please Porzio, it did seem to end his bluster. He knew Teddy had the Chairman's ear. He also assumed that MC was speaking on behalf of the General Counsel. Porzio raised his hands in surrender. He said, "Okay, okay. You can make your damn $5,000 donation for now. But if this guy says one crazy thing about us

The In-House Politician

in the debate, I can guarantee you I will not be voting for any future contributions to him even if he comes out on top."

The meeting adjourned and Teddy didn't think he was bleeding too badly.

As they left the boardroom, Porzio looked over at Teddy and gave him a head nod to come over for further discussions.

Teddy would have preferred that MC was still around, but she had made a hasty exit.

In what amounted to a semi-apology Porzio said, "Hey, listen, DeMarco, sometimes I forget you're the professional politician around here. Sorry if I stepped on any toes today. Anyway, what I wanted to ask you was whether you were thinking about making a contribution to Alex Scarduzo Jr.'s campaign? I know we went a few rounds in the past about his father's business connections, but I don't necessarily want the sins of the father to be visited upon the son, if you catch my drift."

Teddy had a strange look on his face that said, "Could you please repeat that because I thought you said—" He felt like he was in an episode of *Twilight Zone*, but quickly recovered. He said, "Well, Pete, I didn't know you and Alex knew each other."

"We don't," Porzio said angrily, which left Teddy a bit unnerved. "Isn't Alex a Republican, and based on your business relationship with him, he's definitely a friend of the bank, right?"

"Yes, that's right," Teddy said. "We've got an excellent business relationship with Alex and Ocean County."

"Well then, shouldn't we be hedging our bets in this election? Making sure that we've got both sides covered? He's running unopposed, right? Now I know that Alex's chances are slim, the election being in a heavily Democratic district, but we certainly don't want him as an enemy, now do we?"

Once again Teddy thought it curious that Porzio was calling the candidate by his first name. It seemed awkward and all too familiar to him—as if he was holding something back.

Teddy said, "You know, Pete, Alex Jr.'s campaign is financed by his father. As a result, he's pretty flush with cash. In fact, I'm pretty sure he hasn't asked for a dime of outside money—from anyone. Why would we give him money if he doesn't need it and hasn't asked for it? You said yourself we need to conserve our limited funds."

"Okay, okay. Message received. Just think about it. Maybe reach out to him and see if he wants any money from us. I would like to keep things balanced here. I don't want the press to get the impression that this bank sides only with those socialists you always bend over for. Just think about it."

From the smile on Porzio's face, Teddy got the feeling he thought he was making a joke. Porzio then turned his back on Teddy and returned to his office, which was about three steps away from where they were standing.

As Teddy moved in the direction of the elevators, he heard his secretary say, "Mr. Porzio, you have a call from someone who says his name is Buddy and that you know him."

His secretary was in the process of closing the door to his office when Teddy heard Porzio scream into the phone, "I thought I told you never to call me here."

A few things were rattling around inside Teddy's head. First, that MC was a real pistol. Maybe he could find a way to create a position for her in his department. Secondly, what was that all about from

The In-House Politician

Porzio about Alex Scarduzo? All this time he thought Porzio couldn't care less about the politics surrounding the bank's activities. Now he would have to reconsider that opinion. If Porzio didn't actually know Alex Scarduzo Jr., then why was he calling him by his first name? And why would he care about the bank giving him any PAC money, especially if Porzio previously said he wanted nothing to do with the Scarduzo family? Finally, Teddy was wondering who this Buddy person was and why Porzio didn't want him calling at the office.

Paul "Buddy" Wyrough was Porzio's nephew, and was dumber than a post. Buddy was Porzio's sister's son. His sister's name was Portia and she had been left to raise the boy on her own when her husband left town with his girlfriend when Buddy was only five. Porzio helped his sister as much as he could, serving as Buddy's uncle. He tried to find him a reputable prep school, but discovered that no amount of money could get the boy inside those ivy-covered walls. Buddy wasn't very smart. Likewise, after high school Porzio successfully found Buddy a trade school where he trained as a plumber. However, once he graduated and was hired in his first real job, Buddy only lasted two months before he was fired. So after his sister pleaded with him, Porzio was able to find a job for Buddy at 1NEB as an inter-office mail delivery driver. He was responsible for picking up and delivering the bank's mail at various branches. Porzio fervently hoped Buddy wouldn't screw up the job.

Buddy responded to his uncle's tirade with, "I'm sorry, Uncle Peter. But I'm a bit confused with your hand-written instructions. I'm at a pay phone across the street from the campaign headquarters of Alex Scarduzo. I did like you told me and parked the van around the corner so no one could see it. But I just wanted to make sure I've got this right. You want me to hand deliver this unmarked envelope directly to Alex Scarduzo himself?"

Chapter 29

This time Alex came to visit Sally on her turf. He had a message delivered to her through either Nick or Joe. Alex couldn't really tell them apart. For all he knew they could have been twins. One of them hadn't been around recently, but he didn't know which one, or why.

Alex thought that if he had proposed another meeting next to the waste disposal site, Sally would have refused to come. So he told her that he would come alone to her PUMP offices, and he expected her to be alone as well. No witnesses.

He drove himself to the meeting in his personal vehicle with tinted glass. No government license plates to draw unwanted attention. Nick or Joe could have driven him, but he never knew how much English they understood since they hardly ever spoke in his presence. He also didn't know how much they reported back to his father, presumably in their native Sicilian.

The PUMP offices were in a small vacant warehouse in East Newark owned by one of Sally's disciples. It was located on one of those roads running east-west as you enter the city from the Turnpike. Lots of grassy marsh-like acreage just on the fringes of the Meadowlands. As far as warehouses go, this one was smaller than most, but was just right for PUMP. There was a small elevated office in the rear where Sally had a desk, a few chairs, a phone, and a filing cabinet. All were government-issued gun-metal grey. Nothing fancy for them; after all, they were Bolsheviks. The warehouse also held PUMP's two vans, a copier machine, and all

The In-House Politician

the materials they needed to carry out their protests against the evil banking empire.

It was dark when Alex arrived. All the warehouse doors appeared to be closed and the lights were off. "Good deal," he said to himself. "Kessler has finally figured things out." He walked around the building until he found a parked car and a side door near the back of the warehouse with an overhead light. He entered and closed the door behind him. He saw Sally up in the office with her feet up on the desk reading something. This was an unusual sight and Alex had to laugh. All she needed was a fat cigar and some eye shades. This whole clandestine meeting and its location reminded him of a scene out of some film noir. The only thing out of place was Sally.

Alex walked up the few steps and entered her office. Sally saw him coming and removed her feet from the desk. She greeted him graciously with a sincere, "So what the fuck do you want this time?"

"Nice to see you, too," Alex said.

He sat down in one of her government-issue chairs, looked around, and commented on the wonderful décor and cozy atmosphere. "I've seen better accommodations in condemned buildings. Wherever did you find this place?"

"What do you want, Alex?"

"Okay then. I guess we'll dispense with the pleasantries. Actually, I'm here to give you some intel you might find useful. But like everything else in life, it doesn't come free. My sources tell me your good friend Teddy DeMarco has found himself in a real pickle, to put it as politely as I can. Actually, it's more like a shitstorm. Do I have your full attention now? I have here in this envelope the bank's latest mortgage activity report, but I haven't had a chance to review it yet.

It covers the past six months. I'll make you a copy and get it to you in short order."

Sally perked up. "Go on."

"Well it seems the bank has been rejecting most of the Black loan applications that have come in since they made that side deal with your friend, Ogletree. Apparently the credit gods inside 1NEB haven't found too many of your friend's loans they like. And rumor has it that once this information gets out, it's going to be more of a public relations nightmare for them than the last time. But here's the thing. As I understand it, and you can correct me if I've got this wrong, most of the applications are coming in from the African American churches associated with Ogletree's group, right? So, if the rejections are coming out in the numbers reflected in his report, then why hasn't Ogletree made a fuss about it to you? You're inside the campaign, what have you heard? What's more, I have my own theory on why he may not have raised the issue with DeMarco just yet. It may have something to do with a campaign contribution he's been waiting on from your favorite bank."

Sally looked perplexed. But her expression quickly turned to anger. "That son-of-a-bitch! He promised Pastor Lloyd he'd get these loans approved. But wait a second. How do you know all this? Who's giving you this information?"

"Sally, I told you, I've got my sources. And one of those sources provides me with info from someone familiar with what's going on inside the bank. By the way, who are you calling an S.O.B?"

"All three of you. Each of you individually. Take your pick. DeMarco, Ogletree, and you. Are you going to give me that report? You know we have a copier here?"

The In-House Politician

Alex smiled. He had her right where he wanted her. "Settle down now. Settle down. I need to review this report and make sure it's the real deal. Don't want to be making accusations about the bank without solid evidence. I'll get it to you in the next few days. Promise. I just thought you'd want his information ASAP so you could work your magic, or whatever it is you call it. I get confused sometimes."

She hated his sarcasm as much as she hated him. "So how do I know you're not playing me? Having me do your dirty work?"

"C'mon, Sally. I'd have thought by now you'd learned to trust me. Besides, I've got a lot to lose if you actually do take down DeMarco and his bank. But that's a story for another day. I'm telling you what I've heard. And you're welcome."

Sally looked at him plaintively. "Okay. Let's just say for the moment you're right. What do you want in return?"

"You wound me, Sally. I don't think I'm being unreasonable here. I'm guessing this information on the bank could be incendiary, but before we go any further, I think you should also know that Teddy DeMarco just cut a check for $5,000 from his bank's PAC to help Ogletree's campaign. I think the old adage is 'the check's in the mail.'"

"Yeah! I knew about that. I told Lloyd I wasn't happy about it. I lectured him on taking blood money from that bank. And if what you just told me is true, it makes that money even more toxic. His response was that he needed the money and was getting desperate. His campaign funds were on life support, and apparently DeMarco made him some promises of more to come if he does well at the debate."

Then Alex came in for the kill. "But here's the thing. If your guy Ogletree was waiting for that money from DeMarco, all the while knowing about the bank's high rejection rate on all those Black loans coming in from all those Black churches, well, someone of lesser intelligence than me might conclude that your Rev. Ogletree may have taken a payoff from the bank to keep silent. Really, Sally? Can you sit there and tell me that Ogletree didn't know about all those rejections from the other pastors in his group—what's it called?—the Ministry for Justice and Economic Development? Something's not right there."

Sally knew there was more to come. "I'll take this all under advisement. Now, what do you want in return? It's late. Get to it, will you?"

"First of all, I'm just asking that you give me a heads up in advance if you're going to hit DeMarco between the eyes with this. I have business interests I need to protect. But second, and more importantly, if your candidate keeps rising in the polls, he might just end up winning this thing. I'm still not sure where I come down on that, but here's the thing. No pun intended, but God forbid, Ogletree actually ends up as my opponent in the Fall, I'm going to need some dirt on your candidate. Now I've got my own sources for this opposition research, but you're right there inside the campaign. At some point you're going to have to make a decision about whose side you're on. Do you want Ogletree to get elected or do you want to take down DeMarco and 1NEB? You can't have it both ways. But that's your call. So I need for you to get me some dirt on your guy. You have my word I won't use it unless he's running against me. I'll swear that on my firstborn. Promise!"

Sally was contrite. "So you really expect me to trust you? And you think I'm going to give you dirt on my candidate for you to use against him? Really?"

"Let's not go there again, okay? We have a deal. We're in this together. Do I need to remind you that you're on the hook for that last article that placed the bank in the position it's currently in? That fake article put DeMarco together with Ogletree and you signed off on it. That situation couldn't have worked out any better for me if I'd planned it. Their bromance is about to end one way or the other. You can be a hero in the break-up if you play your cards right. Let's talk again when you decide what to do with this little gem I'll be providing you."

As Alex got up to leave he again complimented her on her digs. Sally gave him the middle finger salute.

Chapter 30

Everyone in Pastor Lloyd's campaign knew how much Sally Kessler despised the banking industry in general, and 1NEB specifically. But Rev. Lloyd Ogletree, Democratic candidate for Congress, had thus far successfully parried her attempts at getting him to go after those evil bankers. He knew it was personal for her. He also received advice from his biggest contributor, the very wealthy real estate developer who had maxed out on his political donations, that he would need the banking interests to support his campaign, now, and in the future. Indeed, the banking industry could be a valued source of financial support, and alternatively, they could be a very ruthless adversary if he pissed them off. But Sally kept after it with her friend Lloyd hoping that he would see the light and banish the banks from his campaign.

As a senior advisor in Pastor Lloyd's campaign, Sally had pledged to toe the line and only use the official talking points whenever she was asked a question. And if there was a question that did not fit within the parameters of those talking points, she was ordered to say "no comment," or "you'll have to speak directly with the candidate himself on that issue." These restraints didn't sit well with her, but the success of the campaign thus far meant that something was going right, so she did her best to stay on message.

Inside campaign headquarters was another matter altogether. Sally felt no restraints there, and as a result, some of the Pastor's top aides were not happy keeping her on the team. In fact, Pastor Lloyd's staff did their best to keep her away from the candidate, lest she put ideas in his head that would only result in more conflicts.

But this time was different. Lloyd had actually called her to come in and talk.

Coincidences aside, Sally thought this would be an interesting conversation now that she was armed with the rumor about the large number of minority loan denials issued by 1NEB. She didn't have the written proof yet, but expected it from Scarduzo soon. She reminded herself to play it close to the vest so as not to reveal her source.

In an effort to keep his church responsibilities separate from his political activities, Pastor Lloyd had set up his campaign headquarters in a storefront in Asbury Park. In the realm of wishful thinking, he thought the storefront's close proximity to the Convention Center would be helpful on election night if the Lord blessed him with a victory.

Pastor Lloyd greeted Sally with a hug, which was unsettling to her since he rarely gave one and she rarely accepted one. Sally was never warm and fuzzy, but this time he wanted to make a connection with her. They talked a while about the current situation with his campaign. He was leading in the polls, which qualified him for the televised debate. But his pollsters were saying he might have peaked—unless he could get more air time, and that required money. They said nothing more about his campaign funding since it was a point of contention between them. He didn't know if Sally was aware that a check had arrived from 1NEB, so he avoided that part of the conversation entirely. And she decided not to tip her hand until she heard what he wanted to say. His next words opened the door and Sally walked right on through.

Pastor Lloyd began, "Well, Sally, you were right! Apparently, 1NEB has been rejecting a lot of Black loan applications under its special mortgage program. I've heard a lot about it from my colleagues at the other churches. They haven't wanted to complain about it to me since the bank has also approved some of their loans. It's made homeowners out of some of our brothers and sisters who never thought it was a possibility. No one had the official numbers, so they really didn't know the extent of the bad news. More likely, they didn't want to complain too loudly out of deference to my campaign. So, the bad news about the denials was drowned out by the good news of the few approvals. But now we have proof. Right here in this document, which looks like some sort of spreadsheet prepared by the bank itself. We now know the actual number of minority loans the bank has denied under the program. The question is, what do I do with this information? I want to come clean and beg for forgiveness since the bank's contribution came in yesterday, but I'm not exactly sure what to do. And we're still waiting to hear from the bank on—" He stopped himself. Sally didn't need to know about his mother's loan application. She might get the wrong idea.

He continued. "What I do know is that I just can't stand by and do nothing now that I have this information. The press would have a field day if they ever found out I knew about this and did nothing. And on top of it all, I took campaign funds from the bank. It doesn't paint a pretty picture."

Sally stopped him with her usual, "See, I told you so!"

"Yes! Yes, Sally! I heard you the first thousand times you told me to separate myself from the bank. But your smugness isn't helping me with what to do now."

The In-House Politician

"Can I see that document?"

Pastor Lloyd hesitated for a second before handing it to her. "I'll need that back. I can't let you take that with you. I haven't decided what to do with it yet. That's why I called you in here, to talk about my options."

Sally took a second to look over the report. She assumed it was the same one Scarduzo had in his possession. Was he playing them off against each other? When she looked up from the spreadsheet, she said she had a plan, but first she needed to know the source of the information.

Pastor Lloyd said he didn't know who it was because his direct source, which came to him anonymously through one of his church members, said he shouldn't know who provided it so that he could always claim plausible deniability. But this church member assured Pastor Lloyd that the source had intimate knowledge of the number of loans denied by 1NEB. Apparently, the information came from someone inside the bank.

Sally wasn't happy not knowing who the source was, primarily because she needed proof if Joe Campbell at was going to write another big story. But it was way too early to be thinking about that since such a story now would only hurt Pastor Lloyd's campaign. That is, unless Pastor Lloyd decided to talk directly to the press himself.

When Sally tried to convince him to go to the press with this information, Pastor Lloyd said he wasn't ready to phone a reporter he didn't know, or trust, to make accusations against the bank. He needed more time to think about it and consider his options.

"Lloyd," Sally said, "I hate to tell you this, but the first thing you need to do is to return that contribution you received from the bank.

And you need to do it now, before anyone gets wind of this report. The fact that this information is out means that you're not the only one who knows about it."

She let that last remark sink in for moment. Then she said, "Here's what you should do, and you do should do it immediately. Hold a press conference to announce that you're returning the money from the bank. It should be part of a well-orchestrated press event in which you say that the reason you're returning the bank's money is that you can't keep it with a clear conscience. Then you announce that you're in possession of a report summarizing the number of African American loans the bank has denied under its affordable mortgage plan. I'm telling you, Lloyd, if we plan this properly, and the timing is right, you can go into the debate with an issue no one else has. You'll be a hero taking on the big bank, and I guarantee you'll get a bump in the polls. I can't say how big a bump, but it will certainly move the needle in a positive direction."

"That sounds like a good plan," Pastor Lloyd said, "but how did you know about the money from 1NEB?"

"Really Lloyd?"

"And what if an announcement like that upsets my other big corporate donors? They all know each other, and I've taken money from other banks, as well. How do I explain that away? I'm going to need their support in the general election if I get that far. I don't know about this, Sally. I need to pray on it and take my direction from the Lord. He will guide me to do what's best."

Sally smirked. "How long do you think it will take for the Lord to get back to you? Far be it from me to tell you how to run your campaign, or how to communicate with your God. My God and

I split a long time ago. Lloyd, this is something you need to jump on quickly."

Pastor Lloyd didn't appreciate Sally's sarcasm.

Sally said, "What happens if *The Examiner* gets a whiff of this and writes the story before you return the money to the bank? You're screwed—pardon the expression—because you'll be seen as the candidate who collaborated with the big bank who denied all those loans to your church members. You took the bank's money, then looked the other way when it came to all those denials. It'll definitely cost you much of your support. In fact, dare I say, it might even look like you took a bribe to stay silent about the high number of black rejections." She stopped there. Sally didn't need to go any further with some snarky comment about handcuffs and leg irons. She'd made her points and knew Pastor Lloyd was considering them.

He was still on the fence, not sure what to do. "Sally, I've developed a very good relationship with the bank. They've made loans to some of our brothers and sisters, which is a good story to tell. And the bank supported me with campaign funds to help me continue the good fight. It's like turning your back on a good friend who was there for you when you really needed one. I wouldn't be in this position to move forward without the bank's money, and there's a lot of new Black homeowners who couldn't have qualified for a regular loan at some other bank. And besides, there could be legitimate reasons for all the loan denials the bank has issued. I just don't feel right about this."

"Lloyd! Are you listening to yourself? First off, the bank just gave you that money recently, right? DeMarco didn't have any confidence in you up front. He was waiting to see how you did in the polls before he cut you a check. And believe me, he knows how bad those rejection numbers will look if they ever get out. So he's hoping that you'll look the other way, or turn the other cheek, so to speak—pun intended."

Sally was becoming more frustrated. "Please listen to me, Lloyd. You must understand that the only price DeMarco had to pay to get you to help him and maintain your silence was a small political contribution that he makes to candidates all the time. Your political enemies will call it a bribe. And, you must know that DeMarco is certainly hoping that you screw up in the debate and lose in the primary. Then he doesn't have to give you any more money. And Scarduzo is one of his biggest customers. If you were to actually beat Scarduzo—well, he'll consider Teddy Demarco and 1NEB to be traitors to his election bid. If you win, DeMarco might lose all those accounts. He's trying to buy your silence. He assumed you wouldn't say anything bad about him or the bank as long as he gave you money for your campaign. C'mon, Lloyd! How many times do I have to say it? He's using you to get the loan volume in the door, and he's hoping you keep quiet about the rejections with the donation to the campaign. It was a win-win for DeMarco."

Sally seemed to be getting through to the Pastor, but she needed one more score. "Lloyd, I know you're concerned about campaign finances. I get it. But look at the risk you're taking. Now, I can't guarantee this, but my gut tells me that if you go public with this information and say that you're returning the money to the bank, you'll gain more respect and resulting financial support. I mean it. I think you'll see an increase in campaign donations if you do the right thing and return the money. There are plenty of voters out there who don't like those big bad banks and you'll be speaking

The In-House Politician

directly to them. You gotta go for it, Lloyd. You know it's the right thing to do."

Pastor Lloyd still wasn't convinced by Sally's rant, but he couldn't refute it either. He said, "Well, I used him and the bank, as well. I needed their money for the campaign and the mortgage program helped some of my people. Isn't that what you wanted it to do? Teddy DeMarco came to me to ask for our help with the affordable mortgage program a long time before I officially decided to run for Congress. And it was only after we were helping him with the mortgages that I asked him for the campaign contribution. One was not based on the other. I went to him and asked for the money."

Sally was furious. "Yes, of course! I understand the timing, but that's not what it will look like. Here are the facts, Lloyd. According to this document, 1NEB is denying almost three Black loans for every White loan. There's something seriously wrong with that picture. A lot of people are being discriminated against with those kinds of rejection rates. And if you don't do something about it, then I may have to. Lloyd, I don't want to hurt you or your campaign, but now that I know about these minority denial numbers, I can't sit around and do nothing. Seriously, give the money back as soon as possible, and make a public announcement that you've done it and why. Make this issue work for you, Lloyd. Please! I can handle the press side of it for you."

"Yeah. Right. I've seen how you handle the press," he said.

Pastor Lloyd grabbed the document out of Sally's hand and admonished her once again. "Sally, I know how much you hate that bank, but let's try to be reasonable here, okay? Let's talk about this again tomorrow."

Sally turned to leave and said, "Tomorrow may be too late."

Chapter 31

The televised debate was one week away. Pastor Lloyd knew he had to get out in front of this story before it blew up in his face. He heard what Sally was preaching and it made sense to him now. But the blindside he was going to hit Teddy DeMarco with made him wonder if he could ever be forgiven for what he was about to do.

He went ahead and scheduled a press conference at his campaign HQs for the following day, indicating he had a major announcement to make. The announcement, of course, was all Sally's idea. There was no mercy in her heart for DeMarco and 1NEB.

Pastor Lloyd prayed for guidance, or some kind of sign, perhaps a bolt of lightning so that he could feel just a little bit better. In his mind, he still thought he was betraying Teddy DeMarco. The bank had come through with a nice contribution for his campaign, and had made first-time homeowners out of a good number of God-fearin' Black folks, many of whom were friends and followers of his. But if Sally's interpretation of events was correct, then he had no choice in the matter.

For Pastor Lloyd, though, doing the right thing meant he needed to explain himself to Teddy before the lightning struck. Indeed, he thought it only right that he should give him a heads-up so he could prepare for the in-coming firestorm. He knew Sally wouldn't be happy about it, but she'd get over it. Indeed, he was beginning to agree with his staff that it might be time to separate himself from Sally Kessler, as well as 1NEB.

The In-House Politician

Teddy was sitting at his desk when Kelly leaned her head in and said that Pastor Lloyd Ogletree was on the line. Teddy had a nervous feeling in his gut. There was currently no business outstanding between them, so he couldn't imagine why he was calling. Perhaps he wanted to say thanks for the PAC contribution, or to ask for an update on the status of his Mother's loan. Teddy picked up the phone. "Hey, my friend, good to hear from you. What kind of trouble are you in and how can I help?" That was the last time Teddy joked during the conversation.

Pastor Lloyd began, "Mr. DeMarco, I wanted to call to let you know that my campaign is in the process of separating itself from Sally Kessler and her organization, PUMP. While her heart may be in the right place, and while I may personally agree with many of her positions, I cannot and do not condone how she puts her plans into action. My campaign staff and financial supporters think it would be best if Sally is no longer associated with my campaign. I will be resigning from her board shortly. Now, I would appreciate it if you didn't mention this to her or to anyone else just yet. I need to let her down gently—if that is possible."

Teddy said, "That's a smart move. And don't worry about me spilling the beans. After that last article she approved of in *The Examiner*, we don't talk much."

Pastor Lloyd then moved on to the real reason for his call. "I also wanted to say thank you for all the help you have personally provided me in my efforts to become the next Congressman from this district. And on behalf of my colleagues at MJED, I want to add their thanks for all of the mortgages 1NEB approved to our African American brothers and sisters under the affordable mortgage program." He paused for a moment and let out a big sigh.

Teddy said, "Okay, Pastor Lloyd. You're welcome. Now, I'm waiting for the other shoe to drop. Please be gentle." Teddy could always feel it when bad news was about to be delivered.

"Well, Mr. DeMarco, I'm sure you're aware that in addition to the mortgages your bank approved for our African American brothers and sisters, the bank has also been declining a great many more. For a few months now I've been getting complaints from my fellow pastors in MJED about the high number of rejections they've been witnessing. We've held back on asking you about this, hoping that things might turn around. I'm sure you've kept a tally of the approvals and denials and made some internal assessment as to whether all of those denials were justified, right?"

He didn't wait for an answer. "And what makes matters worse is that our applicants just receive a form letter in the mail saying their loan has been denied, with some boxes checked off for the official reasons. No phone call, no grief counseling, nothing. Just a form letter. I guess that's the most efficient way to operate these days when it comes to communicating bad news, but I think Jesus might not approve of this process. It's a little heartless, don't you agree? A little more compassion is needed."

Teddy was now in full defense mode. He said, "Pastor Lloyd, we know what our batting average is under the affordable mortgage program, and we've been very unhappy with the way some of our folks inside the bank's mortgage department have been applying traditional underwriting guidelines to non-traditional borrowers. Pardon me, I didn't explain that correctly. I meant they're applying traditional underwriting standards to non-traditional credit applicants. But we are, in fact, a bank, and we can only go with what applicants tell us

The In-House Politician

on paper, including their savings and credit histories. Now, when this all started, we spoke with you and your colleagues in MJED, and we agreed to do our very best to approve as many loans as possible. And I can assure you that we're fighting the good fight every day inside the bank to turn around as many denials as we can. But it's a tough battle."

Pastor Lloyd was not surprised by this response. He remained calm, and said, "Mr. DeMarco, everyone in my campaign is advising me to put some distance between myself and your bank. Not necessarily you specifically, but to distance myself from 1NEB. Sorry!"

Teddy's temperature was rising. "Why do I feel the evil hand of Sally Kessler in all this? Has she been bending your ear on how evil we are at the bank?"

"It's true she's not a fan of yours, I'll admit that, but it wasn't only her voice I was listening to in making this decision."

"What decision?" Teddy asked in anguish. "What decision, please tell me what decision you're talking about?"

"I have scheduled a press conference for tomorrow to announce that I am returning the bank's campaign contribution. I will also be admonishing your bank for all the loans you have denied to minority applicants under the affordable mortgage program. I'm in possession of a report on the number of loans you denied to Black and Latino applicants in comparison with White applicants. And it's not good."

Teddy couldn't help himself anymore. His office door was open and he was screaming into the phone so loudly that Kelly came into his office to see if he was having a heart attack. When she saw that he was still alive, she closed the door behind her. Staff on the floor were popping their heads up from inside their cubicles to see and hear what was going on.

Teddy said, "Pastor Lloyd, please forgive me, but WHAT THE HELL! Whatever the problem is, we could've talked it over and worked it out. Instead, you're casting stones for political gain. So what time is this press conference scheduled for tomorrow?"

Pastor Lloyd was shaken by Teddy's outburst. He was expecting a negative reaction, but he didn't think it would be this volatile. He'd only seen Teddy in his collegial, friendly, deal-making mode. He hadn't experienced the four-alarm pounding on the desk, room-clearing, head- exploding Teddy. He tried to calm things down with his soft and gentle response. "I've scheduled it for 10 o'clock tomorrow morning." His soothing voice did not work.

Teddy was having none of it. He screamed again into the phone. "Of course it's at 10 in the morning! The press needs plenty of time to write their hatchet job on us and still make the evening news! You make Judas look like a saint!"

Again, in his gentlest voice, Pastor Lloyd said, "You know, Mr. DeMarco, I didn't have to make this call and give you a heads up. I did it because I think very highly of you personally and didn't want you to get blindsided. You will have some time, albeit limited, to put together your responses to the questions I'm sure you'll be getting from the press. I don't expect you to say thank you, but you do have to understand the predicament your large number of denials has put me in. I couldn't really stand by the bank when the evidence of racial discrimination is pretty clear."

Teddy's chest was about to explode. "Oh, so we've already been convicted of discrimination in the court of public opinion, according to you? Is that right?"

The In-House Politician

Pastor Lloyd was now in full defense mode. "You're a former politician yourself, so you know what it's all about. Please understand. This is not personal."

"Not personal? Really? I can't imagine anything more personal than to accuse me and my bank of racial discrimination before all the facts are out in the open. How about this for not being personal—you may have just gotten me fired from my job! How's that for not being personal? I'll make sure I tell my wife and kids that you said it wasn't personal.

"You know, Pastor Lloyd, I've spent my entire professional life trying to make things better for my constituents, and for our bank's customers and the communities they live and work in. This is like a knife through my heart. If I ever recover from this, and I'm not sure I ever will, it's going to be hard for me to ever think about doing the right thing again, without remembering how all this good work went to shit so fast. I hope you can live with yourself."

Teddy hung up the phone and put his face in his hands. He took a moment and a few deep breaths and felt his pulse. He pulled a handful of Tums from his desk drawer and began to main-line them. He buzzed Kelly to come in and told her to get him in to see the Chairman right away. He said it wasn't a matter of life or death—it was worse than that.

Chapter 32

No doubt Teddy was having a bad day. After that phone call with Pastor Lloyd, he was wondering if these next few days were going to be the worst of his life. You just never know what's down the road. And Tom was about to pile on.

About the same time he saw Teddy heading for the elevator Tom's phone rang. There was sobbing on the other end of the line. He had given Millie Ogletree his personal number so she could call him directly, or leave her voice message on his direct line. No intermediary messenger involved. He couldn't imagine what the problem might be, but she let him know right away. Her loan application had been rejected. She received an adverse action notice in last night's mail, but by the time she composed herself, and presumably had spoken with her brother Pastor Lloyd, it was after regular business hours. So, rather than leaving Tom an ugly voicemail, she decided to wait and call him this morning.

Tom tried not to get too emotionally involved with his customers, but in the case of Millie Ogletree, he had grown very fond of her and her efforts to become a homeowner late in life in order to protect her daughter's and her granddaughter's futures. Tom's specific recollection of events was that Porzio was going to send her file down to Porter and advise him to approve it. Porzio had taken the file from him and said those exact words. Teddy was a witness. They had celebrated their victory, such as it was, in the elevator ride back to their offices. So, why would Millie have

The In-House Politician

received a denial if the bank's Chief Credit Policy Officer, and Porter's boss, approved it?

Under the circumstances, Tom apologized to Millie as best he could, and indicated that it was his understanding that her loan had been approved. His only consolation to her was that there must have been some kind of internal mix-up in the processing system. Trying to remain calm, Tom asked Millie to tell him what boxes were checked off on the adverse action notice indicating the reasons for the denial. By now Millie's sobbing had turned into a whispered reprimand. And he couldn't blame her for it. She told him that both she and her daughter Karen had received separate notices. Both notifications had the same boxes checked off for credit, liquid assets, and other, as the reasons for denial.

It was the "other" that had Tom flummoxed since he thought he knew her file inside out. It was killing him that he might have missed something that would have prevented the loan from being approved. But then, what was the point? The loan was approved by Porzio. What the fuck was going on here? So Tom told Millie that he needed to speak with some folks inside the bank to better understand what might have happened. He asked her to sit tight and be patient until he got back to her. He apologized once again for the misunderstanding. Tom said, if it was in his power to do so, he would get her loan application turned around as quickly as he could.

Tom was well aware that Teddy had received some bad news earlier this morning, he just didn't know what it was all about. But he knew if he liked his paycheck, he should steer clear of him for the time being. The question then became, should Tom go down to Porter's office and slug it out with him directly? He was not about to

253

put a call in to Porzio, since as far as Tom could tell, he still didn't even know his name. That call would have to come from Teddy. So Tom put on his body armor and walked down to Kelly's desk and said he needed to see Teddy. She gave him the look that confirmed his worst fears. No one was getting in to see him today. She said he was currently on his way up to see the Chairman, and he told her to clear his schedule for the rest of the day. So Tom knew right then he was handling this one on his own—at least for now. While he felt the adrenalin pumping through his body, Tom laughed and thought this was why they paid him the big bucks. Right!

If Porter was in his office, the next few minutes might determine whether Tom would still have a job by the end of the day. And as much as he wanted to lay him out in front of all of his minions, Tom decided that would not be the most professional way of handling the situation. But if he failed to get Porter to turn around the file, his job wouldn't be worth two cents to Teddy anyway, so, what the hell. Why not?

When he arrived on the mortgage department's floor, Tom could see Porter was not in his office. He didn't see him elsewhere on the floor, so he was either out for the day, in a meeting elsewhere, or, God forbid, in the men's room. Tom had this scene flash in front of his eyes of so many awful movies where the good guy takes out the bad guy in the men's room. It was just a flash and it quickly passed.

Tom saw that Tina was in her office and thought she might know what had happened with Millie's file. She didn't seem too happy to see him and tried not to make eye contact. But it was too late. Tom was already inside her office.

Conversations on files that had already been decisioned were frowned upon with any mortgage department staff other than Porter himself. His rules. But how did she know what Tom wanted to talk with her about, other than her knowledge of her boss's whereabouts? She didn't, but she still had that guilty look on her face. She said she had seen him earlier in the morning, but didn't know where he was at the moment. They walked together down to Porter's office to investigate further, but the best they could gather was that he was somewhere in the building since his briefcase was behind his desk on the credenza. His assistant confirmed he was in the building, but she did not know where he was at the moment. And Tom was not about to check the men's room.

Tom and Tina walked back to her office. Even though she didn't invite him, he took the liberty and followed her in anyway. He asked her if she was familiar with the Mildred Ogletree file. It was difficult to believe that, due to its political sensitivity, this file had not touched her desk—but you never knew. She was playing for time and said that name didn't ring a bell. She turned and pulled up the file on her computer. And there it was in all its glory. A denial with comments indicating that the file had been underwritten by Tom, with his name in plain sight.

In response to his question, Tina indicated there was no note in the computer file from Peter Porzio's office. The reasons for denial were just as Millie had stated to him on the phone: credit, liquid assets and other. He tried to remain calm and not accuse Tina of anything, but asked her again if she was familiar with the file. She could read his body language and temperament. Tom was close to losing control. Her response was that she now recalled Porter mentioning it in passing, but she was not involved in the final decision. That wasn't a no, in Tom's book.

Just then, Porter poked his head into Tina's office and asked what they were talking about. Tom said, "We were discussing the Mildred Ogletree loan application." Porter's complexion turned ashen and he said, "Why don't you come down to my office? Tina wasn't involved with that file."

Walking to Porter's office, neither of them considered the other person as worthy of proper name recognition. If they had, they would have been courteous enough to at least call each other by their first names—as business colleagues normally do. Tom had no idea how Porter referred to him when he wasn't around, and hopefully Porter had not heard that Tom had nicknamed him Marley. But at this point in their relationship, Tom really didn't give a shit. Most likely, things were about to get ugly.

When they got inside his office, Porter closed the door. Before they both sat down, Tom said, "How is it possible that this file could have been denied when it was approved by your boss, Peter Porzio?"

Porter had a boyish smirk on his face and said, "I don't know anything about that. If the loan was denied, I'm sure it was for legitimate reasons."

It was now time for Tom to actually call him by his name, so that he knew he was as serious as a heart attack. In as firm a voice as he could, Tom said, "Porter, my boss Teddy DeMarco and I met with your boss, Peter Porzio, a week ago. He personally took the file from me at that meeting and indicated to us, in very clear terms, that he was going to send it down to you to approve. Please tell me how that message could have gotten screwed up?"

"Beats the heck out of me," he said smugly. "I wasn't at that meeting, so I'll have to take your word for it."

Tom looked at him with a stare that his wife always laughed at, but he thought it was effective when he needed it in meetings. He said, "So, are you telling me that Peter Porzio had no communication with you on this loan?"

Porter's body language was starting to twist a bit. He said, "That's right. We were a bit surprised when the file came down to us in an interoffice envelope from Peter's office, but that happens from time to time. No big deal. We didn't think anything more about it."

Tom was slowly losing it and there were no other adults in the room. He said, "Really!? There was no note on the file, or follow-up phone call, or email message from Peter advising you to approve this loan?"

"I don't recall any message like that from Peter." He buzzed Tina to ask her to find the hard copy of the Mildred Ogletree file and bring it into his office.

Porter said, "I can assure you if there was a note on the file and we got it wrong, I will personally apologize to the applicant. And if I got it wrong, then I guess I'm in big trouble with Peter, and I can assure you I don't like being in trouble with the Chief Credit Policy Officer."

"Well, I was there at the meeting with Peter and Teddy, and I can assure you that when he took the file from me, we left his office with the full understanding that he was going to tell you to approve the file. His exact words were, 'I'll send it down to Porter and have him put it through the system to spit out the approval.' Those were his exact words. There are all kinds of political ramifications associated with this file, and despite the fact that this specific application is not the strongest one we've seen in the affordable mortgage program, your boss said "Okay." This denial is a nightmare for Teddy and me.

I haven't been able to get the message through to him yet. But I can assure you he's going to go through the roof. How he handles it directly with your boss is up to him. I'm just trying to get this right for the borrower before the shit hits the fan."

At this point, Tina arrived with the file and handed it to Porter. He said, "Thanks," which indicated he no longer needed her. Without being asked, Tina left and closed the door behind her.

When Porter opened the file, on the left side Tom could see his improvised underwriting sheet with his pros and cons columns, as well as his compensating factors on the bottom of the page. Porter smirked and rolled his eyes at this before looking at the opposite side of the file to review the formal reasons for denial listed on the adverse action notice. Then he looked back to the left side of the file and lifted up Tom's underwriting sheet to review all the reasons for denial. Porter then recalled that what he was really looking for was any correspondence in the file from his boss.

He quickly rifled through some of the pages clipped in the file, looked up, and said, "I don't see anything in the file from Peter saying that we should approve this loan. And without anything from him, this loan would certainly be denied. No question about it."

Tom sank down in his chair and thought he was about to commit murder. Fortunately, the feeling passed. He asked if he could see the file since he'd been the one who had underwritten it and had presented it to Peter Porzio for approval. Porter handed it over. But as he was doing so he said, "It's difficult for me to believe that, after reviewing this file, Peter would have told me to approve it."

As much as Tom disliked Porter, he didn't recall ever lying to him about the quality of a loan file. So he came clean and said, "Well, I

The In-House Politician

wouldn't exactly say Peter reviewed the file. It was a quick meeting. Once he found out the loan amount was so small, he really didn't require a full presentation. Teddy reminded him of the political sensitivity of having the loan approved. He took the file from me and said he would take care of it with you."

There was an awkward silence while Tom searched through the file to see if he could find any kind of a message from Porzio. There was nothing. That was when Tom asked Porter to check with his assistant to see if she recalled any note from Porzio attached to the file, which would have come in the interoffice envelope. He got up from his desk and quizzed his assistant, but Tom went with him to make sure the question he asked of her did not include a wink of the eye. She had no recollection of anything from Porzio. She also reminded him that the file had arrived on her desk about a week ago. It was difficult to recall that far back. It seemed like Tina and Porter's secretary had their stories well-rehearsed. Or was Tom just being paranoid?

He had nowhere else to go now. Back in Porter's office, he asked him to review the file with him in the off chance he could convince him of the merits of Millie's application. Why not give it a shot? If Tom was going down, he wasn't going down without a fight.

As Porter looked through the file, all he could do was shake his head. As expected, he said Tom was too generous in giving the applicant credit for $300 a month in income from her housecleaning business. There was no official documentation in the file to support giving her credit for any of that income. It was a cash business and he wouldn't give her credit for any of it, thus increasing her monthly debt to income ratio to an unacceptable level. However, he said he reluctantly let the borrower's debt ratios slide in the reasons for denial.

He also said that the bank had never approved a loan with essentially no equity coming from the borrowers. He could tell it was a gift for the down payment, which had just recently appeared in Pastor Lloyd's account. Porter probably figured the funds had come from the seller, but Tom wasn't about to give him that one for free.

It was clear from Porter's quick study of the file, and from his comments, that he was very familiar with this case. When he learned through Teddy that Porzio had said he could handle the underwriting of Millie's file, Tom knew in his heart of hearts that it wouldn't sit well with his good buddy and head of the mortgage department, Porter McMahon AKA Marley.

It was clear to him that Porter had completed a thorough review of the file just to see if Tom had any business underwriting loans. Tom really didn't care what Porter thought of his abilities. Tom was considering whether Porter had gone rogue and completely disobeyed his boss's direction, or was there some collusion going on between him and his boss? Was it possible that Porzio had winked and let him know he wouldn't be reprimanded if he couldn't find a way to approve the Ogletree loan? Porzio and Teddy weren't exactly bosom buddies. Either way, Teddy was going to explode and Tom would end up taking the brunt of it. And why not? He was responsible for getting this loan through the system.

Before he left Porter's office, Tom wanted to satisfy himself that in some ways, Millie's application had merit, and given the right circumstances, might get a green light. This is what he was in business for—to make homeowners out of folks who really wanted it, but hadn't been dealt a great hand. So he asked Porter why he wouldn't have given Millie credit for her side housecleaning business, and why he couldn't look the other way on the down payment assistance she had received from her brother. Tom admitted there were plenty of credit issues related to Millie's daughter Karen, who, he reminded Porter, had been through a really rough time of it, but seemed to be getting her act together. Millie had good and consistent income from the pension, social security, and rental income. Karen's income from the new job would just be gravy. But Porter shrugged his shoulders and said he understood all the character issues related to this loan. Then, sounding as if he actually wanted to be considered human, said, "I've seen plenty of your affordable mortgage program loans come through the system and we've approved some of them. You've gotten us to reverse our initial decision with a good case for the borrower's character. But in this case, even if we wanted to approve it as a character loan, we couldn't for the other reasons." He put the word "other" in air quotes.

"Yes, I was curious about what those other reasons were." There were no air quotes in Tom's response.

Porter responded with a curt, "Well, it wasn't other reasons, plural—just one other reason. It was the issue of a nearby incompatible land use. We've just been approved for delegated underwriting by Freddie Mac, which means they buy our loans prior to reviewing our underwriting, which is done after the purchase. So, we have to be perfect on all our loans, or they will require that we repurchase them. We recently installed an automated underwriting system that spits out all exceptions to policy, and in this case it identified the subject property as having a nearby incompatible land use."

Tom was incredulous, and began stammering. When he finally got his teeth, tongue, mouth, and brain in sync, he said, "First of all, you know you're not supposed to be using automated underwriting for any of our affordable mortgage program loans. They're to be manually underwritten. We all know that these loans don't fit the standard underwriting criteria you use for your secondary market product. We're not selling any of these loans, and we're using more flexible underwriting guidelines. And secondly, what the fuck is a 'nearby incompatible land use?'" This time Tom did use air quotes.

Porter was a bit shaken with Tom's use of profanity. He got a little red in the face, then recovered, and tried to soldier on. He said, "We're training all our staff on the use of the new automated underwriting system, so all the loans we process go through that system—your loans included. Now, we've coded your loans for manual underwriting after they go through the automated system, so that we can separate them out from the traditional portfolio. This loan was flagged for many different reasons, including the property being located near an incompatible land use."

"Okay," Tom said. "I'll bite. To reiterate, what the fuck is a nearby incompatible land use?"

This time Porter shrugged it off. "A nearby incompatible land use means that the property Mrs. Ogletree was hoping to buy is located close to a non-residential commercial property that will have a detrimental effect on the subject property's future marketability."

Tom said, "You've got to be kidding! What the hell are you talking about? What nearby incompatible land use?"

Porter looked at the appraisal. "In this case, it's a gas station. Apparently, the subject property is located very close to a gas station. According to the appraiser's comments, there appears to be just one property between it and a gas station."

The In-House Politician

Now Tom remembered. Yup! When he left Millie's house, he stopped to get gas in that very same station. It was, in fact, very close to her place.

Tom was now in full Bolshevik mode. Sally Kessler would have been proud of him. He said, "So you're telling me that any person wanting to buy a house, let's say in any given urban neighborhood of this country, which will most likely be near some other non-residential land uses, will be prevented from doing so because of some underwriting theory that assumes its proximity to a non-residential land use will have a detrimental effect on its future value? That's pure unadulterated bullshit! Who thinks this shit up? Is there some geek down there in DC who sits around with his or her made-up algorithm calculating the probability that nearby incompatible land uses are a bad thing for homebuyers? Oh, right! White folks would never want to buy a residential property that's near a gas station! God forbid! No way! Well, that's unless you're a White landlord, looking to rent out the property to some unsuspecting Black folks who don't know any better than to live near a gas station. We still do need gas stations, right? Those Black folks living in that property still need to put gas in their cars to get to their jobs just like the rest of us White folks, right? They've got to pay the rent, right?"

Tom was ranting now, and needed to stop before he said or did something he would regret. He wanted to give Porter McMahon a physical attitude adjustment he would not soon forget. In fact, Tom was remembering how good it felt to take down an opposing running back with a great tackle. His coaches had always instilled in him the need for aggressive behavior when playing defense. Tom was wondering how much longer he could keep those instincts under control.

It was time to leave. He couldn't take any more of this. As he got up, Tom looked at Porter. "Are you going to reach out to your boss to find out if there was some misunderstanding about whether you were supposed approve the loan to Mildred Ogletree?"

Porter had now returned to full automaton mode. "No. I have delegated authority to underwrite and decision all mortgage loans under the terms of the bank's approved credit policy. I received no direction on this loan from Peter and, as such, I don't feel the need to question him about it."

Tom wanted to give Porter the middle finger, but there were too many staff on the floor who might witness his expletive. As he opened the door, Tom turned and said in as loud and sarcastic a tone as he could muster, "Porter, I know we haven't seen eye to eye on a lot of the mortgages we've put through under the affordable mortgage program, but Teddy and I really needed this one. And you knew it. Once again, you've shown us your true colors. Thanks so much for all your help here."

Tom then proceeded to the elevators. When the door opened, he saw Teddy standing there with his head down. They were alone. After the door closed, Tom said, "Sorry to pile on, Teddy, since we assume you got some bad news earlier, but you need to know that Millie Ogletree called me this morning saying her loan had been denied."

Teddy looked up as if seeking divine intervention.

Tom continued. "I just came from a fun meeting with Porter. He claimed he'd heard nothing from Porzio about approving Millie's loan. And get this: as far as Porter is concerned, he sees no reason to follow up with Porzio."

Tom had seen Teddy upset before, when his head was seemingly about to explode. But this was not one of those times. He had a look of resignation, the look of someone about to cry. But he recovered quickly. As the elevator door opened, he said, "Let's meet later this afternoon to debrief. I need some time to—well—"

"Got it. Just let me know what time."

As he walked towards his office, Teddy shook his head and said very calmly, "Can this day get any worse?

Chapter 33

By now Nick was playing the role of go-between with Alex and Sally since Michelle was no longer around. Nick was still dressed in his black funeral attire and was working alone since his brother Joe was on assignment in Italy. Alex didn't ask where Joe was, especially since he couldn't tell them apart anyway.

Nick would deliver handwritten notes from Alex to Sally through all kinds of clandestine operations. Typically, he would sit outside her office waiting for her acolytes to leave and then provide her with the note. Other times, he would follow her walking down the street until she was alone, which scared the hell out of her when he stopped and confronted her. On one occasion, he actually pulled her over at a traffic light by showing her a fake police badge. This really upset her since she thought she was about to be arrested.

But Sally had to hand it to Alex. He was right about 1NEB and the mortgage report that ended up in the hands of Pastor Lloyd. Alex also seemed to have a contact at *The Examiner*, which could be useful to both of them in the future. So she put up with the indignities of being confronted by this weird guy who never said a word and delivered messages from Alex.

This note from Alex was clear and concise. It began with, "Don't ever do that again. I told you I wanted to know in advance if you were going to do anything rash with the information I provided to you. I can't be caught off guard like that. I congratulate you on convincing Ogletree to give the money back to the bank. What else do you have planned?"

The In-House Politician

Sally assumed that Alex was reprimanding her for convincing Pastor Lloyd to hold a press conference related to the bank's high number of minority denials, but she really didn't care what he thought about this development. He could go to hell as far as she was concerned.

It was clear that Alex wanted a response because the delivery man was not leaving until he got one. What was also clear was that Alex had someone inside Pastor Lloyd's campaign. How else could he know that Lloyd was going to announce the return of the bank's donation? She wasn't happy about having to reveal her plans to him, but the delivery guy had a menacing look on his face. Sally wrote a quick note back to Alex saying that she was planning a demonstration in front of 1NEBs headquarters tomorrow to occur right after Pastor Lloyd's press conference. And if he didn't like it, he could go fuck himself.

Chapter 34

Teddy's head was spinning. After hearing from Ogletree and learning of his planned press conference for tomorrow morning the, Chairman had been understanding, but not happy. He gave Teddy the task of coming up with some recommendations on how to increase minority approvals and reducing the denials under the affordable mortgage plan. The Chairman also said he would immediately and separately meet with Peter Porzio to get to the bottom of why there were so many rejections of African American applications.

That Teddy had come away from this meeting still having a job seemed to him like a minor miracle. And since he hadn't known about the Millie Ogletree loan decision at the time of his meeting with the Chairman, he decided to give it some time before piling on Porzio. Teddy would wait until the Chairman had ripped the Vice Chairman and Chief Credit Policy Officer a new one. Porzio would then be ripe for a little heart-to-heart chat.

Kelly knocked on Tom's office door and advised him that Teddy wanted to see him and Althea at 3 pm. She would let Althea know.

Tom was still reeling from the Millie loan decision and his "Come to Jesus" meeting with Porter McMahon. Althea knew that things had turned ugly based on the screaming coming from Teddy's office earlier in the morning. But when Tom advised her on the outcome of his meeting with Porter regarding Millie Ogletree's loan decision, she became a full-fledged member of the hit squad wanting to know what the assassination plans were for Marley. Hell, she had started this whole thing in the first place by introducing the team to Pastor Lloyd and MJED. Now, Millie Ogletree's loan was an unintended casualty, as well as, who knows, the entire relationship with MJED. This was personal to Althea and she was ready for payback.

When they entered Teddy's office, they were pleasantly surprised to find him in a semi-good mood. He wasn't brooding or slamming things around. In fact, there appeared to be a smile on his face. They never knew what to expect from the man.

After Teddy brought them up to speed, primarily for Althea's benefit, he did his best impression of a peacemaker in order to calm her down. He asked Tom to explain what he thought might have happened to Millie's loan. It appeared that Teddy was more interested in how Porter's denial of the loan might have played into Pastor Lloyd's decision to hold the press conference. Tom's response was simple. "I have no idea if Pastor Lloyd even knew about his mother's rejection when he called you. You said he didn't mention it. But he was in possession of a mortgage department report, right? That's all he needed. And some encouragement from Sally, of course. I doubt his mother's loan denial would have been the last straw. My guess is that he already knew what he was going to do."

Teddy seemed nonplussed with Tom's speculation. They were just thinking out loud. He said, "Well, just so you know, I met with the Chairman earlier. I suspect that we'll be getting a more responsive Peter Porzio and Porter McMahon in the near future. And based on this, we should be able to get Millie Ogletree's loan decision turned around in a day or so. I just want to wait on my discussion with Porzio until after he meets with the Chairman. I'd love to be a fly on the wall for that meeting."

Then Teddy got down to business. He said the Chairman wanted to hear from them with recommendations for how to increase the number of minority approvals in the affordable mortgage program. This was a topic Tom had spent plenty of time thinking about, and he was ready with some suggestions. First, he said the bank should consider going to a 100 percent financing product since cash savings for the down payment was the biggest hurdle for most borrowers. Second, he indicated that Teddy should convince the Chairman to move all final credit decisions to his department, thus removing the mortgage department from its authority over the portfolio.

Surprisingly, Teddy did not throw Tom out of his office. Once again, he asked if Tom had always remembered to wear a helmet during his playing days. He looked over at Althea to get her reaction to Tom's proposal. She liked the idea of the department gaining control over the credit approval process, but she had reservations about introducing a 100 percent financing product. She said, "That kind of new product would essentially be an admission that we failed. It would say that the only way income-eligible minorities can qualify for a mortgage is if we give it to them—I mean the whole amount. No sacrifices to be made by these applicants. I think it would send a very bad message."

From his body language, Teddy seemed to agree with Althea and was mulling over his options. "What do you think Scrooge and Marley's response would be to this idea?" he asked. Teddy was using their nicknames more often now since they had shown their true colors.

Tom said, "They'll both shit in their pants at first. I know for sure that Marley will throw a hissy fit thinking that part of his mortgage authority is being taken away from him. But once he realizes that we're relieving him of loans that may end up bringing down the overall performance of his pristine lily-white portfolio, he'll come around and see it as a good thing. He would no longer have the responsibility, or the burden, of our loans. As for Scrooge, I really can't say. You know how much he hates CRA and our agreement with PUMP. He'll complain bitterly to the Chairman about it. But other than that, well, Scrooge is your guy. If you recall, he still doesn't even know my name."

Teddy looked at Tom with a smirk and was mercifully restrained in his comeback. He said, "Tom, I was just trying to protect you. Believe me, you don't want to be on the credit king's radar."

Tom paused for a moment, then continued his pitch. "We're going to need a big win once the news about our high number of minority loan denials goes public tomorrow. You know we're gonna take some heat from Sally Kessler. We need something to keep her off our backs, right?"

Teddy laughed. "That's what I'm afraid of. Anything that makes Sally Kessler happy isn't going to please the powers that be inside this bank. So, this 100 percent financing you're suggesting—you mean the borrowers don't need any down payment? Meaning we finance the entire purchase price? There's no equity coming from the borrowers at all?"

"Yup," Althea chimed in. "And that's why I don't like it."

Teddy said, "No equity from the borrowers violates the very core principles we bankers operate under. Our borrowers have to have some skin in the game. You know I'm right about that, Tom. There's no way any credit officer in this bank is going to be okay with the idea of 100 percent financing. Hell, I'm not good with it either. And while it may not be politically correct to say this, I'm gonna say it anyway. Rental housing may be a right, but homeownership is not. It's a privilege. People need to make some sacrifices and save up money for a down payment and closing costs if they want to become homeowners. The American dream of homeownership is not a freebie. I'm not ready to go to the Chairman with your 100 percent financing recommendation."

Althea agreed. "Amen to that."

Tom wasn't surprised with her response. "Okay then. What about a 97 percent financing product, so our borrowers only need to have a three percent down payment? At the margin, we might get a few more approvals out of it."

Teddy responded quickly. "Yes, yes, I got that. But let's think about that for a minute. How's the profile of a 3 percent down borrower going to look any different than a 5 percent down borrower? And don't tell me the 2 percent difference is going to do it. I'm betting you wouldn't want a portfolio full of 100 percent loans to administer, or 97 percenters for that matter, right?"

Tom didn't have a chance to respond. There was a knock on the door. It was Kelly and she came right in and said, "Alex Scarduzo is on the phone and he says it's very important and time sensitive."

Teddy said, "Tell Alex I'll be right with him."

Althea and Tom took this as their cue to leave.

As they left Teddy said, "We'll get back to this tomorrow."

Chapter 35

Teddy was still trying to recover from the day's events and was in no mood to play the "what's new" game with Alex. Against his better judgment he picked up the phone. After all, Kelly said Alex thought it important enough to interrupt his staff meeting. Teddy was glad he did.

Alex came right out with it. He said, "Hey, my friend. I've got some news that's probably not going to make your day."

Teddy couldn't help himself. "Alex, take a number. Once you tell me your bad news, I'll let you know how it ranks on a scale of 1 to 10. Today has been one of those days you never want to relive. So, take your best shot and let me have it."

Teddy's reaction was not quite what Alex expected. He said, "Well, I'm sorry to be piling on, but you can expect demonstrators from PUMP to be picketing in front of the bank's headquarters tomorrow morning. They're coordinating their protest to occur right after the press conference being held by Pastor Lloyd in the morning. But I guess you already know about that, right?"

"Yes sir," Teddy said. "Got that call earlier today directly from the Man of God himself. So, PUMP is going to protest in front of the bank tomorrow, is that what you're telling me?"

Alex was amazed by the calmness with which Teddy seemed to be taking this revelation. Alex said, "Yes, that's what I'm saying. Sorry."

Teddy needed to end the call as quickly as he could without appearing ungrateful. He thanked Alex for the intel and indicated he needed to get to work on this new development. He purposely did not respond with the typical "I owe you one." That was understood.

But Alex wasn't done yet. "Just one more quick thing. Do you need any help with crowd control tomorrow? We've got some guys here who are pretty good at that kind of thing, if you know what I mean. I can make them available to you for tomorrow's protest, if you need them."

Teddy laughed and said, "Thanks, Alex, but I think our security team here at the bank can handle it. I don't expect the PUMP demonstrators will be armed and dangerous."

Alex reiterated the offer before they hung up. He was proud of himself knowing that he'd collected some IOU points with Teddy, which could be useful in the future. Alex also knew that this was not the time to drill Teddy for having made a PAC contribution to his likely opponent in the election. Ogletree's press conference in the morning would be enough punishment and he guessed that Teddy had learned his lesson. However, Alex was unsure of whether Ogletree's announcement would help him or hurt him. Alex didn't need a martyr rising up from the ashes with more political strength.

Teddy took a deep breath. He was right. The day could get worse, and it did. He thought he still had a good enough relationship with Sally Kessler that she would at least have given him a heads-up before a demonstration in front of the bank. This kind of sneak attack confirmed that they were officially at war. No more pretense and no more mercy. As far as he was concerned, he would make sure the bank held up its end of the agreement—no more, no less. But he would not extend himself or the bank beyond it. He would not negotiate any more agreements with her, ever. He was done with Sally Kessler.

The In-House Politician

And then it dawned on him. How was it that Alex Scarduzo knew about the planned demonstration? But he'd get back to that question later.

Teddy's first call was to the Chairman to let him know about the protest in the morning. He even took the risk of recommending that the Chairman consider working remotely tomorrow so he wouldn't have to interact with PUMP and its picket line. No dice. If Teddy didn't know better, he might have thought the Chairman was looking for an opportunity for a face-to-face debate with the protesters. No matter, though, since the Chairman's limo always brought him into the bank through the underground parking garage. The Chairman and the Bolsheviks would never have to greet each other unless the big boss decided to personally say hello and offer them a toaster for any new deposits.

The Chairman said he would call down to Human Resources Department to have them let all employees know to enter the building from the rear in the morning. There was nothing they could do for the customers except to plan on having the Newark Police Department on site to control the protesters and access to the lobby. The Chairman also advised Teddy that he wanted him to serve as spokesperson if the media wanted someone from the bank to speak in front of the TV cameras.

Teddy also wondered if Pastor Lloyd knew about Sally's planned protest tomorrow. Had Ogletree given Sally the green light to do whatever she thought best to get the message out about the bank's alleged discrimination? Really, what was he thinking? Sally never asked permission. But if Pastor Lloyd knew about the PUMP protest and didn't alert him to it in their earlier phone call, well, then perhaps he was not the kind of person to represent New Jersey in Congress after all. No one, including Pastor Lloyd and Sally Kessler, seemed to want to sit down and talk about these issues. Everyone wanted their 15 minutes of fame, and all at the bank's expense.

Teddy was in a mood to let the whole world know what he thought of Pastor Lloyd Ogletree and Sally Kessler. He needed to draft some remarks just in case the TV cameras were pointed in his direction. This was personal.

Chapter 36

The press conference began promptly at 10 am.

Sally had wanted to attend, but Pastor Lloyd's campaign manager said there might be a conflict since it was her CRA agreement with the bank that had led to all of this. As a result, there might be some awkward questions that might be difficult to answer, especially with her in the room.

Ogletree's campaign staff was trying to let Sally Kessler down easy. All of Pastor Lloyd's advisors were of the opinion that Sally and her comrades were far too radical and might cause some voters and contributors to think twice about the connection between the two camps. And now that Sally was disinvited from the press conference, she decided to hold her own protest, with or without the blessing of Pastor Lloyd. Indeed, Sally hoped she would get some good air time with the TV cameras in front of 1NEB's main office. She had, of course, notified the press.

It was a dark, overcast, and blustery day, so Pastor Lloyd decided to move the press conference inside. There was a podium for him to speak from and plenty of room for the TV cameras. Extra chairs were brought in to seat all the reporters expected.

Pastor Lloyd knew how to play his part. He was dressed in his all-black minister ensemble and his white clerical collar. He was a Man of God, first and foremost, and wanted all the camera shots to reflect this. He looked like he was getting ready to deliver a long sermon—which he was. It just wasn't Sunday and the reporters would not be following his remarks with a chorus of Hallelujahs and Amens.

As he strode up to the podium, Pastor Lloyd rolled up a sheet of paper to hold in his hand as a prop. He used this method many times to personally connect with his audience by speaking without notes. He rehearsed and memorized his message and had prepared a summary of his remarks for distribution to the press. However, he decided not to distribute his written remarks until he finished speaking. These reporters needed to work for their stories by listening to what he had to say, rather than prepare them from the handouts.

After Pastor Lloyd greeted everyone and said thank you to all who were in attendance, he began his remarks. "I'm going to keep this short because I know you all have deadlines to meet. I'm announcing today that I will be returning the campaign contribution I received from First Northeastern Bank. This bank has accomplished some good things for our communities. But these positive accomplishments do not outweigh how the bank has been treating many African American borrowers recently." He paused to heighten the drama. He knew how to deliver a sermon.

He raised his hand, the one holding the rolled-up paper indicating his proof, and continued. "I am in possession of a report here that shows that over the past six months, 1NEB has been denying three African American mortgage applications for every one White application. Additionally, the bank has been rejecting more than two Latino mortgage applications for every White application declined. It's pretty frightening when you look at these numbers in the aggregate. And the bank is doing this under the terms of a formal agreement to provide below-market rate loans with more flexible underwriting

The In-House Politician

standards. Now, some of you might say that's an oversimplification—there may be legitimate reasons for all these denials. Perhaps that's true for some of these applicants, but I doubt it's true for all of them. And I think the message is pretty clear. First Northeastern Bank is discriminating against minority homebuyers and I cannot be a party to this any longer."

Another pause for more drama. "Furthermore, and in full disclosure, my fellow pastors and I, as members of the African American Ministry for Justice and Economic Development, have been working with the bank to get as many new minority homebuyers approved as possible. You see, the bank is operating under the terms of a CRA agreement, in which they agreed to offer some $25 million in mortgages to first-time homebuyers in the cities of New Jersey. In return for entering into this agreement, the bank was permitted to buy another bank and increase its size and market presence.

"When we began working with the bank's staff on what they referred to as this new affordable mortgage program, they explained to us that they would be using more flexible underwriting standards. Those flexible underwriting guidelines included such things as below-market interest rates, low down payments, no mortgage insurance, and a greater understanding of some of the credit issues faced by many first-time minority homebuyers."

He took a long sip of water before continuing. "In order for the bank to reach its goal of $25 million mortgages, representatives of 1NEB came to us, as leaders in the minority community, to help get the word out. We were very successful in helping the bank market this program. But the results are not good. The numbers don't lie. The bank has denied more minority loans than it has approved. A lot more. Now you can't tell me that's just the way it is. If you do, then you have no clue what institutional racism and redlining is all about. And I'll leave it at that."

Pastor Lloyd dropped his head for a moment appearing to gather his thoughts. "One more item for your consideration. When the bank's examiners come in and see what it's been doing, I suspect I won't be the only one calling into question its mortgage lending practices. Now, I don't want to get too far out on a limb on this, because you don't always hear about what's going on in the background between a bank and its regulator. So I would just ask that the regulator in charge of overseeing 1NEB to investigate how this bank has been operating, and to do whatever is necessary to make sure that its discriminatory practices are stopped and the responsible staff be held accountable."

Pastor Lloyd had their full attention. "While we're on the topic of First Northeastern Bank, I would like to single out Mr. Teddy DeMarco at the bank as one of the good guys in all of this. He's tried to do right by all our minority homebuyers, and has always done his best to overturn borderline cases. It's my understanding that Mr. DeMarco is not responsible for the final decisions on these loans. And while I'm not going to tell you how to write your stories, I don't want you to think everyone at 1NEB is bad. Like I said, Teddy DeMarco is one of the good guys there."

Pastor Lloyd walked out from behind the podium and leaned his elbow on its side. It was now time to campaign. "Finally, I want to take a moment to talk about banks acquiring other banks. All these mergers and acquisitions going on in the financial services industry may be good for the shareholders of these banks, but it's not good for our minority communities. Now, I know that I'm never going

The In-House Politician

to stop all these mergers, but I can tell you this. If I get elected, I promise that one of my first pieces of business in Congress will be to do whatever I can to make sure the banking industry is put on notice that we will be expecting more from them. Much more. These huge banks need to understand that we will not sit back and let them further disinvest in our minority communities. You see, whenever these big banks merge, the first thing they do is close branches in the Black and Hispanic neighborhoods. They say these branches are unprofitable and need to be closed in order to save money for the shareholders. We can't let this continue. The banking world needs to work with us to reinvest in our minority communities. And if they don't—well, perhaps Congress needs to strengthen the laws governing these mergers and make sure the banking industry understands what's at stake for them and our communities."

Pastor Lloyd bowed his head. When he looked up, he said, "Again, I thank you all for coming today, and you'll find a summary of my remarks in the back of the room, which you can pick up on your way out. So, with that I'll take a few questions."

The political reporter from *The Examiner* stood up. She was Joe Campbell's colleague. "Rev. Ogletree," she asked, "you seem to have some pretty specific data on the bank's approvals and denials. Can you tell us the source of this information?"

Pastor Lloyd knew this question was coming and was ready for it. "I don't reveal my sources, just like you don't reveal yours. Suffice it to say that we are very confident about the data we have in hand. If I wasn't sure of this, I wouldn't have called this press conference, and I wouldn't be returning the bank's campaign funds. I wasn't born with a silver spoon in my mouth like my opponents. All the campaign dollars I receive are precious. I need every penny I can get my hands on, as long as they come from donors I respect. However, in this case, I must say thanks, but no thanks to 1NEB.

"As for your question, we know this data is valid because most, if not all, the denials were made to applicants coming through our churches located around the state. My fellow pastors and I have been witnessing the large number of denials some time now. So it was time to act."

The Examiner reporter shouted out a follow-up question. "So if you and your fellow pastors are familiar with all the denials, then you're also familiar with all the approvals, as well, right? You aren't giving the bank any credit for making homeowners out of some of your church members? Far be it from me to be defending the bank, but it sounds like the bank's program was pretty generous. So why are you coming down so hard on them? It seems to me that the bank was trying to do the right thing, but, perhaps a lot of your homebuyers just weren't qualified."

Pastor Lloyd said, "Is there a question in there somewhere?"

"Yes," she said. "Did you review with the bank the reasons why so many loans were denied? And when did you get the notion the bank was denying more loans than it was approving? It seems to me that you should have been monitoring the numbers, just like the bank did. And, if you had this information for some time, why did it take you so long before you decided to return the campaign funds to the bank?"

Pastor Lloyd was a bit miffed at all these questions, but knew he couldn't lose his cool in front of the cameras. He took a deep breath and appeared to be getting his thoughts together. He said, "Once a loan is denied, the damage is done. It's impossible for borrowers

The In-House Politician

to improve their credit score fast enough to keep an application in process. It may take months for bad credit issues to be resolved, or for them to save up enough money for the additional down payment and closing costs. In the meantime, the property they were trying to buy has been sold to someone else. When we first met with the bank in order to understand how we might help market the program, we asked them if they would do everything they could to approve as many of our folks' loans as possible. They promised to do so, but you can see the results for yourselves. We have included the numbers of loans approved and denied over the past six months in the copy of my remarks." Pastor Lloyd did his best to avoid answering her last question, the one about why it took him so long to return the contribution. He was hoping no one else would pick up on that either.

For the moment no one else seemed interested in that topic, and that pleased him since there was no good answer to that one. He felt ashamed. He was no longer operating on his true north compass. In fact, Pastor Lloyd was now feeling like he needed to go somewhere and pray. He hadn't told any outright lies today, but he was feeling guilty about the timing of the political contribution and his decision to return the funds to the bank. He was questioning his own character and knew that others would do the same.

He said, "Okay, let's have just one more question."

The final question came from a reporter for the local *Ocean/Monmouth County Gazette*. It was a question Pastor Lloyd was hoping to avoid. The reporter asked, "So Rev. Ogletree, you have qualified for the upcoming debate and are currently leading in the polls. Why would you want to take on the banks? Do you really want the banking industry as an enemy?"

The way the reporter phrased the question left the door wide open. It was time to invoke the Lord. He said, "You see this collar I'm wearing? It doesn't allow me to bend to the will of political contributors. I prayed long and hard about this decision to return the money to the bank. And it wasn't easy. Like I said before, I need every dollar I can generate to get my message out to the voters of this district. My faith in the Lord is unshakable and He gave me the message that I could stand on His shoulders. I have no doubt that I am doing the right thing. The banking industry has nothing to fear from me if it does the right thing. We can work together to make things better as long as they understand that racial discrimination will not be tolerated, and low-income customers need branches in their neighborhoods to access all the same banking services that other folks have."

Pastor Lloyd was feeling good about how he had handled the press conference. But he would have to wait to see how the reporters wrote it up.

The divine inspiration took over. He couldn't help himself. He equated the "love thy neighbor" lesson from the parable of the Good Samaritan to the banking industry's need to love all its customers in the communities it served. And that, he said, "includes all who live in these communities, including the poor."

With that, Rev. Lloyd Ogletree, Pastor of the Evangelical Church of the Living God and Democratic candidate for Congress, adjourned the press conference with a "God bless you all."

Chapter 37

It took Sally Kessler about two hours to pull together her small army of true believers. They were slowly assembling in their warehouse in East Newark.

They still needed to make up a few more signs for this morning's protest. However, some of the PUMP members who had agreed to attend the demonstration were still AWOL. They had to drive in from longer distances, like Short Hills, Summit, and Livingston—the low-income boroughs of Essex County where the median price for a single-family home was somewhere north of a half million dollars. These were Sally's true believers. It is doubtful, however, that any of them, in their white privilege, ever experienced a nearby incompatible land use. And if they did, they promptly had their attorneys make it go away.

The problem with trying to pull off a demonstration like this in the middle of the day, and on a weekday, was that many of Sally's followers had full-time jobs. They couldn't just take the day off to improve the conditions of the poor. This left Sally with only those who were either retired, in college, independently wealthy stay-at-home Moms, and her staff. She was able to get commitments from twenty, but it was now 10:45 am and she had only eleven players in the dugout.

The signs were prepared and ready to go. She couldn't wait any longer for the stragglers since she had notified the press that the demonstration would begin at 11:00 am, and she had no intention of leaving the reporters at the site unattended. Sally did not coordinate the demonstration start time with Pastor Lloyd's press conference, but assumed it would be over by then. Pastor Lloyd's announcement was the trigger she needed for hitting the bank hard.

Sally's soldiers climbed into the two vans. She had planned the demonstration with military precision. Everyone knew their position and responsibility. This wasn't their first rodeo. The drivers of the two vans would pull up to the drop zone in front of the bank, permitting the protesters to quickly exit the vehicles, then the two wheelmen would make a U-turn and pull the vans across the street from the site where they would watch and videotape the proceedings in the event the police or security guards became overzealous in their crowd control measures. PUMP would then have visual proof of any police brutality. The drivers were also stationed there for a quick getaway, if required. This left Sally with nine demonstrators, including herself, four with signs, and the remainder in the supporting roles of marchers, protestors, and loud voices to help keep up the rants and chants.

As the protest began, Teddy's staff watched the events play out from a vantage point just outside of his office. A big picture window that overlooked the main entrance of the bank provided them with a fairly good view. Tom thought one protester's sign was quite clever, and must have taken some time for the Bolsheviks to draft. The sign read,

"If You Need a Loan
There's No Debate
Don't Come Here
They Discriminate!"

Not bad! It needed one fewer syllable, or one more, depending on how you looked at it. Offensive, but still not a bad effort. The rest of the demonstrators' signs were pretty pedestrian. If Tom didn't know any better, they may have been standard signs PUMP kept in the warehouse and brought out for all their generic protests. There was a plain vanilla one that just said "**POWER to the PEOPLE,**" with the required raised fist and PUMP's logo and name on the bottom. And there was one that said, "**OPM – OTHER PEOPLE'S MONEY, THE DRUG BANKS ARE ADDICTED TO.**" Real original.

Tom thought the sign accusing the bank of discrimination to be effective, but offensive. In legal terms, it should have read the bank "allegedly" discriminates. But that was putting too fine a point on it for these Bolsheviks. Up until now, there was no proof of discrimination *per se*. Clearly, the number of minority loans Porter & Company had denied was high, and disproportionate to the number of White loans declined. However, any good banking attorney could make the case that all the loans denied were based on acceptable risk-related underwriting criteria. It was all perception now. The bank was already convicted in the court of public opinion. This was a black eye that would be hard to come back from. It made Tom pause to think that, perhaps, trying to do the right thing came with lots of unintended consequences.

The demonstration continued for about ten minutes before the Newark Police arrived and asked one of the demonstrators if they had a permit. Until then, the bank's security guards had done an excellent job of clearing paths for customers who had no idea what was going on, or there was another entrance around the corner in the rear of the building. Sally Kessler was nearby, but was unavailable to the police for the moment, since she was being interviewed by one of the major New York networks and could not be disturbed. The proximity of Newark to New York made it easy for the networks to hop across the river to see what PUMP was up to.

Next up for Sally was a quick interview with a Newark-based public television station—so the police would have to wait. Sally needed to get her Robin Hood message out before they would be ordered to disperse. And the police were smart enough to not get between Sally Kessler and a TV camera. That could be dangerous on many levels.

Of course they had no permit, which was the only way Sally and PUMP operated. She wanted to maintain the element of surprise. But she had learned, over a lifetime of protests, that when the police ordered you to disperse, it was always a healthy lifestyle choice to comply. Martyrdom was not her style. Scenes of police wielding their nightsticks and loading you into paddy wagons made for good press, but was not appreciated by the donors to the cause. And handcuffs were nasty on the wrists. Once the message had been delivered and the TV interviews concluded, she considered the protest a success. It was time to declare victory and move along.

As the demonstration was breaking up, Kelly tapped Tom on the shoulder and said Tina from the Mortgage Department was on his line. He told Kelly to let her know he'd call her back in a bit. Tom was still hoping to see Sally and her minions get arrested—but no cigar.

One of the onlookers, albeit with a self-interest, was Joe Campbell. He and his editor had talked about the best approach to this story and saw the earlier announcement by Pastor Lloyd as the headline. This demonstration by Sally Kessler and PUMP was just her way of trying to stay in the spotlight and remain relevant. Joe knew of the

The In-House Politician

connection between Sally and Pastor Lloyd, so he and his colleague who had attended the press conference agreed in advance to pool their notes and draft one article combining the two events.

It was now around noon and Teddy seemed to be handling the protest fairly well. He had no idea what Ogletree had said at his press conference and would have to view it on the evening news or wait to read it in tomorrow's edition of *The Examiner*. He called Tom into his office and told him to shut the door. He was on the speaker phone with Tom's favorite attorney, MC. They were summarizing the day's events thus far, and trying to assess the damage. MC was non-committal since she reported to the General Counsel. She indicated that he was a blithering mess, pounding on his desk and ready to jump out the window. According to him, any future acquisitions were now dead in the water. He was ranting that there was no scenario in which the bank's public image could be sufficiently restored for the investor community anytime soon. Or at least until this "discrimination" accusation was put to bed.

As if Tom wasn't in enough trouble already for being the point man on the affordable mortgage program, Teddy now had a new assignment for him, designed specifically to pull the plug on any remaining life-support machine he was relying on to save him. Teddy ordered Tom to call Sally Kessler and let her know the bank was going to sue her and PUMP for defamation since there was no proof of racial discrimination—unless, of course, she made a full and public apology. Tom was to tell her that she and PUMP had ruined the bank's reputation. The only saving grace to this assignment was that MC would be on the call with him, but only as a silent advisor. Her role was to be a witness to the conversation, and to give him hand signals if he was getting in over his head. Tom objected, "Over my head?! Really? MC's the attorney."

Tom stated very clearly that this was not an assignment he thought he was qualified to handle. He said, "Why not have MC make the call and me be the witness? She could introduce herself as bank counsel. Sounds more official than little old me, right?"

"Great idea," Teddy said, "but no. Sally Kessler knows you. She doesn't know MC. So it's gotta be you. And I know what you're thinking: why can't I make the call myself, right? Well, honestly, I need plausible deniability. I can't be the one making the threat. I promise, if this thing goes sideways, I'll protect you. Don't worry! Relax! I just want to put the fear of God in her."

Tom replied, "Well, you're sure putting it in me! So, does this mean that I can't invoke your name as the one who asked me to call her?"

"Really, Tom? She'll know who gave you the order to call. But do your best to keep my name out of it unless she brings me into it."

Then Tom spoke directly into the speaker phone. "MC, do we actually have a case of defamation here?"

She said, "Sure we do. But defamation is always difficult to prove. If she takes it to the press, well, it can make us look pretty bad in light of all that's happened today. Makes it look like we're hitting back because we're guilty. Filing a law suit against her is more of a threat than a reality. We'll have to see how she reacts to it."

Tom looked at Teddy. MC could get away with those remarks because she didn't report to him and, perhaps, she was trying her best to protect Tom from further danger. He would never know. Teddy's mind was made up. He'd been betrayed by someone he considered a colleague in the fight against economic injustice. He

The In-House Politician

worked inside the system, and Sally worked as an outside agitator. She had sucker punched him. He took that personally and wanted his revenge.

Tom was hoping that MC might have instructed Teddy to delay this action until she could discuss his plan with her boss, the General Counsel. She couldn't be sure he wouldn't side with Teddy, if he thought the Bolsheviks' leader might offer an apology based on the fact that there was no official evidence of discrimination. But he could also fire her on the spot for even entertaining the idea. It didn't matter because by the end of their call, MC and Teddy struck a deal to never again mention their conversation about this cockamamie plan. But what about Tom? He was now an unwitting co-conspirator in their crazy plan. And it's always the messenger who gets shot. Once again Teddy looked at Tom and said, "Relax." Then he handed him Sally Kessler's phone number.

MC came down to the conference room. She coached Tom for about thirty seconds about things he could say and things he should avoid. Then he dialed Sally on the speaker phone, with MC quietly listening in.

The call with Sally did not go well, and it had nothing to do with anything Tom said. Sally was not easily intimidated. In fact, she laughed a few times when he said the bank's legal team thought they had a good case of defamation against PUMP as an organization, and against her personally, for the bovine scatology she had planted in the minds of the press and the public. Tom reminded her there was no factual evidence of outright racial discrimination, and the composition of the affordable mortgages closed thus far was over 80 percent minority. The bank had done its part.

Tom ended the call by providing Sally with the message Teddy wanted him to give her, even though he couldn't attribute it to him. Tom said if she made a public retraction of her accusation of racial discrimination, the bank would drop the suit. She hung up on him.

MC and Tom looked at each other for comfort after the call ended. MC said she would report back to Teddy that he had performed well, and had carried the message precisely as requested. Then the phone rang. When Tom picked it up, Sally Kessler was on the other end of the line and she wasn't calling to surrender. She asked, "So Tom, did you have me on speaker phone for that call?"

MC nodded her head and Tom said, "Yes, I did."

"And so, was there someone else in the room listening in on our call?"

Again, MC nodded and Tom responded in the affirmative. Sally said, "So, you didn't have the honesty, integrity, courtesy, or truthfulness to identify that person before we began our conversation?"

Tom was feeling contrite and amazed at the same time. What kind of balls did she have to accuse him of a lack of honesty? His face went completely red and he was embarrassed in front of the one person he never wanted to see him like that. Sally went on to accuse him of double-dealing, just like the bank he worked for. She also said that she was going to let anyone who would listen to never trust Tom Donovan again. And, if and when she ever spoke with Teddy DeMarco again, she would tell him what she thought of Tom Donovan's professional ethics. Then she hung up on him a second time. He was about to hyperventilate, but caught himself.

As Tom walked down the hall to update him on the call with Sally, Teddy came out of his office and greeted him. "Well, we got one piece of good news today. I spoke with Peter and we got Millie's loan turned around. He said he was going to have a personal conversation with Porter. He said he had no idea what happened, but assured me that he wasn't happy about it."

It occurred to Tom that perhaps that was why Tina was calling him. It also occurred to him that Scrooge and Marley might be playing them. Once again, they were a despicable pair.

And it wasn't even five o'clock yet.

Chapter 38

Joe Campbell's colleague at *The Examiner* was doing her best to give Rev. Lloyd Ogletree the benefit of the doubt on why he'd waited so long to make his announcement about severing his relationship with 1NEB. There were still a few unanswered questions. Like, how long had he known about the large number of denials? Even if the bank's campaign contribution was just recently made, why hadn't he returned it immediately? Why make this announcement now? The primary debate was just a few days away and the timing of this announcement would certainly give him a boost in the polls.

Alternatively, Joe had no intention of giving Sally Kessler any benefit of the doubt on why she held the protest in front of the bank, which was timed to coincide with the end of Ogletree's press conference. There had been no communication with Alex Scarduzo about the PUMP demonstration—not that he expected any. Joe understood that Alex didn't want to interfere with Sally doing what she did best, which was to make herself and PUMP appear to be the crazies. Indeed, Sally had called Joe and tried her best Bolshevik guilt trip to get him to write a story about the press conference and protest that would accuse the bank of racial discrimination. When Joe pushed back, Sally had gone so far as to accuse Joe and *The Examiner* as being in collusion with 1NEB, since the bank was one of its biggest advertisers.

Joe and his colleague saw the story as more of a political piece. Ogletree's announcement was the real headline, although there was no proof that 1NEB had purposely discriminated in its mortgage lending activities. Clearly, the bank had denied a lot of minority loan applications, but that wasn't discrimination on the face of it. Their editor made it clear that an accusation of discrimination would have to be proved. But it would not prevent them from using the word in the headline—after all, headlines sold newspapers, and the accusation came from the candidate.

Joe had been trying to reach Teddy DeMarco as a confirmation source ever since Sally Kessler had called and told him the rumors about the bank's high minority rejection rate. But DeMarco was not returning his calls. Now that he was in possession of the report provided from the Ogletree press conference, Joe was pretty sure DeMarco would return his call. Ogletree's press conference and the PUMP demonstration were news, and the story could really hurt the bank's reputation. He knew DeMarco would want to speak with him once he announced he needed a comment on the story before it was published.

It was about 4:00 o'clock when Kelly popped in to let Teddy know that Joe Campbell was calling. Again. Teddy sighed in exasperation and told Kelly to let Mr. Campbell know that he was currently in a meeting, but he would call him back as soon as it ended. Joe's message back through Kelly was that he hoped Mr. DeMarco would get back to him before the close of business, since he was on a deadline and wanted to get his responses to a few questions on the story he was writing. Teddy knew exactly why Joe Campbell was calling, but still let out a big "Fuck!" He apologized to Kelly for the language and told her to get the reporter back on the phone.

After the initial pleasantries, Joe reminded Teddy they had spoken in the past. Joe also gave him what amounted to a small gesture of condolences for how the day had gone for the bank. Teddy said, "Yeah! Thanks. But why do I think our conversation is just going to make matters worse?" As soon he spoke these words, Teddy wanted to recall them. But then again, he also wanted the reporter to understand he wasn't going to lie down and play dead.

"Well, that depends on you, Mr. DeMarco." Joe wanted to keep the interview professional so that Teddy wouldn't try to get too friendly with him. He had a story to write and so far the bank was not looking like the Good Samaritan in all that had transpired.

Teddy asked, "How's that?"

"Well, if I think I'm getting honest and truthful answers to my questions, then you'll get a fair and honest story from our paper. It's as simple as that. I know that your role in the bank is that of chief political and community reinvestment officer. Out here on the street you're known as the bank's in-house politician. Once a politician, always a politician, as they say. I'm not looking for any spin or cliches, Mr. DeMarco. I'm looking for the truth about what happened."

"Fair enough," Teddy said. "What do you need?"

"So, at today's press conference, Ogletree said he was returning the bank's campaign contribution because he could not accept money from a financial institution that discriminated against minority borrowers. His words, not mine. First, I want to get your reaction to his accusation of racial discrimination, and secondly, did the bank make the contribution to Ogletree's campaign in order to obtain his silence on the bank's large number of minority loan denials?"

Teddy found the second question a bit insulting, but was ready for the first question. He took a deep breath to calm himself. He didn't want to come off like some unrepentant banker. So, in full

Kennedyesque fashion, he said, "Let me say this about that." They both chuckled at the famous politician's remarks in advance of answering a question. Teddy said, "First and foremost, you should understand that we approached Ogletree and the members of MJED to obtain their assistance in getting the word out about our affordable mortgage program. Never in a million years did we think we would get the volume of loans we received as a result of that partnership. Now, that's not an excuse for the number of loans we denied, but, well, we were trying to do the right thing and a lot of folks responded to our program. Unfortunately, many of them were unqualified. But let me back up for a minute. Are you aware of the specifics of our affordable mortgage plan?"

"Yes! Yes! Sally Kessler briefed me on all of the terms of your CRA agreement with PUMP a long time ago. It's a great deal, no question about it. But that begs the question. If it's such a great deal, then why did the bank end up rejecting so many of the minority loans it received? Why didn't more people qualify?"

"Joe, you're the head business writer for the paper, right? You understand what it means to underwrite mortgage loans according to long-standing and proven underwriting rules. If a borrower doesn't meet those standards, and by that I mean our even more flexible guidelines, then we can't approve them. Simple as that. We have a fiduciary responsibility to our depositors and shareholders. And we wouldn't be doing anyone any favors if we tried to make homeowners out of borrowers who simply can't afford the payments, or have not demonstrated the ability or desire to repay their debts in the past, right? Additionally, you'd be amazed at how many homebuyers don't have the minimum five percent down payment and closing costs.

They think that somehow we're going to let them save up the money while we're processing their loan. We can't do that."

"That all sounds correct in theory," Joe said, "but the question still remains, why was there so much difference in the quality of Black applications as opposed to the White applications? The income limits were the same for all the applicants, so why, according to Ogletree's report, did you reject three Black applications for every one White application? You need to address the issue of possible racial discrimination in your underwriting, Mr. DeMarco."

Teddy remained calm. Tom had provided him with what he thought was a good response to this question. Teddy said, "You know, Joe, it's that word 'discrimination' that really gets under my skin. Let me ask you this: do you know of any banks that like to deny loans? I mean, really! Think about it. When we take in a mortgage application, we process it, we commission an appraisal and a credit report. We spend a lot of time and money reviewing each and every application that enters our system. The fact is that we lose money on every loan we deny. We only make money on loans we approve and close. So, it makes no sense that we would want to deny a loan for any other reason than the applicant doesn't qualify—doesn't meet our tried and true standards. We want to approve loans, and we bend over backwards to try and approve all the loans we receive, no matter the borrower's race. You have to take my word on this, Joe. We're in business to make loans, not deny them."

Teddy continued. "And here's the point, Joe, on the issue of discrimination. You know the reputation of our Chairman, right? Well, I once heard him say at an officers' meeting, that bankers discriminate all the time. But the only reason we discriminate is in the borrower's

The In-House Politician

ability to repay the loan. It's that simple. And he followed up that statement placing the fear of God in all of the assembled officers by saying that if he ever found one of his officers discriminating on any basis other than the borrower's ability to repay, they would be fired immediately. So if there's anyone in this bank who is denying loans on the basis of race, they're in big trouble and, in all probability, won't be here much longer. I can assure you of that." Teddy smiled. He was wondering if Joe Campbell would use those words in the article, and if so, would Porter be terrified by them?

Joe seemed to be satisfied with the answers, but was still trying to root out the reasons for the high number of minority denials. Joe attempted to drill down further. "Mr. DeMarco, again, that all sounds good, but it still doesn't answer the basic question of why so many minority denials under program? I probably should have come clean earlier, but my colleague spoke with Ogletree after the press conference. He gave us an estimate of the number of Black applications the bank turned down over the last six months. He knows this because most of the denials were to members of the Black churches in MJED."

Teddy was getting frustrated. "Joe, we know what the score is on our denials better than Ogletree. He's just giving you the denials he knows about. He doesn't know how many White and Latino denials there have been in total, and he doesn't know how many total minority approvals there have been. We've received applications from other parts of the state, and some realtors have also sent us some minority customers. And when you add in the numbers from our traditional or conventional portfolio, it can skew the numbers in many different directions, depending on how you look at it."

Joe said, "Well, Ogletree seemed to know quite a lot about the bank's denial numbers—almost as if he had a whistleblower inside the bank providing him with data. But he didn't give up his source—if, in fact, he has one. And we did ask him."

Teddy made a mental note to speak with the Chairman and Porzio about redoubling their efforts to find the leaker inside the bank. And since he didn't trust anyone, Teddy could only speculate on who the source might be. Indeed, his list of candidates was pretty short.

He thought it was time to move on to the reporter's second question. Teddy decided to play offense. "Joe, let me get back to your question about the campaign contribution. You should know that it was Ogletree who approached me about the campaign contribution. He knew I was head of the bank's PAC and he solicited the contribution directly from me. I have a complete recollection of when and where that request took place. I can assure you that when we made the donation, there was no promise exacted from him to keep silent about the denials. In fact, we talked about the underwriting process at the beginning of our relationship and made it clear that while we would try our best to approve every loan we received, it would be an impossible task to hit a home run with all of them. And this was a long time before he asked me for the campaign contribution. You can verify all this with him if you like. As a Man of God, I don't think he will lie to you about the timing."

Teddy was mentally exhausted, but he thought things were going well and didn't want to cut the reporter off. So he paused once again, hoping that Joe Campbell had no more questions. But he wasn't finished yet.

Joe said he wasn't sure if he needed to circle back to Ogletree about the contribution. He had been pretty clear, at the press conference, that he was returning the money because of the large number of minority denials. Joe thought that if Ogletree wanted to accuse the bank of trying to silence him, he would already have stated that fact. However, Joe did think that this issue might resurface in the upcoming TV debate.

"Okay, Mr. DeMarco," Joe said. "I think I have almost everything I need for the article, except that you still haven't answered the question about why so many minority denials? I expect you think I'm beating a dead horse, but the numbers don't lie. There must be something else going on for there to be such a disparity."

Teddy laughed, not because it was funny, but because it was at the heart of the economic injustice and racial disparity issues in the country. He apologized to the reporter and tried to explain himself. "You know, Joe, your question really drills down into the whole debate the industry is having over the standard underwriting guidelines we've been using for years. Do these guidelines make sense for all ethnic populations? Let me give you an example. Many of the properties purchased by our minority homebuyers are located in distressed neighborhoods. And when I say distressed, I mean there could be a few abandoned and dilapidated properties on the same block where these borrowers are buying. In fact, there could be some foreclosures in the vicinity. Appraisers can get real—what's the word I'm looking for here—unforgiving, when it comes to identifying these other properties affecting the value of a buyer's property. And my personal favorite is when an appraiser identifies what's called a 'nearby incompatible land use.' You know what that means?" Teddy didn't wait for an answer. "It means there may be a strip mall, or a corner liquor store, or, God forbid, a corner gas station located close to the subject property. When the appraiser identifies this, and the lender tries to sell the loan to a secondary market investor, well, that loan gets kicked out as a denial for that reason alone. Lenders and investors seem to think that being located near a gas station is going to have a detrimental effect on the value of the subject property, so they say no dice. Now, if you assume that most of the buyers of properties located in these neighborhoods are minorities, well then, you can see why there may be a higher number of denials to minority buyers here. Please understand, I'm not saying it's right, but that's the way the standards are structured. They don't leave much room for discretion."

Teddy didn't want the discussion to end on that note. He continued. "That's just one over-simplified point about the failure of standard underwriting guidelines to satisfy the needs of minority borrowers buying in urban neighborhoods. Then you add in all the disparate economic factors that play out in the typical lower-income minority home buying process. Things like lower pay scales, insufficient time on the job, longer periods of unemployment, lack of savings for down payments and closing costs, and then there's the big one—poor or no credit histories. These issues arise every day on the applications we receive. But we can't solve all the ills of society with one special below-market rate program. We make loans to folks who want to buy homes and have the ability to repay us. There's no great mystery about it. We hate to have to deny any loan. Like I said, we lose money on any loan we reject. So we try to approve every single one of them. But they don't all make it to the finish line for the reasons I just discussed. I don't know what else to say, Joe. That's the business we're in."

The In-House Politician

"You make a good case, Mr. DeMarco. But I thought that Sally Kessler told me that under the terms of the agreement, the bank was supposed to be using more flexible underwriting guidelines, resulting in more qualified applicants. Additionally, there are some folks who think that your regulator in Washington, D.C. might have something to say about the number of minority denials once they come in and review the situation."

Teddy thought things were going well. But once the names of Sally Kessler and the bank's regulator were invoked, he couldn't let that pass. In an official tone he said, "Joe, you know we can't speculate about any regulatory issues just yet. And the fact that you raised Sally Kessler's name in this context means that she was the 'some folks' who planted that idea about any regulatory concerns, right?"

Joe said, "No comment. Well, I guess that's about it. I've appreciated your honesty, Mr. DeMarco, but now I've got a deadline to meet. Thanks again for speaking with me. But before we hang up, I do want to confirm one thing you said earlier. Yes, I am the head business writer for *The Examiner*, so I do in fact understand the underwriting issues you're faced with. As such, you can expect a fair and honest article from us."

"That's all we ask. Thanks."

Teddy was pretty pleased with how he'd handled the questions. On the other hand, he was really pissed. He thought, "How could those two assholes Scrooge and Marley have placed us in this position—having to defend and justify what most of the rest of the world saw as blatant discrimination? I can't believe I had to defend their actions. But we're a team here at 1NEB, and the Chairman wouldn't have it any other way. Just doing my job."

Once he recovered from the call, he decided to try again with the Chairman. He would plead with him to give his department full control over the affordable mortgage portfolio, including all profits and losses. What the hell, CRA was considered a cost of doing business. Why not allow us to show that it could be profitable? Or at least show what the actual costs were.

He also thought this would be a good time for a trip to the Bahamas.

Chapter 39

Teddy thought the overall article wasn't as bad as it could have been. He just hated the headline. It read—CANDIDATE ACCUSES BANK OF DISCRIMINATION. The story quoted Ogletree's words verbatim. And Teddy knew the use of the word "discrimination" was one of those terms that could never be put back in the bottle.

In his estimation, *The Examiner* had published a fair and balanced piece, which he thought gave 1NEB the benefit of the doubt on the issue of discrimination. Could it be that Joe Campbell had a built-in bias against Sally Kessler? Or could Joe's colleague be convinced that Ogletree was looking to get out in front of a bad political situation by giving the campaign contribution back to the bank? It seemed like the timeline for Ogletree's action coincided perfectly with the upcoming TV debate—designed for maximum media exposure—when, in fact, he most likely knew about the high number of African American denials in advance of the announcement. The article also raised the question of why Ogletree would return campaign funds when he stated at the press conference that every dollar was precious. The reporter's skepticism was obvious, but not in the form of an accusation.

Sally Kessler, on the other hand, was furious that Joe Campbell had buried the part about PUMP's demonstration at the bank to the very end of the article. Not only that, but he never even mentioned the group by name. He just referred to them as a protest group. She fumed because she knew no one ever read all the way to the end of a newspaper story. And there was no photo! PUMP had received a few seconds of air time on the NJ Public TV station, as a well as a passing reference on one of the New York station's broadcasting local news. But that wasn't enough to satisfy her. She wanted to let Joe Campbell know what she thought about the article. The only person happy with the story was Rev. Lloyd Ogletree.

Ogletree assumed he would get a bump in the polls from the press announcement and the resulting *Examiner* article. Indeed, the headline itself was worth a few points. But it would be a few more days until the next poll came out.

In the article, Joe and his associate had listed the number of minority loans allegedly approved and denied by 1NEB based on the data provided to them by Ogletree. They indicated that the source of the mortgage data was provided by someone very close to the bank's mortgage department. However, it also mentioned that the candidate would not reveal the source by name. The article told the story about how the bank had approached Ogletree and his colleagues at the Ministry for Justice and Economic Development to assist in promoting the affordable mortgage program to prospective Black homebuyers. And it described how MJED did a good job of getting the word out to the African American community through their church members, families, and friends.

The reporters pointed out how the bank agreed to make $25 million available in low interest mortgages to low-and moderate-income homebuyers in New Jersey cities. And with a little over one year remaining, the bank had already booked $23 million in loans. The article highlighted that the bank had closed approximately 80 percent of all its loans under the program to minority homebuyers.

The article also made it clear that the data on new Black homebuyers under the affordable mortgage program were solid because it was supplied by the members of MJED. The churches kept excellent records on the number of loans approved and denied that passed through their churches. So, while Joe saw fit to disclose the number of Black rejections MJED had offered up, there was no way he was going to say anything about the denial ratios because no one had a confirmed number of White rejections the bank had issued. Those data would eventually be made public through the Home Mortgage Disclosure Act's filings, but it would not be available for some time. He refused to speculate.

Joe Campbell went into some detail about the interview he had conducted with Mr. Theodore J. DeMarco, Executive Vice President at 1NEB. He indicated that Mr. DeMarco gave an honest assessment of the bank's loan denial experience under the affordable mortgage program, and made a coherent case for the high number of minority denials being caused by two elements. The first was the bank's underwriting criteria. Standard underwriting criteria typically used by mortgage lenders did not necessarily line up well with the economic situation for many low and moderate-income borrowers. But rules were rules, and despite the fact that the affordable mortgage program was using more flexible underwriting guidelines, there were still many minority applicants who did not qualify.

The second reason, much like the first, was related to economic conditions in distressed communities where unemployment was high, education levels were lower, and residential properties were not always well maintained. As Mr. DeMarco explained, the vicious cycle of poverty in many minority neighborhoods did not bode well for a high number of loan approvals, even under the bank's more flexible program. What this meant in reality was that a higher number of minority applications were denied—higher than the number of White applications. It was just a fact of life. So yes, Mr. DeMarco admitted, and this was a direct quote, "There were most likely a higher number of minority loan denials when compared to Whites. However, this is not due to racial discrimination. It is due to the unfortunate fact that more minority borrowers applied and did not qualify."

Joe went on to describe how 1NEB had been the first bank to sit down with the protest groups and had come up with a plan to reinvest funds into the distressed communities of New Jersey. The CRA agreement 1NEB negotiated with PUMP was the first and largest in the state. But here's where Joe seemed to be siding with the bank, more than Ogletree and the protest groups. Again, he quoted Mr. DeMarco directly. "1NEB was trying its best to do the right thing. The bank was making every effort to approve as many mortgage loans as it could under the constraints of flexible underwriting guidelines, which were modified to help more borrowers become homeowners."

This statement, coupled with the fact that PUMP was not mentioned by name in the article, sent Sally Kessler into orbit. She was now plotting her next move. Sally might not be able to get even with those reporters from *The Examiner*, but she would make it her life's work to destroy the image of that evil institution of racial discrimination, 1NEB, and its spokesperson, Teddy DeMarco.

Pastor Lloyd struggled with his conscience. Personally, he didn't believe the bank to be evil. He also hoped that nothing he had said or done would cause Teddy DeMarco to lose his job. Despite all that happened, he genuinely liked him.

Alternatively, he was convinced that the tidal wave of bank mergers would not be good for minority communities. More bank mergers would result in more branch closings in minority communities, and this would reduce the number of locations for his folks to do their banking. His constituents would have to travel longer distances to deposit their money and have access to it when they needed it. The scale of merger activity meant that larger banks were growing into behemoths, and the smaller banks were trembling in their boots. Along with the banking industry's inflexible underwriting guidelines, Ogletree now had a second major issue he could use in the upcoming debate.

Chapter 40

Alex had Sally Kessler right where he wanted her—on the edge. He'd been advised by his campaign insider that Ogletree was distancing himself from Sally and PUMP. Likewise, he'd read *The Examiner* article covering Ogletree's press conference and the PUMP demonstration in front of the bank. Alex read the article twice and couldn't find any specific reference to her or to PUMP by name. He knew she was ready to blow. So he decided to help her out—just to seed more chaos into the mix.

His solution was to provide her with three tickets to the Democratic debate. The tickets were placed under the warehouse door inside an envelope addressed to Sally Kessler. No note was included. Alex knew that Sally would assume the tickets came from him, but he didn't want to leave any obvious proof. He knew Sally well enough. She would definitely do something to make her presence known. And Alex was convinced that anything Sally did to disrupt the debate would accrue to his political benefit—eventually.

When Sally arrived at the debate, she was disappointed to find their seats were up in the balcony. It didn't matter, though, since Sally always knew how to use her outside voice inside. She instructed her two hand-picked comrades on how to dress, so as to be as inconspicuous as possible. She didn't want any problems getting past security. Sally thought about trying to get their protest signs in under their coats, but in the end she decided to take no chances and left the signs in the van. Their voices would have to be enough.

The venue selected for the debate by the sponsoring League of Women Voters was perfect. It was an old concert hall and auditorium on the campus of the State University, which was named Little Angel's Hall after one of the school's benefactors whose last name in Italian, in fact, meant little angel. The *LA*, as it was nicknamed, was typically used for small and intimate concerts and lectures, since it held only 1,200 seats, 800 on the main floor and another 400 in the balcony.

The League of Women Voters decorated the *LA's* auditorium in fine patriotic fashion with red, white, and blue bunting everywhere the eye could see. Three podiums stood on the stage with two on either end facing each other at oblique angles and the third in the middle. Thus, the candidates could easily face each other, as well as the moderator sitting off stage in front at a table looking directly at them. The two sides of the stage each held an American flag flanked by the flag of the Great State of New Jersey. A huge banner with the name of the New Jersey League of Women Voters hung on the back of the stage for all to see.

The debate was going to be broadcast by the regional public television station, PBS, and was scheduled for one hour. There was room for as many as five TV cameras, two on either side of the stage and one in the middle behind the moderator. Additionally, there were spots for two more cameras up in the balcony, but PBS decided the three on the main floor were enough. No sense paying for two more camera operators, since it was a political debate. PBS got better ratings for reruns of *Masterpiece Theatre*.

The League had secured the services of Eleanor Morgan, the celebrated anchor of PBS's *News Hour*, as the moderator for the debate. She would bring a measure of decorum and a sense of propriety to the occasion, which was first and foremost in the minds of the sponsor. No one messed with Lady Morgan, as she was referred to off-screen.

The three candidates who had qualified for the debate were provided with 200 tickets each to disperse among their supporters. The remaining tickets were made available to PBS supporters, then the general public on a first-come, first-served basis. The tickets came with a letter admonishing the candidates to advise their supporters that no campaign paraphernalia would be permitted inside the venue, and all attendees would be required to refrain from outbursts of support or opposition.

The candidates were provided an opportunity to come in earlier in the day to get a feel for the auditorium, and to adjust their microphones during a sound check.

As a reward for something Tom had done, the details of which were never disclosed, Teddy tasked him with attending the debate to represent the bank. Along with this wonderful assignment, Teddy made some snide remark about Tom making sure he wore a good power tie since he would be sitting in the front row and would probably be on television. Teddy indicated that Tom's typical Ivy League crest tie just wouldn't do. Tom wasn't insulted. After all, Teddy was a former politician and always looked good on camera.

When he took his seat in the front row, Tom felt a bit embarrassed to be so close to the candidates. More importantly, his proximity to the TV cameras was making him quite nervous about whether or not his tie would meet with Teddy's approval. Tom's wife had selected it, laughing her ass off that he thought the cameras were ever going to pan in his direction. He even shaved a second time. No five o'clock shadow for him. He would be ready for his close-up. Suffice it to say that Tom was sweating through his crisply laundered white shirt.

Before sitting down, Tom turned around to view the audience. That's when he saw Millie Ogletree entering on the other side of the aisle. He assumed the young girl in hand was her granddaughter.

As Millie was about to sit down, Tom waved to her and got her attention. She smiled and nodded back in his direction with an air of pleasant gratitude. However, she made it clear from her body language that no further conversation was necessary. Tom could see that her granddaughter was asking Millie who he was, and, once satisfied with the answer, sat down without ever glancing his way.

Tom felt the need to go over to apologize to Millie, one more time, about how badly her mortgage application had been handled by the bank. But everything had turned out in the end, and Millie was fully engaged in conversations with supporters of her son. She was the matriarch and was basking in the glory of it all. Besides, Tom's paranoia was in full bloom, telling him that the TV cameras should not catch him fraternizing with family members of the subversive Democratic candidate who had taken the bank to the proverbial woodshed. He also knew members of the State Democratic Party were in the audience. He just didn't know who they were, or if they knew he was there representing 1NEB.

Before sitting down, Tom purposely made one last mental note of the audience, since he knew Teddy's first question would be, "So, tell me who was there." As if he didn't already know.

Tom looked at his watch and saw he still had another ten minutes to kill before the debate would begin. He took this opportunity to stretch his legs and hit the necessary room. Whenever he got nervous, well, the adrenaline always sent him to the powder room. As he exited the room, Tom was shocked to see Sally Kessler entering the venue with two of her PUMP acolytes. He watched as all three of them hustled their way up the stairs to the balcony. Fortunately, she did not see him. If she had, who knows what might have happened. She might have singled him out and said some nasty things about him, in what would certainly be her on camera comments after the debate. He felt his paranoia was really getting the better of him.

As he returned to his seat the revelation hit him. It was now becoming clear to him why Teddy didn't want to be anywhere near this televised debate. Plausible deniability reared its ugly head, once again.

Tom now had two unidentified attendees in the seats on either side of him. He introduced himself as being with 1NEB, which was probably a mistake. It may have been his imagination, but both attendees seemed to pull their hands away quickly as if he had cooties. He didn't recognize their names, only that the one sitting on his right was an impeccably dressed elderly woman who introduced herself as a member of the League of Women Voters. The gentleman sitting to his left gave Tom his name, but never advised him of his affiliation. Tom guessed that since he didn't recognize his name, and was not thoroughly impressed by it, then he wasn't worth any more of his time.

It was showtime and the lights slowly dimmed.

Lady Morgan was fitted with a comfortable swivel chair, which permitted her to turn 180 degrees to face the camera located behind her in order to deliver her introductory remarks. She outlined the rules of the debate and set the stage for a no-nonsense back and forth that she would referee fairly and impartially. Each candidate

The In-House Politician

would be given three minutes for their opening remarks, then she would begin the questioning. The candidates would each have two minutes to respond and then one minute for rebuttal. She would alternate the questions between the candidates.

Before she brought the candidates on stage, Lady Morgan admonished the audience to please keep their applause to the initial introductions, and to when the debate ended. She was obviously determined to keep the debate civil. Little did she know there were Bolsheviks up in the balcony.

Sally strategically placed her two comrades in different rows in front of her. This way, no one could assume that the three were members of the same trouble-making gang. Each one of her minions had a specific assignment, and in a specific order. Sally, of course, would be last. Her comrades were perfectly located so that each could easily see her, and she them. She would give a nod when she thought the timing was best for the first comrade to begin his protest. Timing was everything. She didn't want to wait too far into the debate lest their protests became irrelevant. Their disruptions had to begin sooner, rather than later. It was time to make a statement, and she was fully prepared to be arrested tonight, if it came to that.

Security guards were stationed at all the exits and walkways. From time to time, a security guard made his way down the steps in the balcony to try and spot any trouble-makers. Sally and her gang did their best to look inconspicuous.

Rev. Lloyd Ogletree was leading in the polls at 45 percent, so he was assigned the center podium. The two other candidates were Larry Widmer, a retired Federal bureaucrat who had worked for some innocuous alphabet soup agency that no one had ever heard of, and Nancy Smith, a tax attorney practicing for one of the Big Eight accounting firms. Widmer was polling at 15 percent and was the type who always thought he was the smartest guy in the room. Alternatively, Smith was a shy and unassuming character who looked like the local librarian and never thought herself worthy. She came in third, just edging into the debate with 10.5 percent. At this point in the campaign the remainder of the electorate was still undecided.

In the pre-debate warmups, the candidates had pulled numbers out of a hat to determine the order of speaking. Ogletree received the Number 1 position and his team was delighted since he could then set the tone and not be shorted on time.

Despite Teddy's statement at the PAC meeting to the contrary, there was no one more at home in front of a large audience and TV cameras than Rev. Lloyd Ogletree. He also was comforted by the good number of his flock sitting in the audience. But he had to be careful not to work them into a frenzy, so as to turn off the TV voters he was trying to reach. He needed to be a smooth politician: deferential, yet purposeful in his remarks and body language. He also needed to show the voters he could take a punch, as well as deliver one.

Lady Morgan, her palm up in the manner of an offering, said to Pastor Lloyd, "The floor is yours, Rev. Ogletree."

Pastor Lloyd began. "Ladies and Gentlemen and fellow voters of this district, it is time for a change. My name is Rev. Lloyd Ogletree, and I am the pastor of the largest African American church in the State of New Jersey. But all you need to know about my congregation of faithful souls is that they will all be voting for me in this upcoming primary election. The real question is, can I get the rest of you worthy Democrats to vote for me as well? Now, I want to tell you why you should vote for me. Yes, I am new to the political arena, but I can assure you that administering to my congregation of 3,000, and running a church the size of a small university, makes me just as qualified to serve you in this district as your current representative, and next Governor of this great state, Congressman Ed Blake."

Sally didn't waste any time. As Ogletree was making his opening remarks she nodded to the first comrade. As instructed, he'd memorized his rant. No one saw it was coming. He jumped up from his middle seat on the right side of the balcony and began screaming at the top of his lungs… "OGLETREE IS A FRAUD!" He kept repeating this phrase over and over. "OGLETREE IS A FRAUD!" He kept getting louder each time, until he modified the outburst to what Sally had coached him to say, which was, "OGLETREE TAKES BRIBES FROM BANKS!" He repeated this rant a few more times. Everyone in the auditorium had now turned to see where this intrusion was coming from. They finally located him up in the balcony.

By this time, Lady Morgan and the officials from the League were conversing with Security on how best to handle this unwelcome guest. A cadre of security guards hustled down both aisles of the balcony to where the protester stood. As they approached him, they signaled him to come with them. Problem was that his seat was in the middle of the row. Sally had positioned him there knowing it would require the longest time for the security team to remove him. They would have to climb over multiple persons to get to him. In the meantime, he could continue his rants.

As the security guards approached him from both sides, he continued. "OGLETREE IS A FRAUD! HE TAKES BRIBES FROM BANKS!" He kept on repeating it. "OGLETREE IS A

FRAUD! HE TAKES BRIBES FROM BANKS!" He cupped his hands around his mouth to form an imperfect megaphone.

When the security guards reached his row, they asked him politely, but firmly, to come with them. He said, "Sure, no problem. Where are we going?" But he didn't appear to be moving from his location. He started up again. "OGLETREE IS A FRAUD! HE TAKES BRIBES FROM BANKS!"

The security guards were getting rattled. It wasn't going to be easy to forcibly remove this knucklehead without hurting some of the other attendees sitting in the row. So they asked the attendees to get up from their seats to let them get to the protester. While they all obliged, the protester remained in place, screeching out his rants. Meanwhile, the cameras still focused on the stage. The League and PBS were not about to provide the protestor with any free TV face time. Lady Morgan was trying to hold it all together and get back on track. But Sally's plan had worked perfectly. The debate was now a good ten minutes behind schedule.

As Sally's comrade was escorted from his seat, the commotion in the audience took a while to calm down. In the aftermath of this interruption, Tom was asking himself who, or which, organization was out to punish Rev. Ogletree? He was under the impression that Sally and PUMP were still on his campaign team. But Teddy had forgotten to tell Tom about his recent conversation with Pastor Ogletree in which he had indicated his intention to part company with Sally Kessler and PUMP.

Tom turned and strained his neck to see who the protestor was, but it was happening too far up in the darkened balcony. Had the protestor been closer, Tom would have recognized him as one of the

The In-House Politician

PUMP pranksters who had demonstrated in the front of the bank a few days earlier. He just assumed it was one of the Bolsheviks he had witnessed sprinting up the stairs with Sally Kessler earlier.

Needless to say, with all the noise about Ogletree taking bribes from banks, Tom was trying to keep his head down. He was searching the auditorium for the best exit plan in the event he saw anyone with a reporter's notepad moving in his direction. And while he was fairly confident that Teddy had no idea anything like this was going to happen, he was also pretty good at the old duck and cover routine, while leaving Tom out there in the direct line of fire. As the sole representative from 1NEB present at the debate, Tom's name was on the guest list, and it was checked off when he displayed his ticket for the front row. Just taking another one for the team, he thought.

The two other candidates, Widmer and Smith, didn't know how to react to the protest. Alternatively, Rev. Ogletree seemed to be taking it all in stride. The Pastor took a few deep breaths in order to center himself, and just go with the flow. The Lord would help him re-focus, and return to his message. While he wasn't happy with the accusation made by whoever was up there in the balcony—he was pretty sure it was one of Sally's followers—all that shouting did was to move his *mea culpa* up to an earlier spot in his prepared remarks.

The rules of the debate did not permit any of the participants to leave the stage to confer with their team. The candidates had to remain at their podiums while the protester was removed. But Pastor Lloyd looked briefly off stage and saw that his team had written him a sign confirming, "It's PUMP." He acknowledged the recon information with an ever so slight nod of his head.

Lady Morgan swiveled her chair back into moderator mode. She apologized for the interruption and admonished the audience again to remain silent so the debate could continue. She was a pro, but her stoic facial expression did not reflect the churning inside her stomach. Lady Morgan looked at Ogletree and asked him to please continue with his opening remarks.

Pastor Lloyd was at peace with himself and decided before the debate began that he would come clean. He resumed by stating very clearly that what the protester had said was untrue. He continued, "Well, I guess I'm going to have to dispense with the rest of my opening remarks and address the proverbial elephant in the room. First and foremost, I want to say that I forgive that man who seems to want to mislead you with his message. Yes, I received a campaign contribution from First Northeastern Bank. But I want to make this very clear. I solicited that contribution from the bank. The bank did not originate any offer of assistance to me until after I requested it. And I very much needed the bank's money. I was not born with a silver spoon in my mouth and was very appreciative when the bank agreed to financially support my campaign."

Tom slumped down in his seat and looked around to see how many paces it was to the exit.

Pastor Lloyd continued, "And I want to make this abundantly clear, that while the bank did come to me and ask for help to market its affordable mortgage plan, this was prior to my decision to run for Congress. There was never any discussion of a campaign contribution at that time because there was no campaign. We had a great partnership: the bank and our churches. They made a lot of new homeowners out of folks who would normally not qualify for a conventional loan. But over time, it became clear that 1NEB was also denying a very high number of our minority applications. Now here's where the confusion comes in to play. Some say that after I received the campaign contribution from the bank, it took me too long to recognize what the bank was doing. Actually, it was the other way around. I knew about the high number of loan denials being made to my African American brothers and sisters. But I was hoping it wasn't as bad as it looked. And I needed that campaign contribution from the bank. I was greedy and I freely admit that I was wrong. I should have recognized this much earlier."

He paused for a breath—not only for the drama, but to focus, and to look at his watch. He didn't want Lady Morgan cutting him off when he was on a roll. Despite how his team had coached him, it was preaching time now. He was going to let it all hang out and permit the Lord to guide him. He said, "Yes, I sinned and I sinned very badly. And I ask for your forgiveness for my error in judgment. I waited too long before I decided to return the money and admonish the bank. Some of our people suffered: those whose loans were denied. And there were many of them. But I needed the money to continue with my campaign. I only thought about it in self-serving terms."

He paused to determine if he was connecting with the audience. There was complete silence, but he also knew his time was running out. He then nodded to Lady Morgan letting her know he was just about finished. "I also want to apologize to the bank for accusing it of discrimination. The bank is a business, and I truly believe that they were trying to do their best to approve as many loans as they could. But not all of our brothers and sisters had the wherewithal to meet the bank's underwriting standards. It would not have been good for a borrower or the bank if a loan was approved to someone who couldn't afford to repay it."

Sally had heard enough. An apology to the bank from a Black political leader was more than she could handle. She knew it was coming, since her PUMP informant inside the campaign had seen a draft copy of the Pastor's remarks. This time, Sally looked in the opposite direction and nodded to her second comrade. It was his turn to be the disruptor. He stood up and began yelling—although it sounded more like screeching. "LIAR!" He repeated it just as he'd been coached to do by Sally. "LIAR! LIAR! FIRST NORTHEASTERN BANK DISCRIMINATES!" He kept on screaming the same rant.

Tom didn't know what to do. The name of his employer, the one to which he owed allegiance, and who would provide him with future pension benefits, had just been accused of discrimination—for all to hear, both inside the auditorium and out there in TV land. And Tom was the guy at 1NEB responsible for implementing the affordable mortgage program. Someone was coming to lead him away in handcuffs. He was sure of it. He put his head down in his hands and bent over like he was crying and praying at the same time. But no one was looking at him. Fortunately, all their attention was focused on the knucklehead up in the balcony screaming out his Bolshevik bullshit.

Comrade #2 was now being led away. But this time the security detail was not leading the protestor out gently. This was getting tiresome and they looked like they wanted to beat the shit out of him. They were smart enough, however, to know there were lots of eyewitnesses. Even so, they performed their extraction with a bit more aggressiveness than may have been warranted. And just like Comrade #1, he kept up the rant while he was being escorted out of the building. They were true believers, and Sally was very proud of how they had performed under pressure. Another five minutes of air time used up.

Sally was pleased with her attack plan thus far. Her small group of protesters had surgically disrupted the debate to the tune of it now running about 15 minutes behind schedule.

Lady Morgan looked exasperated, to the point of throwing up her hands in disgust. No one, except Sally, knew how many of them were strategically placed inside the venue, and how many more interruptions there might be. Lady Morgan looked at Ogletree and said, "Pastor, I believe the time for your opening remarks has expired. I'm sorry if you were unable to say all that you may have planned, but in order to give your opponent's equal time, we must move on. Thank you, Rev. Ogletree." She turned to Widmer and said, "Mr. Widmer, we would now like to hear your opening remarks."

The former bureaucrat began, "Well, that's going to be a hard act to follow." But when he didn't get a laugh he was savvy enough to let it go. The protesters had done his job for him. His opponent, Ogletree, had lain down on the tracks thinking he could avoid getting run over by the train just by being honest. How naïve, he thought.

Widmer began by listing all of his career accomplishments in government while describing himself as a fiscally conservative Democrat who wanted to reduce taxes wherever possible, but would, of course, support all the current social welfare programs in place.

By the time Lady Morgan got to Nancy Smith's opening remarks the debate was significantly behind schedule. Fortunately, Smith spent her time quickly introducing herself to the voters. She was clearly intimidated by the TV cameras and completed her opening remarks in less than two minutes.

Over the next fifteen minutes, the debate proceeded with Lady Morgan asking the candidates questions on the more important issues of the day. Since all were Democrats, there wasn't much distance between them on how they stood on these topics. They unanimously supported the policies of the young prince currently campaigning for the White House, Bill Clinton. And they all agreed on a woman's right to choose. But here was where Pastor Ogletree had to insert his own religious views on the matter, which permitted him to support the law on the books but still remain personally opposed to abortion.

When the time came to rebut Ogletree's position on abortion, things turned ugly. Alex Scarduzo Jr. had clandestinely provided Widmer and Smith with some nasty opposition research on Ogletree. Widmer used it and went on the attack. His polling numbers told him he needed to get down and dirty to make up some ground. Alternatively, Nancy Smith was too ethical and refused to cite any unsupported allegations.

Widmer said, "Well, Rev. Ogletree, I know that your faith determines your position on this issue. I also know that you've had some personal family issues that you've had to deal with—like at least one child born out of wedlock. I can't imagine how agonizing a decision like that is to go through, but it appears your family made the right choice."

There it was. A pitch in the dirt that Widmer was hoping Ogletree would swing at.

Alex had decided it would be better to use one of the candidates as his surrogate to get the rumor out there. The Sicilian brothers had developed some background information on Karen Ogletree that had not yet been made public. But Pastor Lloyd had never been married,

The In-House Politician

so that didn't make any sense. Unless….. And there was no evidence that Pastor Lloyd's sister Karen had ever had an abortion. People in the audience were all looking at each other and whispering in surprise. Widmer was smart enough to not make an accusation since there was no proof. Just start the rumor and let others speculate. Ogletree would have to respond. This was politics. Rumor and innuendo were king.

After giving the evil eye to Widmer, Lady Morgan turned to Ogletree. "Rev. Ogletree, I assume you want to respond?" She was doing all she could to send a telepathic and body language message to him saying, "Don't be a fool. Let it go."

Whenever Pastor Lloyd preached, emotions always reached a fever pitch. Now he was angry. He took a deep breath and said, "Yes, thank you. I would like to respond to that ridiculous remark."

As he gathered his thoughts, Pastor Lloyd stepped out from behind his podium. He seemed to be moving ever so slightly in the direction of Widmer. His size was enough to intimidate anyone. Widmer also knew that Ogletree had been a boxer in his former life and took a few steps back from his podium. At this point, Pastor Lloyd returned to his podium. He was just using it as a prop for now, hanging on the top of it with one hand. He didn't need the microphone. He looked directly at Widmer, raised his free hand and pointed at him, and said, "God may forgive you. Some of your supporters may forgive you. And perhaps some of my own supporters may forgive you—but rest assured, it's going to take a long time for me to forgive you! You have just shown the voters in this auditorium, and those tuning in, that you have no moral compass. You are despicable! You would rather take a cheap shot at me and my family, than stand here and debate the real issues. You are no gentleman, Sir, and I hope the voters see you for who and what you really are. And that's all I have to say on the matter."

At the end of his takedown of Widmer, there was one very loud and pointed, "You bastard!" from one of Pastor Lloyd's followers. Widmer knew it was for him.

Widmer's face was redder than an apple. He had taken his best shot and it had backfired. He had tried to get inside Ogletree's head with a not so veiled comment about his or Karen's past, but the Pastor had returned fire in a manner that left him looking like a fool.

There were murmurings in the audience. A few outbursts of "You tell'em, Lloyd." Widmer didn't know what hit him. He bowed his head in shameful recognition of his comment. No one in the audience, save Millie and Tom, knew what he was talking about.

Lady Morgan gave a pass to all of Pastor Lloyd's followers for their comments. She tried her best to contain a smile of satisfaction before she turned back to the candidates and said with a sigh, "Okay, let's continue." She never liked Widmer, but she had to be fair.

Chapter 41

In the debate hall, Sally was feeling the pressure. She was all alone now that her two comrades had completed their assignments and been escorted out of the building. No one would come to her aid if things got out of control.

In her mind she had been dismissed by that know-nothing reporter at *The Examiner*. No photo and no mention of her or PUMP in the article about the protest at the bank. And now she and her organization were being rejected by the very candidate she had supported from the beginning. Moreover, *The Examiner* article had semi-justified the high number of minority denials issued by 1NEB as just how the mortgage business works. And Rev. Lloyd Ogletree had now made a pact with the devil by apologizing to the bank for accusing it of discrimination. Everyone was letting the bank off the hook. She had no choice in the matter. This could not go on.

Her watch told her that if Lady Morgan was going to keep the debate to one hour, then time was running out. Sally believed they had been successful in conveying the message that 1NEB was a bank that discriminated against minorities. Also that Ogletree was a liar and a fraud. Whether or not he had taken the bank's campaign contribution in return for keeping quiet about all those loan denials was beside the point. Why let the facts stand in the way of a good protest? PUMP represented the interests of poor people and in her mind Ogletree had abandoned them.

Lady Morgan, needing to shorten the questioning period due to the previous interruptions, was now in the process of asking her final question before the candidates would give their closing statements. And her question could not have been better if Sally had written it herself. She said, "We've heard from all of you tonight, as well as a from a few unwelcome guests, that the banking industry, for good or for bad, seems to be playing a fairly large role in this campaign. If you are elected, please tell us how you will address this same banking industry, and all that it means in helping to grow our economy and to revitalize our distressed cities. Rev. Ogletree, I believe this last question begins with you."

Ogletree was delighted. As he'd advised Teddy, he wanted to take the banking industry to task about its current urge to merge. But thus far in the debate, he hadn't found the right opportunity to opine about what in his mind was a travesty of profits over people. He was ready and began his attack.

"I'm so glad you asked that question," Pastor Lloyd said. "Over the last few years, we've all seen what consolidation in the financial services industry means to our underserved communities, and especially in communities of color. When a giant bank acquires another bank, it ends up closing branches. And typically, the branches that are closed are located in low-and moderate-income communities—again mostly communities of color. A bank justifies this action by saying that a specific branch is underperforming, or its service area overlaps with a branch from the newly acquired bank. The industry says that customers of the closed branch will get the same level of service from the remaining branches nearby. Problem is, those nearby branches are located across town, or over in the next town. Many seniors can't get there to do their banking. People without cars have

The In-House Politician

difficulty getting to their new branch. Loans in the community where the closed branch used to be are no longer available. And it becomes a vicious cycle of more disinvestment, and more decline in that already underserved community. Where does it stop? So, I say to you that when I get to Washington, I intend to introduce legislation that will place a moratorium on…"

The timer went off inside Sally's head. She had positioned herself on the aisle seat in the last row of the balcony that gave her quick access to head down to the railing overlooking the main floor. This was the only way she could be seen and heard by all. Hey, maybe the TV cameras would turn in her direction. That was her plan and she liked her chances.

But there was one big problem. She agreed with what Ogletree had just said. What was she going to shout out in opposition? But she couldn't stop now. As she skipped down the stairs, she stopped herself by putting one hand on the balcony rail and used her free hand to point at Ogletree and accuse him of what she still wasn't sure. The first thing that came out of her mouth was a repeat of the earlier rant. "OGLETREE IS A FRAUD! HE TAKES BRIBES FROM BANKS!" Then she repeated it a few more times as she watched out of the corner of her eye for the approach of the security guards.

Tom knew that voice. From his vantage point, he could only see pieces of what was occurring up in the balcony. It was dark up there and everything was happening in warp speed.

She repeated her rant a few more times.

For the third time, the Bolsheviks had successfully disrupted the debate. All eyes in the auditorium were now focused on Sally Kessler stationed on the edge of the railing in the balcony.

Out of nowhere came the man dressed in black. As he approached Sally, he positioned himself on her right side. He tried to pull her up the aisle. But Sally was having none of it and resisted as hard and as loudly as she could. She screamed and grabbed hold of the railing with a death grip that even the man-in-black couldn't seem to unlock. As she continued her rant against Ogletree, Sally included calls for help. She knew this guy. He was that creep who worked for Alex Scarduzo.

By this time, the security guard was stationed at the top of the stairs. He ordered the man-in-black to back off and away from Sally. But there was no place for him to go. Sally was still resisting.

The security guard pulled his weapon and ordered him to let her go. The guard slowly made his way down the steps towards Sally and her attacker, one careful step at a time. Once the attendees in the balcony saw that a gun had been pulled, all hell broke loose. People screamed and stampeded for the exits.

The man-in-black was no rookie when it came to someone pointing a gun at him. He let go of Sally and put his hands in the air. In that split second when Sally saw that she was free, she kneed him right in the groin. He doubled over in pain and held his groin with both hands. As he bent over, Sally kneed him again. This time her upward motion hit him squarely in the jaw. He fell backwards and tumbled over the railing. As he fell, he tried to grab hold of the railing, but it was too late. He missed and fell headfirst down to the main floor. It was not a pretty sight or sound. Dead on arrival. A case of sudden deceleration trauma.

The debate was over. Mission accomplished by Sally Kessler and her PUMP disciples.

When the police arrived, Sally got her wish and was arrested for causing the man-in-black to fall to his death. The coroner eventually determined it was Nick. He had a New Jersey Waste Hauling, Inc. business card in his wallet.

Sally got all the publicity she ever wanted for herself and PUMP. Problem was that the publicity came in the form of a photo of her perp walk being escorted from the LA in handcuffs. The photo and headline in the next day's *Examiner* was, "PROTEST LEADER CAUSES DEATH OF DEBATE ATTENDEE." This time the article gave her front page, top of the fold publicity. Sally Kessler was charged with manslaughter by the district attorney. None of the witnesses saw it as an accident.

By the time Tom arrived home, his wife had already seen the story on the late-night news. She stood waiting for him at the front door with a glass of his favorite bourbon in hand. She'd poured it when she heard him pull into the driveway.

Chapter 42

When Tom arrived at the office the next morning he was pleasantly surprised that Teddy's first question was not about who was in attendance at the debate. He seemed to be genuinely concerned over Tom's mental health. It's not every day that one witnesses a death at what was supposed to be an event celebrating the country's civil democratic process. And it didn't help that Tom was the only banker sitting in the audience having to listen to all that bullshit about how his bank had tried to bribe Pastor Ogletree. But he weathered the storm without too much trauma.

Teddy had a way about him, always trying to diffuse the stress by inserting some humor into a conversation. He said, "Well, after last night, I guess I owe you a couple of Yankee tickets."

"How about some Yankee tickets," Tom replied, "season tickets for the Giants, and that trip to Disneyworld you thought about offering to Marley."

Tom and Teddy tried to laugh through what was a tragic end for everyone involved. Once they debriefed about the previous night's events, Teddy told Tom to go home and get some rest. But what he really meant was that he didn't want Tom in the office in the event a reporter from *The Examiner* or an investigator from the District Attorney's Office called wanting to interview him about what happened at the debate. There was still a big question hanging out there, like why the bank was being accused of trying to bribe Rev. Ogletree by the crazies from PUMP. And since he was the only representative on the official guest list from 1NEB, Teddy thought Tom should keep his head down and lay low for a while. Teddy would handle the press, and, if need be, any follow-up questions. Tom was okay with this and packed up to leave for home.

As he was heading out, Teddy signaled Tom into the confessional booth to give him an update. He told Tom that after the debate Ogletree indicated he was considering pulling out of the race. Apparently Millie asked him if he really wanted his family slandered and pulled through the mud. She was upset and tried to convince him that God had other plans for him, and that politics should be left to the professionals. His place should be preaching the Word. Millie argued he could do a much better job of effecting change from the pulpit and on the streets, rather than in Washington, DC.

Tom was amazed at how fast Teddy had gathered this intel. The debate was just last night and there was no announcement in the media that Tom had seen or heard. The rumor must have come from Fitz's spies. They were most likely eavesdropping on Ogletree's debriefing.

Tom hoped this rumor was not true. He had come to respect Pastor Lloyd even though he had thought the worst about the bank. Despite all this, Tom believed the Pastor would make an excellent Congressman. Tom's regard for him was partially due to his knowledge of and affection for his mother, Millie.

As Tom drove home and considered the events of the previous night, it seemed inconceivable that Pastor Lloyd would allow someone like Sally Kessler to ruin his political aspirations. Likewise, Tom was amazed at the way Widmer had come up with that scurrilous accusation about how the abortion issue might be something personal in the Ogletree family. Widmer didn't seem smart enough to have come up with something like that on his own.

Chapter 43

Sally Kessler was not made for prison. Despite her hard-nosed reputation for being a bad-ass Bolshevik, she was still a princess at heart. She hoped she could always manage her protest activities without ever seeing the inside of a jail—or at least not for any extended period of time. Sally was fine with little misdemeanor arrests, like protesting without a permit. At worst, her attorney would have her out the next day and PUMP would pay the minimal fine. Indeed, her arrest record for civil disobedience was a badge of honor she wore proudly. But hard time in the slammer for a felony? No thank you. Sally was ready to make a deal if it would get her out of doing the time. The unknowns were, first: what did she have to offer, and second: who might be interested in it? And finally, would they provide her with protection from the Scarduzos?

Sally thought she had some good stuff to use against Alex. But it was her word against his. The deceased just happened to be an employee of the Scarduzo family. His name was Fabrizio Nicolas LiVecchi, who went by Nick or Niki in the U.S. He was one half of the Nick and Joe team who worked for Alex Scarduzo Sr. at New Jersey Waste Hauling, Inc. She'd seen him before as the creepy messenger delivering notes to her from Alex Jr. And while she couldn't actually prove it, it seemed highly probable that Alex Jr. had been the anonymous source providing her with the tickets to debate. Coincidence? Unlikely. The facts were this: Sally had attended the debate on her own volition. Alex was not responsible for any of her actions at the debate. He was not present and had an airtight alibi. Alex was playing cards with his Republican buddies while watching the debate on TV.

Sally was visited by an attorney she'd never heard of who offered to represent her pro bono. And while this attorney never mentioned the Scarduzos by name, when Sally asked, he did not respond. She declined the offer of representation, understanding this guy probably worked for Alex's family. The attorney would then know what she knew and her silence would be the price she would have to pay. Indeed, the only attorneys she could afford were those who might feel sorry for her and take her case pro bono. She might have to be represented by a public defender. Not that using a public defender was beneath her—there were good optics in pleading desperation to the court. However, one never knew how good one of those public defenders was, or how long it would take to get her out on bail. And speaking of bail, she was hoping the judge would be lenient and inclined to release her, but after all, the charge was still manslaughter.

Depending on the bail amount, she hoped her board would agree to put the PUMP headquarters up as collateral, but that might be a problem since they didn't own it. They leased the warehouse from one of her Bolshevik comrades for a dollar a year. And there was no certainty that the owner would say yes to this proposal, assuming it would even cover the bail amount. A few of the PUMP members came to visit her, but none of them included the owner of the PUMP headquarters, or her two comrades in arms from the debate. That neither of her two co-conspirators had come to visit made Sally wonder if they had made a deal to provide evidence against her in return for their freedom from prosecution. Her paranoia was building up and she was getting emotional. Where were all her friends? She'd helped a lot of people during a lifetime of protest and telling truth to power. Alternatively, she'd made a lot of enemies of those same ones in power. She thought they were probably laughing at her now.

Sally had a lot of time to think while she was waiting for her arraignment. In fact, when she thought about what she had done, which resulted in the death of another person, she began to question her instincts. And as if causing the death of another human being wasn't enough, she received a note from Pastor Lloyd saying that he understood why she had come and protested against him at the debate. His note said, "I forgive you."

She began to cry.

Chapter 44

Agent Inbusch personally drove Michelle to her appointment at the bank. He walked her into the lobby but was stopped by a security guard who saw the bulge inside his jacket. Once he flashed his credentials, he was allowed to accompany Michelle to a specified location. There, an assigned bank officer took control. Inbusch was offered a seat in the waiting area where he kept watch for anyone who looked suspicious.

Michelle's bankers in Zurich couldn't have been more accommodating. After completing her withdrawal, she asked if they had any recent copies of the *New York Times*. She longed for some news from back home. In fact, the bank had multiple copies of the *Times*, which dated back one full month. She was given copies to take with her.

She scoured the papers to get herself caught up. One small article buried in the back pages drew her attention. It was a story about how a political debate in New Jersey had resulted in the death of an attendee. The story mentioned that the suspect's name was Sally Kessler, and she had been arrested and charged with manslaughter. The deceased was an employee of New Jersey Waste Hauling, Inc. Michelle didn't recognize the name, but as the former go-between for Alex with Sally, this crime had her former lover's imprints all over it. Once again, no coincidence here.

Michelle really didn't know Sally. In fact, whenever Alex mentioned her name it was always in the form of an insult directed towards her so-called communist leanings. But Michelle felt sorry for Sally and didn't want to see her caught in Alex's web of deceit if she could help it.

Michelle thought it might be time to talk with Agent Inbusch about a timetable for returning home. She was also rethinking the idea of retaining an attorney. If there were things she could offer the FBI, like her notebook, then she needed someone better suited than herself to negotiate the terms of her testimony. In her two years with Alex, she learned that you never gave out any information for free.

She knew Agent Inbusch would not be happy about her hiring an attorney. And he would not be inclined to return her to the States if their case against Scarduzo was not yet ready for prime time. But Michelle was also not inclined to sit around waiting for some hitman to find her in Zurich. It had been six weeks since she had landed in Rome. Officially, her period was now late. It was time to take a pregnancy test and confirm to Inbusch what she already knew. She was carrying Alex Scarduzo's child and preferred American doctors to guide her through the process.

Michelle knew that Agent Inbusch's first question would be "So, are you sure that Alex Scarduzo is the father of your child?"

She was smart enough to understand they already knew the answer to this question. If they were watching her every movement prior to her escape to Italy, then they had a pretty good idea of who she'd slept with. "Yes, Alex was the only man I had relations with before I left for Italy. It has to be him."

Inbusch yelled, "You understand how this complicates things? Goddammit, Michelle! What were you thinking? He's a married man."

Chapter 45

Alex Scarduzo Sr.'s residence had the appearance of an English countryside manor situated within a gated compound. It had all the trappings of a wealthy businessman's preference for the solitude of not having to deal with any neighbors, but who still liked to entertain from time to time. The ten-acre estate was located in Holmdel, best known for its horse farms. But Alex Sr. did not care for the animals. He preferred bocce ball and had installed a court that might have been used two or three times over the years. There was also an Olympic-size pool, pool house, tennis court, basketball court, and a security gatehouse for all visitors to sign in and be announced. Additionally, a separate guesthouse could accommodate up to six visitors.

The mansion included six bedrooms, seven full bathrooms, and two half baths, as well as a room in the south wing for a live-in maid. The kitchen would have made Martha Stewart envious, and included an open-hearth fireplace. The tree-lined drive up to the mansion from the road was approximately the length of two football fields. Different gardening or landscaping activities occurred every day of the week except on weekends. Weekends were for relaxing and entertaining.

On this particular Sunday, Alex Sr. had invited his sister, Morgana, and her family over for a traditional Italian meal with all the chicken, pasta, meatballs and gravy associated with a Sicilian feast. As previously noted, Morgana was married to Anthony Prezutti, who was a lifelong friend and associate of Alex Sr. Prezutti was also a well-known general contractor and godfather to Alex Jr.

Also on the guest list this day were Peter Porzio and his wife Patty. Alex Jr. and Catherine promised to make a brief appearance at some time during the afternoon, depending on Alex's campaign commitments.

This was the first face-to-face meeting between Porzio and Scarduzo Sr. since the wedding of Porzio's son Francis to Scarduzo's niece Leigh Ann three years ago. It was also the first time Porzio and his wife were going to see the Scarduzo estate despite having been invited at least once a year ever since the wedding. Porzio was trying his best to maintain his side of their original covenant, but he had received a private message through the designated intermediary that Alex Scarduzo Sr. needed to speak with him in person. The message said it was urgent. While Porzio didn't like the tone of the message, if Scarduzo thought it was important enough to void their covenant, then perhaps he would agree to attend this one time.

Alex Sr. had the mansion swept every day for listening devices by his company's security expert. After a bug was found inside his office one month earlier, Alex Sr. ordered that all business conversations occur outside in the garden or somewhere else on the vast grounds. He also fired all the help and contractors who had access to the inside of the residence. Alex Sr. took this as a clear sign that the Feds were on to him. As a result, he became much more sensitive to tying up all perceived loose ends wherever they might exist. Indeed, one of those loose ends was to make sure that Peter Porzio and Alex Jr. didn't do or say anything stupid.

The In-House Politician

Once the listening device was discovered and destroyed, the FBI had no further reason to play hide and seek with Scarduzo Sr. A black government-issue SUV with tinted glass was now parked outside the Scarduzo compound 24/7. At times the car was occupied, other times not, but it was always parked within view of the security gatehouse. Once, from his limo window, Alex Sr. asked the agent inside the car to come in for a bite to eat and warm up. It was cold and he knew any agent in there had to be freezing since the car's ignition would be turned on from time to time. There was no response from inside the SUV.

Over the past three years, Porzio had begun to think of Alex Jr. as a hero. Lots of good things were happening in Ocean County as a result of his leadership, with many of his pet projects being constructed by those companies Porzio helped finance. In fact, over the years since the two families were united by marriage, contractors doing business with Ocean County and its young County Executive had received nearly $100 million in construction financing from 1NEB.

In order to accommodate Scarduzo's friends and associates, Porzio had set up an internal lending group of loyal commercial loan officers. He always insisted on final review and approval of the loans. Additionally, he required his officers to insist on large contingency budgets in the loan proposals in order to mitigate the risks associated with these new and relatively unknown customers. As long as the loans were paid as agreed, Porzio and his officers did not ask any questions. Only Porzio thought he knew where the extra reserve dollars were going after disbursement. Indeed, the financial services industry needed a fresh new conservative face in Congress, and this required significant campaign financing.

Porzio was so enthusiastic about Alex Jr.'s campaign he decided to help the young politician in his own way beyond the interim financing arrangement he had made with Sr. In his own mind, Porzio believed he was helping fulfill Sr.'s comment that the Scarduzo family did not plan on losing this election. In fact, Porzio had come up with this plan all on his own. Once advised about it through their intermediary, Scarduzo Sr. confirmed that he liked the idea. Sr. couldn't believe Porzio thought it up all by himself since he had a low opinion of bankers in general, and an even lower opinion of this one. And while he didn't see any great upside to Porzio's plan, Sr. knew it couldn't hurt. It also meant he had the banker right where he wanted him. If Porzio successfully implemented this plan, he would become part of the Scarduzo family circle.

Porzio's plan was to provide the young Republican candidate with reports on the bank's affordable mortgage activity. As the chief credit policy officer of 1NEB he knew he could control Porter McMahon and make sure the bank did not shy away from its tried and true underwriting guidelines. This would result in reports that were not very complimentary when it came to the bank's minority lending goals under the terms of the CRA agreement. Moreover, Porzio believed these reports would eventually lead to DeMarco being placed in the direct line of fire—by the Chairman, the regulators, Ogletree and PUMP. With this bad publicity, he assumed the Chairman would eventually come around to his way of thinking and put DeMarco out of a job, resulting in no more CRA agreements and no more bullshit loans. Porzio was not sure if Alex Jr. would be able to get these ugly reports published, but after the initial false report had made it into *The Examiner*, he assumed the Scarduzos had friends everywhere.

The In-House Politician

The major split between Ogletree and DeMarco, which came as a result of these fraudulent mortgage reports, would also accrue to the benefit of Alex Jr.'s campaign. In Porzio's mind, everyone was coming out a winner. He just worried about being caught as the whistleblower— or snitch, depending on the Chairman's point of view, since no other opinion mattered.

Porzio was not pleased having to travel to Scarduzo's home. The idea of being seen breaking bread with Alex Scarduzo Sr. was making him nervous. Porzio knew well enough to drive cars with tinted glass, but all cars had license plates that could be traced. In fact, Porzio had considered hiring a car service to take him to the Scarduzo estate, but then thought that might be a bit over the top. He told his wife they would not be staying long. Porzio wanted to be cautious.

As he and his wife pulled up to the gatehouse, they passed the black SUV parked down the road opposite the entrance to the Scarduzo estate. He hoped this vehicle was part of the Scarduzo security team. He made a mental note to ask Sr. about it. Porzio's paranoia was getting the better of him and he told himself to calm down.

Dinner was wonderful. Alex Sr.'s personal chef paired all seven courses with the appropriate wine. When dinner was over, Alex Sr. invited Porzio to accompany him outside to discuss some business matters over cigars and digestifs on the terrace. Porzio assumed this was the Sicilian way of doing things.

As the cigars were lit and the cognac poured, Alex Sr. invited the banker to take a walk with him to view his koi pond. Once they were out of earshot of the other guests, Alex Sr. began by saying in a somewhat sarcastic tone, "Peter, I appreciate that you need to keep your distance from a man like me. And I hope you appreciate that I have done my best to keep my side of our agreement. I have kept all my company and personal financing matters away from your bank."

"Alex," Porzio said, "I'm very grateful that you haven't placed me in the position of having to say no to any financing for you or your company. On the other hand, I have very much appreciated the business you've sent us from your colleagues and associates. I hope they've given you good reports on how we've serviced their loan requests. I've established a small cadre of senior lenders who are loyal and who report directly to me. Among other large customer transactions, they're assigned to review deals that come in under our informal referral process. I've schooled all my lenders on why they should require and appreciate the extra-large contingencies in those budgets." Porzio winked at Sr.

They both laughed, knowing nothing further needed to be said on this matter.

"I also wanted to personally thank you for the assistance you have provided my son," Sr. said. "Those bank mortgage reports have been very helpful to him."

"Glad to be of service. We need a Republican Congressman in this district, and I know Alex Jr. will make a great one. But those mortgage reports have helped me inside the bank as well. I don't want to bore you with the internal politics, but I've been able to kill two birds with one stone—the stone being those reports. I've said all along that very few of those people will ever qualify for mortgages. Just not going to happen—and the reports tell that story."

Alex Sr. said, "Yes, yes. That's probably true, but that's not what I wanted to talk to you about. When you arrived you probably noticed that black SUV with government plates parked in front of my property."

"Yes, I did," Porzio said, "and I wanted to ask you about it. But hang on a second, did you say government plates? I thought it might be part of your security detail, or the paparazzi, or some newspaper reporter looking for a story. Oh shit! What kind of fucking mess have you gotten me into?"

Alex Sr. tried to remain calm. No one ever spoke to him in this manner. "Now Peter, you're not in any trouble, at least not as far as I know. But you should probably stop sending any more of those mortgage reports to my son. Just in case they're watching him—or, and this would be most unlikely—they're also watching you. And I won't be sending you any more loan business for a while—until we sort all this out."

Porzio was now in full panic mode. "Okay. So who are 'they'? And please don't tell me it's the Feds."

"Sorry, my friend," Alex Sr. said, "but we do think it's the Feds."

"Goddammit, Scarduzo! I should've known better than to get in bed with you. I can't believe this is happening."

Chapter 46

Porzio knew well enough to not make a scene back at the house. He calmly collected his wife, expressed their gratitude for the wonderful meal, and said their goodbyes. When his wife wanted to know why they needed to leave so abruptly, he said he'd been paged by the Chairman and needed attend to some urgent bank business. His wife, as usual, fell for that little white lie.

Alex Jr. and Catherine were just arriving when Porzio's car sped past them traveling much too fast on the long single-lane driveway. Alex Jr. asked his father who that was leaving at Mach speed. Sr. informed him it was Peter Porzio, his cousin Leigh Ann's father-in-law. Alex Jr. said, "Ah yes, from 1NEB, right? He works with Teddy DeMarco there. Haven't seen much of him since the wedding. Why was he in such a hurry?"

Sr. wasn't in any position to say anything more at that moment. "Peter said there was some crisis the Chairman wanted him to attend to back at the bank."

"Hope it's not anything do with one of our friends who owe him money." Alex said in an attempt at humor.

Scarduzo Sr. did not find his son's remark funny.

After Alex Jr. found his way into the kitchen and sampled some of the chef's wondrous desserts, his mother found him and scolded him for missing an excellent dinner. Alex Jr. reminded her he was in the midst of trying to win an election, but still apologized as good sons are supposed to do.

Sr. signaled to his son that he wanted to see him outside on the terrace. His father took him by the arm and said, "Let's take a walk."

With an eyeroll back to Catherine, Alex Jr. said, "Okay, Dad. But we can't stay long. I've got another rubber chicken dinner commitment tonight and I gave my driver the day off."

Alex Sr. made sure they were out of earshot once again before he turned to his son and said, "You know that banker who just left here in such a hurry? He may be your cousin Leigh Ann's father-in-law, but he's also the guy inside the bank who's been providing you with those mortgage reports. I've kept that information from you to protect both of you. Too many leaks out there. You also know that he's been helping to finance our friends—as long as there's no tracing them back to us directly. It's all on the up and up. Well, maybe a little favoritism here and there, but I haven't had any complaints from anyone we've referred. Have you?"

"Nope. No complaints. But I've left all that referral business for you to handle. It can never come back to me, or my election chances would crash and burn."

"Good to hear—the no complaints part, I mean. But I'm sorry to say the referrals are going to have to stop—at least temporarily. Can't risk it right now. This includes all of our friends and associates. But don't worry. I'll make up for any shortfall in campaign funds with my own money. When you drove up did you see that black SUV parked in front of the property on the opposite side of the road?"

"Sorry, Dad. Catherine was driving and I was taking a bit of a nap. She woke me up just in time to see that banker playing chicken with us on the driveway. Why? What's the matter?"

"Well, I haven't wanted to concern you with this, but we found a listening device in my office a month ago. We destroyed it, of course, but the Feds seem to be sending me a message, and that includes you. They're watching, listening and tailing me wherever I go. So I assume they're doing the same with you."

"You're making this all up, right, Dad? This can't be true. Just a joke, right?"

"Sorry Son, but it's true. I've always tried to be very careful in my business dealings, but I guess I've also made my share of enemies. You can't trust anybody anymore. God knows who I've trusted too much over the years. But somebody has decided that they don't want to pay to play anymore. What can I say, Son? I'm sorry."

Alex Jr. flopped down in a nearby Adirondack chair with a look of astonishment. He knew his father had a reputation for being a powerful man. In Alex Jr.'s younger years, he'd seen the way his father had handled some of those union bosses, and was always impressed at the way he always came out on top. It had occurred to him that his father might have done some things that weren't exactly kosher, but then again, his father didn't tell him everything about the family business either. And he really didn't want to know.

His head in his hands, Jr. said, "You know Dad, I've never been one to criticize your actions, but sending that goon to keep an eye on Sally Kessler at the debate wasn't the smartest thing you've ever done. Look at what happened. The goon is dead and—"

"Hey. That so-called goon was a real person with a real name. His name is Fabrizio Nicholas LiVecchi, and he was completely loyal to me and to you. He might not have been the smartest one in our family, but he was still family. Remember that. And if you want to criticize me for sending him to watch her, then let me say how dumb it was for you to give that commie bitch tickets to the debate in the first place. Did you really think that was a good idea? Look how it ended up."

"Yeah, well, family and loyalty aside, you didn't tell your guy to silence her, did you? Dad, he had your business card in his pocket. Talk about dumb. So the D.A. makes the direct connection to you. Then some anonymous source tells the prosecutor they've seen the dead guy hanging around my campaign. So when they asked me about him, I said I didn't really know him, but that he had volunteered to help out with the campaign. Come to think of it, I haven't seen his buddy around lately. Wonder if he decided to go back home to Sicily, rather than be questioned by the authorities."

"Yeah, something like that."

"Is there more to that you want to share, Dad?

"We'll get back to that later. Please continue, Son."

"Dad, I had everything under control with that bitch Sally Kessler. I had her right where I wanted her doing my bidding inside Ogletree's campaign. Hell, now she's probably cooperating with the Feds and providing them with dirt on me. I'm sure she wants to stay out of jail, so she's probably singing like a bird. But campaign spying is not exactly against the law."

"You might be right about that, Son. I sent one of our attorneys to offer her pro bono legal representation. He didn't reveal who'd sent him. But it didn't matter, she must have figured out the connection because she turned him down."

"Well, of course she turned him down," Alex said. "Kessler's smart enough to figure out we want her to keep silent. So if your attorney didn't say who was paying the bill, then she's scared shitless and is probably asking for protection. How could you have done this to me? Hell, how could you have done this to our family—to Mom and everyone connected to us? You probably just ended my political career. You know once the Feds get involved it's game over. What am I gonna do now?"

"Oh, stop whining! You haven't done anything wrong, as far as I know. Have you? Well, those bank mortgage reports could be a setback if it's ever made public. Do you have that reporter, Joe Campbell, on a short leash? He knows he still owes us, right?"

"Really, Dad? What is it you think he still owes us? Because you paid for all his medical bills when I almost blinded him in prep school? I've given him some juicy stuff about the bank, which he used and never really checked. But that incident from way back in our good old prep school days is still my word against his."

"Okay, Son. We'll figure out a way to keep that reporter in line. But you may have a more serious problem than that. What have you heard from that little chippy who flew off to Italy after you broke it off with her? What's her name? Michelle something? What have you told her about me and our family business that she could be telling the Feds? Anything that could hurt us? And do you know where she is right now?"

Alex Jr. was now in full desperation mode. "How did you know about her, Dad? Really? Did Catherine say something to you about the affair? I can't believe this. How do you know about Michelle?"

"You know, Son, I didn't get to where I am by being uninformed. You weren't very discreet. If Catherine could find out about it, why wouldn't I have known about it? Really? I've got eyes on all my

The In-House Politician

investments. And believe it or not, I consider you to be my most valuable investment. Your election to Congress will be the best thing to ever happen to this family. I'm very proud of your accomplishments. So let's not screw it up now with any further missteps. So, I'm going to ask you again. What can you tell me about the risks we might face with your former side piece?"

"Dad, you don't have to worry about Michelle. I didn't want to tell you this but I had her sign a Non-Disclosure Agreement before she got on that plane. In fact, I paid her a lot of money to keep quiet. If she says one word, she'll lose a ton of money. But to answer your questions, first, I don't know where she is in Europe right now, and second, I don't recall ever saying anything about how you handle the family business other than you were, and continue to be, a tough businessman. People don't like to cross you."

"Well, that NDA was probably a smart thing on your part—to save yourself from embarrassment. But the NDA has no bearing on her testimony in a criminal investigation. The Feds can force her to testify and a judge can order her to answer questions. I thought I raised you better. The first thing I want you to do is get me a copy of that NDA so my attorney can look it over. So how much did you pay her?"

There was a pause in the conversation while they both took a breath.

Sr. continued. "You said before that you hadn't seen Nick's brother Joe around for a while. That's because I sent him over to Italy to find that girl of yours."

"Oh my God! What have you done?"

"And now that you told me about the NDA, I'll tell him to follow the money. You'll need to find out where your attorney wired the funds and let me know."

Alex thought it through, then said, "So, Dad, let me ask you this: what do you intend to do with Michelle if and when your guy finds her?"

Sr. just stared at him. There would be no more discussion on this topic.

Chapter 47

Michelle was not surprised when Inbusch knocked on her door. He had called earlier to say he was coming over. When she answered the door, Inbusch had his serious look on, which told her all she needed to know. It was time to pack.

Inbusch said, "Well, our friend, the one who's been searching for you in Rome, just bought a ticket to Zurich, so Old Man Scarduzo must know about your NDA with Jr. It's time to head back to the States. And we need to leave quickly. He'll arrive here sometime tomorrow, so we don't want to be here then. Besides, we can protect you better back home."

"Really? How's that?"

"We've got lots of safe houses there. We don't have any here in Zurich. We would have to request cooperation from the CIA here to use one of theirs. And they typically don't like to share unless we read them in, and then they'll think we owe them. So let's get moving."

Michelle was convinced and walked to the bedroom to find her suitcase and start packing. As she was leaving the room, she turned and said, "Just one thing. I'll need to hit the bank on our way out of Dodge. I'm not about to leave the rest of those funds here. Never know when I may get back."

After Michelle had closed out her account, Inbusch and his team drove to the Zurich airport. He left an agent behind to help locate and contain the hitman, especially if he decided to return to the States.

There were no issues related to passports or luggage for Michelle and the team upon their arrival at the airport. The Bureau had its own private jet standing by. But just to play it safe, Inbusch recommended that Michelle change in the back of the van. Sunglasses, a wig, a broad-brimmed hat, and a trench coat were all ready for her as a disguise. When she asked Inbusch why this was necessary, he said, "You can never be too careful. We're not sure your man is operating alone. And there are plenty of folks out there with cameras."

Michelle had to laugh at this. She was recalling the nearly identical disguise she wore when she was serving as messenger between Alex and Sally. She wondered if that was where they got the idea. Michelle also decided it was time to talk specifics with Agent Inbusch. There would be plenty of time to discuss these matters on the flight home.

Chapter 48

Three blocks south of the bank's headquarters was a little deli that Teddy liked to frequent. He loved its famous sandwich known as the Sloppy Joe, which included turkey, corned beef, coleslaw, and Russian dressing on rye. It got a little messy on the hands and face, but the waitresses always gave you plenty of napkins to clean-up afterwards. He often went there just to get away from the phones and to read *The Examiner* in peace.

Today he had to get away from colleagues at other banks continuously calling to congratulate him on the arrest and charges against Sally Kessler—as if he'd planned the whole thing himself. No one had heard a word from Sally since the night of her arrest at the debate. She'd somehow found a way to post bail and been released. On the advice of her attorney, she was avoiding the press. Despite the fact that most pundits figured that Sally Kessler and PUMP were gone for good, Teddy didn't see it as a win. He still didn't understand why she had developed such a hatred for him, 1NEB, and the rest of the financial services industry. But that didn't matter to the well-wishers still calling to thank him for putting a stop to Sally and her Bolshevik friends.

As Teddy was walking back to the bank and stepped out from the curb into the intersection, a black government-issue SUV turned the corner and blocked his path. The side door opened and Teddy was invited in. The FBI agent flashed his credentials and said, "Not to worry, Mr. DeMarco. You're not under arrest. We just want to ask you a few questions. It won't take but a minute." All the agents inside wore their regulation grey suits and black aviators.

The agent introduced himself to Teddy as Guy Farrell. He and Inbusch were working together on the team assigned to the Scarduzo investigation.

Teddy got into the SUV and the agent in the front seat got out to close the door behind him. Agent Farrell told the driver to proceed. Teddy asked where they were going. "We don't like to stand still," Farrell said. "Never know who might be watching. We'll have you back in a flash."

No one said a word until the vehicle came to a stop on a street in the industrial section of Newark that held nothing but abandoned warehouses. Great, no witnesses, Teddy thought.

Once the SUV came to a stop, Agent Farrell opened a briefcase and pulled out an envelope containing some large photographs of two men engaged in what appeared to be a heated conversation. He showed one photo to Teddy and asked, "Mr. DeMarco, do you know who the gentleman on the right is?" The agent pointed to Peter Porzio.

Teddy was incredulous, looked at the agent, and said, "Of course, I know him. That's Scrooge, oh shit, sorry, I mean that's Peter Porzio, the bank's Vice Chairman and Chief Credit Policy Officer. But you knew that already, right?"

"Yes," Farrell said. "but we wanted to get confirmation that you know him. How about the other guy in the photo? On the left of Porzio."

"Well, I've never met the man personally," Teddy said, "but I've seen his photo enough to recognize him. That's Alex Scarduzo Sr."

"Correct, Mr. DeMarco. Now, do you have any idea why the Vice Chairman of your bank would be meeting with Alex Scarduzo Sr.?"

Teddy wanted to get out of the vehicle, or alternatively, to summon an attorney. He said, "I have no idea why Peter would be meeting with him. Sorry."

"Okay. Now let me show you this other photo. Can you identify this man?"

Teddy was astonished for just a moment, but recovered quickly. "Sure. That's Alex Scarduzo Jr. I know him well. He's—"

Farrell cut him off. "Yes. We know who he is. Again, we were just confirming that you know who he is. Are you aware that the Porzios and the Scarduzos are related to each other? By marriage? Peter Porzio's son Francis is married to Alex Scarduzo Sr.'s niece Leigh Ann Prezutti."

"No, I didn't know that," Teddy said. "I wasn't invited to the wedding."

Farrell didn't crack a smile. "Cute, Mr. DeMarco. Okay then. Let me get to the point of why we're having this conversation. We know that you do a significant amount of business with Alex Scarduzo Jr. in his capacity as Ocean County Executive. Your bank has done very well by your relationship with him, correct?"

Teddy nodded.

"We also know that Alex Scarduzo Sr. and your Vice Chairman have gone to great lengths to make sure no one can connect them to each other—business-wise, that is. They've done an excellent job of maintaining their distance from each other, personally. But here's the thing. Over the past three years plenty of Old Man Scarduzo's business associates, colleagues, and friends have received financing through your bank because those loan requests were funneled directly to Peter Porzio through an intermediary. Porzio then assigns officers who are loyal to him to underwrite, close and monitor those loans."

"If you say so," Teddy said. "I wouldn't know anything about that—about any commercial loans coming in to the bank, I mean. That's not my side of the business. In fact, I once asked Peter if he wanted me to pursue any commercial loan business with New Jersey Waste Hauling, the Old Man's company, since I was in good standing with Alex, Jr. Porzio nearly took my head off. He said I could do all the business I wanted with Alex Jr. and Ocean County, but to never again mention the idea of 1NEB entertaining any kind of financing relationship with Alex Scarduzo Sr. or his company. So, what you're saying is news to me. And I can't say that it makes a lot of sense to me either." It occurred to Teddy that perhaps he should shut-up and not offer any more intel on Porzio unless he was asked a direct question.

Farrell smiled. "See, I told you, Mr. DeMarco. You're not in any trouble with us. We just wanted to have an informal conversation with you. Okay? One last thing, though. We believe that your friend Alex Scarduzo Jr. has been feeding intel on the bank's mortgage activity to a reporter at *The Examiner*. The reporter's name is Joe Campbell. We know you know him since he interviewed you recently. We also believe that these mortgage reports have been provided to Alex Jr. by your Vice Chairman, Peter Porzio. Not directly, but through an intermediary. What do you think about that?"

Teddy sat back in his seat and said, "Holy shit!"

"Not very eloquent, Mr. DeMarco, but appropriate for the occasion. It's our understanding that these mortgage reports have—oh how shall I put it, not been good for the bank's reputation? And

The In-House Politician

it's not for me to say, but perhaps some of these reports may have been altered to make things appear worse than they actually are. Is that possible, Mr. DeMarco?"

Teddy shook his head in disbelief. "You know, one of my officers thought the same thing—that the reports were doctored. But when we complained to Joe Campbell at *The Examiner*, he wouldn't tell us his source."

"You're welcome," Farrell said. Then he instructed the driver to take them back to where they had picked Teddy up.

"Mr. DeMarco, I hope you fully grasp the importance of keeping this conversation to yourself. You can't mention it to anyone. I repeat, anyone. Not even your wife or your priest. And just so you know, we will most likely be back in touch with you soon. We may need your assistance. We've had the Scarduzo family under surveillance for quite some time. Unfortunately, we believe from these photos that Scarduzo Sr. suspects we're on to him. That's why Porzio met with the Old Man. And we also believe that Sr. alerted his son and your Vice Chairman Porzio to be very careful, which probably means no more false mortgage reports and no more commercial loans to friends of the Scarduzos. But you should continue to go about your normal business routine with both Alex Jr. and with Porzio. We don't want them to think that you're onto them. I know that's a lot to chew on, Mr. DeMarco, but like I said, you're not in any trouble with us. Just keep your head down and your eyes wide open. We'll be in touch."

Teddy was still in disbelief when they dropped him off.

Chapter 49

Walking back to the office, Teddy tried to process what he'd just learned. The information the FBI had given him was beyond astonishing. It was life-changing. They had just informed him that his supposed good friend and biggest customer, Alex Scarduzo Jr., was providing false mortgage reports on the bank's affordable mortgage program to *The Examiner*. Additionally, Peter Porzio, the bank's Vice Chairman and Chief Credit Policy Officer, had been lying to him all along. He was doing business with Alex Scarduzo Sr.'s associates by providing them with financing that only he knew about and carefully controlled. Moreover, Porzio was the traitor inside the bank who had been providing the false mortgage reports to Alex Jr., keeping it all in the family.

How was this possible? Just because Porzio was related to the Scarduzos? Now it made sense to him why Porzio wanted him to consider a PAC contribution to Alex Jr.'s campaign. And it was clear now why Porzio had said in no uncertain terms that 1NEB would never consider any financing for Scarduzo Sr. or his company. He needed to maintain the appearance of some distance while controlling the process.

But Teddy was sworn to secrecy by the FBI. He could confide in no one.

As he entered the lobby and approached the elevator the thought occurred to him that the FBI never mentioned Rev. Lloyd Ogletree's campaign for Congress, and how it might have played into Porzio's and the Scarduzos' illicit activities. It also occurred to him that someone inside the bank was going to end up in jail, or at least summarily fired with no recourse for any future in the financial services industry. And at the moment, Porzio seemed to be the most likely candidate—unless he found some way to worm his way out of it and lay the blame on Porter—or, God forbid—Teddy himself.

Teddy knew that Porzio wasn't smart enough to modify the mortgage reports himself. He had to have an accomplice who was able to alter the reports before they were submitted to Alex Jr. and then Joe Campbell. But the internal candidates were few. Candidate number one was Porter McMahon, of course. But he had nothing to gain from the bank being under a microscope with lots of investigations ending up with his Mortgage Department being accused of racial discrimination. Porter was smug and an asshole, but he didn't seem the type to purposely risk his career.

"Who else could it be?" Teddy asked himself as he exited the elevator. When he arrived at his office he took his messages from Kelly and tried to appear his normal self despite his recent encounter with the Feds. He told Kelly to hold his calls for a while. He needed to think more about what the Feds had told him.

He turned his attention to Alex Jr. What was he going to do about him? If Alex was currently under investigation by the Feds, then Teddy really couldn't have the bank support his candidacy for Congress. But Agent Farrell said he needed to maintain business as usual. No hiccups that might tip off Alex Jr. Then again, Teddy wanted to know how Alex was able to get *The Examiner* to print stories about the bank that were factually untrue. Was Joe Campbell on the Scarduzos' payroll?

Teddy went back into his file to review all *The Examiner's* articles since the original merger, going back nearly five years. They were all written by Joe Campbell—every single one. It made sense to Teddy that, as head business writer for the newspaper, Campbell would most likely be assigned the task of working on stories related to the bank. He had been the one to write the initial piece on the merger, so it made sense for continuity purposes. And when the reporter had interviewed him for the story on the bank's political contribution to Ogletree, which became a huge issue when it was returned, as well as the high number of minority loan denials, well, Teddy had found Campbell to be quite reasonable in how he wrote the final article.

Teddy asked Kelly to have Althea come to his office for a quick meeting ASAP.

When she arrived, he asked Althea to swear a blood oath that she could not tell anyone about the assignment he was about to give her. She consented.

"Okay, here's the deal," he said. "I've been reviewing all the articles written by *The Examiner* since our first merger. They were all written by the same reporter, Joe Campbell. And as you know, these articles were not very complimentary towards our bank. I would like for you to do a quick and dirty background check on Joe Campbell. For example, I want to know when and where he was born, where he went to school, his grades, his parents' occupations, how many siblings, if he's married and has kids, all the professional organizations he's a member of, and all the awards he's been given. Can you do this for me?"

Althea thought a minute. "Well, it's not going to be easy, but there must be a biography on this guy out there somewhere. Once I get my hands on it, I'll probably have to fill in some of the blanks for you.

But that'll be easier once I know the basics. Can I ask why you need this information? And when do you need it by?"

Teddy smiled. "You can ask, but it's better if you don't know. Plausible deniability and all that. Believe me, you don't want to know. As for when, make this your top priority. I'd say I needed it yesterday, but that's a bit cliché. I promise I'll keep your name out of it."

Althea was intrigued, but knew when to keep it to herself. As she left Teddy's office, she said, "I'll keep you posted."

Teddy never looked up or even said, "Thank you." Just a nod.

He sat back in his chair and thought, this is bank business. I'm not violating any orders I received from the Feds today. They never mentioned Ogletree or Joe Campbell. So why not?

Chapter 50

On the flight back, Michelle entered into an informal agreement with Agent Inbusch that would be subject to review by her attorney once they arrived back in the States. She told Inbusch as much as she could remember without any specific prompts from her notebook. She assumed it was information the FBI already had. It included a general discussion of meetings Alex Jr. held with various contractors that she sat in on just to take notes. She was introduced to them as friends of Alex's father. Michelle stated that at each of these meetings there was always a point when Alex would wink at her. This was his sign for her to go powder her nose, or go down to the bar to have a drink and wait for him. There were times she listened in on their conversations from the powder room, since Alex was unaware of how well their voices came through air ducts. Specifics on the dates of these meetings and who attended would be confirmed from her now very valuable notebook.

As part of her informal agreement to cooperate Michelle made it clear she would provide no further information until she was granted full immunity from prosecution. Inbusch often reminded her that if she'd overheard any conversations that were criminal in nature, she could be charged as an accessory if she hadn't reported them at the time. She made it clear to the agent that if she had overheard anything like that, first, she probably didn't understand it to be something bad, so secondly, she never wrote in down. That's why, in her mind, Alex never thought her notebook worthy of being confiscated before she left for Italy.

The In-House Politician

Michelle knew she had a real bargaining chip. And the notebook would not be handed over to the Feds until she had retained an attorney—one who was yet to be selected. Indeed, she feared this process because she didn't know any attorneys, or whether she could trust any of them to keep her secrets safe.

On a separate issue, Michelle wanted to know if the Feds were aware of what was going on between Alex Jr. and Sally Kessler prior to the debate, and Sally's subsequent arrest. She assumed they did, but wanted to confirm it. In fact, the Feds did know about those meetings that soon thereafter resulted in some really nasty articles on 1NEB in *The Examiner*. After Michelle put it all together for Inbusch, she advised him that she would like him to help Sally out of her current predicament, which included her indictment for manslaughter in the death of Niki LiVecchi at the debate.

It wasn't as if Michelle and Sally were good friends. Michelle had merely dressed up in her undercover spy costume and delivered messages to her from Alex. But Michelle felt a certain bond with Sally. They had both been used by him and she wanted revenge—for both of them.

Inbusch was receptive to Michelle's request related to Sally, but indicated it wouldn't be an easy task to accomplish. Sally's case was being handled by the District Attorney, who would not be pleased with the Feds encroaching on his turf. Moreover, Inbusch would have to connect the dots for his bosses in charge of the investigation in order to get the approval to make Sally's case part of theirs. And the only way it would work was if Sally agreed to testify against Alex Scarduzo Jr.

As part of this process, Inbusch said he would need to arrange a meeting with Sally Kessler. He needed this interview with Sally, and her attorney, to be private so as not to risk the locals learning any details about the Scarduzo investigation. He was not inclined to read-in the D.A. unless he had no other choice. It was the kind of tightrope Inbusch had walked many times before, with the biggest risk being too many opportunities for leaks.

Sally was sitting alone in her apartment now with nothing to do and no one to talk to. Some of her former comrades would stop by from time to time just to check up on her, but PUMP was essentially dead in the water without its fearless leader. Likewise, all of PUMP's contributors indicated they wanted to wait and see what happened in Sally's trial before committing to any further funding. Most of Sally's political associates had scattered like cockroaches in the light of day.

Chapter 51

Agents Inbusch and Farrell had been partners and sidekicks for fifteen years ever since they'd teamed up on their first undercover assignment. They were rising stars inside the FBI, known to all as Batman and Robin. Neither one, however, would cop to the subordinate role of Robin. This was their first face-to-face meeting in months since Inbusch had been in Italy and then Zurich protecting Michelle, while Farrell had remained in the States to supervise the Scarduzo surveillance. A few beers wouldn't be enough.

Once Inbusch finished convincing Farrell that the schnitzel in Zurich was better than any he'd tasted in Germany, it was time to get down to business. They had many specific issues to deal with in the investigation, but Michelle's pregnancy seemed to be hitting Inbusch harder. Having spent time with her in Zurich, he found himself in the difficult position of being the male surrogate to this important witness, wanting to keep her and her unborn child safe. But the fact that this child was the offspring of an alleged criminal he was trying to put in jail was not sitting well with him. He knew of no one in the Bureau who ever had a witness and protectee who was carrying the child of the person they were trying to convict. This was new territory for him.

On the other hand, Farrell was on his third marriage and his kids were grown and out of the house. His only concern about Michelle was what she had to offer them in terms of her testimony against the Scarduzos. Likewise, he was hoping her hormones would not kick in at the wrong time—like when she was on the witness stand.

They placed Michelle in a safe house located in Staten Island. This made for easy access back and forth to the FBI Regional Office in Newark. Michelle was provided with round-the-clock protection, as well as a female agent to serve as her companion on all things related to the pregnancy. Michelle was also given access to a Bureau-approved gynecologist who was on the government payroll, who knew how to keep secrets, and who made house calls. She was a former agent who'd served on the Bureau's forensic team, but decided medical school was more to her liking. Michelle's baby bump was beginning to show.

Inbusch came to visit Michelle at least twice a week, always taking a different route to make sure he wasn't being followed. At their most recent meeting he advised her that she no longer needed to worry about the hitman who'd been sent to find her in Europe. Once Giuseppe LiVecchi came up short on her whereabouts in Zurich he decided to take a side trip back to Sicily to visit the family. The Bureau trailed him to his hometown where he met with an untimely death at the hands of some Scarduzo relatives. This was an unfortunate outcome since the Bureau had intended to arrest Giuseppe on conspiracy charges in an attempt to obtain his testimony against Scarduzo Sr. Bad timing for all—but mostly for Giuseppe.

So much for both Nick and Joe being available to assist Alex Jr. with his campaign. However, no one told Alex Jr. of Giuseppe's demise. As far as Sr. was concerned, the less Jr. knew the better. But according to Inbusch, this didn't mean that Scarduzo Sr. hadn't stopped looking for Michelle. It just meant that Sr. was, in fact, tying up loose ends, regardless of distant family relations. The word on the street, as reported by Bureau confidential informants, was that

The In-House Politician

Scarduzo Sr. was very interested in finding Michelle since the Old Man was not convinced she had decided to disappear somewhere in Europe.

Inbusch and Farrell were working on the Scarduzo investigation under the direction of Assistant Attorney General Reggie Willers. According to Willers, they had most the evidence needed to bring an indictment against Alex Scarduzo Jr. in the form of taped conversations, copies of wire transfers, campaign cash deposits, and witnesses to payoffs to gain contracts through a bid-rigging process directed by the Old Man. In fact, the Bureau believed it could prove that a good portion of Alex Jr.'s campaign funds originated out of payments from the large reserves in the construction loan contingencies made by Porzio and his lenders.

But the Feds currently had no one willing to testify against Alex Jr. who had specific knowledge of his illicit activities. There were many subpoenas waiting to be issued, but the Feds needed to turn Michelle Mitchell, Sally Kessler, and Peter Porzio into willing witnesses. They believed they had Michelle's testimony locked up, and would soon have Sally Kessler's as well. But Peter Porzio, Vice Chairman and Chief Credit Policy Officer of the 1NEB was the big fish they needed to reel in.

The threesome of Inbusch, Farrell, and Willers decided it was time to bring in some of the important witnesses to determine where the holes were in the case, and how they were going to be filled.

When Kelly poked her head into Teddy's office and said she had a Mr. Guy Farrell on the phone, his initial reaction was to tell her to take a message. Kelly did as she was told, but then returned with a certain timidity that Teddy rarely witnessed. "Teddy," Kelly said, "I think you'll want to take this gentleman's call. He stated very firmly that you two met for lunch a few days ago, and that he was following up on the matter you discussed with him. He said you'd definitely want to talk with him."

Then it dawned on Teddy who this Mr. Guy Farrell was. The FBI agent hadn't given him a business card, or his phone number. It occurred to him there was probably a good reason for this. He smiled at Kelly and told her to put Mr. Farrell through. And to please shut the door.

Chapter 52

TJ Bara was a retired FBI agent who was a legend in the annals of the Bureau's recent history. His resume included the takedown of some of the most notorious mobsters in the New York area. However, Bara was so bored with the daily routine of endless paperwork and surveillance that he decided to join the Bureau's New York-based SWAT team for a little more excitement. As a result, he retired from the Bureau on a medical disability in the mid '80s after having blown out a knee repelling out of a helicopter on a classified mission. As a graduate of Fordham Law School when he joined the Bureau, he could write his own ticket and joined a very prestigious Newark-based law firm.

Teddy first met Bara on the softball field when the two competed against each other. Teddy was the captain of the 1NEB team, while Bara served as captain of his law firm's team. Teddy's ego was such that he considered himself the best player in the league—until he saw Bara play. As a shortstop, Teddy had the range and arm to outplay anyone in the infield. But because of his bad knee, Bara couldn't play any position requiring those same fielding skills, so he stationed himself at first base. He sure could hit the ball, though, and Teddy was impressed. After one very long and tedious game that ended in a tie due to darkness, the two went out for a beer and a lifetime friendship ensued.

As a result of his call from Agent Farrell, Teddy reached out to Bara to set up a time to meet with him the next day. After the hugs and questions about their respective families, Bara quipped, "So what kind of trouble are you in and how can I help?"

Teddy got right down to business. "Well, do you still have any friends in the regional office here?"

"Is that a serious question?" Bara said. "They have my retirement photo hanging on the wall of fame there. Now, to be quite honest, there are a few there who won't return my phone calls, but they're not the ones you'd want to talk to in the first place. Lots of jealous guys in that office. The fact is, many of the stories about me have been twisted and exaggerated over the years—and not in good way."

"Okay then," Teddy said. "I wanted to get your take on the fact that an agent recently contacted me and said he wanted me to come in and speak with them about an ongoing investigation. Our initial conversation took place in the back of his SUV last week. He showed me a few photographs he needed me to confirm. He said I was not a target of their investigation, and that they only wanted to speak with me on background. He called me yesterday and wants me to come in to talk."

Bara sat up straight in his chair. "Yeah, that's what they always say. What's his name—the agent?"

"Guy Farrell."

"I know him. He's a boy scout—honest and trustworthy. Let me ask you this, did he swear you to secrecy? Did he say you can't talk with anyone about the case except them? Because that's unadulterated bullshit when you're talking with your attorney. The attorney-client privilege is sacred, more sacred than inside the confessional booth with your priest. You got a dollar in that skinny wallet of yours?"

The In-House Politician

Teddy paused a moment, then knew exactly where this was going. "Let me see. Yep, there's at least one George Washington in here."

Bara said, "Give it to me."

Teddy complied and they shook hands.

"Okay. You're now represented by counsel. Now tell me what you know about the case."

Teddy explained as much as he knew about the investigation based on the photos he'd been shown, and the allegation that Peter Porzio was not the person he appeared to be. Bara said he knew Agent Farrell fairly well. They'd had a few beers in the past and said that he was a good guy and could be trusted. "But in the words of the Great Communicator," Bara said, "trust, but verify."

"Okay, here's what your dollar gets you today in the form of my legal services. And keep in mind I'm trying to save you a whole lot of money. You don't want to know what we charge by the hour. In any case, I will call Farrell. First off, do I have your permission to call him?" He didn't wait for a response. "We know each other well enough that I suspect he'll tell me what information they want from you. Now, if after I've spoken with Farrell I get the sense that he's pulling my chain, then I'm going to recommend that I go with you when you meet with him. Okay?"

Teddy nodded. He had every confidence in his friend and now attorney.

"Oh and one more thing," Bara said. "At some point, you'll probably be introduced to Farrell's partner. His name is Inbusch. They're a team—known as Batman and Robin. And don't ask me which one is which. I don't think they even know."

Chapter 53

As instructed, Teddy arrived at the Federal Building at precisely 9:50 am. His name was on the list to gain access to the underground parking garage. He was directed to a parking spot designated for visitors, then took the elevator up to the lobby where he passed through security. On the other side of the security checkpoint was a rather ominous looking agent dressed in a traditional grey government business suit, including the bulging side-arm. He signaled Teddy to follow him. Together they rode the elevator up to the sixth floor. The chaperone never introduced himself or uttered a word.

When the elevator doors opened, the agent said, "Follow me." He led Teddy to an unattractive conference room. He pointed out the coffee available on the credenza, and left Teddy alone to ponder what might be coming next. Teddy had found himself in some pretty tense public meetings during his political career, but none of them measured up to the anxiety he was currently feeling about being part of a federal investigation. But despite his nerves, he was feeling a lot better after he'd heard back from Bara. His attorney said that based on his conversation with Agent Farrell, he was convinced Teddy was not in any trouble. The former agent said it was okay to cooperate with these guys. They were pros and always got their man.

Teddy was not impressed with the quality of the coffee, and knew he wouldn't be able to finish it. He walked over to the window with a distant view of the incoming and outgoing flights at Newark airport.

The In-House Politician

A second later the door to the conference room opened and in walked Agent Guy Farrell with another man who was introduced to Teddy as Agent Stephen Inbusch. There were no pleasantries. However, Agent Farrell said, with a wink, "By the way, I spoke with your attorney TJ Bara. He's the best. I hope he's not gouging you with his normal fees?"

Agent Farrell thanked Teddy for his assumed cooperation, and handed the meeting over to Inbusch.

"Mr. DeMarco," Inbusch said, "Agent Farrell here tells me he gave you a little background on our current investigation. There are lots of moving parts to it, and in order to maintain the highest level of secrecy, we will not be able to tell you what they are. Suffice it to say that since your Vice Chairman Peter Porzio is one of the targets of our investigation, we are very interested in learning more about your understanding of his role at the bank, and how he may have used his position to further the alleged criminal activities of both Alex Scarduzo Sr. and his son, Alex Scarduzo Jr. So let's begin with how the two of you interact in your respective roles at the bank."

The agent paused a moment, then continued. "Do you mind if we record this conversation?"

This gave Teddy the opportunity he was looking for. He granted them permission to record the conversation under one condition. He wanted one more assurance, on the record, as loud and as clear as they could make it for him. He said, "You may begin recording, but I would like for you to state on the record that I am not a target of your investigation. I'm here voluntarily, and my sole purpose is to provide you with background information. Correct?"

"Mr. DeMarco," Inbusch said, "I can understand why you might feel nervous, but rest assured we are just asking for your help to better understand how things work inside the bank. You have important background information we need to confirm. That's all. You are not under investigation. Please believe me when I say your cooperation is requested on a purely voluntary basis. You have nothing to fear from us. And what's more, we expect you'll be reporting on our conduct back to your attorney, TJ Bara. Rest assured, we don't want him for an enemy. He put you up to that, right?"

Teddy nodded. "So that's a no. I'm not a target of your investigation?"

Inbusch said, "No, Mr. DeMarco, you are not a target of our investigation."

Agent Inbusch, clearly frustrated said, "Shall we continue?"

"What would you like to know?" Teddy said.

After twenty minutes of explaining how he interacted with Peter Porzio and the bank's mortgage department, Teddy made sure the two agents clearly understood that he had no specific dealings with the Vice Chairman on any of his commercial lending lines of business. He also made it clear that he interacted with Porzio only when he needed to overrule a residential loan denial by Porter McMahon, or whenever the bank's Political Action Committee met. As Teddy ended his explanation, he thought it necessary to add that he felt bad for the bank's chairman, who had placed the highest level of confidence in Peter Porzio as his #2 and top credit policy official inside 1NEB. "Our chairman will be devastated when all this comes out."

Inbusch responded. "Mr. DeMarco, we don't make the rules. We just enforce them. Peter Porzio chose to do what he did, and

The In-House Politician

now he'll have to face the consequences. Now, there is a chance that Porzio might come out of this without being—"

"Better not say any more about that right now," Farrell interrupted. "We don't want Mr. DeMarco to misunderstand Porzio's situation."

Inbusch nodded. "One more thing, Mr. DeMarco. You mentioned something about coming into contact with Porzio whenever the bank's PAC met? Can you tell us more about that?"

Teddy said, "Well, our Chairman has given me the responsibility of overseeing the bank's PAC. I'm responsible for convening all PAC meetings, and putting forth my recommendations for candidates we should support—financially, that is. At the last meeting of the PAC, I brought in a recommendation to contribute to Rev. Lloyd Ogletree, the African American pastor and Democratic candidate in the same district where Alex Jr. is running. Ogletree approached me for the contribution and when I presented it to the PAC, Porzio pushed back a bit. Part of it was my fault for insinuating that Ogletree might not be successful and that—well, he wasn't a great friend of the banking industry. I tried to make the case that we were covering all the bases with our African American customers. Also, I might have suggested that if Ogletree did well in the televised debate and moved up in the polls, we might want to give him another larger contribution. As a result, Porzio went into orbit."

Teddy gathered his thoughts. "Fortunately, one of our attorneys made the case better than I did, and Porzio finally came around—at least for the initial contribution. But he wasn't happy about it. Anyway, after the meeting was over, Porzio asked me privately if I would consider making a similar PAC contribution to Alex Scarduzo Jr. Porzio said he wanted the bank to balance its contributions

377

between the Republicans and the Democrats. He didn't want the bank to appear to be taking sides in the election. I was a bit curious about this request because Porzio used the candidate's first name a few times as if he knew him personally—you know, Alex Scarduzo Jr. I was shocked to learn that Porzio even knew who was running in the race. He never showed any interest one way or the other about politics—other than his own conservative leanings and a desire to only support candidates who were friends of the bank."

Agents Farrell and Inbusch looked at each other with the kind of body language that said this was new and interesting intelligence.

"And how did you respond to Porzio's request?" Inbusch asked.

"I said that I was unaware that he even knew Alex, which he immediately denied. I also reminded him that Alex's campaign was flush with cash from his father, and he had never asked us for a contribution. I said that we needed to conserve as much PAC cash as possible. He seemed to be okay with this."

Again, the two agents seemed interested in this new development. "Okay," Inbusch said. "That's something we may want to revisit. Thanks."

Now it was Farrell's turn to ask the question he'd been waiting for since the meeting began. In fact, with the exception of the PAC story, they already knew most of the information Teddy had recited to them. They were just trying to make him feel comfortable and to make sure they had it right. Farrell laid it out. "So, Mr. DeMarco, here's the thing. It's not our job to police how you do your business when it comes to making mortgages. We have other people in the Department of Justice who are responsible for that sort of thing, and believe me when I say, that they've heard about your bank's problems. But your mortgage business is only a part of our investigation as it relates to the fraudulent mortgage reports Porzio was feeding Scarduzo Jr. We do know that 1NEB has been getting ripped in the press, as well as by some politicians—and by this we mean *The Examiner* and Rev. Lloyd Ogletree—for what appears to be on the surface a large number of loan denials to African American applicants. Do I have this right?"

Teddy was embarrassed. "Yes, that's right, but—"

"We also know how much you bankers like to keep your reputation as clean as Mother Theresa's," Farrell said. "The only time you guys like to see your bank's name in the press is when the Little League team you sponsored wins the championship, right?"

Teddy nodded.

The agent got up from his chair in an effort to stretch his legs. This just added to the drama in the room. Farrell said, "Well, you should know we believe that Scarduzo Sr. has told both his son, and your Vice Chairman Porzio to cool it with any more ugly mortgage reports being provided to *The Examiner*. Our guess is that he thinks, and correctly so, that we're on to Alex Jr.'s plan to help take down your bank with these bad mortgage reports."

Teddy held his hands up to signal a timeout. He said, "Sorry, but I don't follow. How did Alex Jr. think he was going to take down 1NEB with some bad mortgage reports?"

"You're right about that, Mr. DeMarco." Farrell said. "Alex Jr. most likely knew these stories in the press wouldn't really hurt you or the bank that much. He was just trying to make nice with—and it's a good thing you're sitting down—he was just trying to form an alliance with your good friend and ballbuster, Sally Kessler. In return for Alex Jr. getting those ugly mortgage reports printed in *The Examiner*, which made Kessler very happy, we think she agreed to provide him with insider information on Rev. Lloyd Ogletree's campaign. Of course, that all ended when Kessler was arrested for manslaughter in the death of one of Scarduzo's men at the debate. And didn't she accuse Ogletree of taking a bribe from 1NEB at that debate?"

Teddy was in a state of shock. It took him a moment to recover. "How do you know all this?" he asked. "I mean about Alex Jr. working with Sally Kessler to make us look bad?"

Farrell looked over at Inbusch, who nodded his approval. He said, "Because she told us that. And by the way, she says hello. She said she was just doing her job. I expect you know what she means by that. For your information, Sally Kessler has agreed to become a witness against Alex Scarduzo Jr. And in return for her testimony, we will be downgrading the manslaughter charge against her to something less. After all, we could make a case that the whole thing was accidental and in self-defense since she supposedly feared for her life."

"Holy shit," was all that Teddy could say in astonishment.

Farrell reminded Teddy once again that he was sworn to silence.

The two agents looked at each other and indicated they needed to talk privately. When they returned it was Agent Inbusch's turn to tag in. "So here's the deal, Mr. DeMarco. We need to get Peter Porzio on the record admitting to providing those false mortgage reports to Alex Jr. And since we're convinced they've been instructed to keep silent by Old Man Scarduzo, we have to come up with an alternative plan to get Porzio to talk. We would like to plant another article in *The Examiner*, specifically with Joe Campbell. We believe there's some connection between the reporter and Alex Jr. that provides him with some leverage over

Campbell. And you know as well as we do the article Campbell published on the first anniversary of your bank's agreement with Sally Kessler's group was pure bullshit. For some reason Campbell looked the other way and ran the story anyway."

It was all coming back to Teddy now. "That's right. One of my guys, Tom Donovan, was quite upset about the numbers quoted in that first year report. Although we never got any answers about it from Campbell or the newspaper because we—well, really me, missed an opportunity to question it before it was published. However, I'm still curious about who gave Porzio those bogus reports that ended up in *The Examiner*."

Inbusch had a big grin on his face. "We might be able to fill in that blank for you, Mr. DeMarco."

The agent went over to the conference room phone and pushed a few numbers. "Send her in."

A few seconds later the door opened and Tina Washington walked in. At first, Teddy didn't recognize her, but then he put it together. This was the young lady who assisted Porter McMahon in the mortgage department. She was responsible for underwriting many of their affordable mortgages. Indeed, Tom and Althea had spoken very highly of her despite her having to cow-tow to Porter's bigotry and his take-no-prisoners approach to the processing of their loans. While Teddy was not at a loss for words, he thought it best to remain quiet and let the other players in the room explain it all.

Agent Farrell asked Tina to sit down at the end of the conference room table opposite Teddy. He looked at Teddy, then at Tina, and asked, "You two know each other?"

Tina did not smile. She seemed just as nervous as Teddy.

Teddy remained silent. It occurred to him there were now two of them inside 1NEB who were playing nice with the FBI.

Farrell said, "For your information Mr. DeMarco, this investigation has been ongoing for quite some time. I'm going to speed past the introductions since I can see from the look on your faces that you two do know each other. For your information, Tina came to us through an intermediary, and reported she'd been approached by one of the bank's top officers to make up the initial false mortgage report. This officer requested—no, make that ordered her to pull together a mortgage report that would appear to be real, but would make the bank look bad under the terms of your agreement with Sally Kessler. The report had to be believable, so as not to be dismissed as nonsense. So to answer your earlier question, Tina here is the person who provided that initial false mortgage report to Porzio, who gave it to Alex Jr., who then gave it to Joe Campbell. Tina did this at our request and has been working with us ever since. She is the one providing all the loan data for those nasty stories about the bank. But we asked her to do it, to continue to play the role Porzio wanted from her. Tina says her job hasn't been all that difficult since, after that original bogus article, all of the information in the form of specific mortgage reports have all been pretty close to the actual numbers. Just a few tweaks here and there. She blames her boss for it all. She says this guy Porter McMahon is the person inside the bank responsible for denying all those minority mortgage applications."

Teddy smiled now, and greeted his colleague. "Nice to meet you formally, Tina. Tom Donovan and Althea McBride in my department have said nice things about you and how you've been able to help turn around a few border-line loans—you know, from Porter's evil hand."

The In-House Politician

This appeared to place Tina in a better mood. She laughed at Teddy's description of her boss and said, "Yes, I've been working a lot with Tom, and to a lesser extent Althea. I like them both very much. We've tried our best to reverse some of Porter's decisions, but he's a tough nut to crack."

Farrell wanted to get things back on track. He said, "Okay, that's enough for the reunion. No more talk about mortgages. Oh, one last thing. Tina, can you fill in Mr. DeMarco about how you were approached by Porzio?"

Tina looked down at her feet, not wanting to make eye contact. She paused for a moment, then looked up at Teddy and stated very clearly, "Mr. Porzio contacted me and said he would make sure I was promoted to Porter's job as head of the mortgage department if I helped him. He said the bank's reputation would take a hit once the reports were published, and that Porter would be the scapegoat for all the Black loan denials. Porzio also said the bank would need someone like me to take over and run the department. I'm assuming when he said someone like me, he meant because I'm Black."

Tina took a breath. "I really didn't want to do what he asked me to do. That's not the way I was raised. He basically threatened to end my career if I didn't cooperate. But he also sold it to me as a way of getting rid of Porter. I then talked with a friend of my family who's an attorney, and he counseled me to speak with the FBI."

"You should know," Farrell said, "that Peter Porzio was on our radar screen because of his family connection with the Scarduzos. We were suspicious of some commercial loans he was making to some associates of Scarduzo Sr. But until Tina came to us, we never made the connection between Porzio and Alex Jr. That's when we put it all together with her story about the false mortgage report. We followed the report through the various handoffs and saw it as an opportunity to flip your Vice Chairman. Oh, and sorry about the bad press. After this is all over, we'll make it right with your regulator—about the initial false report. Can't help you with the remaining denials."

Farrell looked at Teddy, and in his most patriotic tenor, said, "Mr. DeMarco, that's one brave young lady. Don't you agree? Tina is risking a lot by informing on Porzio. Chances are she'll pay a heavy price for coming forward. But we're going to do everything in our power to keep her safe and make sure that your Chairman knows how much we appreciated her service in this case. What do you say, Mr. DeMarco? You think you can help us take down the Scarduzos?"

"Well," Teddy said, "I don't understand how I fit into your plans, whatever they may be. I just told you that I don't have anything to do with Porzio's commercial lending activities. And while I'm not happy learning that Alex Scarduzo Jr., who I considered a friend, was conspiring with my worst enemy to bring me and my bank down, I'm still not sure how I can help you. But if you see a role for me to play—one that's not too dangerous—please, by all means, let me know."

Inbusch and Farrell looked at each other and smirked. It was the kind of body language that let Teddy know his response did not convey any profile in courage. Agent Farrell, now in a more exasperated tone, said, "Mr. DeMarco, your role in our plan is the least dangerous of all who are involved. We need for you to do two things, and one of them may never occur. The first is, if Joe Campbell does publish another story on the bank's poor mortgage performance, we want you to confirm the data. That's all. Now, we don't think he'll do another story on your bank, but anything's possible."

Teddy asked the obvious question. "Why wouldn't he write another bad story about the bank? Seems to me we've been selling a lot of newspapers for *The Examiner* recently."

"Too risky for him," Farrell said. "We're pretty sure there's some bad blood between Alex Jr. and the reporter Joe Campbell. While we don't know this for sure, we're betting that Alex Jr. doesn't want any more articles published, especially now that Sally Kessler is no longer in his corner."

"And the second item?" Teddy asked.

"We would like for you to follow through with your proposed second PAC contribution to Ogletree. First, it will give you an opportunity to make up with the candidate. But more importantly, from our perspective, we believe it will set off Porzio to do something really stupid. We'll be listening and waiting. Can you do that for us, Mr. DeMarco? Or do you need to check with your attorney first?"

Farrell's sarcasm was not lost on Teddy, and he looked embarrassed.

Chapter 54

Agent Farrell was all revved up from too much coffee and the excitement of coming up with a plan he was confident would flip Peter Porzio. The Feds did not mention a second part of their plan to Tina since it was related to Porzio's commercial lending activities since it did not involve her. However, because Teddy would be involved in setting the trap for Porzio, they thought it appropriate to read him in.

This second complaint was based on some suspicious activities the Feds had been monitoring. They believed that funds from loans being made to associates of Scarduzo Sr. were ending up as illegal cash contributions to Alex Jr.'s campaign. By following the money, the Feds were convinced they had discovered Porzio's involvement in this scheme due to his encouragement of large loan reserves, and orders to his lending officers to look the other way when these reserves were disbursed without sufficient back-up documentation. The Feds had successfully turned one of Scarduzo's associates who had been an early recipient of a loan from one of Porzio's lenders. Additionally, when the time was right, they would subpoena this lending officer to confirm his boss's order to keep silent on the large reserves. The Feds would then charge Porzio with a second count of conspiracy to violate federal election campaign laws along with Scarduzo Sr. by illegally channeling these funds into the political campaign Alex Jr. The Feds knew this charge would be more difficult to prove against Porzio since he would most likely claim he was unaware of how these

The In-House Politician

reserve funds were being used. But the Feds needed to pile on the charges in order to get Porzio to flip.

Before the Feds brought Tina into the room to go over their plan, Teddy wanted some clarification. Teddy said, "If I may, it seems to me that providing false mortgage reports to a third party, in this case from Porzio to Alex Jr., is not a major crime, is it? And the issue of Porzio encouraging his lenders to increase the size of the reserves in those commercial loans, is that really a game changer in trying to get Porzio to flip? I'm sure when this all comes out, Porzio will be dismissed from the bank, but this doesn't seem to me to be a crime in which he's going to serve a lot of jail time. What am I missing?"

The agents looked at each other, then whispered something. Farrell said, "One moment please, Mr. DeMarco."

While they were waiting for Farrell to return, Tina entered the room with an escort. When Farrell returned he was accompanied by a man with no suit jacket, his sleeves rolled up, and his tie askew. He had the appearance of a man who had just been saved from too many depositions, too many subpoenas, and too many cases. Sure enough, this man was introduced to Teddy as Assistant Attorney General Reginald K. Willers. He was the man in charge of the Scarduzo investigation.

Willers looked at Tina. "Good to see you again, Ms. Washington."

Tina returned his greeting with a smile and a nod.

Willers then looked at Teddy. "Mr. DeMarco. Your reputation precedes you. I've followed your previous political career and your subsequent success with 1NEB. Very impressive. Sorry to make your acquaintance under these circumstances. Agent Farrell tells me you've agreed to join our team. Is that correct?"

Teddy was still unsure of his role, and hadn't exactly volunteered to storm the beaches, but thought it best to play along. He nodded his assent.

Willers continued. "Well that's a good thing because what I'm about to tell you both is that your Vice Chairman Peter Porzio is not the prime target in this investigation. But he knows just enough to be an important witness. As you guessed, Mr. DeMarco, he's an accessory to their crimes, and will probably not to go to jail if he cooperates. But we'll be playing hardball with him until he fully understands how much trouble he's in. Our goal here is to flip your Vice Chairman and have him testify against the Scarduzos."

Chapter 55

Michelle was beside herself. She couldn't believe what she was hearing from Inbusch. She began to scream at him. "You know back in Zurich it occurred to me that you guys might have been using me as bait. Well, it seems I was right. I can't believe this. No way. I'm not agreeing to that. You can't put me and my baby in that position!"

Inbusch understood why she was so upset. This wasn't his idea. It came directly from his boss, Willers, and there wasn't much he could do about it, except to have his objection noted for the record. Willers was proposing they place an article in *The Examiner* as a follow-up to her disappearance, which would ask the pointed question, "Where is Michelle Mitchell?" It had been seven months since she left for Italy, and the rumors about an affair between her and Alex Jr. were running rampant. No one knew her whereabouts, but the sharks were circling the candidate.

At every campaign stop the question was being raised about whether there had been an extra-marital affair between them, and if not, why couldn't she be located to deny it. In fact, some Ocean County employees who were not fans of Alex Jr. implied to the press there was plenty of circumstantial evidence proving that the two always traveled together—on business, that is. Moreover, Catherine Whitman Scarduzo no longer answered the phone at home since most of the calls were from reporters wanting to interview her. And her husband, the candidate, was getting hammered in the polls.

He knew it was only a matter of time until the NDA found its way into the press.

So Willers decided it was time to throw more fuel on the fire. He was of the opinion that a well-placed story in *The Examiner* stating the Feds were still searching for Michele would precipitate some kind of reaction from the Scarduzo family. Indeed, it might cause the targets of their investigation to make a dumb mistake. And the Feds would be there to spring into action.

Inbusch attempted to quiet Michelle down. It wouldn't be good if one of the neighbors close to the safe house called the local police to report screaming coming from inside the residence. Michelle got the message and began to sob. Inbusch summoned the female agent to take Michelle into the bedroom to calm her down.

About ten minutes later Michelle came out with the female agent and sat down opposite Inbusch. The female agent then removed herself to give them some privacy. Michelle looked at Inbusch with her sad and reddened eyes while placing her hand on her extended belly. Her mood was not lost on Inbusch. She asked a series of questions. "What makes you think I'm still news? And why do you think *The Examiner* is going to agree to do a story on my whereabouts? Who cares about me except the Scarduzos?"

Inbusch was pleased to see she appeared calm, and was now thinking more clearly. He was also happy he had real answers to her questions. He said, "First, you should know that you are news. We've done our best to keep you away from the papers and from watching the news. Believe me, all of those less than truthful rags you can buy at the check-out counter are in full speculation mode about your affair with Alex Jr. There are also rumors as to where your body might be buried. One of them has your body in one of the Scarduzo landfills, while another has you at the bottom of Lake Como. And as to why we think *The Examiner* will print the story, well, have you ever heard of a reporter for the paper by the name of Joe Campbell?"

Michelle thought for a moment. She recalled hearing his name in passing from Alex Jr. when they were together, but nothing more than that.

"Well," Inbusch said, "it seems there's some kind of connection between your former lover and this reporter. Alex and Joe Campbell attended the same prep school at the same time. Our investigation has found that Alex Jr. almost blinded Campbell in a fight. But of course, Old Man Scarduzo paid a lot of money to make the case go away, and keep Jr. from being expelled. There has to be a lot more to the story on what triggered Jr. to do what he did to Campbell. But whatever it was, it seems to have provided Jr. with some sort of leverage over this reporter. We mean to confront Campbell with our knowledge of their history and use it to our advantage. We will convince him to do the story. And if he says no, then we threaten to go to his editor with this information. If necessary, we can strike some kind of deal with Campbell to provide him with an exclusive on the investigation once its completed. Of course, we're not going to tell them the details of the investigation or that we have you in a safe place—alive and well. We'll just say that we're still actively looking for you. We may even set up a reward and a hot-line for information on your whereabouts. It'll lend more credibility to the story."

He paused a moment. "So have I answered your questions?"

Michelle was stunned. Not so much about Alex having almost blinded someone, or that he was using some unknown leverage over a newspaper reporter. She was most upset over the fact that people were speculating that she was already dead, and that her body would never be found. It gave her the chills. She said, "I guess. But I'm not clear on what you think will happen as a result of this story about me. And you still haven't allayed my fears."

Inbusch knew he had to be careful in how he responded. He couldn't reveal to her the listening devices they planted inside the Scarduzo estate had been discovered and destroyed. This might upset her again. He said, "Well, we're not actually sure how they will react to the news, but we expect they will do something stupid. Just remember that as long as you remain under our protection, I promise they won't find you."

Michelle shook her head in disagreement. "How certain are you of that? That they'll never find me?"

Inbusch stated, "I'd bet my life on it."

Michelle said, "Good. Because it sounds like you're betting mine."

Chapter 56

Buddy was confused and wasn't sure what to do. A woman he didn't know stopped him outside the bank just as he was about to pull out of the parking lot in his delivery run. He was all loaded up with the interoffice mail and ready to make his rounds when the woman chased him down and told him she had something for him from Vice Chairman Porzio. He rolled down the window and listened to her pitch. She said the Vice Chairman wanted to make sure this got to him before he left for his deliveries. She appeared to be out of breath, and indicated how thankful she was she'd found him before he'd left. She said, "Vice Chairman Porzio said you would know what to do with this. I'm glad I found you before you left. You know how he gets."

Tina improvised this last statement. If it had been anyone other than Buddy—well, someone else might have been suspicious of how she knew "how he gets."

There was nothing written on the outside of the plain manilla envelope. On the inside was another envelope—this one addressed to Alex Scarduzo Jr. Buddy's confusion was based on the fact that he'd always met his Uncle Peter somewhere outside the bank whenever he wanted him to personally deliver an envelope to the candidate. Tina said to him, "The Vice Chairman said not to worry. He's busy with all-day meetings and wanted to make sure this got delivered today. You can call him to confirm if you like." The Feds were taking a big risk in assuming that Buddy would not be inclined to disturb his uncle again.

Buddy recalled the last time he questioned his uncle when he called him to confirm the assignment. His uncle nearly took his head off by reminding him in no uncertain terms to never call him directly on a bank line. This seemed to satisfy Buddy, who never asked Tina for her name. However, she made sure her fake I.D. badge was in plain sight for him to see. The name on the badge read Meryle Bonavito-Asaro just to make it more difficult for him to remember. Not that Buddy would ever think to ask for her name, or even remember it—but just in case. Additionally, it was a sunny day affording Tina the opportunity to hide behind sunglasses and to put her hair up underneath a baseball cap.

The Feds were ready to follow Buddy to make sure the delivery was made. The team was impressed that he did not immediately drive to Alex Jr.'s campaign headquarters. He took his normal delivery route and then, as instructed, delivered the envelope to the candidate. The Feds had made sure the candidate would not be in his campaign offices this day, since it would have risked Alex Jr. interrogating Buddy.

As instructed Buddy always parked around the corner in a narrow alleyway. He understood that some level of secrecy was involved because his uncle didn't want the vehicle with its 1NEB logo to be spotted. Buddy handed the envelope to Alex's campaign manager and pointed to the note inside that said "Personal and Confidential. For the candidate's eyes only."

Chapter 57

As Joe Campbell was leaving *The Examiner* offices for the day, Inbusch and Farrell corralled him their van. There was nothing subtle about their invitation techniques, and no ability for the reporter to escape. Inside the black government-issue SUV the two agents flashed their credentials, then indicated they just wanted to have a brief conversation with him.

Joe said, "What's this all about?"

Inbusch took the diplomatic approach. "Mr. Campbell, is it okay if I call you Joe?" He didn't wait for an answer. "We would like to request your help with something. As you know, we've been searching for Michelle Mitchell for quite some time, but thus far we haven't had any luck. We thought if *The Examiner* put out a piece asking for anyone with information on her whereabouts to come forward, we might get lucky. And we're offering a $10,000 reward for any information leading to her location. So, what do you say? Can you help us out here?"

"Wasn't she supposedly Alex Scarduzo's mistress?" Joe asked. "Why do you need to find her? Last I heard she'd gone missing over in Italy, right?"

Inbusch said, "Let's just say she's an important witness in an ongoing investigation. We really can't say any more than that. She's been underground for seven months now, and it's been a few months since your paper published the last story about her disappearance."

"What makes you think she's back in States?"

"We have no idea if she's returned," said Inbusch, "but we're open to that possibility. We're working with Italian authorities to do the same over there."

Joe knew Alex would not be happy if he wrote another story about Michelle. "Sorry, guys, but newspapers are not typically in the business of helping the government do its job—especially those agencies who arrest and prosecute people. It's part of our code of ethics to stay impartial. So I'll have to decline. May I go now?"

The agents looked at each other and laughed. Now it was Farrell's turn to play hardball. He said, "Congratulations, Joe. We've heard some crackerjack excuses from reporters, but that one is pure unadulterated bullshit. Now here's the deal. We were hoping you would cooperate voluntarily, but, well, it looks like you're going to need a little inducement."

Joe began to feel nervous, thinking he was about to get worked over by these Feds.

Farrell said, "Joe, we know you have a longstanding relationship with Alex Scarduzo Jr. He's your old prep school buddy. And he's the reason you have to wear that eye patch sometimes, right? Now, what would happen if your editor found out about how you colluded with Scarduzo on that piece you wrote about 1NEB? You know as well as we do those numbers were false. But you published the article anyway."

Joe was weighing his options. He was not in a good place. What would Scarduzo do to him if he wrote the article? Alternatively, if the Feds revealed his connection with Scarduzo to his editor, his career at *The Examiner* would be over.

The agents could tell the reporter was wavering. Farrell looked over to Inbusch and he nodded. "Okay, Joe. We're willing to sweeten

The In-House Politician

the pot if that's what it takes. If you write this story, we'll agree to give you an exclusive once the investigation is concluded. We're not at liberty to provide you with any more details about it now, but let's just say this could be a big story for you. Who knows, it might even make your career."

Joe knew the Fed's investigation was related to Alex Scarduzo. Why else would they be hunting for Michelle Mitchell? He also knew this investigation and story would ultimately come back to bite him. The Feds knew about his connection to Scarduzo and the false article he had published about 1NEB. But this last promise for an exclusive on the investigation was too good to pass up. He was still a reporter, first and foremost. It sealed the deal and he agreed to write the story.

Joe thought if Alex contacted him after the story appeared, his excuse would be that his editor was still upset over the original 1NEB article, which had set off lots of angry accusations from all sorts of interested parties. He'd say his editor was looking for something juicy and the "Missing Michelle" story fit the bill.

But Alex was too smart to contact him directly. A day after the story appeared, there was a knock on Joe's door. When he opened it, a young man indicated he had a message for Mr. Campbell. The message was delivered orally. He said, "Your friend wants to remind you to never write another story about Michelle Mitchell without speaking with him first." The messenger then turned and left.

The article had Old Man Scarduzo in a rage. Everything seemed to be falling apart. The story indicated that the Feds were still searching for Michelle Mitchell. But this didn't make any sense since his contacts were positive she was not to be found anywhere in the Europe. She had been there—that was confirmed, but then she vanished. In fact, Giuseppe LiVecchi had paid the ultimate price for not completing the assignment of locating and disposing of her body. This could mean only one thing. The Feds already had her in protective custody, and she was singing like a bird. By virtue of the article, the Feds were hoping to draw them out. Scarduzo Sr. knew when he was being played.

Adding to Sr.'s alarm was that Alex Jr. was in receipt of a new mortgage report from Peter Porzio. But Sr. had ordered Porzio to stand down. What's more, Alex Jr. made the cardinal sin of calling his father on an unsecure phone line to ask him what he should do with the new report. Scarduzo Sr. instructed his son in as calm a voice as he could muster to burn it. If there was anyone listening in on the conversation, Sr. wanted them to know he was on to them. No hysterics on his end. Sr. knew his phone was clean, but his son's? Alex Jr. was a politician working with many campaign supporters and county employees who could not be trusted. There were times when Sr. wondered about his son's common sense. He indicated to Jr. that he should come by to visit his mother, which was always code for they needed to meet ASAP.

Chapter 58

It was time for Teddy and Tina to act out their respective roles in the amateur Shakespearean play drafted for them by the Feds. It was agreed that Teddy and Tina would have final editing authority over the script since they worked with Porzio, and had a much better sense of how he might react to certain situations. The overall goal was to get Porzio so nervous that he would do or say something to incriminate himself. Of course, the script included certain trigger words designed to set him off.

Act I, Scene I was Teddy calling a meeting of the bank's PAC on a day when he knew the Chairman would be out of the office. Teddy couldn't risk the Chairman attending the PAC meeting. There was no telling how a consistently honest and brilliant thinker who always wanted to do the right thing would react to two of his top officers going after each other. Teddy and the Feds didn't want to place the Chairman in this position—each for their own separate reasons.

Act I, Scene II would be Tina meeting with Porzio, presumably at his request due to the PAC meeting leading him to her. Tina would be wearing a wire at this meeting. After being admonished and most likely threatened by Porzio, Tina would then say she'd had enough of doing his dirty work and needed greater assurances of how she would be protected and how soon his promises of her career advancement would be fulfilled. Tina would tell Porzio a fabricated story that she'd been approached by another lender to head up their underwriting department with a title of vice president and lots more money. She would threaten to leave unless Porzio could find a way to move the timetable up for her promotion.

Willers, along with Agents Inbusch and Farrell, had met with Teddy a few times to make sure he was on board with how to play his role. During this interim rehearsal period, Teddy visited with Margaret Tilley, the Chairman's personal assistant. She had worked for the Chairman for the past twenty years and was considered his alter ego. Margaret understood Teddy's role in the bank, and had accommodated him on previous occasions with information on the Chairman's schedule, that she didn't share with others she didn't trust or like. She also understood how much the Chairman relied on Teddy to be the public face of the bank, and did her best to interpret the fine line between providing too much information versus not enough. She was very good at her job.

Margaret gave Teddy a few dates when the Chairman would be out of the office for the entire day. But that was the extent of it. No reasons were given as to why he would be out, and Teddy was fine with that. He assumed the Chairman was meeting privately with investment bankers on the lookout for his next acquisition.

A meeting of the PAC was set for a date Teddy knew would be acceptable to Porzio and corresponded with when the Chairman would be out. The Vice Chairman held his regularly scheduled senior commercial lenders meeting on Wednesdays at 10 am. So Teddy zeroed in on this date and scheduled the PAC meeting for 11 am that same day.

All the PAC members had arrived and taken their traditional seats in the boardroom. Teddy was getting anxious since Porzio was still absent. As he got up to check on the Vice Chairman, whose office

The In-House Politician

was next door, he saw him hanging up the phone and signaling he would be there momentarily.

Porzio entered the room and moved directly to the head of the table, once again assuming the role of chair for the meeting. Teddy knew the drill and had become accustomed to it even though he had called the meeting and it was his agenda. Teddy's nerves were about as frayed as when he'd heard from Ogletree telling him he was returning the bank's contribution and accusing the bank of discrimination. But today was a different kind of nervousness. If he screwed this up, it could cause a whole Federal investigation to crash and burn. And the Feds were not the forgiving types.

Porzio, always in a pleasant mood, looked at Teddy and barked, "Okay, DeMarco. You called this meeting. Let's get started."

Teddy said, "Gentlemen, and our esteemed MC, you will recall the last time we met, Peter indicated that if I was going to recommend we contribute more funds to Rev. Lloyd Ogletree's campaign, we should meet again to review the situation."

He didn't get any further in his presentation when the grumbling began. Porzio looked like he was about to get up and leave, but Teddy pleaded with him to stay and hear what he had to say. The events of the televised debate were still fresh in everyone's mind. Another officer laughed out loud and said, "DeMarco, didn't this Ogletree guy return the last donation you tried to give him? Didn't he also accuse us of discrimination? You're not seriously thinking about giving him more money, are you? Hell, he didn't keep the last check! And all that bullshit about us trying to bribe him. Really?"

Porzio didn't need to say anything. The officers in the room were all in agreement and thought Teddy's idea was a joke. One officer said the meeting was a waste of his time and was about to leave. That's when Teddy stood up and said, "You're all going to want to hear what I have to say. If any of you leave this meeting and we don't have a quorum, I'll have no choice but to inform our Chairman, who is keenly aware we are meeting today."

This last statement, while being true, might have been a bit of an exaggeration, especially the "keenly aware" part. But it did the trick. No one left the room and Teddy had everyone's attention.

Teddy continued. "We are all familiar with what happened with our last contribution to Rev. Ogletree. But I think it would be wise to review a few important items that have occurred since then, which I believe sheds a different light on the situation. First, Ogletree apologized to us at the debate, and to me personally. Second, Ogletree will win the Democratic nomination, and will most likely be the next Congressman in this district. We don't want him as an enemy."

Porzio was fuming. "Now wait a second, DeMarco. You can't say that for sure. I think Alex Scarduzo has a legitimate shot at winning the election against your guy Ogletree."

Teddy responded quickly. "Peter, no Republican has won in that district in the last thirty years. It's a Democratic stronghold. What's more, Scarduzo, has been dropping like a rock in the polls since rumors started about an affair he allegedly had with one of his political aides. And if that wasn't bad enough, that aide has gone missing over in Italy. I can say with a high level of confidence that Ogletree will win, period."

One of the officers piped up, "You know that wasn't much of an apology from Ogletree."

The In-House Politician

Teddy said, "I have the transcript here of the debate if you'd like me to read it back to you—just for the record."

The officer shook his head. "I watched the debate. The whole thing was bullshit. Weren't those protestors the ones you negotiated that CRA agreement with? And isn't that agreement the source of all those rejections to all those Black applicants?"

The reaction from the officers was exactly what Teddy had predicted and what Willers was hoping for. It was lighting a fire under Porzio.

"Gentlemen." Teddy said. "Please. Settle down. Please listen to me before you start judging. Those denial ratios cited by Rev. Ogletree in his press conference were pretty close to the truth. We still don't know how he got hold of that report, and we're still looking for the leaker. You should all know that our Chairman took to heart what Rev. Ogletree said about us in his press conference and his remarks at the debate—despite the protestors' interruptions. And what's more, we understand our regulators in Washington have also been made aware of these rather large disparities in the number of African American denials in comparison to the number of White denials. We expect they'll be digging into this to a much greater extent in their upcoming examinations, which are due to occur in the next six months. If any of this holds up another acquisition—well, I wouldn't want to be on the receiving end of that blame game."

Porzio couldn't contain himself and didn't seem to care that MC was in the room. "DeMarco, this is all your fault. If it wasn't for all those shitty loan applications coming into the bank under the terms of that fucking CRA agreement with those commie friends of yours, we wouldn't be in this mess."

Teddy remained calm. "Peter, the only way our last merger was approved was when we entered into that agreement with PUMP. If you recall, it was written in as a condition of the merger approval by the regulators." This was a fine legal point that no one in the room except MC would have remembered. Teddy looked at MC and gave her a subtle wink. She understood and did not correct him.

It was time for Teddy to close the deal. "Rev. Ogletree has asked me if we would consider making another contribution. He is in dire need of money for the Fall campaign, and I think we should consider it for the following reasons. First, he has apologized for accusing us of discrimination, and has admitted he may have been wrong. He has stated it is possible all those Black loan applications that were rejected may have been denied for legitimate reasons. He doesn't want to judge us without knowing all the facts. And separate and apart from Rev. Ogletree's admission is that our Chairman wants to know why so many loans were declined. So, we will be establishing an internal review team, an independent audit group if you will, to look into the reasons why we had so many minority denials. Rev. Ogletree will be appointing one of his fellow pastors active in the Ministry for Justice and Economic Development to sit on this audit team. Likewise, I am hereby asking MC to be part of the team. And finally, we have our eye on a retired Federal bank examiner to come in and head it up."

Teddy paused a moment and took a breath. He looked toward MC. She was smiling and gave him a thumbs up to serve. He was now waiting for Porzio's response. Right on time, Porzio bellowed, "I was not aware of this. Has the Chairman approved this? If so, he hasn't made me aware of it. At least not yet." There was a certain alarm in his voice.

The In-House Politician

"The recommendation is with the Chairman as we speak." Teddy said. "But we've talked about it and I can't see any reason why he would say no to the proposal. He wants to get to the bottom of this. And as for you not being in the loop, Peter, doesn't the Mortgage Department report directly to you? Isn't Porter McMahon one of your guys? And all of those mortgage reports that somehow ended up in the hands of *The Examiner* and of Ogletree, aren't they produced by your folks in the Mortgage Department? It only stands to reason the leaker is someone close to the Mortgage Department, wouldn't you agree?"

All the officers sitting around the table looked at Porzio to see his next move.

The Vice Chairman pounded on the table. "I said it before, and I'll say it again. This is all your fault, DeMarco. We wouldn't have had all those denials if it weren't for that cockamamie agreement you entered into with those radicals. How do we know you didn't give those damning reports to the press yourself? Huh? How do we know it wasn't you?"

Always fast on his feet, Teddy returned fire. "Peter. Do you actually hear yourself? The Chairman hired me to be the guy who puts the best face on all things external and political. He hasn't fired me yet, and he's had plenty of opportunity to. What's more, he gave me a vote of confidence just the other day by asking for my recommendations on how we can improve the number of approvals to minority applicants. We're working on those recommendations for him as we speak."

Teddy was feeling confident. "Okay. The second reason we should consider for making a contribution to Rev. Ogletree's campaign is that he has agreed to not make any public announcement of it. The contribution will be made anonymously. Of course, if someone wanted to bring it to light, the Federal Election Commission makes all donations public in its reports, so anyone could find out about it if they really wanted to know. But Rev. Ogletree has made it clear to me, and to our Chairman, that he wants to build bridges with the financial services industry. He said he's learned two very important lessons the hard way in his short political career. The first is that if you take on the issue of what the big banks are doing to the little guys, you can gain lots of political support from the voters. We are not held in very high esteem with the public."

He paused for dramatic effect. Most of the officers sitting around the table held very high opinions of themselves, and of the roles they played at 1NEB. They were not accustomed to hearing that the general public did not share their opinion of themselves.

Teddy continued. "The other lesson he learned was that you can lose a lot of corporate financial support when you take on the big banks. He said after he publicly accused us of discrimination, funding from all his corporate sponsors seemed to dry up rather quickly. I assured him we had nothing to do with it. So he wants to be friends again. He promises to be a kinder and gentler candidate when it comes to banking industry issues. But he also promises that he will continue to protest against the closing of branches in low-income communities whenever there's a merger. We agreed to disagree on this issue, and to come up with solutions that make sense for both of us."

Porzio seemed to have calmed down a bit, which was not the plan. So, Teddy needed one more big push. He said, "One thing we all agreed on was that we would redouble our efforts to find the leaker

The In-House Politician

who provided those false mortgage reports to *The Examiner*. The Chairman has made it clear that whenever this person is identified, he or she will be made an example of."

This last statement was a risk. Teddy had discussed the situation with the Chairman, who had indicated his concern. But no one, including Teddy, knew what the Chairman meant when he said "be made an example of." As far as Teddy knew this could mean the person was going to be given a medal by the Chairman for uncovering what certainly appeared to be either institutional or personal discriminatory underwriting practices in the bank's Mortgage Department.

Teddy had done his job. "It's time to vote. I am recommending that we give Rev. Lloyd Ogletree, Democratic candidate for Congress, $15,000 as an amount he can use as a match from other donors. As part of this contribution, Rev. Ogletree will agree not to make it public. 1NEB will remain anonymous. You will note I have recommended an increase from $10,000 up to $15,000 since, as you recall, he returned the original $5,000 to us. Are there any other questions I can answer for you before we vote?" He paused. "Okay. Seeing none, let's vote. All in favor, please signify by raising your hand."

Teddy counted seven affirmative votes.

"All those against? I see one vote against. Let the record show the vote was approved by a vote of seven to one, with Vice Chairman Porzio dissenting. Thank you, gentlemen, and you too, MC."

As Porzio got up from the table, he glared at Teddy. He pointed his finger at him for all the officers to see, and repeated his rant. "This is all your fault, DeMarco. I hope you're happy with yourself." Porzio then turned and stomped out of the room.

Chapter 59

Porzio reacted just as the Feds had predicted. Teddy had set the stage by revealing that the bank, with the support of the Chairman, was redoubling its efforts to hunt down the internal leaker. As a result, Porzio would have to contact Tina to make certain they had their stories straight. After Porter McMahon, she would surely be one of the persons of interest the new audit team would interview. He needed to move quickly to tie up his own loose ends.

The Feds had coached Tina to respond calmly. No hysterics. Porzio would need to see a young woman who was confident. They were uncomfortable with Tina hanging out there all alone with no one available for back-up should Porzio do something completely out of character and attempt to silence her. The team knew that Porzio believed intimidation was his powerful tool to keep her in line, but the Feds had no way of planting anyone near her office to keep her safe. Tina knew the risks, however, and decided she'd take her chances.

Within twenty minutes after the conclusion of the PAC meeting, Porzio phoned Tina. There was no way he could visit her in person. He was the king and no one could see him meeting with someone as lowly as Tina—least of all in her office. Staff would get the wrong idea.

Tina recognized the number, so she let the call go through to her voice mail. But Porzio was too smart to leave a message. He would continue calling until she picked up. This gave Tina time to reach the Feds and let them know their timetable would have to be moved up.

Within thirty minutes Tina was meeting with the Feds in the bank's underground parking garage to have them plant a wire on her. Once all the details were covered, she was ready to answer the call from Porzio.

When Tina picked up the phone, Porzio said only eight words. "We need to meet. Same place. One hour."

Chapter 60

Tina was ready. They would meet in Branch Brook Park at the north end of Newark, the same location Porzio had used when he first approached her. When she advised the agents where they were going to meet, they couldn't contain their excitement. Porzio could not have made their surveillance any easier—both the audio and the visual. They just needed to switch cars. Their government-issue black SUV was hard to miss, and needed something a little less obvious.

As with their initial meeting, they arrived separately. Porzio was taking no chances that his car might be bugged. Likewise, the Feds did not want Tina alone in his car, not knowing what he might have in mind for her. The specific location in the park was the same as before. There was a bench just opposite the lake on the pathway, which seemed to be perfectly situated for clandestine meetings like this one. It was another scene right out of a grade B spy movie.

Tina arrived and made her way to the bench. Porzio had arrived earlier, and had been walking around the lake to make sure no one else was trying to eavesdrop on them. Once he was confident they were alone, he proceeded to the bench. There were no pleasantries.

"I don't know if you've heard," Porzio began, "but there's going to be an internal investigation to uncover the person responsible for all the false mortgage reports."

Tina looked directly at him and said, "Really? I thought that search had already begun. You have something planned to cover both of our tracks, I hope?"

The In-House Politician

Porzio was impressed by Tina's demeanor. She was calm and wasn't making this easy. He said, "What do you mean? Covering what tracks?" He had a feeling she might be trying to trap him. He really wanted to frisk her to determine if she was wearing a wire, but couldn't bring himself to believe it had come to that.

Tina had been coached on how to react to his denial. It was important for her to make him feel comfortable. She needed him to think she was part of his team and understood the risks for both of them. In as calm a voice as she could muster she said, "Listen, Mr. Porzio. I fully understand the situation you have placed us in, and I've accepted the risks. But if they interview me, I need to know what you want me to say that will make sense and not place me under any further suspicion. So what do I tell them?"

Porzio mumbled something unintelligible. He was thinking now. Apparently he hadn't formulated a plan yet. His ego was such that he never thought anyone would ever question his motives.

Both of them were now playing their respective roles—assuming someone was listening to their every word. Only Tina knew for sure.

She was on the spot now and needed to show her cards. "You should know, Mr. Porzio, that I'm getting a bit tired of waiting for your promises of being promoted to Porter's job. So far your plan that he was going to take the fall for all the minority loan denials, and then I would get his job seems to have backfired on you. Wouldn't you agree?"

Porzio was still in denial mode. "I don't recall ever promising you Porter's job. You're living in some kind of fantasy world. I would never have said that. Besides, it would be your word against mine. And who do you think wins that one?"

Tina said, "Why? Because I'm Black and a woman? You know what? I've about had it with you. I see no reason why I shouldn't come clean with this new audit team and tell them how you ordered me to make up that false mortgage report, and in return, you promising me Porter McMahon's job."

Porzio was rocking back and forth trying to solve his Tina problem in his head. "Really? Are you playing the race card with me? It was your department that rejected all those Black loans, not me. You had every opportunity to do a better job in that regard. So you saw an opportunity to make the bank look bad hoping—just hoping that you wouldn't be found out, place the blame on Porter, and possibly be in line for his job—that is, if he got fired as a result of all those loan rejections. You should have done a better job of controlling Porter's instincts. It's your fault. So you put out those bad mortgage reports in the hope that Porter would be fired. You were trying to get him fired all along, weren't you? And then you would come riding in as the new Black hero and set things right. Do I have that right?"

Porzio was beginning to think that his unscripted, spontaneous accusations were working. At least they were working in his own mind—and to anyone else who might be listening.

Tina knew she was losing him. She had to do something quickly. She decided to go off script. "Okay, Mr. Porzio. I got it. You have all the power and I have none. They'll believe you over me. Got it. So how do we both come out of this without too much damage? I mean, the fact is, Porter McMahon reports directly to you. He will say he was just underwriting those loans in the manner he thought you wanted him to—strictly by the book, with no exceptions. There's no way Porter goes down without some of the stench leaching on

The In-House Politician

to you. You were the man in charge, right? Going up the line? What kind of supervision did you provide to Porter? Or did you leave him alone? Either way—you get torched. I know Porter well enough to say he's not going down without a fight."

The Feds were listening intently to their conversation. Now that she had gone off script they were feeling doomed.

But then Porzio forgot what he had just told himself about not saying anything incriminating. He was buying into her logic. "So what do you have in mind, young lady?" he said so condescendingly Tina wanted to punch him in the face.

She recovered fast. The response to his question was obvious to her, but not to Porzio. At least not yet. Tina looked at him and said, "We need to find a way to lay all this off on Porter."

Porzio laughed at this. He was thinking perhaps she wasn't trying to lay a trap for him after all. If she was looking for a way out that would help them both, then maybe he had misjudged her. "And how do you propose to accomplish that?"

"Give me a second to think this through."

Porzio looked at his watch. "I need to get back to the office. I have another meeting in 30 minutes."

Tina was feeling emboldened. "Excuse me, but you're the one who called this meeting."

Staff never talked to him like that, but he knew she was right.

"How about this?" Tina said. "You say you came to me to ask for my help to keep an eye on Porter since word had gotten back to you that he'd gone rogue. He was denying too many minority loan applications, and the bank was going to find itself in a public relations nightmare. When Porter found out you were having me spy on him, instead of fearing the public relations problems, he wanted to make sure they actually happened. So he doubled down hoping the bad press would lead to Teddy DeMarco and his staff getting fired since they were responsible for that damn CRA agreement with those PUMP crazies."

Porzio was loving it. "Yeah! You know, I was just at a meeting in which I said that very same thing. DeMarco and his commie friends were responsible for all this going sideways. Too bad we can't find a way to put this off on him."

Tina was stunned, but then remembered Teddy thought Porzio might try something like this. She said, "I really don't know how we could manage that. No one would believe it. He and his staff are the in-house liberals always trying to save the world. That wouldn't fly."

"I suppose you're right," Porzio agreed. "We'll have to sacrifice Porter. You know I never liked that little piss-ant anyway. He's actually less charming than me, if that's possible. So smug. Oh well, please continue."

"You know, Mr. Porzio, there's one big hole in this plan, which I'm not sure I can fill in because I don't know how it all worked. I gave those mortgage reports to you. So how did they end up in *The Examiner*?"

The Feds were all smiling. Tina was pretty good at improvising and had circled back.

Porzio considered his response very carefully. "Well, I've got a contact who knows someone at the newspaper."

Tina said, "Okay, so if Porter is the one being accused, what's his answer to that same question? Who did he give the false mortgage reports to at *The Examiner*? When Porter denies it, won't the audit team ask the

The In-House Politician

folks at the newspaper who gave them the reports? Oh wait, reporters never give up their sources even under pain of death. So if the reporter declines to say who gave him the reports, can't the audit team ask the reporter to eliminate bank staff who weren't responsible for providing him with the reports? You know—by a process of elimination?"

"I don't think it works that way," Porzio said, "but you may be on to something. We'll need to figure that out."

Tina knew her time was running out and needed a home run. "You know, Mr. Porzio, in order for me to help us plan this out so that we escape with our jobs and reputations intact, I should know what the process was. The newspaper is the real wild card here. The reporter wrote stories he didn't properly confirm. Seemed kind of funny to me all those reports I prepared for you ended up in the press. We'll need to come up with an answer about that if we're going to be successful in pinning this all on Porter."

Porzio wasn't thinking now. All he wanted to do was to get out of there and back to the office. He couldn't be AWOL without a good alibi. He just blurted it out. "I have a politician friend who provided them to the reporter at *The Examiner.*"

He was walking away now. The only thing they had settled on was that they would plan to lay it all on Porter.

Tina raised her voice. "Well that doesn't help us with the Porter plan, does it? This politician is your friend, not Porter's. And is that politician Alex Scarduzo Jr?"

Porzio stopped in his tracks and looked back at Tina. He had a sense of foreboding. "What makes you say that?"

"Because I live in the same Congressional district where Scarduzo and Ogletree are battling it out. It only makes sense that stories making our bank look bad would be something Scarduzo could use in his campaign against Ogletree."

Porzio walked back towards Tina. "And how did you come to that conclusion?"

Tina said, "Well, if the bank is getting bad press because of too many minority loan rejections, that would cause a rift between Ogletree and DeMarco. And that's exactly what eventually happened, right?"

"Yeah! So what?" Porzio said.

"Well, it only makes sense that Scarduzo could make good use of those false reports to drive a wedge between Ogletree and DeMarco. Both of them came out looking bad."

Porzio was pleased with himself. This young lady he'd recruited saw how well his plan had worked. But he needed to get back to the office now. "Yes. My politician friend is Alex Scarduzo Jr. I provided him with the reports and he gave them to his reporter contact at the paper. It seemed like a good idea at the time—being good for Alex's campaign. At the same time, the bad press made DeMarco and his people look bad because of all the promises they made to Ogletree. I thought all those minority loan rejections would get DeMarco fired. But now we're facing an internal investigation."

Tina fired back. "You got me into this mess. We can try to get out of it together, but you're the one who ordered me to produce that initial false mortgage report. And now I'm screwed."

Porzio couldn't help himself. "Yeah! So what? So what if I ordered you to do that? Actually, I would rather call it an inducement. This whole thing can still work out in our favor, if we play our cards right. Porter McMahon is gone, you end up head of the mortgage department, and the bank is rid of DeMarco and his gang of lefties."

And that was it. The Feds in the car were congratulating themselves. They now had Peter Porzio on tape admitting to ordering fraudulent mortgage reports and providing them to Alex Scarduzo Jr., Republican candidate for Congress.

With a nod from Willers, Agents Inbusch and Farrell moved in and arrested Peter Porzio charging him with conspiracy to defraud the bank and its investors. Whether it would result in him serving any jail time would be up to him. The charges against him were serious, but would they be enough to entice him to flip on the Scarduzos?

Chapter 61

Porzio made a deal with the Feds. Between his taped admission and the testimony of Tina and Buddy, the Feds had him, and squeezed hard. He agreed to testify about providing the false mortgage reports to Alex Jr. He would also be helpful in making the case against Alex Sr. for using the loan reserves as illicit contributions to Jr.'s campaign, even though Porzio claimed he never knew where the funds ended up. In return for his testimony Porzio's attorney negotiated a deal in which he would plead guilty to a lesser charge and not have to serve any jail time.

The arrest of Peter Porzio left 1NEB without a chief credit policy officer. Initially, the Chairman took pity on him and left the position open temporarily. The Chairman was an ethical man who believed Porzio was innocent until proven guilty. His plan was to place Porzio on paid leave until the trials were completed. However, once the Chairman learned his Chief Credit Policy Officer had pled guilty, Porzio was immediately terminated for cause.

Porzio's attorney tried to get him out of the charges he faced in the Scarduzo Sr. trial. His argument was that Porzio was unaware of the final destination of the large reserves being disbursed in loans to all the Scarduzo associates. But testimony from one of Porzio's commercial loan officers indicating the reserves were well above normal, and were regularly disbursed without any evidence of cost overruns, made the argument frivolous—especially for someone who maintained the reputation of having complete control over all his credit operations.

Additionally, Alex Jr.'s campaign manager confirmed the receipt of significant amounts of unreported cash contributions with no questions being asked. As a result, Willers insisted that Porzio also testify against Sr. or be charged as an accessory.

Once the Scarduzos were arrested and indicted for the alleged kickbacks and illicit campaign contributions, the Feds searched their respective homes and offices and found more incriminating evidence. After completing their forensic analysis, the Feds determined that in addition to the charges of conspiracy to commit bank and election campaign fraud, the Scarduzos would also be charged with tax evasion, bribery, and money laundering.

Chapter 62

While waiting for the trial to begin, Michelle Mitchell went into labor. This was a serious problem for the Feds since her condition required that she deliver in a hospital, which was notoriously unsecure. Indeed, the Scarduzos were still expecting to see Michele's name on the witness list and were anxious to determine where she was being held by the Feds. When word got back that a Jane Doe, fitting the description of Michelle, had been admitted to St. Francis Hospital in Staten Island with a cadre of official looking guards—well, this was of special interest to the defendants.

The Scarduzo spies could not get near Michelle's room. The best they could do was to show fake press credentials and ask questions to staff at the front desk. When federal agents showed up with their holstered guns to answer their questions, the spies turned and ran. They had their confirmation.

It turned out to be a false alarm. And the spies never got close enough to obtain any photos since the Feds had set up a rather impressive system of decoys leaving Scarduzo's with nothing.

Chapter 63

The Scarduzo trials were about to begin.

Teddy was not required to be a witness at the trial of Alex Jr. since Willers believed the testimony of Tina and Buddy would be sufficient to connect the dots for the jury on how the bank was reluctantly brought into the Fed's investigation of the Scarduzos. Even without Teddy's involvement, however, the bank's name was front and center in much of the testimony. Specifically, four 1NEB employees played key roles. But the Fed's flipping of Peter Porzio was the headliner.

Willers used the testimony of Tina Washington and Buddy Wyrough to seal the deal with Porzio, as well. And now that the trial was beginning, he wanted the jury to see Porzio as a convincing and conniving witness. Thus, Willers needed to accentuate the insensitivity of its primary, albeit hostile witness, Peter Porzio. He believed the callousness of Porzio on display would make him a more reliable witness.

Willers began by putting Tina Washington on the stand in order to illustrate how the Feds used her as a vehicle into the alleged criminal activities of the Scarduzos.

Once Tina was sworn in and her position in the mortgage department was established with the judge and jury, Willers said, "Ms. Washington, would you please describe your relationship with Mr. Porzio?"

Tina said, "As an employee in the mortgage department, I reported to him indirectly through my boss, Porter McMahon, who I reported to directly."

Willers continued. "Please tell us what happened on August 31, 1992."

"Mr. Porzio called and asked me to meet with him. He also said I should not let my boss, Porter McMahon, or anyone else know about the meeting."

"And where did this meeting occur?"

"At Branch Brook Park in North Newark."

"What happened at this meeting?" Willers asked.

"Mr. Porzio said he wanted me to develop a mortgage report that indicated all of the Black applications that had come in under the special mortgage program during the first year of the agreement had been declined."

Willers continued. "And were in fact all of the Black applications declined during that first year?"

"No," Tina responded. "None of them were declined. But none of them had been approved either. As I recall, there were only five or ten loan applications from African Americans in process at the time of the report."

"And did Mr. Porzio say why he wanted you to develop this report?"

"He said the bank should never have agreed to make these kinds of loans, it wasn't good for the bank or the borrowers, and it was important that we did all we could to make sure the agreement failed."

Willers continued. "Did Mr. Porzio say anything else?"

"Yes, he said that if everything worked out as planned, my boss, Porter McMahon, the head of the mortgage department, would most likely be fired since he was directly responsible for denying all of the African American loans. Then he said that once Porter was fired, he would promote me into his job."

"What did you do then?"

"Well, I knew what he was asking me to do wasn't kosher. But he also implied that if I didn't help him, it wouldn't be good for my career. He threatened to have me fired. So, then I met my friend's father who is an attorney in the Department of Justice. He introduced me to Agent Farrell of the FBI. And the rest is, well—"

"And as result of your meeting with Agent Farrell, what did you do?" Willers asked.

"Agent Farrell told me to go ahead and produce the report Mr. Porzio wanted and to continue to play along with his plans."

"Now, would you please tell the court what happened after you provided this false report to Mr. Porzio?"

Tina smiled. "On Sunday, September 20th, which was three weeks after we met, a story appeared in *The Examiner* essentially declaring that the bank had not done its job under the terms of the agreement. It claimed all the African American loans had been rejected."

Willers walked back to the prosecutor's table and picked up copies of the newspaper article published on Sunday, September 20, 1992 and asked the judge to enter them into evidence.

Agent Guy Farrell was next in line to testify for the prosecution.

"Agent Farrell, will you please tell the court what happened after you were introduced to Tina Washington?" Willers said.

"Well, the Bureau had the Scarduzo family under surveillance for some time, but we weren't able to find a way inside their organization."

The defense attorney immediately stood up. "Judge, we object to the characterization of the Scarduzo family as an 'organization,' and all the unsavory connotations associated with that term. Also, Alex Scarduzo Sr. is not on trial here."

"Sustained," the judge said and directed Willers to no longer use the term 'organization' to characterize the Scarduzo family. He ignored the reference to the head of the family, Alex Scarduzo Jr.

Willers turned back to his witness, and said, "Please continue, Agent Farrell."

"Well, we knew about the connection between Porzio and the Scarduzo family. When Ms. Washington came to us, we saw it as an opportunity to use Porzio as a possible witness against the defendant. We just had to build the case. So we brought Ms. Washington in as a confidential informant and asked her to continue to do whatever Peter Porzio asked her to do. Eventually, things came to a head and Porzio admitted to providing the fraudulent mortgage reports to the defendant, Alex Scarduzo Jr."

"Thank you, Agent Farrell."

Next was Buddy Wyrough. Willers proceeded slowly with the young man, knowing he needed time to process the questions. He also understood that Buddy was very fragile and upset that he was being asked to say bad things about his uncle—the man who had helped raise him.

Willers began. "Mr. Wyrough, is it okay if I call you Buddy?"

Buddy nodded, but the judge told him he needed to say "yes."

Willers tried to calm him down. "I just have a couple of quick questions for you. So, Buddy, would you please tell the court how you are related to Mr. Peter Porzio?"

"Peter Porzio is my uncle. He and my mother are brother and sister."

"Thank you, Buddy. Now, what is your job at the bank?" Willers asked.

The In-House Politician

"I drive a van around to the bank's branches and deliver the interoffice mail to them."

"Okay. That's good." Willers said. "Now did your uncle ever ask you to do something unusual for him?"

Buddy put his head down, knowing this was the bad part he was going to have to say about his uncle. "Yes, he took me out for lunch one day and said there might be times he needed me to drop mail off to a location that was not one of the bank's branches."

"And what else did he say about these deliveries?" Willers continued.

"Well, he said they were a secret just between the two of us, and that it was no big deal. He reminded me that he was responsible for getting me the job, and if anyone ever questioned me about it, he would handle it for me and make any problem go away."

"What else did your uncle tell you about these deliveries?"

"He said that when I arrived at the location I should park in the alley on the side of the building so no one could see the bank's logo on the side of the van. Oh, I almost forgot. He also told me to never call him on a direct bank line. If I ever had a question about a delivery, he said I should call him on his pager and he would call me back. But he forgot to give me his pager number. The first time I got a little confused about his directions, so I called him at the bank. His secretary answered the phone and when Uncle Peter got on the line he was really mad at me for doing that."

"Okay, Buddy. You're doing fine. Now this is really important. Can you tell us the actual date when you made the first secret delivery for your uncle?"

"Well, I didn't really remember when it was, but I always kept a log of my deliveries. When I went back to look at the log I remembered that it was on a Tuesday in September, specifically September 15th."

"And are you sure about the date, Buddy?" Willers asked.

Buddy was feeling confident. "Yes sir. I'm sure, because I put a note on the log explaining why I was late to my last branch delivery that day."

"Why did you need to do that?"

"Because the branch manager yelled at me for being late that day, and I just wanted to make a note in case she complained about it to my boss."

Willers was smiling now. "Okay, Buddy. Last question. Will you please tell us the location of that secret delivery?"

Buddy put his head down again in resignation. "It was the campaign headquarters of Alex Scarduzo Jr."

"Thank you, Buddy. That's all I have for this witness."

The stage was now set to put Porzio to take the witness stand. Once he was sworn in, Willers made certain the first order of business was to have Porzio come clean about of the deal he'd been granted by the Feds. He began by asking Porzio to explain why he was testifying on behalf of the prosecution. "Mr. Porzio, will you please let the court know why you are here today?"

Porzio said, "I'm here because you subpoenaed me, and because I agreed to testify under the terms of an agreement you offered me."

"For the record, Mr. Porzio, you pleaded guilty to charges of defrauding your former employer, First Northeastern Bank, is that correct?" Willers said.

"Yes."

"Okay then, Mr. Porzio, please tell us how you're involved in this case."

Porzio's body language made it clear he was not happy to be there. "When Alex announced he was running for Congress I thought I might be able to help him with his campaign."

"And how were you going to do that?" Willers asked.

"Well, I thought if I provided him with some information about how badly the bank was performing in making loans to African Americans under the terms of the special CRA agreement, it might give him an edge against his expected opponent Rev. Ogletree. At the same time, I thought these reports could also help me get rid of those liberals inside the bank who actually developed the special mortgage agreement."

"Thank you, Mr. Porzio," said Willers. "Now, who did the bank made this special mortgage agreement with?"

"The name of the organization was People United for Movement and Progress, or PUMP for short."

"Mr. Porzio," Willers continued, "as chief credit policy officer of the bank at that time, is it fair to say that you were not a fan of the bank's agreement with PUMP?"

"Yes, you could say that."

"And why was that?"

"Because the mortgages they agreed to make were high risk and low return. They only agreed to make them because the bank was required to as part of an agreement to merge with another bank. There's a law on the books called CRA that allows groups like PUMP to blackmail the bank into making these kinds of loans. And if the bank doesn't agree to make the loans, it's possible the merger could be held up, or even turned down by the regulators in Washington."

Willers did not want to confuse the jurors with details of the CRA law. "Mr. Porzio, your characterization of blackmail is your personal opinion, which might be challenged by others both inside and outside the bank, correct?"

"Yes, there are those who say it's just a cost of doing business."

"Okay then," Willers continued, "so personally you had lots of problems with the kind of loans your bank was making. But the bank did agree to it, right?"

"Yes."

"And when you said 'they' before, weren't you referring to the same officers at the bank you worked with every day? Weren't you all on the same team there—working together to implement this merger?"

"Yes, I suppose," Porzio grumbled.

Willers was drilling hard. "So, if the merger was approved and the bank had willingly entered into the agreement, why were you so opposed to it? Other than the fact that these mortgages were less profitable, as you said earlier?"

Porzio knew where this was headed and wanted it to be over. "Because these mortgages were being made in high-risk neighborhoods to high-risk borrowers, that's why."

"Would it be fair to say that not making loans in those neighborhoods, and to the African Americans who live there, is a practice called redlining?" Willers said.

"It's been called that, yes."

"So once you started to see a lot of African American loans coming in, you thought it would be helpful to the defendant if you

The In-House Politician

provided him with a false report on the number of loans the bank was declining to these Black applicants, right?"

Porzio took a deep breath before answering. "Yes, that's right."

"But the fact of the matter was that at the time you provided this mortgage report to the defendant, things were not as bad as this report indicated, were they?"

"That's right."

"So you made up a false report on the bank's performance, threatened Tina Washington into helping you prepare the report, then provided it to the defendant. Do I have the process correct?"

"Yes."

Willers was wrapping things up. "Mr. Porzio, at the time you provided the initial false report to the defendant, did you have any knowledge, or any idea of what he might do with it? I mean what's a politician running for office going to do with a mortgage report like this?"

"I thought he might be able to use it in his campaign against his opponent."

"And is that because his opponent was Black?"

"No, it was because he was a Democrat."

"Ah, I see," said Willers. "So, again, I ask you, how did you think the defendant was going to use this false mortgage report?"

"Well, I thought he might use it as a wedge between himself and his opponent, Ogletree."

"How so?

"If Ogletree saw the bank was declining a lot of Black loan applications, then he might attack the bank on this issue," Porzio said. "Ogletree would then appear to be a radical and Alex could accuse him of only looking out for the interests of his Black voters.

And if Ogletree attacked the bank, then the bank wouldn't give him any money to support his campaign against Alex."

"But that plan backfired, didn't it?" Willers said.

"Yes, it did, initially."

"Please explain what happened."

"Ogletree and his churches met with the liberals inside our bank and made a side arrangement to help promote those high-risk mortgages. As a result, we received a lot of applications from African Americans."

"But you kept on providing those false reports to the defendant, didn't you?"

"Yes, but after the first one, the rest weren't that inaccurate," Porzio said trying to defend his actions.

"That wasn't necessarily a good thing, though, was it?" Willers said. "In fact, the bank was declining a lot of the African American loans that were coming in under the agreement, right?"

"Yes, that's right. But all those loans should have been declined. They didn't meet our standards."

Willers said, "In fact, at the worst point, the bank was declining approximately three African American loans to every one White loan. But let's leave that assessment to your regulators, who I'm sure will be looking into the bank's record there." He paused for a second. "Okay, a few more questions, Mr. Porzio. Did the defendant know you were the person inside the bank who was providing him with these false mortgage reports?"

"Not that I'm aware of. I didn't tell him."

"So," Willers said, "who else knew about your plan to provide these reports to the defendant?"

The In-House Politician

"I ran the plan by Alex's father, Alex Scarduzo Sr. He liked the idea."

"Before you provided the defendant with these false mortgage reports did you know he had a contact at *The Examiner*?" Willers asked.

Porzio smirked. "Not specifically, but most politicians at Alex's level have a whole posse of reporters following them around looking for stories."

"So you weren't surprised to see the original false mortgage report you provided to the defendant published in *The Examiner*, correct?" Willers said.

"Correct."

"Oh, and one final point of reference, just to confirm, Mr. Porzio. You are related by marriage to the Scarduzo family. Your son is married to the defendant's cousin, right?"

"Yes, that's correct."

"Thank you, Mr. Porzio." He turned to the judge. "No more questions for this witness."

At the conclusion of Porzio's testimony the judge called for the midday recess. All the reporters scrambled out of the courtroom to file their stories. The press was going to have a field day with the revelation that the former vice chairman and chief credit policy officer of First Northeastern Bank was the leaker, as well as the person primarily responsible for unwittingly providing the FBI with a route inside of Alex Scarduzo Jr.'s alleged criminal activities as the former Ocean County Executive and candidate for Congress.

The final bank employee to testify was David Helman, one of Porzio's young commercial lending officers. He was a tall lanky young man and former college basketball player whom Teddy had seen perform on the court. When Helman applied for a job at the bank, Teddy recommended him to Porzio's #2 in the commercial lending department. Helman turned out to be a wiz at the job and became a rising star in the commercial lending side of the bank. As a result, Porzio recruited him to join the special lending unit he was putting together for the loans coming in from the Scarduzo family associates. Helman was the only member of this group who agreed to testify against Porzio. The remainder of the lenders in the unit did not want to appear to be ratting out their boss. Rumors inside the bank, however, were that Teddy had convinced the young man to cooperate with the Feds by reminding him that the Chairman had his eye on this unit, and was wondering how they could have given Porzio a complete pass on how the loans were structured. Teddy counseled him that redemption might be the only key to keeping his job at the bank.

When court resumed, Willers called him to the stand. "Mr. Helman, please let us know what you relationship was with Mr. Peter Porzio."

"I'm a commercial lending officer at the bank, and a few years ago Mr. Porzio put together a special lending unit that reported directly to him. The purpose of the unit was to review large transactions that came into the bank through him. Typically, these loans were in excess of $10 million. Many were even larger."

"And did Mr. Porzio ever reveal to you where these loans originated?"

"No, he did not. Whenever a new loan came in he just assigned it to one of us in the group."

"Can you please tell us," Willers asked, "was there anything unusual about how these loans were structured?"

"Yes. Most of the loans came in with very large contingencies, or reserves in layman's terms."

"Can you please explain that?"

Helman smiled. "Sure. Typically, when a loan comes in, we see a reserve of five percent, or, in some cases as high as eight or ten percent of the total budget. But these loans were coming in with reserves of fifteen percent and higher."

"And were you concerned about these loans with larger than normal reserves?" Willers asked.

"Yes, but the boss—I mean, Mr. Porzio told us not to worry about it. He liked larger than normal reserves, and as long as the loans were paying as agreed, then no problem, it was all good according to him."

"So Mr. Porzio told you to ignore these large reserves, is that correct?"

"Yes sir."

"But that wasn't all he told you do to with these reserves, was it?" Willers continued.

"No. Mr. Porzio told us to disburse the same percentage amount from the reserve account as it related to each draw amount requested. Let me give you an example. So if the total loan amount was $10 million and the specific draw amount was $2 million, which is twenty percent of the loan amount, then we were authorized to permit a draw amount equal to twenty percent of the reserve account, or in this example $400,000."

"And why was this unusual?" Willers said.

"Because a lender doesn't typically disburse funds from a reserve account unless there's a specific issue to be addressed. It could be a cost overrun, or some other unforeseen project-related expense. But he told us not to worry about it."

"Last question for you, Mr. Helman," Willers said. "Did you ever ask the customer what these reserve funds were being used for, if there wasn't any documentation?"

"No sir. I did not," Helman said.

"And why not?"

"Because I didn't want to know."

"Thank you, Mr. Helman. No more questions."

With the testimony of Porzio, Willers had successfully placed the false mortgage reports in the hands of the defendant, Alex Scarduzo Jr. These false mortgage reports published in *The Examiner* created a chain of events that eventually led to his arrest by the FBI. Likewise, the testimony of David Helman set the stage for Willers to eventually prove that the defendant was the beneficiary of illegal campaign contributions. The source of these illegal and undisclosed cash contributions was from the reserves disbursed to the Scarduzo associates.

Chapter 64

Sally Kessler was next in line to take the witness stand. Inbusch was very persuasive with the District Attorney handling her case from the debate. He made it clear the Feds considered Sally Kessler to be an important witness in their case against Alex Scarduzo Jr. He also convinced the D.A. that the man who fell to his death at the debate, an employee of the Scarduzos, had been harassing Kessler. The agent indicated a case could be made that Sally Kessler feared for her life and had reacted in self-defense.

The speed with which the D.A. handed over her case was a surprise to everyone. Inbusch would learn later that the D.A. was eager to recuse himself since anyone with basic research skills could discover that Alex Scarduzo Sr. was a significant contributor to his re-election bid. Moreover, the D.A. believed that if anything happened to Sally Kessler before or during the trial, it would be the FBI's responsibility. Not his.

Teddy was advised of the date Sally would be testifying. He wanted to be there to hear what she would say about the evils of the banking industry, and 1NEB specifically. He hoped her testimony would be the whole truth and nothing but the truth. He'd been watching too many TV courtroom dramas.

When Teddy entered the courtroom, Sally noticed him right away. At first she was upset and embarrassed since she didn't want it to appear as if he and his bank had won their little war. Then it occurred to her that, in fact, she had lost and he had won—at least for now.

The idea that Teddy DeMarco and his big bank had beaten her, made her angry. On many occasions since her arrest she'd thought about how she might get even with him. In her mind, it was ultimately Teddy's fault she'd accidentally caused a person's death at the debate. She wanted her revenge.

Sally thought testifying would be just like standing in front of a microphone and reporting on all the evils being perpetrated on poor people. Indeed, she even liked the way she looked today, despite her appearing completely out of character. The Feds had dressed her in a spiffy new business suit making her look less like Che Guevara and more like a young Bette Midler, ready for her close-up.

Willers began Sally's testimony similar to Porzio's. He had her set the record straight by admitting she was testifying under the terms of a plea bargain. Sally had agreed to a deal in which the original charge of manslaughter in the first degree was reduced to involuntary manslaughter. As long as she testified truthfully, she would not serve any jail time. But she would be placed on probation for five years, and she would still be a convicted felon.

Willers said, "Ms. Kessler, would you please tell us how you came to be involved with the defendant?"

Sally said, "He approached me through an intermediary, who said I should meet with him because he had information on 1NEB that I might find useful."

"And did you meet with the defendant?" Willers continued.

"Yes, I did."

"Can you please tell us where and when this meeting took place?"

"It occurred on the evening on September 16th, 1992 at one

The In-House Politician

of his companies' landfill sites. His intermediary provided me with directions. It looked and smelled horrible."

"Understood. And what happened at this meeting?" Willers said.

"Alex gave me a copy of what appeared to be a bank-produced spreadsheet on the number of mortgages it had made during the first year of operations under the terms of our agreement."

"Thank you, Ms. Kessler. We'll get back to that agreement in a second. Now, what did the defendant say he was going to do with that report?"

"He said he was going to get it published and that I should keep the copy so I would be prepared if I was asked to confirm it."

"And did the defendant say where he was going to get it published?"

"No. And I didn't think he could get it published."

"Why not?"

"Because the report made no sense—the actual numbers, I mean. But it did appear to have been produced by the bank."

"Ms. Kessler, would it be fair to say that you were not particularly fond of Alex Scarduzo Jr.?"

"Yes, you could say that. In fact, we hated each other with a passion."

"And why did you dislike each other so much?"

"We come from two completely different political sides of the aisle. He's a conservative Republican politician and I am a liberal Democratic operative. He's made it clear he thinks I'm some kind of communist loser."

"What do you mean by describing yourself as an operative?" Willers asked.

"I am, or at least was, the Executive Director of a nonprofit called PUMP, which stands for People United for Movement and Progress."

"And briefly what is the mission of PUMP?"

"We advocate for many things, like economic justice, higher pay scales for low-income workers, low-income housing, and we monitor and hold banks to their obligations under the Federal Community Reinvestment Act, or CRA."

Willers asked Sally to describe her understanding of the requirements of the CRA, and how PUMP had negotiated an agreement with 1NEB to make mortgages to low- and moderate income homebuyers.

When she finished, Willers thanked her for the details. "So, when the defendant approached you with his plan, you were in the middle of this agreement you had negotiated with 1NEB, correct?"

"Well, actually it was more towards the beginning, rather than the middle. We negotiated a three-year agreement with 1NEB, and he approached me just after we completed the first year."

"So if you were still in the midst of an agreement with 1NEB, why didn't you just say no to the defendant and let the bank do what it needed to do over the next two years?"

"Based on the report he showed me, I believed the bank needed a swift kick in the pants in order to get its attention and take its job seriously. And bad publicity can do that."

"So you didn't think the bank was taking its job seriously enough under the terms of your agreement?"

"That's correct. Based on the numbers in the report, I had no reason to believe the bank was doing what it needed to do to meet its goals under the terms of the agreement."

"And what made you think the numbers in the report were correct?"

"Because the report appeared to have been produced by the bank itself."

"And how did you come to this conclusion?"

"Well, I've seen lots of bank reports before and they all have similarly recognizable notes and water marks on the bottom of each page."

"So getting back to your relationship with the defendant," Willers said, "if you hated him so much, why did you agree to confirm the false mortgage reports when you were asked to do so by *The Examiner*?"

"I didn't know at the time the report was actually false. And assuming it was correct, I felt it needed to be made public. My feelings about Alex Scarduzo Jr. didn't enter into my decision to confirm it. I was eager to assist in any plan that might bring down 1NEB."

Willers was becoming frustrated with Sally. He was not prepared for her to go off on a vendetta against 1NEB. He wanted her to stay focused on the defendant. But he couldn't leave her last statement unchallenged.

"I'm sorry, could you please explain that last statement? You said you wanted to bring down 1NEB."

"Yes, I did."

"And why is that?"

"Because banks have all the money, and they construct these crazy rules to prevent the people who really need it, to ever get it. So we needed to make an example of one of these big banks to show the world how the banking business operates, and that it will never be fair to hard-working low- and moderate-income people who just want to get ahead, move up, and live better lives. That's why. This time it just happened to be 1NEB that needed to be tweaked."

"So we'll leave the discussion of how you intend to reform the entire banking business for another day. Let's move on, okay?"

But Sally wasn't ready to move on. She looked out into the courtroom and saw her nemesis, Teddy DeMarco, smiling and just sitting there. She wanted to crush him.

"No. It's not okay!" she yelled. "1NEB and its henchman Teddy DeMarco are the real reason we're here today." Sally stood up and pointed her finger at Teddy. "You're the evil genius who always wriggles his way out of these situations when your bank is guilty of redlining, mortgage discrimination, and buying off politicians who should be shutting you down, rather than coddling you."

Willers requested for the judge to have Sally sit down and be quiet.

When she finally sat down, the judge admonished her and asked if she needed a moment to compose herself.

Sally stared at Teddy again with fire in her eyes, but turned to the judge and said no, she was fine to continue.

Willers wasn't so sure and requested a short recess to confer with his witness. The judge granted him a ten-minute recess.

Teddy sat frozen in his seat. He didn't want to leave the courtroom for fear Sally might have more to say about him and the bank. While remaining in his seat, he benefited from a certain level of courtroom decorum, whereby the reporters would not approach him until he was outside.

When court resumed, Sally was ready to move on.

Willers continued. "Now, please tell us what the defendant wanted you to do after you agreed to help him."

"Well, he didn't make any specific request at our first meeting. He knew he needed to prove himself to me. It was only after the story appeared in *The Examiner* and we met for a second time, that he told me he wanted me to spy for him inside the campaign of his expected political opponent, Rev. Lloyd Ogletree."

"But at that time, when you and the defendant met, Rev. Ogletree had not yet announced he was running, correct?"

"That's right," Sally said. "Ogletree was still considering his options at that time."

"So what made the defendant think Rev. Ogletree was going to be his opponent?"

"Well, he told me that Teddy DeMarco from 1NEB had met with Ogletree at a very private, hush hush dinner. He thought that DeMarco was going to help finance Ogletree's campaign through the bank's Political Action Committee. But like I said before, Ogletree had not yet decided to run at that time—or at least he hadn't announced it to me."

"Why would Rev. Ogletree have announced it to you before anyone else?" Willers asked.

"Because I was one of his top advisors and he sat on my PUMP board of directors. We actually trusted each other back then."

Willers saw the judge looking at his watch. He wanted to make sure he got all of Sally's testimony in before court adjourned for the day. He tried to speed things up a bit. He said, "Now Ms. Kessler, can you please tell us how the defendant was going to use the false mortgage reports to his benefit?"

Sally sat up straight in the witness chair as if she was looking for a TV camera. "Alex is a very good politician. He can anticipate the kind of reaction he'll get from putting something out there, like those false mortgage reports. He knew that if—and I guess now I should say when—the reports were published, they would eventually drive a wedge between his opponent, Ogletree, and Teddy DeMarco at 1NEB. But what he didn't anticipate was that the initial false report drew Ogletree towards the bank. The bad press from the article caused DeMarco to propose they join forces to promote the bank's special mortgage program, the one he had negotiated with me—I mean PUMP."

"And then what happened?"

"Well, around the same time Ogletree announced his candidacy, two things occurred. First, the bank began receiving lots of minority loan applications, but they kept on rejecting most of them. Second, Ogletree received a campaign contribution from 1NEB, which took on the appearance of a bribe since he was a bit late in his recognition that the bank was denying all these minority loans. Finally, Ogletree made the decision to get out in front of the situation and to hold a press conference announcing he was returning the campaign contribution to 1NEB. I was proud of him at the time. In fact, I'd like to think I may have had something to do with his decision to return the money and let the press know about how many minority loans the bank had denied. He accused the bank of mortgage discrimination, and rightly so."

Again, Willers felt he had to steer Sally back to why she was testifying. "Please tell us how all of these events eventually played into the hands of the defendant."

"Pretty simple." Sally said. "As he continued to feed *The Examiner* with false mortgage reports from the bank, his political opponent found himself in a real bind. Ogletree had to decide if he was going to look the other way, knowing how many loans were being rejected

The In-House Politician

by the bank, or if he was he going to denounce the bank, return its money, and risk having his corporate contributions dry up if he accused the bank of mortgage discrimination. Alex was the puppet master. He benefited politically by all the bad press Ogletree received from before, during, and after the debate."

Willers knew this was a risk, but he felt he needed to have Sally come clean before the defendant's attorney drew it out of her. He said, "So, Ms. Kessler, you mentioned the televised debate. I'm sure the defense will ask you about this on cross-examination, but for our purposes here and now, would you please tell us what happened at the debate."

Sally withdrew into herself. She didn't want to talk about what happened at the debate with her arrest in the death of Scarduzo's man, Fabrizio Nicolas LiVecchi. She said, "My organization PUMP protested at the debate and accused Ogletree of taking a bribe from 1NEB."

Teddy was bowing his head now, trying to avoid eye contact with anyone. He knew it wasn't true, and Ogletree knew it wasn't true, but this didn't matter to the story she was telling and to the reporters covering the trial. Teddy was hoping this statement wouldn't be the headline in tomorrow's edition of *The Examiner*.

Sally continued. "But in the end, supposedly, it wasn't true. I don't know all the facts." She couldn't resist that last jab at Teddy and his bank.

"And what happened after that?" Willers asked.

Sally was nearly in tears. "Well, one of Alex's men attacked me. We struggled, but he ended up falling over the balcony railing onto the main floor."

"And just to be clear, this man who attacked you, he worked for the defendant, and delivered messages from him to you, is that correct?"

"Yes."

"And at the debate this man tried to stop you from protesting—he tried to physically restrain you?"

Sally was sobbing now. "Yes, that's right."

"And this man died as a result of the fall from the balcony where he attacked you?"

"Yes, yes. I'm sorry! I was just protecting myself. I was defending myself—it was an accident."

"Thank you, Ms. Kessler. I know this is difficult for you. Now, getting back to the

defendant, is it your testimony that he intended to use the false mortgage reports to drive a wedge between Rev. Ogletree and his supporters on the basis of the large number of minority loans being denied by 1NEB?"

Before Sally could answer, the defense attorney objected. "Judge, please, there's no way this witness could have known what the defendant's intentions were with the use of the bank reports."

The judge said, "Overruled. Please continue Ms. Kessler."

Sally said, "The bad publicity resulting from the large number of minority loan denials ended up with Ogletree being accused of taking a bribe. So, yes, I would say he was successful with his plan to weaken his opponent. He tried to recruit me as a spy. It was clear to me that he would use whatever weapon he had available to win the election—whatever the costs and by whatever means necessary."

The defense objected again.

"Sustained," the judge responded. "The jury is advised to disregard the witnesses' last statement."

"Thank you, Ms. Kessler." Willers turned to the judge. "I have no more questions for this witness."

With the completion of Sally Kessler's testimony, Willers believed he had made the case that the defendant, Alex Scarduzo Jr., intended to use the fraudulent mortgage reports to hurt his opponent's campaign.

Teddy was pleased he had scheduled time to come and listen to Sally's diatribe and verbal vendetta, even though he was unhappy she had pointed him out in the courtroom. He achieved some level of satisfaction in the proof that the initial published report was false, ultimately leading to all the dominos falling. However, he was not very happy with the number of times Sally brought up the bank's name in her testimony. Willers would later disclose to Teddy that when Sally saw him enter the courtroom, it seemed to enrage her and make her go off the rails. He apologized and said it was not his intention to have her criticize the bank as much as she did, but—well, he knew her better than they did. It should have been expected. Willers implied it might have been better if Teddy had not been in the courtroom. No one could control Sally Kessler, who blamed the banking business for everything except sunrises and sunsets.

When Teddy left the courtroom, reporters were quick to place microphones in front of him. They asked him what he thought of her testimony, and her grievances against 1NEB. "I have to be honest with you, Sally Kessler said some things in there today that made me cringe. She doesn't understand how banks operate. But I would also say there were some elements in her testimony that I will bring back to our leadership for further consideration. Thank you."

The next questions came in rapid fire. "Mr. DeMarco, what can you tell us about Vice Chairman Peter Porzio? Why didn't anyone inside the bank know what he was doing? Don't you have internal controls to prevent that kind of thing from happening?"

Teddy looked at the reporter with contempt. "No comment," he said.

Chapter 65

Michelle Mitchell was scheduled to testify the following day. When called to the witness stand, she was escorted into the courtroom through a side entrance by Agents Inbusch and Farrell. Alex had mentioned to Catherine about Michelle's possible role in the trial, but not her condition. When she came face-to-face with Michelle, Catherine let out a loud scream and nearly fainted

The judge called for order.

Immediately, Alex's attorney stood up. "Your honor, the defense objects to this witness."

The judge said, "On what basis?"

His attorney looked over at Alex, shrugged his shoulders. He whispered to him, "We have to do this." Alex put his head down in his hands in resignation.

The defense attorney said, "Your honor, as you can clearly see this witness is with child. We would like the court to order a DNA test to determine if the child was fathered by the defendant, which we believe it was. If the test confirms that this witness is, in fact, the mother of the defendant's child, we would move to strike this witness from testifying on the basis of the spousal privilege."

Catherine got up from her seat, pointed her finger at Alex, and yelled, "You bastard! We're done!" Then she turned and stomped out of the courtroom. She had never been so humiliated in her life. She would be filing for a divorce whether Alex was convicted or not.

Once again the judge had to restore order. As the courtroom quieted, the judge asked, "Was the defendant ever legally married to this witness?"

"No, your honor, and in anticipation of your next question, they were never in a common law marriage either."

"So let me get this straight," the judge said. "The defense is objecting to this witness on the basis of the possibly the child may be the defendant's, do I have this right?"

"That is correct, your honor. And the defense will stipulate that there was, in fact, an affair between the two."

The judge laughed briefly. "The motion to strike this witness and your objection based on a possible spousal privilege is denied. And if your client wants to know if the child is his, he can order a DNA test at his own expense. Now, let's move on."

Willers correctly assumed the judge would determine this objection to be frivolous and rule in the prosecution's favor. What he wasn't happy about was that his fears about a leak were front and center. How did the defense know about Michelle's hospital visit? They had taken pains to keep the whole maternal process a secret, but someone had found out and tipped off the Scarduzos. He made a mental note to speak with Agents Inbusch and Farrell about how best to protect Michelle Mitchell. And if this meant moving her to a new location, they would do so.

Willers then began his examination of the prosecution's star witness.

"Ms. Mitchell," Willers asked, "would you please describe your relationship with the defendant?"

Michelle proceeded to tell her story about initially being hired to work for NJ Waste Hauling, and then coming over to work directly

The In-House Politician

for the defendant in his role as Ocean County Executive. She said that not long after the defendant announced his run for Congress he asked her to come and serve as his assistant in the campaign.

"Ms. Mitchell, for the record, did you have an affair with defendant?" Willers asked.

"Yes."

"And when did this affair begin?"

Michelle appeared to be trying to recall the specific date, but it was all for show. The date was ingrained in her memory. "It was at a political fundraiser Alex attended in Atlantic City. I accompanied him to this meeting as I always did in my role as his assistant. After a reception that evening, which included a few cocktails, Alex asked me to come up to his room to finish up some correspondence he wanted to get out of the way. And that's when it happened. You know—that's when the affair began."

"Thank you," Willers said. "I think we all understand what you mean. But can you please be a bit more specific as to when this occurred?"

"Well, I can be more specific if I can take a look at my notebook."

The defense attorney rose. "Your honor. Once again we object to this witness. She is clearly a jilted lover who will go to any length to get even with my client."

The judge said, "Overruled. How about we let the jury decide on the witness' motivation."

Willers indicated to the judge and the defense that he was entering Michelle's notebook into evidence. The defense had no objection since they had previously reviewed it in discovery and had already lost a pretrial motion to suppress it on the basis that it could have been written by the witness after the fact.

"Once again, for the record, we object, your honor," the attorney said. "This witness either hates the defendant and wants to get even with him, or is still in love with him and thinks if she can't have him, then no one can."

"Sit down," the judge demanded. "I have decided to permit this witnesses' testimony, so no more objections. Do you understand me?"

The defense attorney took his seat and Willers continued.

"Ms. Mitchell, when did the affair begin with the defendant?"

Michelle turned a few pages performing her act for the jury. She found the correct page and said, "It was March 22nd, 1991. There's an entry here for that date about the meeting in Atlantic City. My notes indicate that we stayed at Resorts International."

Willers said, "And what else do your notes tell you about that specific meeting?"

Michelle took a deep breath, then continued. "Well, a few things happened that night. The first was that Alex asked me to come to his room to work with him on some campaign correspondence. Then he proceeded to tell me he loved me and wanted to spend as much time with me as possible. He said that if I came over to work full-time for him in the campaign, we would have more time to spend together. He also said that after he won the election, he would take me with him to Washington where I would be with him constantly. He also said he had an understanding with his wife that she would never move to D.C. because she didn't want their daughters to have to change schools."

Willers decided it was time to drop the other bombshell. "Ms. Mitchell, would you please tell the court if you were in love with the defendant?"

"Well, at first things were a lot of fun. All the meetings, all the travel, and all the wining and dining, and all the—well, you know."

"And to the best of your knowledge, who was paying for all of this?"

"Well, initially we were on the Ocean County tab, and after he announced his candidacy, it was all paid for out of campaign funds."

"And then what happened?" Willers asked.

"Alex's wife found out about the affair and she told him to dump me, or face a real hurtful and politically devastating public divorce."

"What did the defendant do then?"

Tears were welling up in Michelle's eyes. "Alex broke it off with me. And a few days later, I got on a plane to Rome."

"Did you hate the defendant for ending the affair?"

"Yes, I did at first. But then I figured it was just a fling. Nothing more."

"So you don't hate him now?"

"No. I don't."

"Why not?

"There was a very nice settlement included in our break-up," Michelle said.

"Please tell us about this settlement."

As expected, the defense attorney objected, but the judge had previously overruled and ordered Michelle Mitchell to answer the prosecution's questions, despite the NDA.

Michelle said, "Alex demanded that I sign a Non-Disclosure Agreement, and I did. The NDA provided me with $2 million as long as I agreed to never talk about the affair—to anyone—ever."

Willers picked up the document and asked the judge permission to enter it into evidence. As he gave the document to the judge, he said, "Your honor, please recall that in pretrial motions you reviewed this NDA for the purpose of determining the witnesses' testimony. You determined there was nothing in this NDA that prevented the witness from testifying in this criminal proceeding."

The judge nodded and accepted the document.

Willers said, "Okay. Now you arrive in Rome richer by $2 million, you think. Then what happened?"

"The FBI interrupted my trip by confronting me while I was on a train to Zurich. The agent advised me they needed my assistance in their case against Alex Scarduzo Jr. They painted a very dire situation for me if I didn't testify. They showed me a photo of a man they said was a hitman employed by Alex's father, who'd been sent to find me and kill me."

The courtroom erupted again and the judge pounded his gavel in an attempt to restore order.

The defense attorney rose immediately. "Judge, we object to the prosecution's characterization of the man in the photo as a 'hitman.' We will stipulate that the man in the photo was an employee of the Scarduzos, but there is no evidence he traveled to Italy for any other reason than a vacation."

"Sustained," the judge said. "There will be no further discussion of the alleged hitman." But Willers had done his job. He'd planted the idea in the heads of the jury and there was no taking it back.

Despite his inability to get Michelle's testimony on the record about fearing for her life, Willers was nevertheless a happy man. He could not believe how stupid Alex Jr. was for never having asked Michelle to turn over her notebook as part of the NDA.

Willers continued. "Now, Ms. Mitchell, can we get back to the notebook? Specifically, please tell us about what happened on February 22nd, 1992."

"There was a big meeting that day, which was held in Alex's hotel suite. The meeting included Anthony Prezutti—Alex's godfather, and Richard Napolitano, both close friends of Alex's father. Alex told me they were in the construction business and had just been approved for some big projects."

"Now Ms. Mitchell, this is very important. Were you physically in attendance at this meeting? Were you actually present in the room."

"Yes, I was for most of it."

"Now why would the defendant want to have you in this meeting if he didn't want his affair with you to be known?" Willers asked.

"Well, I got the impression there was some kind of macho code between all these guys. Like they all knew what was happening, and it was no big deal. Like it happened all the time, and maybe they had their own affairs going on. Who knows? Anyway, I also got the impression that Alex wanted to show me off—like some kind of trophy, you know? Alex even told me what he wanted me to wear—a sexy short black dress I'd worn before that he really liked to see me in. He also reminded me to bring my notebook to the meeting so he could always say I was just there to take notes."

"And then what happened?" Willers asked.

"Alex and I had agreed to a sign from him indicating when it was time for me to excuse myself. He would give me a wink. It meant I was to go down to the bar and wait for him. He would meet me there when he was done. But before I left the suite I hit the little girl's room to you know—powder my nose. But I could still hear their conversation through the air vents."

"And what did you hear?" Willers said.

"Both of the men said they wanted to make contributions to Alex's political campaign because they definitely wanted to see him in Congress, and also because they owed his father for helping them out in their businesses. They were grateful and wanted to repay his kindness by supporting his son. I also heard them say it was important for Alex to win in order to keep that—and here they used the 'N' word to describe Rev. Ogletree—out of Congress."

"Okay, Ms. Mitchell. Again, this is very important." Willers said. "During the course of this meeting, or when you exited the suite, did you ever see any money change hands?"

"No. I did not."

"But there's more to that story, isn't there, Ms. Mitchell?

"Yes. When Alex came down and met me at the bar, he had a pretty big wad of cash in his hand, and a big grin on his face, like he'd just won the lottery."

The defense objected. But the judge allowed it.

"Please tell us why this is important."

"Well, despite the fact that we had separate rooms—you know, just for show—I spent most of my time in Alex's suite and bedroom. I never saw a stash of cash like that anywhere in the room."

Willers asked, "Was there a safe in the room?"

"Yes sir, there was. But whenever Alex wanted to place some important documents in the safe, or retrieve them, he would always ask me to do it. He said he could never remember the code. So I made up my own access code to the safe."

The In-House Politician

"So when Alex met you at the bar with this big wad of cash in hand, did he say where it came from?" Willers asked.

"No, he did not. But the money wasn't in the safe before the meeting because he'd asked me to get some documents out of it to review."

There was murmuring in the courtroom at this revelation. The judge pounded his gavel.

Michelle's testimony went on for some time. It included references to notes from other meetings she had attended. Her notes were damning because they included dates and names of Scarduzo Sr.'s friends who Alex agreed to meet with ostensibly to give them an audience and to collect their campaign support—in cash. They all had the same story. Alex's father had been very good to them and their businesses, and had referred them to 1NEB for financing. They all claimed that the financing they received from the bank was very generous. Indeed, all of Michelle's testimony on the dates and names of the attendees at the meetings were corroborated by hotel records verifying that Alex, Michelle, and the other meeting attendees were all registered at the hotel on those same dates. Willers found it amazing that it never occurred to these knuckleheads to register under aliases.

Willers was feeling pretty good, but now he needed to pull things together for the jury. He said, "Thank you for that, Ms. Mitchell. Now a few final questions. Taking notes and being the defendant's girlfriend were not your only jobs, were they?"

Michelle said, "No, they were not."

"What else did the defendant ask you to do for him?"

"Around the time his campaign was revving up, Alex asked me to deliver a message to Sally Kessler. He asked me to dress up in some kind of costume—like Ingrid Bergman in *Casablanca*—you know, in a trench coat, sunglasses and a fedora. He said it was for my own protection, so Kessler wouldn't recognize me. But the whole thing was crazy. She laughed at my costume. It was embarrassing."

Willers said, "And what was the message from the defendant to Sally Kessler?"

"Alex told me to tell Sally she should meet with him because he could help her and had some important information to share. But the meeting had to be private and just between the two of them."

"And then what happened?"

"It wasn't long after that Alex's wife found out about us and he broke it off with me. Then I left for Rome."

Willers thanked Michelle for her testimony and said, "No more questions for this witness."

With the completion of Michelle Mitchell's testimony, Willers believed he had established that Alex Scarduzo Jr. was a corrupt politician taking fraudulent campaign contributions from his father's friends. Michelle's notebook was the key piece of evidence linking the dates and the names of the collaborators in this criminal activity.

Chapter 66

The final straw was the reporter, Joe Campbell.

He testified that it was Alex Scarduzo Jr. who provided him with the fraudulent mortgage reports. The reporter knew he would have to fall on his sword, and that his career at *The Examiner* was over. Under oath, he provided the background story about himself and Alex Jr. He admitted to having harassed the defendant in a prep school hazing incident, which resulted in Alex attacking him and his nearly losing an eye.

During the trial, Alex Jr. was allowed to remain on the ballot for the Congressional election, but no one expected anyone to vote for him. The Ocean County Board of Freeholders, however, were not so forgiving. They voted to terminate his contract as County Executive, and replaced him with a deputy on an interim basis until they could hold a new election. Alex Jr. was out of options.

Alex Scarduzo Jr. was convicted on all counts; including conspiracy to commit bank fraud, conspiracy to commit campaign election fraud, tax evasion, money laundering, and bribery.

There was still the big question as to whether Alex Jr. would flip on his father—if, in fact, the Feds were inclined to offer him such a deal. At best, it might reduce his sentence by a few years, but he was still going to do some serious prison time. After all, the thinking went, Alex Jr. was just a pawn in his father's desire for power. Sr. wanted the Scarduzo family name to mean something more than just trash collections and landfills. As it turned out, the Feds were not so inclined. They believed they had a good enough case against Sr. even without Jr.'s testimony.

The trial for Sr. lasted another two months, but Alex Jr. never did testify against his father. He would do the time. Alex Scarduzo Sr. was also convicted on all counts.

Alex Scarduzo Sr. was sentenced to twenty years; while Alex Jr. received a somewhat lighter sentence of fifteen years. Sr.'s sentence was longer since it was proven he was the mastermind behind all the criminal election campaign activities.

Michelle Mitchell believed there was no need to inform Alex Jr. of the fact that he was the father of her child. She never wanted him to know—ever. She would ignore any request for a paternity test—and why not—since she was about to enter the Feds Witness Protection Program—never to be seen or heard from again. But the best part was that the Feds had never seen a situation in which their protectee entered the program with close to $2 million. She would need to be very careful in how and where she invested her money—wherever she eventually landed.

Chapter 67

Once it was determined Peter Porzio was serving as a witness against the Scarduzos, his phone never stopped ringing—before and during the trials. The callers, of course, never revealed themselves and their messages never lasted long enough to be traced. However, there was no doubt about their purpose, which was to intimidate and pressure Porzio into breaking his deal with Feds. But Porzio would never agree to spend time in jail and take the heat for someone else—no less someone like Alex Scarduzo Sr.

In a pretrial motion prior to the start of Alex Jr.'s trial, Porzio's attorney tried to get the judge to drop the charges against him on the basis of entrapment by the Feds. But his confession to Tina was on tape, which was difficult to refute. And the combination of Tina's and Buddy's testimony closed the door on Porzio.

Porzio's attorney also tried to get him out of the charges he faced in the Scarduzo Sr. trial. The argument was that Porzio claimed to be unaware of the final destination of the large reserves being disbursed to the Scarduzo associates. But the testimony of David Helman indicating the reserves were well above normal, and were regularly disbursed without any evidence of cost overruns, made the argument frivolous for someone who maintained the reputation of having complete control over his credit operations. Moreover, Alex Jr.'s campaign manager confirmed the receipt of significant cash contributions from various sources including the candidate's father in amounts that matched up well with the dates and amounts of disbursed loan reserves. And no one asked any questions. On the witness stand Porzio broke down when the Feds highlighted his extremely poor judgement that no banker could ever excuse.

Peter Porzio, the former Vice Chairman and Chief Credit Policy Officer of 1NEB was now a convicted felon. As a first offender, however, he would not serve any jail time. Still, he was now out of a job, and his reputation was ruined.

Porzio's wife Patty knew he was on the edge. No one was coming to his defense and he was at the lowest point in his life. She refused to leave him alone out of fear of what he might do to himself.

Two weeks after the end of Sr.'s trial, Patty Porzio received a call from her sister-in-law Portia. Buddy was having an anxiety attack and was beside himself. It finally occurred to him what his testimony had done to his Uncle.

Portia said, "Patty, please come over quickly. I need your help with Buddy. I'm afraid he might do something to hurt himself, and possibly me, too. Please. I need you!"

"I'm really sorry," Patty said, "but I don't want to leave Peter alone. He's in the same place Buddy's in. He's just keeping it inside and not talking about it. Can't you call 911 and say you have an emergency? They're professionals and know how to handle situations like this."

"Buddy's locked himself in his room," Portia said, "and he's throwing things around and banging his head against the wall. I don't want to call the police. They'll just break the door down. And I don't know if he's got a gun in there. I can't be sure. I would ask Peter to come over, but I don't think Buddy would believe him—you know, that he forgives him and that everything will be alright."

Porzio overheard their conversation and told Patty go help his sister. It was important and he couldn't do it.

Patty wasn't convinced. "Are you sure? I'll try not to be too long. When I get home, I'll make your favorite dinner. Okay?"

After Patty left, Porzio wrote out his brief note. It said, "I'm sorry. You'll be better off without me." He then walked out to the garage, connected a hose to the exhaust pipe, closed the windows of his car, and then turned the engine on. He wanted to end his life in the most painless way he knew how. He couldn't stand the humiliation.

Chapter 68

A few weeks after the trials ended, Teddy decided he wanted to debrief. He selected a date and advised Kelly to cancel all his appointments for that day. Althea and Tom were chosen to be part of this painful ordeal. Teddy secured a small meeting room at Mayfair Farms in West Orange for all three of them to spend the day away from the bank decompressing and debriefing about what had transpired over the last four-plus years. Teddy wanted to do some heartfelt searching on what went wrong, and what, if anything, went right. He also wanted them to laugh and to cry if the occasion warranted—that is, if the two macho men were up to it. He wanted to talk about the future, but in order to get there, he believed they needed to review their past mistakes.

They spent the early morning eating and laughing, while Teddy tried to pull together an outline based on what they all remembered as the most important events. Then Teddy hit them right between the eyes with the proverbial question, "So how did we get here?"

This was a whole new Teddy. Althea and Tom looked at each other. Tom said, "Who are you, man? And what have you done with our boss, Teddy DeMarco?"

That comment got the ball rolling with a laugh or two.

But Teddy was completely serious. He repeated the question. "I know it sounds hokey, but I really want to know what happened and how it happened. Maybe I can get us started."

He paused for a moment to gather his thoughts. "You two know that I attended Alex Jr.'s trial on the day when Sally Kessler testified, right?"

The In-House Politician

"Well, I knew you attended," Tom said, "but I wasn't aware of the reason why you went that day."

Althea said, "That must have been tough for you."

Teddy laughed at first, but then said sincerely, "It was one of the toughest days of my life. When Sally was asked by the prosecutor to defend why she did what she did—you know—becoming Alex Jr.'s accomplice and agreeing to confirm the bogus minority denial numbers, she actually said she considered me a traitor to all poor people. She said I sold out and went over to the dark side when I became a banker. She gave testimony about our personal history. I won't bore you with the details. You've heard it all before. She really went off on me as turning my back to the cause of helping the underprivileged when I took the position at the bank and resigned from politics. Then she really lit into the banking industry as a whole. She said we're structured in a way that would never help poor people and never benefit communities of color. We're only concerned with big returns for our shareholders. Indeed, anything that gets in the way of that is considered high risk and low reward, and thus we won't take those products on. She actually said that – 'high risk and low reward.' I gotta say I was impressed with that. What do you think about that?"

Althea said, "Well, first things first. You know as well as we do that she's not wrong about our business model. And secondly, you can't beat yourself up over what Sally Kessler thinks of you. She has the same opinion about every banker, not just you. We're all evil in her mind. You just happened to be the one banker she actually had a personal relationship with when you were her counselor and when she worked in your campaigns. You two were on the same team back then. But when you took the job here, she must have been crushed. It's only natural she would have some hard feelings about that, right?"

Tom chimed in. "Yup. Remember what she said to me when you had me call her after the demonstration in front of the bank? She despises me as well as you. And she doesn't even know me that well."

Teddy smiled. "Yeah. Sorry about that."

Tom shook his head. "Teddy, you do understand the Feds had the Scarduzos under investigation well before you negotiated the agreement with Sally and her Bolshevik friends. And it was a pure coincidence that Rev. Ogletree decided to run for Congress against Alex Jr. A perfect storm—the investigation, the politics, and the greed. Then the agreement with PUMP just poured fuel on the fire. It's like Althea said—don't beat yourself up over it. Sally hates us all. The circumstances were such that the crisis became unavoidable. And not to pile on, but Scrooge and Marley didn't exactly care for us either. We asked them to approve loans that were completely out of their comfort zone."

Teddy said, "But what if Porter McMahon actually had a conscience and had played ball with us and approved more of those borderline applications? And what if we had a chief credit policy officer who wasn't a crook, and not such a hard ass when it came to those same loans? Everyone, including the Chairman, knew that the agreement was the right thing to do. The original $25 million was nothing more than a drop in the bucket. It was just impossible to change their mindsets. And I still can't reconcile how much of it was pure out and out racism, and how much of it was ultra-conservative underwriting."

Althea said, "Woulda, shoulda, coulda. Come on, Teddy. You can make up all the hypotheticals and excuses you want, but I say it was both.

It was equal parts bigotry and conservative underwriting. The bigotry leads to the unforgiving underwriting. I truly believe that someday we'll find out that rat bastard Marley is a member of the Klan."

Teddy and Tom looked at each other and laughed. They were glad Althea said what they were both thinking. "Yeah," Teddy said. "I'd love to see a current background check on Marley. I wonder what other perversions are on his rap sheet."

Tom tried to get things back on track. "How about we look at the timeline?

They both agreed.

Tom spent the next 30 minutes or so trying to place the important events in their proper sequence. When he was done, both Teddy and Althea congratulated him for what he had recalled and when each event occurred.

Teddy looked amazed. "You know, Tom, maybe you should write a book about this whole sordid tale. Just make sure I come out looking like a hero in the end. Okay?"

Althea still looked puzzled. "Yeah. That was a good summary. But there's still some pieces missing."

"Well sure," Teddy said. "There's Alex's affair with Michelle Mitchell. But that's not part of our story. But the one thing I still can't figure out is, how Ogletree got his hands on that damn mortgage report? He never did tell us his source, did he? I can't believe it was Sally since she was just as surprised as he was with the numbers. And she was on her way out the door of his campaign at the time. I guess it could have been Tina Washington, but I'm sure the Feds never approved of it. If it was her, she would have done it all on her own, right?"

"That's right," Althea said, "but that's not what I was thinking about. I mean, the Scarduzos were accused of some rather nasty business practices, to say the least. And while the Feds couldn't prove it, it was pretty clear that Sr. was trying to eliminate Michelle Mitchell. But when they couldn't find her, they made sure that dude Giuseppe, or whatever his name was, paid the ultimate price and never made it out of Sicily. All those illegal activities were going on for some time, according to the transcripts I read."

Teddy jumped in. "Wait. What did you just say? You read the transcripts? How did you get your hands on them?"

Althea looked down at her feet, a bit embarrassed. "Well, it just so happens that my Dad has an old friend who works for the Department of Justice and called in a favor. He defended the request on the basis of him wanting to make sure there was nothing in there that could come back to bite me in the ass—so to speak. Sorry, I forgot to mention that."

Teddy laughed. "Really? Don't you think the Feds would have let us know if anyone besides yours truly was going to be part of their investigation?"

Althea shrugged. "My Dad just made that story up so his friend would have a legitimate reason to give it to him. He wasn't really worried about it, and neither was I. I just wanted to read through the transcripts. Call me crazy. Maybe someday I'll go to law school. You never know."

"Okay," Tom said. "So you read the transcripts. Where are you going with all this?"

"I'm not certain about this," Althea said, "but it's my reading of the transcripts that the Feds really didn't have anything on the Scarduzos except some assumptions based on circumstantial evidence. It wasn't until Tina gave them a heads up about Scrooge, which led them to Alex Jr. That made the connection for them. In fact, one could say that 1NEB and Tina Washington were primarily responsible for bringing down the Scarduzos. Tina got the Feds inside. She opened the door and gave them Scrooge, who in turn gave them Jr. and Sr. I think Tina is the real hero in this story. But I'm sure she'd rather keep that a secret. She didn't know anything about the Scarduzos when she went to the Feds. And she didn't know anything about the relationship between Alex Jr. and Joe Campbell at *The Examiner*. I hope the Feds are doing whatever they can to keep her safe."

The conversation went back and forth over the rest of the morning. Althea and Tom were convinced that Marley would never have come around to look at the affordable mortgage loans in more favorable terms. It just wasn't in his nature. Even if Scrooge had given him a pass and said he wouldn't hold him responsible for the performance of the loans under the agreement, he couldn't change. But Teddy kept on wanting to give Marley the benefit of the doubt. He said Marley was just doing his job, or at least the job he thought he was supposed to be doing.

Tom wasn't buying it. "Yes, Marley had the personality of a rock, but you can't convict him for his lack of charm. It was Scrooge who was trying to bury Teddy and the rest of us. He saw it as an opportunity to help Alex Jr., and to take us down at the same time. How did we not know that Scrooge was related to Alex Scarduzo Jr.?"

Teddy shook his head in disgust.

There came a knock on the door. Lunch was being delivered. And it came at the right moment. They were all mentally exhausted and needed a break.

Teddy, being Teddy, left the room to call Kelly to see if anyone was looking for him. While he had made it clear Tom and Althea should keep their calendars clear for the whole day, apparently the same rule did not apply to him. When he returned, he said we would spend another hour or so together, but then he needed to get back to the office. He ordered Althea and Tom to take the rest of the day off when they were done.

The next hour was basically a rehash of the underwriting issues that became the problems for so many of the minority applicants—like the down payment and cash for closing costs. And the two years on the job requirement. Credit histories and acceptable debt loads. And Tom's personal favorite—nearby incompatible land uses, and all the other cockamamie items listed by appraisers who were not up to the task of reviewing urban-based single family properties.

At the end of the discussion, Teddy said he wanted Tom to pull together a list of the changes that would be needed in the bank's standard underwriting guidelines in order to move the Chairman on his pledge of giving them additional funding. Teddy would ask the Chairman to give his department complete responsibility for the marketing and underwriting of these new affordable mortgages, with the Mortgage Department serving as the back office.

Tom said he would be glad to handle this new assignment, but that it might take some time.

"How much time?" Teddy asked.

"Well," Tom said, "I need to review all the rejected loan files to establish the primary reasons they were denied. It might take about a week or two. I won't really know until I get into those files."

The In-House Politician

Teddy had that serious coaching look on his face. It's the look no player ever wants to see. It means the coach is about to let you know how badly you just screwed up. Teddy's response was crystal clear. "Tom, listen to me. You have two days to get this done. There are rumors that by the end of next week the Chairman will be announcing a new Interim Chief Credit Policy Officer to replace Scrooge. I want to get those underwriting changes up to the Chairman by the end of this week. He'll do one of two things with them. He'll either review and personally approve them, or he'll sit on them until he appoints the new interim chief. My bet is that since this is all fresh in his mind, he'll personally approve them. He won't want to test the new interim with something like this. Too much history. The Chairman wants to be involved in the next round of our affordable mortgages. And I will remind him that someone needs to speak with Marley about his new responsibilities of working cooperatively with us. Capisce? Two days. Who knows, you might even get a meeting with the Chairman to go over the proposed guidelines. And I can assure you the Chairman does give a rat's ass about our loans. Oh, and I promise to introduce you to him."

Tom was glad he didn't tell him to relax.

Chapter 69

Teddy and Pastor Lloyd made peace with each other. Teddy had made good on his promise to provide him with a sizeable campaign contribution. And despite the Chairman's reluctance to any involvement in political matters, Teddy arranged a personal meeting between him and Pastor Lloyd. While he had to get down on his knees to beg the Chairman to participate in the meeting, Teddy knew that under the pain of death there would be no public statements from the bank about it. If the candidate wanted to put something out in the press, that was up to him, but the Chairman made it clear 1NEB would have nothing to say publicly about the meeting between the two men.

When they met, Pastor Lloyd was effusive in his praise for Teddy—to the point where Teddy finally had to intervene. Pastor Lloyd went on to apologize for all the past issues he had created in reaction to the clandestine mortgage reports. The Chairman was gracious in his response, indicating he had every right to take the bank to task over its high number of minority loan denials. Furthermore, the Chairman said the bank was currently going through an internal review to determine how it had happened, and to come up with solutions to improve the process. And that was all the Chairman wanted to say about the matter since he was still in shock over the Peter Porzio affair, and how badly the bank's reputation had been affected by it.

The two men shook hands and ended their meeting with an agreement to disagree on how best to handle the closing of branches in underserved communities after mergers were concluded. The Chairman reminded Pastor Lloyd that closing a branch was never easy, but was merely a business decision, pure and simple. Pastor Lloyd smiled and said, "It's never that pure and simple for my people."

As Teddy walked him to his waiting car, Pastor Lloyd turned and said, "You know, Mr. DeMarco, I guess it's about time I take you up on your offer to call you Teddy."

"Yes. I'd say that's long overdue. But what do I call you?"

The Pastor winked at him and said, "Well, hopefully soon you can call me Congressman-elect. Oh, and by the way, I hope to see you at my campaign headquarters on election night. I don't want to jinx things, but I hope it will be a night of celebration. And I have you to partially thank for it."

"I wouldn't miss it." Teddy said. "And can I bring Tom and Althea? You know my two staffers who were with me at the first meeting? I know they'd love to be part of your special night."

Pastor Lloyd said, "Certainly. By all means. Please bring Althea. You know that all my friends in MJED have a certain fondness for her, if you catch my drift. And Tom is welcome, too. I'm sure my mother would like to thank him again for the mortgage approval."

Epilogue

It was election night and the polls were closing. There was never any doubt as to who would be the next Congressman from the district. It's difficult to call it a landslide since the Republican opponent was serving time and did not campaign from his prison cell. The New Jersey Republican Committee never took Alex Scarduzo Jr.'s name off the ballot, despite his conviction. He even received close to fifty votes, presumably from family members and Sr.'s friends. Rev. Lloyd Ogletree was now the Congressman-elect and the party had begun.

Teddy, Althea and Tom all drove separately since each would be heading in different directions after the celebration ended in Asbury Park. They hoped it wouldn't be a late night since the candidate was scheduled to make his victory speech early at 8:30 pm right after the polls closed. There would be a quick receiving line and then all could depart. The real party had started earlier in the evening when all of Pastor Lloyd's supporters greeted and congratulated each other with a little bubbly and lots of smiles.

When Teddy entered the room, it was as if Moses was parting the Red Sea. Many of Ogletree's supporters knew the two men were back on speaking terms, but none thought anyone from 1NEB would show up for the celebration. After Teddy shook a few hands and took an obligatory glass of champagne, his eyes focused on the young Black woman staring at him from across the room. Indeed, only a few of the real insiders knew the name of Tina Washington, and that she worked for 1NEB. Teddy acknowledged her presence with a smile, a nod of approval, and a long-distance toast of his glass. Tina responded in kind.

Althea was making the rounds and re-acquainted herself with all the same gentlemen admirers who had attended the original MJED meeting. This time, however, Mr. Zeus was a bit more reserved since, when he came over to greet Althea, he was accompanied by his wife. Teddy saw Althea from a distance and made his way over to join their conversation.

Deacon Isaac recognized Tom from the original MJED meeting and came over to introduce himself. He wanted to thank Tom personally again for all the hard work he'd put in getting Millie Ogletree's mortgage approved.

"So how are things going with Millie and Karen? Tom asked. "Everything good with the property? Is the renter a good tenant?"

Deacon Isaac said, "Why don't you ask her herself? I'll bring you over to her."

Millie was excited to see Tom. She gave him a big hug and introduced him to all her guests. She put her arm around him and said, "You all should know this young man probably saved my daughter Karen's life. If he hadn't approved the mortgage for the two of us to buy Deacon Isaac's property, well, she might still be out on the—" Millie stopped herself before she went too far.

Tom asked Millie if Karen was in the room, but she shook her head and said, "No. She couldn't make it tonight. It's a school night, you know."

Millie took Tom by the arm and asked if she could have a brief private conversation. Tom agreed and they found a not so quiet little corner where they hoped they wouldn't be disturbed.

Once they sat down, Tom began by saying, "You know, all the time we were negotiating your mortgage application you always called me Mr. Donovan, never Tom. I appreciate that you've finally broken from the formality."

Millie smiled. "You became Tom in my book once the loan was closed. And I thank the good Lord every day that He put the two of us together. I was blessed with you, Tom. But that's not what I wanted to talk about. I was introduced earlier to that nice young woman from your bank standing over there. Her name is Tina Washington, but I guess you knew that. She said she had a little something to do with my mortgage. So we got to talking about the reasons for the original loan denial. She seemed to be quite familiar with it. And she was trying her best to explain to me what the other reason was for the rejection. Something about a nearby incompatible land use, if I heard her correctly."

Tom looked embarrassed. "Yes. You heard her correctly. When I first learned about that being one of the reasons for your denial, I went a bit crazy and had a—pardon the expression—Come to Jesus meeting with Tina's boss, the head of the Mortgage Department."

Millie laughed. "I forgive you and would say that Jesus intervened and showed this head of your Mortgage Department the right path to take."

"Right," Tom said. "But it was a pretty stressful situation. During the process, I could have used a little lightning from Mr. Zeus over there." Tom pointed to the gentleman speaking with Althea.

"Tom, what are you talking about?"

He said, "Oh, nothing, it's not important."

Then Millie got to heart of the matter. "So, I'm thinking this so-called nearby incompatible land use item is about the most ridiculous thing I've ever heard. Are you telling me there are lending officers out there who believe this kind of bigotry has any effect on whether people will pay their monthly mortgage bills? That's crazy!"

"I couldn't agree with you more. It's nuts, but unfortunately I don't make the rules."

Millie was like a dog with a bone. "So who do I have to speak with to make this craziness go away?"

Tom didn't hesitate. "Your son, Millie. Your son. With any luck, your son, the Congressman-Elect, will be appointed to sit on the House Banking Committee to replace Blake. All Congressman Ogletree has to do is bring it up at the committee level and ask someone to come in and testify as to why this relic is still around."

Millie leaned in to hug Tom once again. "You see. Just like I said before. I was blessed to be paired up with you."

By now Teddy had made his way through the crowd of supporters to find Tina. They shook hands and Teddy began the conversation by whispering, "The last time we saw each other Willers was planning your takedown of Porzio. Congratulations! Nice job—even if that's not the most appropriate thing to say. Just between us, Porzio was a scumbag. Tom Donovan and I went to war with him and your boss on many occasions over the past few years. I wasn't sorry to see him go. But his death was still a tragedy."

Tina nodded, but didn't really want to say anything more on the topic.

Teddy continued. "So, can I ask you what's going to happen now—I mean with your job at the bank?"

Again Tina was not very forthcoming. She didn't know whom to trust. "As I understand it, the Chairman wants to meet with me personally. There's also a rumor flying around that Porter's on his way out. And then you can add in that an interim chief credit policy officer is about to be named. So to answer your question, I don't have a clue what's next for me. But Willers told me that there's no way they can fire me for being the leaker on Porzio. What he did was against the law. I guess they could still ding me for not taking my complaint up the line. But who was I supposed to talk to? Make an appointment with the Chairman?"

They both laughed at this, but Teddy knew Tina was not in a good place. The best he could come up with was, "Listen, if Porter survives this whole thing, and you need to get out of the Mortgage Department, just let me know. I'm sure Tom would love to have you working beside him on the next round of affordable mortgages we've been promised by the Chairman."

Althea joined them. "So how are you holding up, girlfriend?"

Before Tina could answer, they were joined by Simone. Tina and Simone hugged as if they hadn't seen each other in years. Simone said, "I was hoping to see you here tonight. Great celebration, right?"

A distinguished-looking middle-aged Black man approached the group. Tina gave him a brief hug and said, "Good to see you, Mr. Martin."

Tina turned to the group and made all of the required introductions. "This is my friend Simone's father, Mr. Michael Martin. And this is Simone Martin, my best friend from high school."

Simone put her arm around Tina and said, "And we're still best friends, right?"

Simone's father then looked at Althea and said, "I know this young lady quite well. She's my goddaughter."

Althea and Mr. Martin hugged, then reverted to their best impression of respectability.

The In-House Politician

Then Teddy asked the question. "So, Mr. Martin, how do you know the Congressman-elect?"

Mr. Martin said, "I'm a member of Pastor Lloyd's church. In the past, I've done some pro bono legal work for the church and Pastor Lloyd. But it was all in the time before he announced his candidacy. I couldn't do any more work for him after that."

"Oh? Why not?" Teddy asked.

Mr. Martin said, "Because I'm an attorney who works for the Department of Justice. I'm sure you're familiar with The Hatch Act and all that no politics nonsense while on the government payroll rule, right?"

Teddy was quite familiar with the rules from his previous career in politics. But now he was even more curious. "Did I also hear you say you're Althea's godfather? Now that's quite a coincidence, isn't it, Althea?" He was staring directly at her.

Simone's father was looking for a quick exit strategy. He saw someone on the other side of the room and excused himself. But before he left, he took Althea's arm and said very clearly so Teddy could hear him, "Please give my best to your father. Tell him I'll be in touch soon. We have our 50th Reunion coming up next year, and I'm chairman of the fundraising committee. I'll need him to dig deep into that skinny wallet of his. Love you, kid."

As he turned to leave, he whispered in Althea's ear, "Were those transcripts helpful?"

She winked and said, "Yes, they were. Thank you, Uncle Mike."

The room was buzzing. Congressman-elect Rev. Lloyd Ogletree was being introduced and everyone was looking towards the podium. It was time to celebrate.

About the Author

William (Bill) is a graduate of Colgate University and holds a Master's in Urban Planning from New York University. He spent his entire career in the financial services industry as a banker and bank regulator. The last fifteen years of his professional life were spent in Washington, D.C. working for the nation's premier bank regulatory agency.

Other Short Stories by William Robert Reeves:

Meeting with Scrooge (Wilderness House Literary Review 2022)

Cleo in ¾ Time (Penmen Review 2022)

Made in the USA
Coppell, TX
07 October 2024

38289748R00288